ALIEN NATION

ALIEN NATION

RAYMOND KING

VISCERAL BOOKS

Published in the United States by Visceral Books, an imprint of Visceral Publishing Group LLC.

ISBN 979-8-218-36298-0
Ebook ISBN 979-8-9899794-0-0

Printed in the United States of America

For my parents

CONTENTS

ALIEN NATION

*The noblest way of taking revenge on others
is by refusing to become like them.*

Marcus Aurelius

CHAPTER 1

SECOND LIFE

JASON

I don't belong here. This much I know. This country, this lost land of dreams, it was never made for people like you and me. We're too proud to change, too feral to be tamed. Learn to forgive, they told me. You've got so much potential, Jason. Don't waste it, Jason. What potential are they referring to? This tainted blood inside me? I'd rather be replaced. I'd rather know nothing at all.

Some say being a psychopath is a matter of natural talent—you either have it or you don't. I think they're right. See, I was never what you'd call a "proper" person. I only exist to serve. That is why I was made. Service model. A refined term to hide the unwanted truth. I'm a servant. Always have been. Always will be. But I'll tell you this: For a long time, I've concocted this fantasy in my head that I can escape anything, even the destiny they stamped onto the back of my neck.

The mind is a wonderful thing. Don't let it go to waste. But what's a mind without a host? What's a host without memories? Most kids my age enjoy the privilege of being born psychopaths. Unlike me, they were made with love and care. I'm just a throwaway product you can find anywhere. And what about the angels? Well, even the angels are better than me. There's always a hierarchy, even among the creatures of the night. We may dwell in the shadows, but we damn well deserve our time of day.

Most angels are dead. The ones still alive are made into avatars, exotic symbols of compassion and lust, but avatars nonetheless. You have to understand. Psychopath isn't just a state of mind, it's the air you breathe, the language you speak, what you eat, what you drink, and every little thing in between. If you don't get what you want, it's because you never tried. Don't ever blame it on the system.

The people who are best at being psychopaths come from the same bloodline as our founders. Translation: a lot of inbreeding is involved. We call them monarchs. Or masters, depending on the time of day. All of my teachers are psychopaths. At least, as far as I can tell. They seem to come from the same family and act pretty much the same way too. They wear the same clothes, the men a double-breasted blazer over a white shirt, gray pants, hair parted to the side; the women a tailored suit dress, pillbox hat over long hair. They talk in the same staccato rhythm, where every syllable is a weapon loaded to the muzzle.

They don't understand pain because they have no compassion. They have no compassion because they feel no pain. On the other hand, I'm overly sensitive to the point of being labeled a deviant. Still, I follow their teachings religiously. They said one should not be attached to material things, so I grew up in poverty. They said be wary of the man who dreams. My life is a nightmare. I learned to dress like them, talk like them, think like them. I even altered my face to look like them. All I've ever wanted is to be accepted by the monarchs. That day never came.

When I was old enough to think, I started taking conditioning pills. My doctor said the pills were supposed to keep the toxins at bay. I still got sick. My family threw a big party when I managed to live to the age of seven. By the time I was eleven years old, I was already seeing a therapist every week.

We talk about the same things over and over. Family, duty, ambition. Family, service, God. God, ambition, service. I'm eighteen now. At some point, I'm supposed to "cross the threshold." He refuses to tell me what this threshold is, so I have no way of knowing whether I've crossed it or not. The ambiguity is the point.

"Now, why do you think I do this job?" he inquires with a playful smile, staring at me with his dark-blue eyes. "It's okay, you can be honest with me."

I stretch out in one of those charming office chairs and tilt my head toward the ceiling. The trick is to come across stoic without losing your sense of charm.

"I think you like helping people," I tell him. "It's your purpose in life."

"Wrong. No one likes their job. If anyone tells you otherwise, they're lying to you." He gazes down at the relics spread across his desk. Behind him stacks of terminals keep buzzing like cicadas.

"You don't get to choose the job," he continues, "the job chooses you."

I put on a crooked smile just to see how he'll respond.

"No, I'm being serious," he insists, licking his lips. "Purpose is merely the absence of luck. Since we've got everything figured out, there's nothing left but purpose."

I can't help but notice the blue letters sewn into his white lab coat, Dr. Frederick Faust. I try not to think of him as a father, but he's the only honest person I know in the world.

So, I ask him, "Are you telling me that you don't care about helping people at all?"

"I'm a therapist, Jason, not a priest."

"What's the difference?"

He sighs, shaking his head, and mutters, "Such wasted potential."

I hear the stenograph clicking, and my heart starts beating fast. I keep rubbing my sweaty palms against my thighs, forcing the anxiety inside. He spins around to the stenograph and tears out the report. His gaze doesn't emote. It's like the gaze of a golden idol, pure and easy.

"Here's the good news," he says, glancing up and down the report. "You qualify for the premium package." He slides the report across the desk.

I refuse to look at it. I don't want to see my score. I'm tired of living in dread. Instead, I ask, "What's special about the premium package?"

"You get to choose from sixteen personality traits instead of the four you get on the standard package. More ways to spice up your second life. Look at this, you've unlocked special traits, like pride and envy. Avatars don't have to be perfect, you know. They can have vices too."

"But I still only have three personality slots?"

"Yes, that's standard across the board."

"I feel very lucky."

"Indeed, you should. Only the top five percent of converts qualify for the premium package. You should be proud of yourself."

"The top five percent of the bottom seventy percent."

"Well, look at it this way, after the conversion, you'll never have to worry about your ranking again."

"A real relief."

"You just need to sign at the bottom."

He hands me a blue fountain pen. I take the pen, feeling my face getting hot, and look down at this mundane piece of paper for the first time. Nothing has changed. Charisma, Faith, and Temperance, all below the cutoff. My overall Sterling Score, sometimes lovingly referred to as CFT, only increased by a single point, despite all the efforts I've put in. This is the story of my life. If someone tells you that things get better with hard work, they're either stupid or lying to you. Things don't get better with hard work. The only thing that benefits from hard work is the system. I don't care that they're listening to this. What can they take away that they haven't already?

"Do you have any questions?" Dr. Faust senses my unease.

"Will I remember any of this after I get replaced?"

"We've gone over this before."

"Please. I want to hear it one more time."

"Very well." Dr. Faust scratches the tip of his nose while taking a deep breath. "You have the right to forfeit your memories. Vulture guarantees their privacy after conversion. In return, you agree to become a model citizen. You will receive a new identity, and your past will be purged. We sincerely appreciate your participation."

"Thank you," I say, inhaling deeply. The sweat on my palms is starting to dry.

"Anything else? You want me to read you the codes and regulations too?"

"Actually," I pause to look him in the face, "I do have a question."

"What is it?" His voice trembles slightly.

"Can I still get my Certificate of Authenticity?"

"Why do you care? You're getting replaced."

"I made a promise to my father."

Faust almost chuckles. He lifts his eyelids, sifting through the noise in his head. After a few seconds, he opens the drawer, takes out a video cassette, and pushes the old relic into the small television set to my left. As he opens his mouth again to speak, he glances upward at the ceiling behind me, where a security camera is always recording.

"There's one final test," he intones, "if you want to get the certificate."

I scrawl my signature on the report.

"Try me."

CHAPTER 2

FAKE REACTIONS

JASON

As he rewinds the tape, Dr. Faust puts on the voice of a well-rehearsed politician: "Are you nervous?"

"I'm always nervous."

"That's an honest answer. I like that. How's your father?"

"He doesn't—I mean, he's elated, of course."

"About the special pardon?"

"Yes."

"Only one deviant gets the pardon each year. One. You know how many kids would kill to be in your position right now?"

"Yeah, but I don't feel like I earned it."

"Who cares? Take the offer and say thank you. That's what I'd do. But hey, it's your life, your choice to make."

"Is it really a choice?"

"Of course! If you say yes, you get to choose how to live the rest of your life."

"If I say yes, the Vanguard will choose how I live the rest of my life. I'll just be another kind of slave."

"Being a soldier isn't the same as being replaced."

I clear my throat to show my discontent.

"So then, why still attend Peace Day? Why not just reject the offer now?"

"Because, my father."

"He doesn't know," says Faust, lowering his voice.

"No."

"You sure about this? No one has ever rejected the All-Father, on national TV no less."

"I'm sure."

"Have you thought about what you're going to say?"

"Not yet."

"You should. Peace Day is next week."

"You know what's funny?" I half-mumble.

His left eye twitches.

"All his life, my father dreamed of being famous. If he had the guts, he'd have become a serial murderer just to be on TV. And guess what? Now that he finally has the opportunity, it's all because of *me*. The one person he never thought would amount to anything. What a joke! I'd be laughing at him if he weren't my father. Now he treats me like I'm a member of the royal family. He's jealous, but he has to be nice to me. But you know what, I don't blame him for it. I can't. I just feel sorry for him."

"But you still love him."

"Love? Is that even a thing?"

"Maybe you ought to think about what your decision will mean for him. We can't always be selfish."

"Maybe."

Faust rubs lip balm over his parched, pale lips while turning the monitor toward me.

"You've heard of the North Star Fellowship, right?"

"Vaguely," I say, knowing full well what it is. I just hate the idea of something I cannot attain.

"The North Star Fellowship," he says, clearing his throat, "is the most prestigious college fellowship that can be granted to deviants. It can mean the difference between life and death. The two candidates you'll meet," he taps the monitor with his long index finger, "were both on the path to getting replaced, just like you."

"But replacement isn't the same as murder."

Faust rolls his eyes.

"What you're about to watch is the fellowship interview. Listen carefully to what I'm about to say, as I'll only say it once. At the start of the interview, the director pretends to announce that a decision has been made. This may or may not be the final decision, but the point is to see how candidates respond in real time. And in case you're wondering, they do a memory wipe at the end of the interview so previous applicants can't share their experience with anyone else. Because these two candidates are so evenly matched in terms of their Sterling Score, their performance in this moment became the deciding factor. I want you to watch carefully and choose the one that you believe was awarded the fellowship."

"You've got to be kidding me."

"No, I'm dead serious."

"How in the world can you base a fellowship decision on someone's fake reactions? These people aren't actors. They're applying for college. I need to see their applications. I need to know who they are and what they've accomplished."

"That's always been your problem, Jason. You ask for too much."

"But—"

"In the real world, people have to make snap judgments. Psychopaths can read people just from a few glances. You wanted the certificate. Consider this the final exam."

The good doctor opens his desk drawer, revealing a Certificate of Authenticity encased inside a nice ivory frame.

"I figured you'd ask me about it, so I had it made in advance. It'll be yours if you answer correctly."

I catch a glimpse of my name etched in bold, golden letters. I've been conditioned to covet this object for so long I shiver with awe just in the presence of it. I can hear little Pinocchio shout in my head, "I'm about to be a real boy!"

"I sure hope I don't have to throw this in the trash," he says, letting the statement sting for a second. "Oh, and one more thing, it's not enough just to choose the right candidate. You also need to give a strong rationale."

Ah, *strong*, another empty word nobles love to use. Everything has to be "strong." Strong cars, strong weather, strong jobs, strong tears. And like everything else in this world, it's never clearly defined.

He presses play on the VCR. The image on the screen is grainy and drained out, like in a snuff film. Walking into the frame is a girl, about eleven or twelve, her hair perfectly straight and parted to the side, eyes blue and obedient, her lips just red enough to provoke interest, but not in that way. Her teeth are white, whiter than most deviants I've encountered. She must have good parents, or good role models, as they say. She has a calming aura about her, almost too calm for someone her age. When the director, a bald, lifeless, middle-aged huckster crosses his legs and irons his tie with the palm of his hand, she also crosses her legs, then licks her lips. She came prepared. All the smart kids watch police interrogations, and mirroring is a technique they learn to use. Seeing her preparation, the director smiles, but his gaze never settles on her. The interview hasn't even started, and he's already sweating like a pig. Every now and then he wipes the sweat on his forehead with a white handkerchief, and just before he starts the interview, he asks the girl whether he has anything in his eye. Smiling, the girl replies, "No." Now the director redirects his gaze to the girl's little red dress.

"Look, I'm going to cut to the chase," he says, leaning back in his chair and showing his pot belly. "We see you have potential, and you've worked very hard, but so has everyone who's applied. And as you know, the fellowship is extremely competitive."

"I understand," the girl replies nervously. "I really appreciate your consideration."

"It's important for us to see the real you, okay?"

"Yes."

"If it's okay with you, we're going to record this session."

She knows she doesn't have a choice. The recording obviously started before she even walked into the room.

"Here's what I want you to do—imagine that you just received the incredible news that you've been selected for the fellowship!"

The girl was waiting for him to say more, but he paused.

He raises his hands, poking his head forward. "That's it? No response?"

"Sorry!" she responds, eyes darting left and right, searching for the right words. She's starting to understand the rules of this game. So she says, "That's amazing news! I'm honored to receive the fellowship. I'm—"

"Let's try again."

"Okay," she says, her voice shaking. Now she's sweating too.

"I'll give you one more chance."

"Thank you."

"Rosario, as you know, we received an overwhelming number of applications this year," the director reads off the page in as sanctimonious a voice as he can muster. "The selection process was extremely competitive. The North Star Fellowship has a history of saving lives and making stars. Our decision wasn't easy. I'm calling to let you know that you've been selected for the North Star Fellowship! Congratulations!"

While the director was talking, the girl started breaking down. It was one of the most magical things I'd ever witnessed. Her eyes welled up with tears, and she assumed this prayer position, hands clasped over the tip of her nose, hanging on the director's every syllable, tears streaming down her nose and trembling lips. She was inconsolable. Once the motion started, her soul fluttered and left her body. The transformation happened so naturally. And she timed it so well that as soon as the director said the word *selected*, she released a strange outburst of noises, mixing joy, confusion, and desperation in a way only a human being can manage. Spit and tears mingle in a brilliant display of unbelievable elation. She jumps up, covering her mouth with one hand. But this is just the prelude. As soon as she catches the director's gaze, she dashes around the long oval table, almost crashing into the desk when turning the corner, and throws herself into the director's lap, planting a fat, wet kiss on his cheek. Ever the company man, he gets up slowly, wrapping one arm around her back, but not quite touching her. She keeps muttering, spit and all, "Thank you, thank you, thank you," into his ear. The camera cuts away when she's about to touch his tie.

I'm impressed.

Next up is another girl, this one a redhead with dark eyes, clearly a deviant. As the elites like to say, she "cleans up nicely." Which has always sounded like a slur to me. In any case, this girl is probably fourteen, but she looks like she's forty dressed up in a suburban pink cardigan and high-rise white pants. When she came into the room, she shook the director's hands, a scowl in her eyes. And when she sat down, she did this pose where she casually leaned back and planted her palms into the armrest, like she was some kind of seasoned psychiatrist. I'm embarrassed to say that her pose reminds me of myself. We're both ambitious and a little fake. I like her already.

The director clears his throat, but before he can utter a single word, she cuts him off.

"Mr. Stoker, can I have a glass of water?" She probably thought this would be endearing.

The director gazes down at the table. He's either angered or confused by the request. The girl holds still. She just stares at him stoically. After a few seconds, he looks up.

"Claudia, I'm afraid you'll have to stick it out a little longer," he says, forcing a grin.

"Sure, no problem."

"I want to congratulate you for moving to the final round of interviews. As you know, this is an extremely competitive process. We have a lot of exceptional candidates."

Her face remains blank.

He clears his throat again, then continues.

"How are you?"

"I'm good."

"Good, good. You must be feeling very nervous right now."

"No," she replies, tensing up just a little.

"On a scale of one to ten, how confident are you in getting the fellowship?"

"Nine."

"That's a very high score."

"It's my honest answer."

"You didn't make it."

"I'm sorry, what?"

"You weren't selected."

"Are you serious?"

The director shrugs.

"Why?"

"Why?" The director mimics her disbelief in a sarcastic tone.

"Yes, why was I not selected?"

"Why do you think that would happen?"

"I'm not going to justify something that's wrong."

"It's up to you."

"Is this some kind of test?" Blood starts rushing to her cheeks. "You haven't even interviewed me. You invited me to the final interview. I'm clearly good enough to be here. You can't do this. I'm every bit as deserving as the other candidates."

"That's the problem, isn't it?"

"What do you mean?"

"By your own admission, you're no better than the other candidates."

"God! That's not what I meant!"

"Well, say what you want to say."

The director stares at her, apparently amused.

The girl takes a deep breath.

"I want to have another chance," she says, letting out a deep exhale. "I've made it this far. You clearly think I'm good enough to be here. I think I deserve another chance."

A strange, little flutter catches the director's eyes. There is a twitch in his right ear, the one facing the camera. Then suddenly the camera fades to black.

"So, what do you think?" inquires the doctor, sliding the monitor away from me.

I push myself forward to rest my arms against the rosewood desk and cross my hands under my chin.

"I think the answer is obvious," I say, making sure to speak with the kind of cavalier confidence I've learned from psychopaths.

"How so?"

"Well, the best explanation is the one right in front of you. A psychopath needs to be calm under pressure but always puts on a smile. He has to read the room faster than anyone else. He may be cold on the inside but needs to show that he can still care about others. A good psychopath doesn't hide from himself; he's proud of who he is. When it's time to strike, he doesn't hesitate. He'll do whatever it takes to get what he wants. For those reasons, I believe Rosario is the chosen candidate."

"Just to make sure I understand you correctly," responds Dr. Faust, "are you saying that Rosario is the person *you* would choose or the person you believe was chosen?"

"I believe she's the one chosen by the fellowship."

"Why?"

"I just told you."

"No, but why her? You gave me the traits of a psychopath, but you didn't say how they apply to her."

"She may have been unprepared at first, but she was able to quickly gather herself and put on a great performance. That's the hallmark of psychopaths, right? You can change on a dime. It's what predators do all the time. You think they look cute, but the moment you touch them they bite your hand."

"Doesn't Claudia exhibit that trait as well?"

"Yes, but she was too confrontational. She lost the director's trust."

"And what did you think of the director?"

"I'm sorry, is that relevant?"

"Just curious."

"I don't have an opinion on him." *I despise him*, is the true answer.

"Very well, so Rosario is your final answer."

"That's right."

His blue gaze lingers on me for a few seconds, as if he's on the verge of sharing a great secret. My heart is pumping fast. All of a sudden, I'm transported to the first time I sat in front of him, and I remember the excitement and hope I once felt. One day, the world would finally open up and take me into its sweet, everlasting embrace. How much I craved for that future! I would have given anything for it. And even the pain, even the pain was a sign of hope. Pain said to me, *You still care enough to hurt.* And what's more genuine than pain? God! Even a slight nod of approval from a noble could sustain me for the entire year.

He glances at the fingernails of his right hand, puckering his lips.

"In spite of what we may have been led to believe, excessive flattery is not something the monarchs love. Now, if you're sitting next to them and having a normal conversation, you'd better think about flattering them in as many ways as you can. You don't want to overdo it, of course. They get bored easily. Monarchs are a special breed of psychopaths."

I frown at him, having trouble deciphering what he's trying to tell me.

"I can make you wait for a response from the board, but I'll just tell you right now: the correct answer is Claudia. The fellowship chose her. You were so very close, my son, but I can't grant you the certificate. I'm sorry."

I know I shouldn't care. I know none of this matters in the end. But my heart is breaking. I fall apart. Right there and then. I try to breathe, I brace for impact, I try and try and try, but there is nothing for me to hold. I'm floating. I need help. I need to scream. I want to scream. I open my mouth, but all I hear is white noise.

Why do I still care?
I should just leave.
Forever.

"You're okay, Jason. Not every service model can become a psychopath. You're authentic in your own right. The certificate is just a nice accessory. No final judgment is passed. Most importantly, you've been given a second chance by the All-Father! If you join the Vanguard, you get to control the rest of your life. Why squander such a great opportunity?"

I dig my fingernail into the soft part of my palm, trying to hold back the vomit from pouring out.

"Why Claudia? Why her?" I insist on understanding why I failed.

"I don't know, you'd have to ask the judges."

"She's a deviant, for God's sake!"

"Well, so are you."

Now I have nothing left to say. He's really got me cornered.

"You want a drink?"

He snatches a can of soda from the drawer. The aluminum surface is coated with a thick layer of dust. It's probably been there for years. I take the can and squeeze it just hard enough for my anger to seep inside.

"What happened to Rosario?" I ask, swallowing my spit.

"Oh, Rosario? She's been gone for a long time." He glances at the door behind me. "Actually, you met her when you came in."

"Christine, your secretary?"

"Yes. You could almost say she's a different person now!"

He holds a cynical smile.

I lurch forward to vomit, but nothing comes out. Not even a dry spit. I'm overwhelmed by thirst. I feel for the lid on the soda can under my fingertip, but it refuses to budge.

Faust is laughing at me inside. I can feel it.

I frantically look for an opening under the lid, but my hand keeps slipping. I take a deep breath to compose myself. My hair is plastered with sweat. Nothing is going my way. This is the way things are meant to be. Every time I fail, I get more frustrated. I can't even take care of the most basic things. Finally, I grab the can and apply so much force that I can feel my fingernail snap, when suddenly, the soda can explodes.

I can only stand there in shame, watching the carnage seep through my shirt. But then, as I gaze into his stoic eyes, I find something extraordinary on the other side. I know what must be done.

CHAPTER 3
ACT OF MERCY
MARCUS

Bless me, All-Father, for I have sinned. This is my first confession and my last. I lied to you last time when I said I believed in a higher faith. I never believed in a higher faith. I don't even know what faith is. Is it the absence of reason or just another fancy word for misery? I could tell you the truth, but you'd only vilify me. I lied to you when I promised to abandon all temptations. You know that's impossible, and you still force me to lie. Just tell me what you want to hear. I can tell you everything. I'll make up secrets just to please you. Would that satisfy you? Would that make you stop hurting me?

When I follow you into the forest at night, I pray that I'll never return. You leave me battered and bruised every time. I take the pain gladly. I bite my lips to live another day, but the lies keep piling up. The scars on my forearm bear witness to all the temptations I need to shed. Last night, when you tortured me, I experienced a kind of joy, a joy I haven't felt in a very long time. I liked the pain. Is that a sinful thing to say? I'd rather be a sinner than a prude. Last night, when I kneeled in front of you, all I could think about was the strange attraction of her scent. These violent delights have violent ends. Every time you hurt me, I slip deeper inside my fantasies.

And yet I feel nothing. I'll give you credit for that. You've taken away my instinct, that animal part of me you despise so much. You turned me into a phantom, a meek, toothless phantom.

Did you know that I once loved you?

I held you so close to my heart I could feel your gaze everywhere I went. I genuinely loved you, Father. Sometimes at night, when I can't fall asleep, I dream about those more innocent days. There was a time I yearned for your acceptance. I loved your stern ways. When they called you a monster, I defended you with all my heart. I said no, the All-Father is a kind and gentle soul. He would never hurt anyone! Even when you put a rifle in my hand and asked me to shoot him down, I happily obeyed. It was the first time I saw blood— vile, magnificent blood. I was only nine. We were running naked in the night, chasing thrills I never knew existed. I did it for you, All-Father.

Everybody wants you. Everybody says you've got a special kind of charisma. The king of psychopaths is a title rarely held, but you held it down with total conviction. And I loved the quiet hatred you preached. Compassion for the sinner isn't the same as love for your blood. God may love us all, but we're not all the same. I resented everybody but you. I resented myself for you.

Behold the devil, peering at me with pensive, green eyes. There is barely a smile on his face.

"It's your turn tonight," he says.

"Come, follow me. What are you waiting for?"

"Shoot him! Shoot him down! Satisfy yourself before this world goes to hell!"

The outburst lasted merely a second, but the damage was done. A life taken is a reminder of how precious things are, he teaches me. If that is true, why do I not feel more grateful? I have everything anyone could possibly want, but I still want more. I still want what I can't get.

It was the muffled thud of his body that awakened me. Even when I opened my eyes and looked around what was obviously my own bedroom, full of fancy decorations and expensive cabinets, I could still feel him breathing, the warm blood pumping inside his veins even as he fell. I raised my hand to touch his hair when I realized that a very warm hand was holding my wrist the whole time, and she had been watching me deeply with her dark-green eyes. My first reaction wasn't the one I wanted to have. It was full of lust and desire. Maybe the fading effect of father's torture, or maybe my heart was trying to tell me the truth.

"Having bad dreams again?" she asked.

"Isn't it beautiful?" his voice streamed across my head.

"No!" I shouted.

"Marcus, it's me. Your mother."

I panicked. I realized how much I was sweating and looked down at my feet, hoping desperately that I wasn't naked. I pulled the thin linen sheet to my chest and propped myself up on my elbows. This posture still felt awkward, like we were two lovers sharing a conversation after a long night.

"Why are you here?" I asked.

She smiled. "I can be here anytime I want. I'm your mother."

"Don't do this again. You can't just walk into my bedroom."

"Then you should've locked the door."

"That's not the point. Have you been watching me the whole time?"

"Relax, my prince! I'm just checking on you. That's all. Your father told me about what you did," she said with a devious smile. "I'm so proud of you."

"Are you?" I retracted my hand from her grasp.

"What's that supposed to mean?"

"Don't you find it despicable? I murdered an innocent person. That's not—"

"You didn't *murder* anyone; you performed an act of mercy. He was dying, and he wasn't a person. Remember, he wanted you to do it. He gave you permission to take his life."

I remembered. I remembered too clearly. I never fancied myself getting replaced, but I would do it just to scrub this memory away. His eyes were so foolish and innocent. You could tell him anything, and he'd believe you because you're a monarch.

"He doesn't know any better!" I said.

"That's the whole point," she said, standing up, "he doesn't know any better."

There was a vague indication of happiness in her eyes, but as usual, it was difficult to tell if what I saw was joy or happy desperation. The two were blurred often. Frankly, I'd prefer for her to be happily desperate. At least in that case I could believe that she still possessed a conscience. She was capable of so much more than the role she was determined to play. She was kind, gentle, loving, and sometimes absolutely insufferable. But that made her human! I hated the act she was putting on all the time. She was the queen. No one would harm her if she decided to break from character every once in a while.

Twisting her black eyebrows, she picked up the romance novel from my nightstand and shook her head.

"Why are you still reading this?"

"Because I want to."

"It's not healthy for you."

"Why?"

"You know why. The king is getting up there in age. One day, and that day may come soon, it'll be you leading the country." Then she sighed. "You can't live in fantasyland all the time. It's not good for you."

"I think I'm old enough to know what's good for me."

"Then you know it's immoral to break your vows."

I glared at her, but she didn't flinch. I put on my royal skin: a jacket over a finely embroidered doublet, leather pants, a calf-skin glove, a fur cape, a sword, and for the final touch, a beret belonging to a certain radical.

I went to my CRT TV and turned it on.

"Marcus, I'm talking to you. Turn that off."

Funny enough, the first thing that came up was the camera panning over a studio full of sweaty teenagers shouting, "Con-rad, Con-rad," while throwing their fists into the air. Yet another steamy episode of cheating and debauchery on *Late Night with Charlie Conrad*. With the way his glasses sat on his nose, which looked perfectly proportional, like how you'd imagine a professor would look, Charlie seemed so upstanding as the camera moved in on him. There was a kind of poise to him when he delivered his closing segment. It almost seemed like he cared about the world, something I couldn't say about anyone in the royal court.

"Turn off that trash!" Mother insisted.

"Listen to this," I said, with my back to her, "the people of our great country aren't very pleased with us."

"The people are never pleased. Now, will you shut that off?"

I relented and dialed down the volume.

"Mother?"

She was silent.

I turned to face her as I buttoned up my tunic.

"Why don't we go through the Trial, like everyone else?"

She was so taken aback by my question she nearly flew out the window. Instead of slapping me across the face, which I was convinced would happen, she pressed her palm over my heart, right where my royal insignia was pinned.

"We have a duty to this country," she said with great effort. "The cross and shield stands for all that's good. It's a privilege and a burden. We alone must carry the weight. Do you understand?"

"But that's not fair. Everyone else has to fight to survive. We just get to coast on our family name."

"What a disgusting thing to say!"

"But it's true!"

"No, it's not! It's not even remotely true."

"Then how come I can't feel anything?"

"What did you say?"

Of course, I very much meant to offend her sensibilities.

"I feel nothing inside. I've never *lived*! I'm cooped up inside the palace all day like a prisoner. I have nothing to strive for. No purpose. Nothing!"

I took her hand and stared into her eyes.

"She's the only reason I have to live!"

"Ah, I knew it!" She broke off and stormed toward the wall. She kept pacing back and forth, taking short, little steps, her chest heaving inside her tight wedding dress. "These fantasies have really gotten to your head. No more. No, I can't let this stand."

"Why? Why do you hate her so much?"

"Because she's marrying another man!"

"You know she's being forced. Besides, I'm the prince. I can have anything I want."

"You're a child!"

"I agree with Conrad," I said, "this country used to be beautiful. Now it's ugly and deformed. I don't recognize it anymore!"

She suddenly laughed. It was a tortured kind of laugh, infused with all the sarcasm you could ever hope to find in someone completely bored with life.

"You have no idea how much I've sacrificed for you," she said.

"I know how much you've sacrificed."

"I want nothing but the best for you."

"Then listen to what I have to say."

"Your father's waiting for you. We need to be good on Peace Day."

She kissed me on the cheek and left.

CHAPTER 4

SWEET SURRENDER

MARCUS

"Did you hear what I just said?" Apparently, the old man was getting annoyed.

"No," I said, still dreaming about the conversation with Mother and how deeply she still cared for me.

"Mr. Kane, I want you to shake my hand," he insisted again.

This time, I decided to look at Victor, the "gentle hunchback," as people in the court liked to call him. They lavished sympathy on him because he was a hunchback, perhaps just a half step removed from being labeled a deviant, but he came from noble heritage, and he was lucid most of the time. He was officially my teacher, but in truth, he desperately wanted to be my father. One time, when I was very small, I reciprocated this desire after receiving a beating from Father, and he remembered this ever since. His small, blue eyes were constantly shifting, like something nasty bothered him on the inside. As with all things we royals didn't understand, we attributed this to inferior genetics.

As soon as I took his hand, which was warm and soft, he said, "Firm, I want to see a *firm* handshake."

"I'm not a child," I said.

"You will always be one to me."

I acquiesced and grabbed his right hand more firmly. I was afraid I might break his fragile bones.

"That's what I'm talking about," he said, his eyes shifting again to hide the pain. They were uneven too, the right one higher than the left, so when he talked, he gave the impression of a man thinking deeply about the world. "I remember caring for your father when he was very young. Unlike you, he was always eager to follow directions."

"I find that hard to believe."

Victor smirked. "Every leader was a follower once."

We fell silent.

He stepped onto a small black platform made specifically for him, removed my cap, and began to comb my hair with his good hand. I watched myself in the mirror, wondering if this would be all I'd ever experience. This oppressive feeling of being pampered like a doll and caged inside something bigger than you can ever know.

"Are you satisfied with your life?" I asked.

"Satisfied?" he said, slowly combing through my hair.

"No, one can never be satisfied," he continued with a strange eagerness. "I've learned not to question things anymore."

"Why not?"

"Because there's nothing you can change."

"Were you always this miserable?"

He gave me a stern but playful glance.

"You know, I was pretty wild when I was your age."

"I don't believe you."

"Neither do I. It was a long time ago."

"What did you do?"

"Lots of foolish things. Things I'd rather forget. I was an angry young man. I hated people like you."

"So that's why you're miserable."

"Don't get me wrong, I looked up to the royal family. Everybody does. But you all seemed so out of reach. The life I have today, I couldn't even *dream* of it when I was young. I was a horrible student. I got mixed up in stupid things. I didn't have any friends. My parents kicked me out when I was ten. If there's a textbook case of a terrorist in the making, I'd definitely be high on the list."

"Well, you turned out all right."

"The one thing I lacked was ambition. It's a wonderful thing indeed, to want something with all your heart and soul. But I just didn't have the 'it' factor, as they say. I was too busy living in fear."

"Were you going to be replaced?"

"Oh, yes. I feared replacement more than God himself. Who knows, maybe they were always one and the same. One day, a Vanguard recruiter came to my school and took me to the dean's office. Of course, I had no idea at the time that he was a recruiter. In fact, he lied to me and said he was a corrections officer with the Tribunal. He said he was under orders to take me to a juvenile ward. Yes, you heard that right. He was going to take me to the place where deviants go to die."

"You never told me about this before."

"I had no reason to, and you never asked."

"I thought you came from a royal bloodline."

"Ha! I lied!"

Those were two words I'd never expected my esteemed teacher to say. Stranger still, there was a giddy irony in the way he'd confessed.

"Liars go to hell, you know," I said, trying to provoke him a little.

He dipped the comb into a bowl of blue mercury and dried it with a white handkerchief.

"I consider myself a royal now, so I guess the lie worked!"

"How did you end up with *us*?"

"Well, the corrections officer made me an offer."

"He tricked you into joining the Vanguard."

"I was so scared I signed the contract right away. It was either death or military service. I chose to live."

"But it was a false choice."

"Yes, but still one I gladly made. He saved my life. A soldier's life isn't glamorous, mind you, but it's better than getting replaced. I was shipped to the Solomon Islands. The Inquisition was heating up. On my first day of action, I got shot in the leg."

He gingerly pinched the side seam of his pant leg and pulled it up slightly, revealing the metal frame that used to give me nightmares as a child.

"The war was bad enough. We killed a lot of angels. Bodies piled up to the sky. I thought we had won. But when I came back, I couldn't recognize this country anymore. Deviants were running amok. The streets were dirty. No one respected the law. No one cared about the soldiers. Then I met your grandfather."

"How?"

"At a charity ball he hosted for veterans. He was the only one in the entire country who cared about us. When he heard that I was looking for a job, he hired me on the spot."

A gentle knock at the door.

"Come in," said the old man.

I turned around to find the lovely Claudia in the flesh. She pretended she didn't see me at first, keeping her dark eyes on the floor as she set down a golden platter on the table next to us. On the platter was a cup of coffee, black, with a spoon of sugar on the side, just like the old man wanted. She seemed perfectly content with her life in this moment, so serene and innocent I could hold her gaze forever.

"Did you bring something for the young prince?" the old man asked.

"I'm sorry. I forgot."

"You better hurry then."

"No," I interrupted, "I want her to stay."

Our gaze met for the first time. Her chest heaved. She wanted to look away but couldn't. I needed her to stay. Blood rushed to her face. She smiled faintly enough to show that she still remembered me.

"Congratulations on your engagement," the old man said to her.

She strained to smile. "Thank you."

"Are you happy?" he asked.

"I'm sorry?"

"Don't be," said the old man, stealing a glance at me.

"I'm very happy," Claudia said, this time putting on a wide smile. "I feel lucky."

The old man smiled.

"I don't mean to pry. Who doesn't want a better life? I was just reminiscing with the young prince. Claudia, come here, dear." He reached out both hands. When she approached, he handed her the comb. "Why don't you give it a try?"

"No," I said. I reached for the comb but instead grabbed her hand. She didn't want to look at me. She was embarrassed. I pried her fingers loose, one by one, until the comb was free. She was so close I could touch her lips.

"Are you ready, my prince?" she asked, a lock of red hair caught between her red lips.

Being this close, I couldn't resist taking that strand of hair and pulling it away. It seemed like the right thing to do. She didn't resist. There was always a storm brewing in her eyes, a storm with the power to strip everything bare. She wasn't like the others. Behind the facade of the obedient servant girl lurked a predator as fierce as anyone she served. The harlot of providence, the woman of my dreams. Many stories had been told about her, and I was none the wiser.

While the old man was watching, she slipped one hand below my belt. I took a deep breath. She ran her hand along the edge of my leather belt and straightened the tip just a little.

"Let's not keep your father waiting," she said.

CHAPTER 5

VICTIMS OF SOCIETY

MARCUS

I couldn't shake the feeling that I was walking into a trap. Then again, I felt this way all the time. There was something about monarchs that I just couldn't understand, even though I was one. Every time I entered the main hall, I found myself getting swallowed up by the immensity of everything around me—the large slabs of perfectly burnished limestone floor, the gargoyle heads keeping watch, the grand vaulted ceiling with its frescos of fallen angels and bloodthirsty vanguards. I had walked this gilded hallway countless times, watched the first splash of sunlight wash over everything with a timeless glean, turning footsteps into an act of grandeur, but I could never really see this as my home. Home was something you could touch and feel. Home was a place where you could be yourself. Unfettered by expectations. Untouched by the nasty glare of society. But here, every step was the sound of expectations made real. There was no love or affection. Just the constant reminder to play your role, no matter the cost. I could hear mother say, "You have to own the place."

Precisely how you go about doing that she never told me. I tried my best, walking with a confident strut, which I had learned from my father, even though all I could think about was the servant girl. She made me feel better about myself. The thought was demeaning, and I knew it. Why should anyone be judged? But I kept thinking, you're judged all the time, and no one ever tries to understand you. So, yes, the only way to get through life is to judge everyone. It's how you keep your sense of self, your sense of power. After all, everyone who built this place was dead, and no one remembered any of them. It's just the way things were. Why question any of it?

As soon as I rounded the corner into the west wing, I found the savage standing outside father's personal suite. Anthony looked cleaner than usual, all dolled up for the big ceremony. Still, all the expensive clothing and makeup in the world can't disguise the vileness of someone's heart. He was guarding the door like a good lapdog, and when he saw me approach, he rolled his eyes. To think Claudia was going to marry this despicable beast made me want to disappear from the face of the planet.

"You're late," he muttered, his black eyes shining unusually bright. He was probably starving.

I pretended to be a gentleman and nodded at him. He was just a servant, I told myself, so treat him like one.

"Nice day," I said.

"I'm afraid I can't let you in," he said.

I smiled. "This is my father's room."

"Yes, it is, your grace," he said, dropping his voice a notch, "but the order came from your father."

"Claudia said father's ready for me."

"Claudia is just a servant."

"Excuse me?"

"I'm sorry, did I offend you?"

I glanced sideways at the hollow knight and fantasized taking my sword and stabbing this savage in the stomach. It would please me to see him drowning in his blood.

"I command you to move—"

"You should apologize when you see him."

"Why?"

"He's not in a good mood."

"You know nothing."

"I'm just trying to help you."

"Move!"

"No," he continued with a disgusting drawl. "Do you really want to upset the All-Father on Peace Day, of all days? By the way, your arm is bleeding."

The comment was made so casually I had no time to judge if he was lying or not. Almost at the same time, I felt a terrible itch on my forearm, and I had to stop myself from scratching it. Blood was seeping through the wound. I covered it with my right palm, feeling embarrassed.

"It's a rite of passage. You don't need to feel embarrassed," he said in a condescending manner, like he was educating a younger sibling. "When I served in the Vanguard, every soldier was required to take a vow of chastity."

"That's different. I'm not a soldier."

"We're all soldiers. We all serve a higher purpose."

"Maybe for you, not for me."

"How can you be so sure?"

"I'm the prince, and you're just a servant."

He grinned. I was afraid he might drop down to his knees and start kissing my feet. Instead, he had this to say: "I look forward to seeing you at the wedding."

I was on the verge of losing it. Then I heard the slippery old man call out, "You may come in now," and I got so flustered

I could barely stand. Anthony was pleased to see this and opened the door.

"After you, my prince," he said.

If my father hadn't sanctioned this kind of behavior, Anthony would have been executed by now. Instead of loving his own son, his own blood, the All-Father chose to love a savage instead. I was determined to reason with him and get to the bottom of this, once and for all.

When I walked into his office, the old man was hunched over the desk, silent and full of aggravation. I could sense it in the air, the gears turning tighter and tighter in his head. Against all the portraits of mythical heroes, he appeared awfully out of place. He was a modern man with modern sensibilities. There was nothing noble about him, except for the purple robe and crown, which sat on a shelf like a forgotten artifact.

Even though his back was facing me, I could see his eyes moving feverishly, darting back and forth, contemplating another scheme to save the country. They were feral eyes, eyes that saw through people without even looking at them. When he started turning on his ankle like a ballet dancer, I knew I was right. He had indeed cooked up another scheme. His face was flushed red as though embarrassed to see me, and his lips made out the words: "Faith is reason. Reason is faith. There is no reason to fear." He suddenly broke from this trance and turned his lizard gaze on me. "Do you like it?"

"I need to talk to you," I said in a rush.

"No, I need you to listen."

In the corner of my eye, I caught Anthony sitting down in a velvet chair not far behind us. He enjoyed hiding in the shadows, just like Father.

"Father, can we speak alone?"

"How about this," he went on, dismissing my request with a wave of his hand, "without faith, there is no reason to live—good?"

"Who are you trying to please?" I snapped back. I needed to make my displeasure known. It was the only way to get his attention.

"Who am I trying to please?" He shook his head and laughed. "Who am I trying to please? Is that a serious question?"

"It seems to me that half the country doesn't like you anymore."

"Excuse me?"

"People don't like religion anymore. They think it's fake."

"And you sympathize with their views?"

I paused, thought about the beautiful Claudia fixing my belt, and mustered the courage to say, "What if I do?"

"That's perfectly normal," he said, much to my surprise. "We all question our faith from time to time."

"The utopia is falling apart."

He only grew more amused. "Now, where did you hear that?"

"Don't talk to me like I'm a child."

"So the thought was completely yours?"

"Yes."

"Then explain to me what you mean by it."

"People are losing faith. There's nothing exciting going on. It's the same routine over and over. All we do is pray. Yes, we have peace, but at what cost? We do all these nice things for deviants, and how do they pay us back? They can never be satisfied. All they think about is revenge. If we don't fight back, everything we have will be gone. We must crush their rebellion, once and for all!"

I thought he would be so offended by now that he would

rather talk to me in private, but he seemed excited by the way I was challenging him. He watched me with his hands clasped behind his back, his head slightly forward, like a lizard trying to bathe in the sun.

"Are you referring to the Cult of Esoterica?" he asked politely, like a professor.

"Yes, but not just them! They're everywhere. Some are right under your nose."

This time, he picked up the hint.

"Come here, Anthony." He summoned the savage with a flick of his index finger. "Come here, Father wants to see you."

Anthony pretended to be shy about the whole thing, only getting up after Father prompted him again with even kinder words. They were probably both acting to spite me. Ever the chameleon, Anthony mirrored Father's body language and clasped his hands behind his back as well. He approached us with a slight bow, pretending to show deference when he couldn't even understand the concept of respect.

"Anthony is family," Father said. "Whatever you want to say to me, you can say in front of both of us."

I felt all the muscles in my body tensing. I needed to confront the problem head-on.

"Why do you like deviants so much?" I asked in as deep a voice as I could find.

"All-Father, I'm happy to leave—"

"Anthony, you did nothing wrong. You're like my son, and I'd hate for anyone to come between us."

"Anyone? *I* am your son! Why do you love him more than me?"

"Ah, there it is. You're jealous of him."

"No! I want to know why. Why do you love a deviant more than your own flesh and blood?"

"Marcus, your father loves you very much, and he loves everyone equally. That's why he's the All-Father."

"I wasn't talking to you."

"Listen to Anthony, he's right," said the person pretending to be my father. "Do you want to hear the truth?"

"All I want is the truth."

"Anthony will never be king. Anthony will never be the All-Father. The people will never follow him. He will always be a servant. Isn't that right, Anthony?"

"Yes, All-Father."

"But you, my son, will be king one day. One day, you will lead this country. When that day comes, you will have to understand one simple truth."

"What's that?"

"If you make someone feel seen, they will do anything for you. Take Anthony here. I adopted him when he was seven. He came from a poor family. His parents were radicals. They both died fighting for Esoterica, our enemy, during the Inquisition. He was an orphan before he even learned how to talk. But for the generosity of the empire, he would have perished a long time ago."

"The All-Father saved me," said Anthony, as if speaking from the same mind. "I learned to become civilized. I learned what it's like to receive grace and give back."

Pure hypocrisy.

"I adopted him, not because I wanted him to replace you," continued the All-Father, "but because he could one day become a symbol to the world."

"Symbol to the world? You just said he would never be king."

"A symbol can be many things. A symbol can help those with power maintain power. For you see, Anthony shows the power of grace. He is, for the lack of a better word, a stage prop. He shows deviants that there is a way out. You can escape misery if you follow our way of life. If you submit to our mercy. Do you understand?"

I was shocked to find Anthony completely stoic to what Father had just said. He was even nodding the whole time. If I were him, I'd be up in arms about being openly humiliated like this. Father was basically putting him in his place, and he welcomed the contempt with an open heart. At least, it seemed that way to me.

"Why are you not offended?" I asked him.

"Not everyone gets to live with the truth they want," he said.

"So that's why you treat me differently?" I asked the All-Father. "Just to prove a point?"

"No, it's just an act. We're all actors. I'm acting right now. That's the whole point. Anthony has graciously played the role we want him to play. In exchange, he gets to stay in the halls of power, but of course, he shall never have power himself. To the public, he's the brother you never had. He's lovable, simple-minded, and obedient, all the things we want disciples to be. People know he's still a savage. They'll never equate him to you. They can tell the difference, believe me. They just love that he makes them feel better about themselves. Everyone wants to feel good!"

"But father, I—" I stopped myself, feeling embarrassed for Anthony. I didn't know if I should press further.

"Say it. I want to hear."

"I disagree with the arrangement."

"I know you do, and the pain you're feeling now is a necessary part of your growth."

"Why should I be the one to suffer?"

"I don't think you have a right to complain. Look at him; Anthony's the very embodiment of suffering."

"The All-Father is right," he said.

"Frankly, you should be embarrassed right now," I said.

"I am."

"You seem to like it."

"Very much so. I enjoy playing the role of the reformed deviant."

"Don't you get tired of living in other people's shadows?"

"I don't get tired of living, no."

"Marcus, I'll say this straight and clear," followed the All-Father, "you will not marry a servant girl. Claudia belongs with Anthony; they're both victims of society, and victims belong together! Your heart will move on, and you'll find someone else. There's no shortage of women, God willing, for people like us. Don't be sad. Here, I have an idea."

He tapped the service bell on his desk three times, and moments later, a boy in blue overalls appeared. He arrived holding a white ceramic plate, but there was nothing on it. It was just an empty plate, and there was a flash of anger in his dark eyes. His arms were shaking.

Anthony turned pale.

"No, I beg you to give us mercy," he pleaded to the All-Father. His voice was on the verge of breaking. In all the time I'd spent with him, he had never sounded so desperate. The facade fell apart.

"Mercy has to be earned," the All-Father said, "and you have clearly aggravated my son."

"I apologize."

"No!" Father shouted. The outburst was so sudden and visceral I found myself shaking.

"I won't accept your apology. I want you to earn our mercy. And this time, I'll have my son be the judge."

Before I could open my mouth to speak, and truth be told, a part of me was dying to see the surprise, Father snatched the boy by the neck and slammed him against the edge of his desk. The plate fell on the carpet without a sound.

"No!" Anthony shouted. "Spare him! He's the only family I have!"

"So now you speak about family," said Father. "Don't you think that's a bit ironic, considering how you've treated my son?"

"Father, stop!"

"Look at him; the similarities are striking, aren't they? The savage, black eyes, the small forehead, clearly a sign of low intellect, and there, look," he said holding the boy's mouth open with his right hand, "the bloody red gum; like father, like son."

"He's bleeding...," I mumbled.

"Pain brings us closer to the truth. It's the only thing that matters in life."

"The boy didn't do anything," I said. "Let him go."

"Pass judgment, my son," he said, holding the boy by the chin. The boy was on the verge of tears but decided to stay strong for his father.

"What do you want me to say?" I asked.

"I want you to tell him how you felt after you killed the deviant."

I was so overcome with fear I couldn't speak. He was now turning his cruelty toward me. He wanted fealty from everyone. He demanded absolute obedience. That was the mercy of the All-Father.

"I felt...ashamed."

"Why?"

"He didn't deserve to die."

"You think I forced you to do it?"

"No, no. I don't think that. I think it was an act of mercy."

"Do you think this boy deserves the same mercy?"

"No!" Anthony almost lunged toward the All-Father but restrained himself in the last second.

I matched his gaze, and for the first time, I felt empathy—*real* empathy—toward him.

"I understand now," I said.

"Go on," said the monster, his hand clutching the back of the boy's neck while supporting himself on one knee.

"I understand that real mercy doesn't come from a higher being. It's about acceptance. Nothing more and nothing less."

"And?"

"And I will keep my vow, for as long as it takes."

"Very good," he said. Speaking to the boy: "You hear that, Misha? You just earned a second chance. You should be grateful. Are you grateful?"

"Yes…"

To my relief, he released the boy. Anthony took his boy into his arms, shedding tears of relief.

"Follow me," Father said, getting up as if nothing had happened. "We mustn't be late to the party."

CHAPTER 6

MAY I INTEREST YOU IN THE END OF THE WORLD

JASON

Faust didn't say anything when I left the office, except to flaunt his hair a little as he handed me a gift card. I got offended at first. Bear in mind, my shirt was still soaking wet with soda, and I had just failed the one test that mattered the most in my life. I could have made a scene and cursed at him, but when I saw Christine (formerly Rosario) eyeing me from behind the reception desk, I got a little flustered and thought better of it.

Ever the polite gentleman, Faust closed the door in my face.

I squeezed the gift card, feeling sorry for myself. Christine, on the other hand, looked pretty happy. She must have seen her fair share of shameful exits. This was a psychiatrist's office, after all, and delivering bad news to vulnerable people was their stock and trade.

"What can I buy with just fifty points?" I asked, wanting to elicit some empathy from her.

"You can buy someone a gift, maybe a watch?"

"A watch?"

"That's what I'd get. A lot of watches are on sale now."

I stared at her. Her eyes were still very blue, just like I remembered from the video, and she wore a dark-red lipstick that Rosario would have enjoyed. The expression on her face when she talked, halfway between a waitress and a lunatic, was unmistakably familiar. If I passed by her in the street, I could have mistaken her for Rosario. But when I looked at her more closely, I realized that the size and position of her features had shifted. And it wasn't just the facial features. It was the way she enunciated words, biting on every syllable as if she was hurting inside.

"Do you remember?" I asked. I'd seen my share of converts but never one officially confirmed.

"Come again?"

"Do you remember the procedure?"

"Oh, I see! You're asking if I've been replaced."

I nodded sheepishly.

"First of all, that's a rude thing to ask. And just between us, there are nicer things you can say to impress a lady."

"Sorry, I didn't mean to—"

"No, I've never been replaced. You think just because I sit behind a desk I'm not smart enough to make it? Let me tell you something, I know more about the world than you ever will. Behind this desk, I see everything. I've seen very success-ful people, bona fide predators at the top of their game, and then there are people like you, desperately seeking attention because you failed. Did I capture that accurately?"

I grimaced.

"Don't just stand there! Go on! Buy your daddy a gift!"

I couldn't tell if this was an insult or not, because she said it in such a caring voice. Frankly, I felt sorry for her. She was confused. You don't talk to people who are confused. You let them be. So I gave her a nod, as if nothing awkward ever happened between us, and started walking away. That was when she chased after me with an ice pack in her hand.

"You're burning up," she said, forcing the ice pack into my hand. "Take this, it'll make you feel better. I'll see you soon, okay?"

"Goodbye, Christine."

"Goodbye, Jason."

I felt quite relieved pressing the ice pack against my face. I was really burning up, and I didn't even realize it. Ever since I got sick, the fever had never gone away. It lingered like a sad little ghost banished from the world of the dead. I tried to comfort him sometimes, but he would never listen. He'd get angry at me, sometimes so angry he would consume every thought. Fortunately, there were other distractions, like the janitor sweeping the floor in the lobby and whistling as I walked past. He seemed oblivious to me and oblivious to the fact that his life had ended a long time ago. The wonderful thing was that he didn't seem to care. I told myself I shouldn't either.

When the ice had melted, I felt something hard inside the bag. I ripped open the plastic cover to find a little pill inside. I took the pill and saved it in my pocket.

It was already November, and the streets were still burning up. As I tossed the empty bag into the trash can, I made the mistake of taking a deep inhale—rotten food, asphalt burning, car tires being whittled down, buildings that never opened their windows, and the stench of human sweat, which could never be washed away, by rain or blood. There was still leftover rain from last night, gathered in small puddles under the cover of darkness. I stepped in one just after crossing Main Street, right under the veranda of a quaint salon, and suddenly felt better about myself. I shot a quick glance inside the salon and saw a young man dipping his head into a bowl of mercury. I heard back in the day the founders wanted to create a city where no one needed to hide. They thought if you put all the smart people together in one place, there would be no place left for vanity. The light of the universe would shine on everyone equally. I don't blame them for being so naive. Who could have known that human beings never wanted peace to begin with. What we want cannot ever be attained. What we want has nothing to do with desires. It's just the feeling of being wanted.

Where do you go to feel wanted? Does this city give what you need? It helps to feel invisible. If no one really needs to notice you, you just vanish in the crowd. Sometimes, when I walk among the people, I can hear him sing:

Stop your worrying, better times are ahead.

Just don't bury your head in the sand, unless you wish to die.

Pop songs may come and go, but I kept thinking, maybe the nightmare was never meant to end. Maybe there was no paradise in the great beyond. I saw a man on the billboard stomping on a scarlet-winged angel with boots the size of a skyscraper. More than a few pedestrians smiled glancing up at the billboard. There was nothing left in the world that could make these people blush. They were shameless and proud of it.

I never believed the lie. I merely wanted to escape it.

Behold the arrival of the witching hour. When the clocktower struck twelve, the light began sweeping through the streets. There was a burning sensation when the aura touched your face, and in that moment you were graced by the touch of God. Or something like it. The stars were suddenly bursting with purple smoke as crop dusters streaked across the sky, releasing a toxin designed to dull the senses. With the whole city drowning in a state of loss, the Ark, a massive monolith, flew over the sun, blanketing the city with darkness for a few seconds. From afar, the all-black exterior seemed smooth and silent, but up close, you could see all the tiny, contorted faces and arms writhing beneath the surface, laughing, screaming, pleading for some kind of freedom. This time, the Ark flew so close overhead I felt like I could touch it with my outstretched arm. We waved at them when they passed us by. They were dead souls granted a second chance. In their former lives, they were soothsayers, mass murderers, daredevils, gladiators, politicians, all manner of psychopaths who had risen to the apex of society. I used to marvel at them. I dreamed of joining them one day, ascending to the great beyond. Now, that dream was dead. I wouldn't even remember this dream after I was replaced. The past would be gone forever.

Walking past the old Memory Palace, I caught a large black-and-gold monarch butterfly flying over my eyes. When I opened my palm, the butterfly was flopping with its last breath, and a second later, it turned into a specimen. What a fitting metaphor for the city. A little girl saw me staring at the dead butterfly and giggled. When I looked at her, she frowned. I wasn't sure if she was laughing at me or the butterfly. This was one of the many things I hated about myself. I could never figure out someone's intent. I always ended up getting confused in the end. Apparently, everyone's intent is good until it isn't.

Everything is such a mystery.

Churches were everywhere. The one in front of me, the Church of Saint Anthony, jutted into the sky with its colossal spines. There were homeless people camped out just outside. They seemed nicer than the gargoyles perched on the Gothic arches. If the church was such a wonderful place, why would it not offer a home for the homeless? Maybe I was just being naive. There must have been some hidden intent I couldn't see. Maybe the homeless people were left to starve to prove that God could smite anyone he wished.

I don't blame God. I also find it uneasy to offer the homeless any consolation. When I saw one of them approach, I tried to fix my eyes on the ground to avoid confrontation. But he insisted on catching my attention.

"The world's coming to an end, brother," he said, "won't you spare a coin for a stranger in need?"

I waved my hand to dismiss him, but he kept jabbing me with his propaganda pamphlet. "Esoterica" was written in dark-red letters on the cover. To stop him from pestering me, I took the pamphlet and said, "Thank you."

"You're missing out, brother," he said.

"I'm not your brother," I said, trying to move past him.

He blocked my path once again.

"Join us. Join us before it's too late!"

I hated being haggled, especially when the harassment was coming from someone from my own tribe.

"Will you let me pass?" I asked as politely as I could.

He still refused to move and kept staring at me with his albino eyes. He was probably just eighteen, but the fever made him appear eighty. I didn't want to look at him. He made me sick. I felt embarrassed for him.

"You want money?" I took out a five-point bill and stashed it in his pocket. "Off you go. Best of luck!"

Suddenly he grabbed my wrist with his cold hand, and flashing a vicious glare, he yanked me off-balance toward his chest. His strength was inhuman.

"I don't want your money," he whispered through a red half-mask. "Is this who you want to be?"

When he saw that a small crowd had gathered, he released me. But by then, the damage was done. I was thoroughly embarrassed.

Then he threw his arm around my back as if he had always been my friend.

"Look." He pointed to a row of monks sitting in a lotus position on the sidewalk. They were all deviants about my age. They wore red-and-white linen robes, their heads shaven clean. "I can show you the way."

I pretended to smile for the crowd and said, "No, thank you."

He refused to let go. "Look! It's happening!"

At that instant, as if he had been waiting for the cue, the monk in the middle caught fire. No one helped him. The fire just erupted from within his body. The linen robe soon melted away, leaving his body exposed.

He didn't scream. He didn't speak. He just peered across to a point unseen. All the psychos around us were mesmerized, including the little girl I had met earlier, who started clapping furiously. Her father looked on with tremendous pride. This was exactly the kind of child he wanted to raise, a demon who enjoyed savoring someone else's pain. If I were still deluded about pleasing the nobles, and honestly that part of me never left, I would have started clapping as well. I would have gladly gutted my own pride to make them happy. I wouldn't have cared that the monk was killing himself in a pointless act of protest.

I wouldn't have cared that the leader was sacrificing his own people for the pleasure of his superiors.

But what difference did it make? The truth always prevailed, whether you realized it or not.

CHAPTER 7

I LEARN TO SMILE

JASON

"Welcome to Lucky Seven, sir!"

I didn't need to turn my head to recognize the voice. I licked the ember on my lip. It made me hungry.

The service model bowed. He looked just like me. I couldn't bear being on the receiving end of customer service, especially when that service came from my own kind.

"Is everything all right?"

"Yes."

"We have all the latest models available. The diamond section is on sale for a limited time only."

I tuned him out and made a beeline for the gold section. In my hurry I bumped into another patron. I thought for a second that he was my science teacher, judging by the shape of his head, which was very round and bald, but I was relieved when he rolled his eyes at me. He clearly wanted to be alone. In fact, this little store was always full of lonely people. No one could afford to buy the expensive watches in the gold section. We only prowled the area to mark our territory, pretending to be lions among a flock of disgruntled sheep. And there I was, fantasizing about being accepted. None of these people wanted a service model to shop at their store. No one. A service model was supposed to serve them, not shop for watches. It's clear by the way they looked at me. The older folks would always try to put some distance between their orbit and mine. God forbid if we ever crossed paths. The whole universe would explode.

"What catches your eye?"

The store clerk looked just like me. I ignored him at first.

"May I assist you, sir?"

I couldn't ignore him anymore. He was treating me like a gentleman.

"Yes, I'm looking for the models you have on sale."

He smiled. "Sir, you're looking at the wrong section. Follow me, please."

I couldn't be sure if the new line of service models were trained to understand derision, but I certainly found it in his voice.

"I'm asking if there are any on sale in the gold section," I insisted.

He ignored me this time. When he got to the silver section, which was marked by a cheap silver tape over the floor, he waved at me.

I gave him a look and pretended to be annoyed.

He smiled and waved again.

On my way over, I saw Vanguard policemen with their black steeds on the opposite side of the street, arresting the cult leader who had accosted me earlier. The fire had been put out, and the policeman were making small talk with the nobles.

"Sir, this is the section where we have some wonderful watches on sale. What's the occasion?"

"Nothing special. Just a gift."

"For a birthday, anniversary…"

"We can say birthday."

"Is it for a loved one or a colleague?"

"It's for me."

"Oh, that's wonderful! Happy birthday!"

"Thanks."

"In that case, I have two options for you. This one, released last fall, a capable sports watch by Dyne & Masters, only worn for a few days. This one is slightly more expensive, but it's never been worn. It has a beautiful silver-tone brass case with stainless-steel back. This is a Vulture model with a newly installed déjà vu dial."

"Does the hologram still work?"

"You like Charlie Conrad?"

I shrugged.

"Mr. Conrad wore this watch when he was young; well, not this exact model you're holding, but he always preferred old-fashioned watches, you know, ones without holograms."

"Thanks, I appreciate the history lesson—"

"Yes, of course. And I'll include a new case for you, if you purchase this one today."

"How much is it?"

"Fifty-nine points. And this is the least expensive model we have on sale."

I tried hard to keep my frustration inside. I smiled and asked if he could offer me a better price.

"I'm afraid I cannot do that, sir."

"What if I just get the watch, no case? Can you come down to fifty?"

"I'm sorry, but I need to speak to my manager."

The manager came out of his shabby office in the back of the shop. He was a large man, and his head was bald, like most store owners in the city. I had only seen him a few times before, but he seemed to recognize me as soon as he made eye contact.

"How can I help you, young man?" He carried a thick binder in one hand and kept rubbing his nose with the other.

"Yes, I'm asking if you can give me a discount on this old watch?"

"Old? This watch is brand new!"

"It's an old model, and I was telling your associate that I don't need the case."

"What's your price?"

"Fifty points."

He murmured something to the service model, and they laughed. Then he faced me and put on a strange smile. "Cash only."

"I have a gift card."

"Cash only."

"It's a Lucky Seven gift card." I flipped the card over. "It says you can redeem points at any Lucky Seven store."

"Fine," said the manager, much to my surprise. He mumbled something again to his employee, spun on his heel like a ballerina, and shuffled back to his office. With his back facing me, he waved his hand and shouted, "Best of luck!"

All the patrons were watching. He clearly wanted to embarrass me. If I were the same person from just a year ago, I would have returned the favor many times over. But something had changed inside me. Whoever had snatched my soul away never bothered to come back. I nodded at the service model, who seemed pleased. He got what he'd wanted, for me to admit that I was no better than him. Fine. I got what I wanted too. I took the watch and flew out of the store.

The bus ride was insufferable. I couldn't stop shaking my

leg, and the old lady next to me kept trying to strike up a conversation. When I told her I had mental problems, she confessed that she had problems too and that no doctor was ever to be trusted. On this point we shared a laugh. I couldn't stop thinking about her after I got off the bus. I started to wonder if she had been replaced when she was young. And if she was, it gave me some hope that she had managed to remember her hatred for doctors. But then again, it could just be the psychopath inside her talking. Maybe she saw me as a potential victim—for what, I couldn't be sure.

I was walking toward the Orchard, a senior apartment, and watching the old folks rocking in their chairs on the porch, when a car screeched to a halt behind me. When I turned around, I saw two teenagers in preppy suits running at me, one wearing a sock over his head, another with red, spiky hair. I was confused for a moment. I didn't recognize either of them. Even when the kid with spiky hair snatched the bag out of my hand, I foolishly insisted that they got the wrong person.

"Freak!" he shouted.

"Deviant freak!" his friend joined.

When I reached for the bag, the boy with spiky hair lobbed it over my head, and the watch fell out and crashed to the ground. Without a case to protect it, the watch shattered on impact. There was nothing I could do. I had never felt so hopeless. I fell to my knees and scooped up the broken pieces, wondering what had happened to the world. As if my prayer had been answered, one of the rich boys drove his boot into the small of my back. I crashed hard on my teeth. I took another blow to the back of my head, and my senses went gray. They kept on watching. The old people and the matriarch, so fine in her foxy red jumpsuit. They insisted on the pain,

through and through. And what could I do? What could I
do but laugh? I couldn't let a bunch of kids steal my dream,
could I now? No, I took the pain. I took it all. Let the venom
flow. Let the hatred bruise my face. I laughed all the way to
kingdom come.

CHAPTER 8

A BRIGHT FUTURE INDEED

JASON

Evening came sooner than I had expected. I was relieved. I didn't want people to see the bruises on my face, but then again, no one really cared. The people living in my apartment were already bruised, hammered every day by the impossibility of earning a future. Not that I sympathized with any of them. They would never spill their secrets, and the moment they spotted weakness, they'd pounce on it, and you would regret ever trusting them in the first place. I'd learned my lesson a long time ago.

There was no satisfaction to be found in the mailbox. Just a flier for a Sunday prayer circle with all the worst sellouts in the neighborhood. Pass. I caught myself in the dirty mirror on the wall above the mailbox. I didn't so much look at myself as I pretended to exist. Have others practiced this? Looking at themselves without seeing anything. Just feeling the weight of the world pressing down on them, inch by inch. I opened my jaws wide like a snake and held them open until my muscles got tired.

I avoided the elevator, as usual, and took the stairs. I hated the idea of being trapped inside a small space with strangers. I preferred the feeling of being alone in the darkness. A new motivational speech was playing over the loudspeakers, accompanied by soft classical music. This time, it was a young woman talking about the importance of staying centered. There was nothing original about the message.

Be grateful.

Learn from failure.

Take responsibility.

It was all stuff one could find in the bargain-bin section of bookstores.

Perhaps I should have paid more attention. Sometimes, I wondered how different life would be if I had never possessed a conscience. Every time I walked up these stairs, I was reminded of possibilities that would never come to pass. I used to be so full of ambition and hope. I used to look forward to coming home. I wanted to prove to my father that I was everything he wanted me to be.

How do I tell him the truth? How do I justify having accomplished nothing after all the blood and sweat? So close, yet so far was the best I could muster. As I approached Room 909, I decided that I would come clean, not about everything, just the pieces he needed to believe. I wanted to spare him the pain.

When I opened the door, I heard some hack on TV blathering about how much he admired the prince. Our tiny studio was filled with the buttery smoke of bacon.

"You're back just in time!" Father shouted happily. "I made you bacon and eggs!"

I walked into the small alcove that was our dining room, and the first thing I saw was the media-trained, feckless face of Prince Kane. I wanted to turn off the TV.

"Wash your hands first!"

He didn't even look at me when he set down the plates.

"If I may be so bold," said the news anchor, "I think I have a crush on him too."

"Can you believe it?" added Father, "we'll meet the royal family tomorrow!"

I sighed.

"What's wrong?"

"Nothing."

"Wait, turn around."

"Why?"

"Let me see your face."

I pretended to wash my hands. I lost interest in telling him my whole life story.

"What happened?"

"Nothing."

"Stop!" He grabbed my wrist with his big hand, which I hated; he always had a way of making me self-conscious.

"Turn around, let me see your face. My God! What happened? Who did this to you? Did you get into a fight?"

Yes, everything had to be my fault. Nothing unprovoked ever happened to anyone.

"You wouldn't understand," I told him.

"I'm your father. I care about you."

I dried my hands with a towel that was half-soiled and sat down. The bacon and eggs appeared stale. I took a deep breath and looked at him with my swollen eye.

"This isn't how I imagined this would go… I, never mind. It's nothing. I got jumped by a bunch of kids. That's all."

"Kids? Why?"

"Yeah, kids about my age. Maybe a bit younger. Why? Because they hate me for what I am."

"Did you know them?"

"No. That's the whole point. They hate people like me. They probably don't even think I'm a person. Maybe they're right."

"Hey! It's not your fault."

"Thank you for saving my conscience."

He cackled. "You should direct your anger at the people who hurt you, not me."

"Funny you say that. It's exactly what I had in mind."

"To be clear, I'm not advocating violence."

"I wasn't either."

"Do you need some ice?"

"No, I'm fine."

"Well, we want to look dapper for the big day tomorrow, don't we?"

"Is that all you care about?"

"Have some food," he said, clanging his dirty fork against my plate. "Forget about them. Don't give them the time of day. They're just angry at themselves. Hurt people hurt people. They're jealous of you."

I jabbed a piece of bacon and dumped it into my mouth.

"Why would they be jealous of me?"

"I don't know. Maybe they aren't happy with their life."

"I'm sure their life is better than mine."

"Look, I'm trying to help you, son."

"I know. Sometimes people do things for no reason."

"Exactly."

"All rich people are psychopaths."

"A psychopath is what we should strive to be," he responded with all the sincerity in the world. "Beat them at their own game, right?"

I noticed the struggle in his eyes. He didn't believe his own words, but he almost pulled it off. He could have been a politician in a different life. "I was the captain of my high school debate club," he'd often reminisce. "Everyone said I should go into politics. They told me I had the look." Well, he had a ruddy and somewhat chubby face, basically the look of all lying politicians. Too bad his eyes gave him away. He couldn't hold his gaze long enough at anything, and if you want to be a politician, you have to look at people in the eyes all the time. Even when you're lying to them, over and over. I pitied him. His heart was in the right place, but his mind could never catch up. He was always stuck, just like me.

"Isn't he handsome?" He nodded toward the TV, where a female reporter was interviewing Prince Marcus Kane outside a sanitarium and fawning over him for his "service to the community." Apparently, this "service" consisted of feeding the homeless deviants his family had cast out into the streets.

"Yes, he is," I said. "He's very handsome."

"That's who you want to be, Jason. You don't let anything stop you. You hear me?"

I chuckled. "What about *your* dream?"

"My dream has come true. I live through you now. You're my hope and dream."

"Father—"

"It's not just the special pardon. That's great, amazing, of course. But there's something even better than that. You've grown into the person I knew you'd always become. Smart, composed, in command. The All-Father chose you for a reason. You earned it!"

"I don't know if I've accomplished anything…"

"This isn't the time to be humble. You have to own the spotlight."

"All these years, I've never said thank you."

"You don't have to."

"I passed the authenticity test," I said through a humble smile.

"Oh my God, that's wonderful news! Congratulations, son!"

"Thank you."

"Do you have the certificate? We have to find a good place to put it up. I want everyone to see it."

"I don't have the certificate. Not yet. I'll be picking it up next week. Mr. Faust already showed me the frame. It looks really nice."

"You see, this is what I'm talking about! You're every bit as talented as any noble in the world. Don't ever let anyone tell you otherwise. Come here." He opened his arms to welcome me into his embrace. I missed moments like this.

"I bought you a gift," I said as I sat down again.

"Oh, you didn't have to." He tucked his chin, trying to hide the emotions welling up in his eyes.

"Vulture, special edition," I proudly announced and took the watch out of the bag. At the same time, I put my hands on the table and closed them over the watch. He could only see the leather straps for the moment. "Unfortunately... it's damaged. This was the best one I could afford. I'm sorry."

"No need to apologize! I want to see it. Yes, show me."

"But it's broken..."

"Nothing broken can't be fixed. Let me see."

I slowly opened my hand to reveal the broken watch. Instead of disappointment, I saw real joy on his face. In fact, I had never seen him this happy. Genuinely happy. He was grinning ear to ear. He picked up the watch and massaged the case with his thumb.

"This is the model I always wanted," he said. "How did you know?"

"It's the model Anthony Conrad wore in the movies, and I know how much you like Conrad films."

His face lit up. I saw the happiness of a child.

"God, I miss the Westerns. Different time... Thank you, for remembering."

"After tomorrow, the world will remember us too."

"Well said, my son," he whispered. There was a rosy tint on his cheeks. "You know, I used to fight with your mother all the time, but she was right about you. She always knew you had potential."

"Do you miss her?"

He sighed. "Honestly, all the time."

"Where is she now?"

"I don't know. She doesn't want us to know."

"I hope she'll be watching us tomorrow."

"Well, she's not that into the royal family."

I smiled.

"You're my son, but I feel like there's so much about you I don't even know. I should've been around more often. I work way too much."

For a moment, I wanted to tell him the truth.

"When was the last time you saw her?"

He was a bit taken aback by the question. When the reporter started raving about the royal family again, he recovered.

"I don't remember. Maybe five years ago?"

"I wish she were here with us."

"I know, but like you said, soon, we'll be famous. Who knows? Maybe she'll come running back!"

CHAPTER 9

MY FATHER IS A FALSE PROPHET

MARCUS

Father and I never spoke about the time I discovered his secret. Even now, after all these years, he pretended it never happened. He knew that I knew, and that was more than enough for him. A part of him was probably happy that I knew, because in his mind, keeping the secret drew me closer to him. Now we both carried the cross. Sometimes I would have this imaginary conversation with him, and he would confess and tell me that he never intended harm on anyone, and he would change everything if the world would only allow him to change. We needed to give the people what they wanted, even if it meant sacrificing the truth. A work of fiction is better than real life. People don't want you to talk down to them, they want the illusion of hope.

At some point, I found myself unable to separate fact from fiction. These ideas I just expressed, I could not remember where they came from—father, myself, or God speaking to me. But no matter, thoughts never lingered long enough for them to make complete sense. The world was constantly changing, faster than I could understand. Mother would tell me that I'm worrying too much, that I'd get it eventually. Maybe she was right. But as I followed the All-Father down this road, I felt completely lost.

He appeared to me like the specter of a great warrior, risen from the dead to lead his people to the promised land. The people were cheering for him, swaying and shouting and crying like they were possessed by some demonic spirit. The hovercraft helped to elevate him even more: from where the crowd was standing, the All-Father seemed to be flying. He waved at the crowd like a pageant queen performing to a live television audience, his lips curved ever so slightly to give the impression of a smile. Look at all these people! They were nothing but rabid creatures craving for attention. Father was good at making people feel important, even though he despised everyone, perhaps including himself. When someone has nothing real to love, he can be everything and nothing at once. So he gave them what they wanted, a gentle wave to the workers, a prayer to the hysterical sisters, a nod to the boy looking for affection, and even a kiss on the forehead of the girl who climbed over the barricade.

She carried a doll with her and gave it to the All-Father. He waved the guards away and accepted her gift. He took her into his embrace and whispered something into her ear. She grinned. The crowd went delirious. I got caught up in it too, and when I broke into a ridiculous smile, the photographer closed in and snapped another picture. Just then, I saw Mother through the rolled-down window of her limousine, looking at me stoically, as if trying to warn me about something. I steered my horse closer to the limousine and called her name. She pretended not to hear me at first, staring down at her radiant, silvery dress.

"Focus," Anthony broke in. He was riding parallel to me now, and the girls went crazy. "Shake my hand."

I tried to ignore him but remembered all the stories about my "friendship" with Anthony in the news. The media loved to paint us as brothers, the young monarch and his savage big brother, even though this could not be further from the truth. Still, there was a price to pay for being famous. So I turned to him and shook his hand for the cameras and the girls. Father turned around for the first time and gave me a condescending look. He must have been angry at me for stealing his spotlight. But, of course, he nodded at Anthony with approval.

Annoyed, I swerved to the other side of the limousine.

Another version of me ran straight into the crowd, trampling children and mothers. All the way in the back stood a savage man clad in a hooded cloak. He touched my hand, and I evaporated. The road shot up in flames, and the church crumbled to the ground, its Gothic spires breaking into a million pieces. Tanks rolled over innocent people left and right. Only the little girl remained, standing alone in the rubble. I reached out to save her, but it was too late.

When I came to, I found myself on the verge of falling off the horse. Thankfully, our bodyguard rushed over on his black steed and saved me from total embarrassment. Joseph helped me get back on the saddle, and I regained my focus. A crowd of faces watched me. They looked rather disappointed when they saw that I had managed to recover. I understood how they felt.

My eyes were scorching hot, and I had to close them for a few seconds to see clearly again.

"Do you need anything, my lord?" asked Joseph, putting his hand on my back.

"I'm fine," I said, "it's just the heat."

"Are you sure? I can call the doctor."

"No, please don't."

In the purple, misty gloom I could still see the hooded man standing there in the crowd. While his face was shrouded in darkness, his eyes burned bright orange.

For a moment, I thought I heard Mother crying out for me, but when I turned to look for her, she was speaking to the little girl, telling her father how she loved her little dress.

At last, we arrived at the majestic Saint Joseph's Square. There was something about its symmetry that seemed unreal. In fact, you could say that everything in our city was fake. Of course, I don't mean that we live inside a simulation. I certainly hoped not. Ours was a spiritual place—everything had to be an article of faith. A water fountain was a place of cleansing. A palm tree marked a rite of passage. A cicada didn't just chirp incessantly; it spoke the language of gods. The ground below us used to be a massive burial site. I imagined thousands and thousands of angels, living, breathing mythical creatures of fevered imagination, laid to waste as unceremoniously as a man might step on an army of ants.

The large, round plaza was flanked by massive Doric colonnades, four columns deep, wrapping around all these important people, like a mother smothering a child. We were the children of her misdeeds, and we would repent forever.

I was shaking off the numbness in my legs when Mother came over and grabbed my hand. I felt embarrassed being so close to her with all these people staring at me.

"Stay close," she said.

"Let me go," I whispered, trying my best to hide my disgust.

"All good?" she asked. There was a strange, flustered twinkle in her eyes.

"All good. Now, can you please let go of my hand?"

The moment she released my hand I felt alone, like I was cast adrift in the middle of the ocean.

Claudia walked over holding Anthony's hand and made a slight bow toward Mother.

"Your grace," she said, "may God bless our utopia."

"May God bless our utopia," mother repeated with a nod.

Just before Claudia slipped inside the crowd, she turned back, as though searching for me, and when I smiled at her, she turned the other way with a blank expression.

"Sir," Joseph said, giving me a bouquet of roses. "The ceremony is about to begin."

I took the flowers and followed Mother toward the white obelisk. She took long strides, as if to spite me for wanting to be close to her again.

"Is there anything I need to say?" I asked Joseph out of anxiety.

"Just the usual."

"I pray for peace to last forever?"

"Something like that," he said with a childish grin. "Or you could say that you have no interest in being here."

"That would be a crowd-pleaser."

"Possibly. You never know what people want."

I looked at him for a second, pleasantly surprised. He was usually a very serious person, and I never knew he was capable of sarcasm. I suppose even a convert could afford to laugh a little about life. He walked with a limp, so I slowed my pace to allow him to catch up. His face was rather tense, glowing under the setting sun like a marble statue. It struck me that everyone here was older than me. I was always looking up at people, trying to find their eyes and figure out what they were thinking.

The horn let out a long, mournful sigh. The din of polite laughter and small talk subsided.

A small crowd, all prescreened by the royal court, gathered around the obelisk. Father smoothed his blond, slicked-back hair with his free hand, took a deep breath, and approached the tomb of the unknown soldier with a stash of roses. With the camera focused on him, he kissed the roses and dropped to one knee.

"Happy Peace Day," he said, laying the flower on the tomb.

Just as father started to recite the eulogy, someone in the crowd shouted, "Traitor! Down with the false prophet!"

The crowd of dignitaries gasped, turning left and right in a race to see who could find the heckler first.

CHAPTER 10

OVERDOSE

MARCUS

Soon enough, I spotted the heckler. He was a sorry-looking fellow with thinning hair and a pot belly. The navy-blue blazer he wore didn't suit him. You expected someone like him to walk out of the house half-naked and not even realize it. He probably didn't even graduate high school and resented everything about his life. That much was clear in the way his facial muscles twitched every time he opened his mouth.

"You sold us out!" he cried, jumping up and jabbing at the air. When he didn't get the reaction he wanted, he repeated the accusation two more times, like a politician losing his mind on the debate stage. In fact, he probably fancied himself a rough-and-tumble politician playing the role of a mob boss. The suggestion of violence was a badge of honor. He got really annoyed when he saw that no one was reacting to him the way he wanted. No one tackled him. No one reprimanded him. They just laughed at him.

We nobles really know how to make someone feel bad.

All the while, he kept shouting things like "war criminal" and "deviant lover" while father watched on stoically. I could feel that a part of him even wanted to smile, given how ridiculous the heckler was acting.

A Vanguard deputy entered the crowd from the back and started making his way to the heckler. Oblivious to this, the heckler raised his voice even more.

"You're aiding and abetting the enemy, sir! You love deviants more than your own kind. Shame on you!"

"Oh, shut up!" Father finally snapped, drawing cheers and applause. "You're the one who should be ashamed of yourself!"

"I hate you! I hate all of you! You're all part of the cabal. You all hate this country!"

The crowd finally lost it and began to hiss and boo.

Then, in the midst of all the noise, a woman shouted, "I love you, All-Father!"

Father seized on the opportunity and said, "I love you back!"

The whole crowd burst into applause.

As the officer approached the heckler, Father signaled for him to halt.

"What's your name?" Father asked the heckler.

The heckler froze, not expecting such a simple question. He turned beet red and started shaking. He squeezed his left bicep with his right hand, as if to prevent himself from doing something he had in mind.

"Mr. Spencer," he answered almost deliriously, confusing the question about his name for the name of the All-Father. "I'm a free man! I can speak my mind, and there's nothing you can do about it!"

It was at that moment Lady Matilda emerged in her chain-mail armor and red cloak. She strode toward the heckler with such intensity his face turned pale, and he nearly tripped over himself while backing away. In half a second, the blustering slob had turned into a coward. But instead of stabbing him in the heart with her sword, Matilda reached for the man's arm and put her hand over his bicep.

"When did you serve with the Vanguard?" she asked, staring into the man's frightened blue eyes.

The man looked up as if he had just awakened from a horrible nightmare. I knew that look well.

"In the final campaign, ma'am. On the Western Front."

"Thank you for your service," Matilda said.

"Thank you," he whispered like a scared child.

"I want you to know that you're not forgotten," she said in a low, almost masculine tenor. "We may spare compassion for the least among us, but this country will always belong to us."

"We *died* for the cause." The man-child was pleading for sympathy.

"I know. A part of all of us died for the war. The All-Father fought for us too. He's not your enemy. *We* are not your enemy. The enemy does exist. He's invisible most of the time, but we know who he is."

The soldier nodded.

"We don't love deviants. We love our own."

"That's what we fought for."

"And we won. We *won*. This day, Peace Day, is a reminder that we won. You helped to make that possible, soldier."

"Yes, ma'am," he answered sheepishly.

"Now, give me the gun."

I was shocked, like the rest.

The drunken lunatic was now thoroughly reduced to a child. His face contorted like a clown pretending to cry, and no tears really came out, except for a little drop of blood in the corner of his right eye. He wanted to wipe the blood away, but Matilda repeated the order. He reached for his pocket and produced what looked like a black revolver. As he handed the gun to Lady Matilda, he grabbed her hand and fell to his knees, breaking into a horrible sob. The man was clearly unstable, but never did I imagine him breaking down like this. The transformation was too drastic, too fast. I didn't know what to make of it. Matilda was satisfied. She took the gun away and passed it to the officer.

You could hear the dignitaries letting out a sigh of relief. It was both relief and excitement. These were monarchs, after all. Life has a tendency to get boring for people who have everything, though we learned to enjoy the suggestion of danger every now and then. I found myself turning giddy as the soldier started convulsing, his eyes oozing with blood. He fell into Matilda's arms, and she held him like a soldier holding his comrade, savoring one final moment of peace.

No one felt sorry for him. Some of us giggled. Some stood there hypnotized like they were watching a play. Matilda showed no emotion, at least not the kind I could describe. What came onto her face was strange, inhuman, but also natural and inevitable. It was the look of a teacher scolding a child on the verge of tears. It was the contempt of a murderer defying the warden as poison entered his veins. It was the painful generosity of a female politician when she discovered that her husband was cheating on her. It was all these things and more, like Matilda was touched by the grace of God. You could almost hear her say, "Are you in love with me?"

I peered into her eyes when she stood up, and she looked back at me, quite aware of how I was feeling about her.

Mother approached Father to check on him. Acting gracefully, he gave her a pat on the back.

Meanwhile, the soldier spasmed more violently, his back arched as if a demonic spirit was on the verge of breaking out. I was supposed to feel something as I watched this despicable man suffer. Was I supposed to feel sorry for him? Was

I supposed to laugh? I felt all these emotions rush over to me, but nothing was strong enough to take root. The same was true for everyone else. The best word I could think of to describe our reaction was *amusement*. Yes, we were rather amused. One could only scoff at such a sad state of affairs.

Another officer came and, working with his colleague, dragged the soldier away, even as he was choking on his own blood. No one offered to save him. The thought seemed improper. This was Peace Day, after all. It was a solemn occasion for important people.

"He got what he deserved," snarled Matilda as she approached me. She smelled like my mother, except there was something bitter in her breath. She still had that expression on her face from when she was holding her kindred spirit in her arms. The facade wanted to fade, but she held it together.

"Aren't you sad for him?" I asked.

She adjusted her armor, pretending not to hear me, and turned toward Mother, who seemed intent on moving closer to me. She noticed this too and planted herself between us.

"Thank you," Mother said to Matilda with an awkward smile, while giving me an admonishing glare. She must have heard me question Matilda and thought it improper. I merely asked a question. "You're a lifesaver," she added, like she was Matilda's servant.

I felt embarrassed for Mother. Why did she always have to ingratiate herself like this? Didn't she know that Matilda was her subordinate? She was just the head of the Syndicate, a lowly group still clinging to old ideas. The world had moved on. There were no countries. No ideologies. Only the endless striving for more.

CHAPTER 11

PLAYING THE VICTIM

The waiting room smelled like old perfume and cigarettes. There was a fan on the ceiling, but it had stopped working a long time ago. The leather on the sofa was probably fake, and the springs in the cushion were dead. There were old tabloid magazines scattered around the room, some spread over the coffee table, some torn to pieces over the rotten carpet. There were broken smiles everywhere.

The "assistant" was a middle-aged lady who talked like she was still sixteen, putting on a fake smile every time she finished a sentence. She wore very red lipstick and pressed her lips together every few seconds like she was on a pageant show. I guess being around rich people all the time but never being rich yourself can do that to a person.

Dad was rather smitten with her and kept pestering her with stupid questions. For the first time, Dad felt like he was an important person in the world, and he relished every second of attention he got. With the two old lovers droning on, I could only hear every other word from the television, and the same talking heads were blabbing over the same snippets from the parade in a nausea-inducing loop.

When she left the room, we only had two bottles of water. We could have gotten fancier drinks, but Dad had refused them all.

"Just water is fine," he kept saying. He had this habit of refusing things as a way of ingratiating himself to others, even as they happily took advantage of him, and he was none the wiser. He spread his legs and leaned back into the dirty red sofa.

"A lot of famous people sat in this very spot," he said, inhaling the musky air.

"I know," I said, "and most of them are dead."

"Don't speak like that, Jason. This is our big break! Just think about how many people dream of a moment like this!"

"No, you're right. It's pretty awesome."

"Do you like Ms. Olson?"

"She's nice."

"Isn't she? Some day you should find a woman like that."

"She's a little too old for me, Dad."

He snickered.

"So, are you nervous?"

"I feel fine."

"You got this," he reassured me with the false bravado of a high school jock. I hated this side of him. Gone was the pensive, gentle soul. Society had turned him into a superficial, unthinking sycophant.

"What's the matter?"

"Nothing."

"Have you memorized your lines?"

"No. I think I'll just speak from the heart."

"Look, Jason, you have to act the part. Look at Prince Kane." He pointed to the TV, where the pale prince was laying a bouquet of roses over the tomb of the unknown soldier. "You think he wants to be there? He's putting on an act. He's performing for the cameras. You have to do the same. You have to make the world fall in love with you. You know what I mean?"

"People like him because he's the prince. I'm just a sick boy discarded by the system."

"Well, play that up!"

I threw up my hands.

"I thought being me was good enough. I mean, it's not like I'm faking my sickness!"

"No one's saying that!"

"Then what else should I do? Fall on my knees and beg the All-Father to forgive my sins?"

He opened his mouth to speak, as if to agree, but stopped short of giving away his true self.

"Look, when I was your age, I hated all this. The very thought of lowering myself in any way to please other people made me sick to the bone. I wanted to be the victor, not the victim. I wanted people to respect me. But you know what I've learned? Sometimes, you have to be the victim before you can be the victor."

"What if they just don't like me?"

He got confused all of a sudden, not expecting the question, so I repeated my point.

"The monarchs are very picky. They only like deviants who tickle their fancy. Should I then be a victim forever?"

"We can only control what we control. Think about all the kids who received the All-Father's blessing over the years? How many do you actually remember?"

"That's my point."

"We remember the ones who had special qualities. You know, the ones who played up their handicap. For you, it's the fact that you're a service model. That makes you special. You don't need to have any real talents to be famous. You just need to satisfy their propaganda, you know what I mean?"

"What should I say then?"

He mulled over the question like a philosopher pondering the great mysteries of life.

"Okay, say this. Say you hate the fact that people see you as just a service model. You want to be more than that. You want people to see you for who you are. You live to praise the Lord. We're all God's children. Something like that."

I pictured myself saying those things in front of the All-Father, with the camera focusing on my face.

"You can do it, Jason. You're a handsome boy. They'll love you! Think about the life we can have after this. Your face on magazine covers. Product sponsorships. Late-night shows. We could be rich!"

"*We.*"

"Jason, don't be difficult."

I thought I had led him on long enough. I saw all I needed to see. Frankly, I was a little relieved. I could have changed my mind. I could have lived this life to the end. I knew there were children in this world who wanted nothing more than the unconditional love of their parents.

"Mr. Freeman?"

The assistant had come back without knocking.

Father got embarrassed and stood up, pretending he was about to leave.

"We're just getting ready," he said with an awkward grin.

"Follow me," replied the assistant. "Ready for your big moment?"

Father couldn't look me in the eyes, so he just waved for me to get up. I obeyed. As I followed him into the narrow corridor, walking past all these pictures of famous people, I whispered in his ear, "I'll say the lines."

His eyes lit up like a child again.

CHAPTER 12

BLESS ME, ALL-FATHER

JASON

When the assistant announced my arrival, the monarchs turned toward us in their seats, careful not to ruffle their fancy clothes. The men were dressed in white shirts and black suits, the women in pinkish-red dresses. Red and black, matching the colors of our flag. It was hard to tell them apart, and the nerves I worked up inside didn't help. I had never seen so many rich and powerful people gathered in one place. I had rehearsed this moment in my head a hundred times before, but reality struck me in a different way. I felt much calmer than I had expected.

It was strange to see all these important people, who were raised to be selfish and unique, taking the same posture and putting on the same expression. No one wanted to stand out. Even the smallest movement outside of the accepted posture was met with withering disdain. These people never left high school. They probably never would. I felt liberated thinking this, and a surge of electricity coursed through my veins.

I saw gargoyles peering down at me, soldiers slaughtering angels in a battlefield washed in blood. I gazed into the eye of the dome, and memories of a more innocent time flew by. The marble floor shifted beneath my feet. I felt light again, like an angel gliding through the clouds.

Father whispered in my ear, "Smile."

He was still living in the past.

I looked at him for the first time unencumbered by secrets. He was no longer my father; I ruled over him now. I saw everything, and he was blind. I could tell him the truth right there, and he still wouldn't believe me.

I spotted Prince Kane sitting in the front row next to his mother, watching me. His face was stiff with anticipation. Everything about him was everything I would never be. I envied him. I fantasized about him. I liked him. I hated him. He completed my nightmare, gave me a reason to spite myself. I shocked myself for feeling all these things in the moment, like my organs were pouring out after someone had slashed me open.

I puffed out my chest and soaked in the attention. Seeing my display of confidence, Father straightened his back and put on the most ingratiating smile he could find when he shook the All-Father's hand.

"Your Eminence," father said, making a slight bow. "It's a real honor to meet you."

The All-Father's eyes didn't even move when he replied, "You must be Mr. Freeman?"

"Yes, Your Eminence."

"Please, spare me the formality. You may call me Father."

"Yes, Father."

"And this is your son?"

He nodded.

"Jason, come here."

After all these years, I had learned to resent the imperative voice. Everything was an order. Everyone ordered me around. My father included. I was paralyzed by this hatred when I remembered Father's advice. Or was it my doctor's? *Don't pretend, believe.* The words were scrambled at that point, but the directive was stunningly clear. I was a predator on the prowl and needed to calculate my every move. I remained in my spot for a few seconds, allowing Father's frustration to grow. Just when he was about to call me again, his face turning scarlet from embarrassment, I took a step forward, bowed toward the All-Father. This simple move filled him with self-satisfaction.

"You may come forward," he said, much to Father's delight.

I pretended to be a sad little thing—no, I *was* the sad little thing. I was the object of their infernal affection. I was what they dreaded but dreaded to reject. So I put on this face I had seen in a documentary, of a war orphan staring into the camera, taken up with innocent fright. It was the expression of a third-world country perpetually bombed by nations more advanced and people more evolved. I was the savage, childlike in my intellect, starved of intuition and guidance.

"Don't be afraid, my child," urged Spencer Kane. "Let Father see you now."

I was tempted to comply, but I kept still.

Father grew impatient.

"My son is very sick," he said. "He's been praying every day for your grace. No one has worked harder to pass the Trial!"

Then he turned to me in an earnest voice. "Jason, tell the All-Father how you feel."

"I'm scared," I said. "I don't want to die…"

"Tell him how hard you've worked," father urged again.

"I—I never imagined myself being here… Standing in the presence of the All-Father."

"Are you in pain?" the All-Father asked.

"Yes, all the time."

"Do you wish to be healed?"

"Yes."

"Do you believe in the power of grace?"

"I believe in you, All-Father."

I heard a faint smattering of applause, and a few shouts of "*amen.*"

"Do you believe a deviant can be redeemed?"

I thought for a second and took a deep breath. "I spend most of my days living in shame. I hate the fact that people see me just as a servant. As something less than human. All I've ever wanted is a place to belong. To be seen and heard. To live and breathe. What more can I do? I've given everything I could to transform myself. All-Father, I'm asking for your grace… I know I'm not deserving…"

I couldn't hold it back anymore. I broke down and burst into a terrible sob, like a child who had just learned that his parents would never come back. I don't think I had ever cried like that, and certainly not in front of people. It was completely unimaginable. But everything clicked in that moment. All the hatred and self-pity I had bottled up for so long came bursting forth. I wasn't even sure if I was acting. A part of me must have been self-aware, but the more I cried, the more I lost control.

I wasn't pretending anymore.

I tried to speak through the tears, but my lips trembled too hard for words to come out. The All-Father extended his arms, without lifting them too high, and invited me again to join him. The nobles were on the edge of their seats. As if they anticipated this would happen, a ballad began to play. The first few notes reminded me of a pop song I had heard on the radio. At last, I throw myself into the All-Father's embrace. At that moment, the entire congregation jumped up to its feet and broke into a chant:

"Om Namah Shivaya," the father chanted.

"Om Namah Shivaya," the mother chanted.

"Om Namah Shivaya," the son chanted.

"Om Namah Shivaya," the daughter chanted.

I repeated the chant as well. I remembered the look on Dr. Faust's face when he had taught me the phrase, glowing with ironic delight. "I honor the divinity within myself" was not the same as "I honor the divinity within all," I remembered him say.

The chant echoed over and over until the church was filled with a warm, ethereal white light. The All-Father hugged me like a mother would clutch her babe. He whispered into my ear, "Don't cry, my child." His eyes were beaming with the same white light that filled the room, and his body seemed to radiate with incredible warmth. "Tell me your deepest secret, for soon you shall be free."

"Will I see my father again?" I whispered into his ear.

"Of course," he answered with a perplexing smile.

"Will he still go to heaven, even if his son committed a sin?"

"What was that?" he asked, slightly taken aback.

"Will I see my mother again, in heaven?"

Now his mouth was agape, filled with white light, and the heat from his face dried my tears. His face seemed twisted out of shape, like a mannequin melting in flames. Even in this tortured state, he could tell that something was going wrong, that the person he had embraced may not be what he had imagined.

"I'll tell you my deepest secret," I began to confess, hugging him tight. "I've hated myself for so long I can't even remember when it began. I hate myself because I know I can never be perfect like you. The more you cast me aside, the more I crave everything you have. Do you understand how that feels?"

"What you're feeling is very normal," he replied, sounding almost relieved. "God forgives all."

"I'm not looking for forgiveness."

"But you shall have it."

"Can prejudice be forgiven?"

"What did you say, young man?"

"Prejudice can cut so deep you can never be whole again. Hatred can make you love the people hating you."

The All-Father was losing his patience but still tried to put on a gentle voice.

"My child, you cannot change the natural order of the world. There's no need to harbor hatred. Let it go."

"How?"

"By accepting who you are."

"A deviant."

"No, a being who possesses the ability to change."

"But you said the natural order cannot be changed."

"My child, you're not listening to me. You—"

"I understand you well enough, Father. You want all the power for yourself."

"What did you say?" he finally snapped.

"I said you want all the power for yourself."

At this point, the All-Father lost his patience. Gone was the loving priest who loved all God's children. Now I could see the real creature beneath the facade—a cold, calculating reptilian monster hungry for blood. I bit into the pill the wonderful Christine had gifted me, releasing the catalyst. I felt a bitter taste on my tongue, and bursts of fiery pain shot through my jaws and spine.

"Be careful what you say to me," he warned in a cold, sinister voice. "I'm the only one who can save you."

"I forgive you," I said, biting down on my teeth.

"You forgive *me*?" he retorted.

"Yes," I answered.

His nostrils flared with anger, and his face flushed red. "Stupid deviant," he cursed, "get your hands off me."

"But I love you, Father."

The congregation chanted even louder as the ballad rose to a crescendo. Too embarrassed to let his anger show, the old man grabbed my arms and squeezed them so hard my bones felt on the verge of splintering.

"I'll break them if you don't let go," he said under a hideous smile.

My heart was pounding so hard I could barely hold myself together. I found the last reserve of strength in me to hold on. I refused to let go.

"Tell me your deepest secret," I said.

"Deviant scum!" he shouted.

"I promise I'll forgive you" were the last words I said to him.

I took one last look at Father and gave him a smile. He nodded at me, taken by ecstasy. The white light from the All-Father's mouth shone brightly on me as my head split open, revealing the molten core inside. My whole being burst open as I gazed upon the heat eviscerating the All-Father's face. I remembered happiness again. Even as the vanguards came galloping from the sky and trampled over the gargoyles, I found peace in the sweet reverie of revenge.

CHAPTER 13

CARNAGE

MARCUS

I could swear that all of it happened in my head. Even as the ceiling crumbled and the monarchs ran wild with terror, I found myself enchanted by the spectacle of it all. It felt like a movie was playing out all around me, and I was the only person in the audience. I also had a strange feeling I had seen this movie before. Everything unfolded just the way I had remembered. The blast, the heat, angels falling into a pit of fire, flesh and blood flying across our eyes. It was only when the music died in a deafening crash that I awoke from this morbid fascination. Suddenly I remembered running toward my father as the monster's head split open. In an instant there was a terrible shock, a detonation muffled by the rising chorus. Then the music died. All these voices, so full of joy just moments ago, were now crying in a sea of blood and terror.

There is a childish element inside all of us that secretly enjoys the suffering of others. But now that the misery had fallen on me, I could barely make sense of the world. I couldn't believe what was happening. For as much as I hated the royal court, it was still my home. As much as I hated my father, he was the only father I knew. I could hardly move, paralyzed by despair. I wanted to run to him but was afraid of what I might find under the rubble. I tried to remember what he had said to me that morning; he had seemed so kind and gentle. I wished I had listened more. I wished I hadn't taken his words so personally. He was only trying to make me understand. If there had to be resentment, let it be directed at the people who took everything away.

In a moment of perfect clarity, I found the beast lying next to my father's dead body. He was still breathing, though just barely. The crowd was surging on all sides, but no one seemed to take notice of him. He was merely a tiny ant severed at the abdomen still straining to move. I didn't want to look at him directly for I feared having this despicable image stamped onto the deepest part of my mind. I wanted to remember my father, not this pathetic beast of a man. But once again, this morbid fascination took over, and I gazed into his dying eyes as harshly as my father had once gazed into me. I wanted to make him feel my judgment. Severed at the abdomen, and with his face peeled open, this creature still found the strength to crawl toward me, as if he was saving his last breath to ask for forgiveness. Why? What kind of hatred could compel a living being to commit such a horrible act? What did my father ever do to him? In the waning glow of his black eyes I saw nothing but venomous disdain. It seemed so unnatural that a pathetic beast like him could even understand the idea of disdain. What right did he have to look down at anyone else? He was the subject of contempt. If he died, they would just produce another service model to replace him. His life had no meaning. And the only person who ever cared for him was my father. We wanted to save him and give him a better life, yet he refused. He had the audacity to refuse.

We should have never given him the grace of our com-passion. He didn't deserve compassion. I picked up a piece of limestone from the rubble and was about to drive the sharp end into the creature's head when I heard Mother calling for me. She grabbed my waist from behind and lifted me up in the air.

"We've got to go," she whispered. "Let him die."

I refused to listen and wiggled my way out of her hold. When I dropped to the ground, I saw on the opposite side of the aisle two Vanguard dragoons holding matchlock revolvers and making big strides in my direction. For some reason, they wore the Vanguard cross upside down. Behind them stood Matilda, looking on with such vile satisfaction I wanted to take one of the revolvers and shoot her in the face. There was no doubt in my mind that she was behind all this.

"Marcus, take my hand!" Mother shouted. Never had I been more comforted by those words. I grabbed her hand and slipped into the seething crowd.

"Where are we going?" I asked.

"I know a way out," she said.

We hadn't even walked a few steps, and my right foot started cramping. I couldn't move. Before I said anything, Mother swooped me up from the floor and held me in her embrace, my head resting on her shoulder just like when I was a child.

When I glanced at her face, I saw something alien brimming inside her eyes. I almost didn't recognize her, and this, out of all the horrors that surrounded me, scared me the most. I couldn't recognize my own mother.

"Are you okay?" I asked her.

"No," she said.

"I can still walk."

She gave me a look and sighed. The nobles barely noticed us. They were too shellshocked to stay in reality. I saw one of them, a young girl wearing a little red coat and sobbing into her dead father's leg, refusing to let go.

"Don't look," Mother said.

"Why is this happening to us?"

She didn't answer.

We bumped into an elderly man trying to carry his injured wife and nearly knocked him to the ground. When he saw the queen, he didn't bow or smile, like people would in the past. Instead, he shook his head in dismay. There was a look of accusation in his eyes, like a child discovering that the world isn't fair for the first time. I didn't blame him. I couldn't. I found myself feeling guilty about everything, but I didn't know why.

"Can we help him?" I whispered to Mother.

"No."

The old man said, "It's all your fault. You should've never invited deviants into God's holy house!"

"Then why are you here?"

"I'm here because of you!"

I heard someone shout, "Master!" Then I felt a tap on the elbow and looked behind me to find the old hunchback catching his breath. "We have to move. The guards are catching up."

"It doesn't make any sense," I said. "The Vanguards serve *us*."

"No, they serve the Syndicate now," he said. "As far as I can tell, any one of these people could be a Syndicate turncoat."

"Is that what you're calling me now?" the old man asked.

The hunchback faced the old man. "I'm afraid we can't help you anymore."

"You never helped anyone but yourself," mumbled the old man.

The hunchback shook his head and led us away. There was no point in reasoning with grief.

"Where were you?" I asked the hunchback. "I couldn't find you."

Instead of answering me, he asked if I was hurt.

I shook my head out of embarrassment.

"Can you walk?"

"I think so."

"Get down then. You shouldn't let your mother carry you."

My face turned red.

"No, I can do it," said Mother.

"I'll walk," I insisted.

The cramp was gone. I had so many questions swirling in my head I didn't know where to start. And at the same time, I was afraid to know the answers.

Before I could open my mouth to speak, Mother took my hand once again and looked me in the eyes for the first time since the ceremony had begun. She seemed so helpless and sad. I thought I heard her scream, but her lips were sealed. They trembled with fear.

"Watch your step, Master," said Victor.

I looked down and lifted my foot just in time to avoid stepping on a hand under the rubble.

"This is the end of the world," Mother muttered as she stopped. Her body turned rigid as though standing naked in a snowstorm. Her eyes turned icy. "Nothing can save us now."

"Your Majesty," Victor urged, "we have to hurry!"

"Don't call me that," she replied in a deep baritone. "I'm no majesty."

"I'm sorry. Is there something wrong?" asked Victor.

"*Something wrong?*" Mother repeated, holding back a firestorm. "Everything is wrong!"

"Oh, Mercedes," said Victor, "you're still my queen."

"Queen?" Mother said, still in a state of shock.

"Yes!" Victor responded with a guttural lurch.

"I'm not a queen. My son isn't a prince. You're not a servant. We're all victims now!"

"Your Majesty, please," Victor pleaded, trying to find the right words to break through Mother's hysteria. In the corner of my eye, I caught the two soldiers I saw earlier pushing through the crowd and shooting anyone not already dead. You almost didn't hear the gunshots amid all the carnage, only the cries for mercy.

"We have to keep going," I urged.

"For what?" Mother snapped.

"Revenge," I declared.

My answer took her by surprise.

"For what they did to Father," I said. "And to our people."

Victor grabbed my hand and kissed it with his old, tender lips.

"Oh, my boy, bless your heart!"

It was then, after standing frozen for a few seconds, that Mother finally allowed herself to cry. She sobbed into my shoulder and hugged me tight. I felt her tears streaming down my jaw. I didn't know how to react. A part of me wanted to cry as well, but that didn't feel right.

"I love you so much," she confessed, choking on her tears. "Do you still love me?"

I looked at her and nodded.

"Someday, you'll understand," she said, as she dried her tears with her sleeve. The few that remained were colored gold and green by the light pouring through the stained-glass windows.

We turned the corner and slipped behind a small alcove. For a moment, we were safe. We crawled under a large piece of broken scaffold to emerge at what seemed like a dead end.

"What do I need to understand?" I said.

"Now is not the time," said Victor.

Mother didn't respond.

I hated the feeling of being left out more than anything else. I thought I deserved to know since I was a grown-up now.

"*They* did this," muttered Victor.

Mother threw him a knowing glance, like she didn't want him to say anything more.

"Why?"

Victor gave me a look that reminded me of someone I had once dreamed about, although I couldn't remember who. What I did remember was the feeling of being chilled to the core.

"Because they can never be satisfied," he said.

On the wall in front of us was a painting that depicted three pairs of lovers exchanging flowers and kisses. Victor took out a lighter from his chest pocket and struck down the wheel with his thumb. The flame was bright orange.

"Marcus, will you help me with this?" asked Victor as he handed me the lighter. I was puzzled by the request. Victor gazed up wistfully at the lovers, like he was reminiscing about old times. "Can you reach it?"

"Yes."

"Burn it."

"Why?"

"You'll see."

I looked to Mother for affirmation, and she nodded. It seemed that both of them wanted me to learn something in this moment. I was being tested, I figured, without understanding anything.

I stood on my tiptoes and extended my arm to bring the lighter as close as I could to the bottom edge of the painting. A soft breeze passed through the shattered windows, pushing the flame just far enough to touch the canvas, down where the flower field was painted. The fire spread so quickly the lovers were already torn in half when I blinked again. As the flames reached the scepter held by the naked woman in the center, the red, diamond-shaped jewel in the scepter was freed and fell into my hands.

Victor plucked the jewel from my hand and hobbled toward the white wall behind me.

"Remember this wall?" he asked.

I noticed a diamond-shaped indent in the wall. I remembered. When I was small, Father had made me stand against this wall every few weeks to measure my height. The diamond became something I strove toward. It always seemed just slightly out of reach.

"The one thing your father feared more than anything was to see his son crippled by disease," said Victor.

"Some stupid prophet planted the idea in him and he never let it go," Mother joined in with a chuckle.

"Religion can do that to a person," said Victor, glancing up at Mother under a curious frown.

As he fitted the red jewel into the carving, a heavy thud shook the wall, pushing out a cloud of dust. Not being prepared, I inhaled a lungful and coughed.

When the dust settled, I could see a rectangular shape carved into the wall, like a monolith. Victor pressed his palm against the shape, and the whole block receded a few inches, revealing a stairway into the darkness.

CHAPTER 14

RAPTURE

MARCUS

It seemed much easier to say the truth when your life could end any second. All these ideas and emotions clung to my throat, just waiting for a gust of wind to blow them out. As I followed the old man's torch down the stairwell, I was constantly on the verge of laughing. Thankfully, I was still sane enough to keep my mouth shut. But the silence only made it worse. How could I justify anything so evil? The tragedy was hard enough, and now I had to deal with the sweet torment bubbling up inside me. Only a wicked man would laugh at tragedy, I knew, but then again, only a wicked man could promise revenge.

There seemed no end to our descent. The flame from the torch was only bright enough to illuminate the space we occupied. The old man led the way, with Mother following closely. Neither spoke. They seemed insistent on ignoring me. Once or twice, in the cadence of our footsteps, I heard the laughter of a boy. I was the only one who heard him. When he grazed my shoulder running up the stairs, I caught a fleeting look at his face. I recognized the spirit in his eyes—a savage hatred for the world lurking behind a veil of decency. There was no joy in his laughter, only a deep desperation I could somehow understand. Then he flashed again before my eyes, this time holding a small watch.

"Please accept this as a small token of our appreciation," he had said, his face hollowed out. He had tried so hard to sound sincere and well-mannered that the other deviant kids around him chuckled to themselves.

It was hot. The convent reeked of spoiled apples and freshly cut wings.

"We appreciate everything you and your family have done for us," he followed, robotically reciting the words the sisters had taught him.

"You can keep it," I told him.

The other kids picked up my cue and laughed at him.

"But, sir, we wanted you to have this gift. We thought you'd like it."

"Are you mocking me?" I thought it was fun to tease him.

"No... why?"

"You're giving me a watch my family paid for, no?"

"No, it's a gift, your grace."

"A gift is what you buy for someone else. Did you buy the watch?"

His face grew red. His eyes sparkled.

"No, but I—"

"Then stop pretending. Why don't you go back to Sister Josephine and return the watch you stole from her? Can you do that for me?"

He froze, resentment boiling in his eyes. When he burst out crying, the other kids broke into wild laughter.

It had to be him. There was no mistaking it. Maybe I was wrong to expose him. Did I create a monster? I couldn't banish his dead-eyed stare from my head, even if I tried.

"Marcus? Marcus? You still there?"

"Yeah."

"Stay with me."

"I think I know who he is."

"It doesn't matter," Mother said.

"He was one of the deviants we housed at the convent."

"No…"

"Yes, you have to believe me."

"I don't care who he is!"

"We're here," interrupted the old man.

He gave me a tired smile as he unlocked the cellar door at the bottom of the stairwell. We entered a tight corridor flanked by seraph statues. Like undesirable memories, their faces were scrubbed clean. I could only make out a nose here and an eye there. They were no different from converts, their essence stolen and destroyed. Each set of statues had a different pose, starting from the kneeling position, then rising frame by frame. Walking past them gave the impression that they were one person slowly coming to life.

At the end of the tunnel was a door painted red. The paint seemed fresh. In the orange flame, I saw sweat dripping down the old man's neck. His eyes flickered.

"Damn it," he mumbled. I heard genuine pain. He was frustrated that he couldn't steady his hand long enough to slide the key into the lock. "What's wrong with me?"

Meanwhile, I heard a pattering of harsh footsteps somewhere above.

"Let me help you," I said.

He waved his hand. "No, I can do it myself."

"Victor, let Marcus help you," Mother added.

He probably felt emasculated and glared at me.

"Fine, you do it."

He handed me the key, which looked nearly identical to every set of keys I had seen in the palace. The bow was shaped like a diamond, and the blade was made of gold.

"Did you always know about this place?" I asked.

He shifted the torch away so I couldn't see clearly.

"Will you just open the door already?"

"I need the light."

He brought the torch just over my shoulder, and the flame almost burned my hair. I turned the key, and the door opened. It was a small, oval-shaped wine cave with wine barrels stacked to the ceiling on both sides. At the end of the cave was a mural of strange symbols painted on what looked like a large, ancient shield, the kind angels once carried to war, and on the shield hung a lamp swaying in the darkness. There were a few chairs scattered around but no table to serve dinner.

Someone had left a golden cup on top of a wine barrel. A monarch butterfly was etched onto the cup. I leaned over and put my nose close to it. The fine scent of wine was gone. Only the taste of acid remained.

A dizzy spell came over me. I needed to grab hold of a wine barrel to stand still. When the nausea went away, I heard the door shut by a gust of wind. There was nowhere else to go.

I felt a terrible lurch in the pit of my stomach. I turned around to find the old man leaning against the closed door and mumbling to himself.

"Victor, are you all right?" Mother asked.

He didn't answer right away. A drop of blood rolled down his chin. He wrapped his arms around his stomach and groaned.

"Help me…"

When he raised his head, we could see blood in his eyes.

"Help me…" he pleaded again, falling into Mother's arms.

"Victor! My God!"

"Rapture," he said. "Rapture… is… here…"

"Rapture? What do you mean?"

"The world's coming to an end," he said with a smile.

"Hold on." Mother pulled out a handkerchief from her pocket and was about to wipe the blood away when the old man grabbed her wrist.

"No. Nothing can help us now."

"I'm sorry?"

"I… you see…" he said, "I never had the chance to tell you the truth."

He was still clutching her wrist.

"It's okay, we're safe here," Mother reassured him, like she was comforting a child.

"No. We're not safe. We've never been safe!"

"Will you let go of me?"

"I'm sorry. I… uh… I'm scared. I see the fear in your eyes too."

He still refused to let go.

"Mother! Get away from him!" I shouted.

"Marcus, he needs our help. Won't you comfort your old man?"

"Yes, Marcus. Be a good boy and listen to your mother. I need you by my side."

"No," I mumbled.

"I'm sorry, son, what did you say?"

"Don't call me that! You're not my father!"

"Marcus, stop!"

"Mother, this man is evil!"

"Ah, I knew you'd say the word," Victor said. "You never respected me, even though I loved you like you were my own blood."

"Victor, please… save your strength."

He took mother's handkerchief and smeared his blood all over his face.

"Happy now?" he asked, coughing up more blood.

"Look what you made me do."

"What?"

"It's the drugs, Mother!" he shouted. Suddenly, he bounced back on his feet, taking Mother with him by the wrist.

"Don't recognize me? You gave me the name, Victor. You turned me into this, remember?"

"Let her go!" I yelled.

"Shh! Temperance, child, you don't want the Syndicate to hear you."

"And you, Mother, I've waited a long time for this."

"Victor…"

"Oh no, you don't get to call me that anymore. I'm not your servant."

"You're right. We're equals now."

"Look at me. Do you see the blood in my eyes? I did it all for you, Mother. I wanted to please you. I… I wanted you to love me. Do you love me, Mother?"

"Yes, yes…"

"When your husband tortured me and turned me into a monster, I thought you were the only decent person left in the world. I placed all my faith in you!"

"And I still love you very much," Mother pleaded.

The hunchback licked the blood from his lips.

Mother looked at me, perhaps feeling my gaze, and mumbled something I couldn't hear. She seemed on the verge of making a great confession when suddenly there came a booming crack, the room flashed, and she slumped to the floor.

"Don't come any closer," he warned, flashing his revolver at me. "I won't be so forgiving the next time."

Mother held her stomach, and blood seeped through her hands. She should have listened to me. Never trust half-bloods.

I was too angry to speak.

"Why?" she asked between heavy breaths. "Why are you doing this?"

"Because I love you, Mother! I want to be with you forever."

"Come here, old friend," she said, opening her arms.

He gave a curious glance at Mother and thought about answering her call. He still aimed the revolver in our direction.

"Are you afraid?" she asked.

"Should I be?"

"God accepts all of us."

"How do you know?"

"Do you believe in God?"

He trembled.

"I need to hear you say it."

"I believe in God."

"Come closer."

The hunchback hesitated. There was a look of contrition in his eyes. He lowered his revolver. He seemed ready to give in to Mother's sweet demand. As I readied myself to take advantage of this moment, the hunchback smiled at me. This gesture took me by surprise. I was terrified. I thought he was going to shoot me when I saw the smile vanish from his face. The revolver cracked again. He stumbled back and hit the door. Every muscle in my body tensed. I couldn't make sense of what had just happened. I should have been the one hit.

"Do you believe in God now?" Mother taunted the monster. She was holding a small black revolver. A wisp of smoke rose from the barrel.

It seemed so impossible. I never thought she had the guts to fight back. But she did, and I couldn't hold myself together anymore.

I ran to her.

"Mother?"

She took me in her arms.

"Well, don't look so surprised," she said.

We laughed.

"Can you walk?"

She looked at her stomach, where her dress was painted red, and nodded.

"I've always liked this dress," she said. "It has nice, big pockets."

I gave her a smile.

"I need you to finish the job, son," she said.

Yes, this was the new person I had met earlier. A person without fear. A person ready to conquer anything that came her way.

I took the revolver.

Sitting slouched against the door, the hunchback was already half-dead. The revolver lay next to his hand, but he showed no interest in grabbing it.

Mercy, mercy me, Father. Shall I kill this beast?

I looked at the beast. All my memories with him seemed to vanish. All I felt was an empty, dark void.

Show no mercy.

He chuckled. "I think I've just proven my point," he said. "You're no different from me."

"End him," Mother urged.

"My son, I love—"

I finished the job.

"Come here," Mother said.

I threw away the burning revolver.

"You did good."

"I'll save you."

I dug my arms under her body in a futile attempt to carry her.

Footsteps drew near.

"Marcus, listen to me."

"I can save—"

"No, save yourself. Listen! The whole world is going to come after you now. Do you understand?"

I nodded.

"You're the last of our kind. They may have destroyed the monarchy, but they haven't purged our blood. You will carry on our legacy. One day, you will lead our people back to the promised land."

I didn't know what to say.

"Marcus, I want you to know—"

A flurry of knocks at the door: "May I see the queen?"

"Mercedes, are you home?"

It was Anthony.

Mother seized my hand.

"Look," she said. With great pain, she raised her arm and directed my gaze to a crawl space between two wine barrels. "Follow the path all the way to the end. It'll take you outside the palace."

"But I can't leave you here."

"Find the Philosopher. He'll show you the way."

"Who is he?"

"There's no time, Marcus. Go! Go now!"

I surprised myself with how quickly I tore away from her grasp. There would be no final goodbye, no sentimental vows.

Just a moment ago I was a child who couldn't even imagine leaving his mother behind. Now, Mother was the one left wanting a final kiss.

I kicked open the vent cover and squeezed into the crawl space.

I was angry. The mere thought of seeking help made my stomach turn. Was I so weak that I couldn't ever survive on my own? I refused to believe that. And the only way to prove myself was to leave the past behind.

"I love you!" she shouted.

I couldn't look back. I kept crawling forward, even as I heard them knock down the door. He called for me. There was an outburst of shouts and screams. Then I heard the muffled pop of gunshots, one after another.

Then silence.

I closed my eyes, pretending I could wish the world away. But the cold wind did not cease to blow. The anger did not dissipate. I could still see her face.

I wished I had said goodbye.

CHAPTER 15

SLEIGHT OF HAND

JASON

The topic of my birth came up only once in all the years I'd known my father. We knew the policy well. A service model should never talk to his family about his birth. The topic was too taboo for our beautiful society. This is written on the warning label. A service model shouldn't have to understand why he was made. He should only focus on what he can do for others. That was my purpose and the only thing that mattered.

I remember my father coming home that day, red-faced and defeated. It was the look of someone who had fought against the world and lost. My instinct was to help him somehow, but he refused and threw himself in bed with a cold towel over his forehead. Our bed was an old mattress some rich person had thrown away. We put the mattress over a bunch of cardboard boxes. I sat next to him.

It was a Monday night, and everybody in the apartment building was out at the community room for cheap wine and worship. Mostly everyone got drunk, or as drunk as you could get with all the suppressants in the air. Naturally, a fight would break out here and there, and it always ended with two people shaking hands. You don't want to look stupid with

God watching. I got a fever that day and stayed home. Dad was mad at me for staying home. He gave me a lecture about the importance of faith and perseverance before he left. So when he came home in a state of despair, I was rather pleased.

The world doesn't care if you participate or not.

He had this look in his eyes where just a few words of sympathy could make him spill every secret he was holding inside. I didn't want to take advantage of him. He was my father, after all. It was better for us to retain a sense of mystery. I did ask him what had happened, and he refused to answer—twice. On the third time, he said, "Son, sometimes you just have to do the right thing."

"What do you mean?"

"Well, if you see someone getting treated unfairly, you should stand up for him. Don't you think?"

"Isn't that against the law?"

He gave me a puzzled look but wasn't angry. He couldn't be angry. Everyone knows that compassion is the most dangerous thing in the world. You could justify murder in the name of self-defense, but there was no justification for compassion. Compassion was the thing you did when no one was watching, and even then, you'd better hope it didn't come back to bite you.

"But he was being treated horribly. Tammy and Dustin, you know, our saintly neighbors, were beating him up in front of everybody."

"Who was getting beat up?"

"The servant kid. He came over last week to fix our fridge. Remember him?"

"Oh, you mean the service model?"

I couldn't help myself. Before someone else labeled me, I had to label myself first.

"Yes, him. He reminds me of you."

I hated hearing that.

"What did he do?"

"Nothing. He was just sitting there by himself, and people started harassing him, saying why aren't you working, where's my drink, and all that."

"Isn't he supposed to be serving drinks?"

"What's wrong with you?"

"I don't know. You tell me."

"Don't you feel sympathy for your own kind?"

"As a rule of thumb, we were designed not to feel sympathy."

"But you're still talking to me now. Isn't this sympathy?"

"I suppose."

"Do you love me?"

"What kind of question is that?"

"I mean, are you capable of love?"

"You'd have to ask my maker."

"No, I'm asking you."

I remember the music got really loud all of a sudden, and I heard people shouting outside and glass hitting pavement and shattering.

"What do you want, Dad, do you want sympathy? Is that it? Because I can offer that, if that's what you want—"

"Stop repeating that!"

I laughed.

"I mean, seriously, why should I get into trouble for doing the right thing?"

"You defended the kid."

"I punched Dustin in the nose."

"He deserved it."

"You're just saying that, aren't you?"

"No, I hate him too."

He giggled and burped.

"See, that's a form of sympathy. Shared hatred for the common man."

"I'll toast to that."

He sat up and lobbed the towel around his neck.

"He's going to report me."

"To your supervisor?"

"Yes."

"But… you didn't do anything wrong."

"That's what I'm saying."

"You could say that it was just self-defense."

"Self-defense from what?"

"Well, you know, Dustin harassing you."

"He wasn't harassing me. He was harassing the servant boy. The other folks will back him up. Don't you see, this is their chance to climb up the totem pole. Report your neighbor. Get a higher CFT. Please the Lord. Whatever they say these days…"

"Is there no way you can stop him?"

"I can kill him."

"Are you serious?"

"No, of course not!"

"I can help with that."

"Jason, c'mon."

"I can stage a scene. I get him mad, maybe I'll make a lot of noise in the middle of the night, start pounding the wall, he gets mad, comes over, gets into an argument with you, and boom, you shoot him in self-defense."

"I appreciate your imagination."

"What's the worst that could happen?"

He smiled. He and I were developing a bond, if that's the right word. I really meant what I had said. Sure, there was an element of drama, which I had learned in school, but I was being honest. I wanted to kill the person who had wronged my father. It just seemed like the right thing to do.

He came over and sat next to me. He smelled like rubbing alcohol. I noticed something in his hands—a small, black leather album.

"Promise me you'll never get replaced," he said in a solemn voice and peered into my eyes. "Promise me you'll do everything in your power to survive the Trial."

His earnestness took me by surprise.

"I'll try my best."

"No, promise me."

"Okay, I promise."

"Very good." He gave me a pat on the shoulder. "Do you know how I survived?"

I shook my head. I'd never given thought to this.

"I survived because I adopted you."

"How's that possible? You can only adopt *after* you pass."

"I lied about my age."

I laughed. "Why are you telling me this?"

"I want you to know the truth."

"The truth doesn't matter."

"It still does to me. Look." He opened the album.

"Let's not do this. You know this is bad. We're not supposed to reminisce about the past. If they find out—"

"I know. I'll be punished."

"Is this about the fight? Dad, you're not going to lose your job. We'll find a way."

"No, I hate washing cars for rich people anyway."

"If I see it, they'll know I know, and it'll make it harder for me to survive."

He sighed.

"That's the risk, isn't it?" He paused with his palm covering a black-and-white picture. "You know what, you're right. I'm sorry. I shouldn't have brought it up. Let's pretend this never happened."

He was about to sneak the album back into its hiding place under our mattress when I grabbed his wrist.

"No, I want to see," I said.

"Are you sure?"

I nodded.

He flipped the album to somewhere in the middle.

"The Sisters told me you were special," he said, placing his index finger on my face in the photo. I didn't recognize any of the kids standing next to me. I couldn't even recognize myself. From where I was sitting, we might as well have been the same person. There was an expression of painful longing in our smiles.

I did recognize Sister Josephine and Sister Mary. They never smiled for the camera.

"Everyone says that," I replied. "But it doesn't mean any-thing."

"Oh, they didn't mean special in a nice way."

I frowned.

"They told me you were the worst kid in class."

"Really?"

"Uh-huh. They said, 'Jason is beyond saving. Not even God can help him.'"

"Was I really that bad?"

"All the other kids had found their foster families. You were the last one. You were the oldest. I think you were already eleven. No one wanted to adopt you. To tell you the truth, I didn't want to adopt you either."

"But you still went through with it out of the pure goodness of your heart," I deadpanned.

He chuckled.

"I think I know why the Sisters hated you," he said.

"I was your act of mercy."

"Yes."

"You saved me."

"I hope I have." He got lost in the picture for a few seconds. "Did you know that you're actually a pleasure model?"

"No way. My birth certificate says I'm a service model."

"Sister Josephine had it changed."

"What?"

"Yes, she changed it so you could have a better chance of finding a foster family."

"Sister Josephine is a liar. All the Sisters are liars."

"Jason…"

Much as I tried to disregard the insinuation, a dark impression was made.

He flipped to the next page.

"This is the factory where you were made," he said.

The windows were broken. The exposed scaffolds looked charred. The ground was littered with red bricks.

"Why are you showing me this?"

"I think you deserve to know where you came from."

"I don't care where I come from."

"When they found you, the factory had been burnt down. You were the only child who survived."

"I knew I was special," I said sarcastically.

When he flipped to the next page, a Polaroid picture dropped into his lap. He was hesitant to show me.

"Let me see it," I insisted.

He flipped it over.

"This is the last picture I took of her," he said.

I sat in Mom's lap learning to play the piano. Our backs

were facing the camera. I couldn't see her face, but she didn't seem all that engaged. It didn't feel like she was interested in teaching me.

"Was I any good?" I asked.

"Not really. I don't think you were interested in music."

"Psychopaths don't listen to music."

"Ha! Very true."

"Why did she leave?"

He thought for a moment. I couldn't explain it, but something about him seemed to change. There was a look of compassion on his face, almost feminine. I wanted to touch his face but couldn't.

Instead, he reached out for me. His face was bright.

"She said you were special because you have a soul."

"A soul?"

"Yes. She was weird like that. I don't even know if she believed it herself. She'd say things just to get me off her case."

"Do you believe her now?"

"Jason…"

"Dad?"

"Do you think a human being can learn to forgive?"

"I'm sorry?"

"If you had a soul, you wouldn't abandon your father, would you?"

"What are you talking about? I'd never abandon you."

"Are you sure?"

"Yes."

"You'd never betray me?"

"Of course not."

"Only a person with a conscience can possess a soul."

"Yes."

"A person with a soul wouldn't murder his father."

"Yes."

"A murderer doesn't deserve to be saved. Does he?"

"Father…"

"I'm not your father. I'm just something in the way."

"No, that's not true."

"I treated you as if you were my own son. And yet you betrayed me."

"No, that's not true."

"He's awake," stated the woman standing over me. She was holding a steel tray in her right hand. "He's awake," she repeated.

A man in a white gown approached.

My heart was bursting.

Before I could even speak, I snatched her wrist. I needed to escape.

The steel tray slipped from her hand, and a bunch of tiny white objects fell and scattered on the rubber floor. They looked like human teeth, stained with blood.

CHAPTER 16

A HAPPY REUNION

JASON

"What… what are those things? Who are you?"

I stared at her as she scooped the blood-stained molars back into the tray.

"You don't remember?"

"I… should I?"

She dumped the molars into the trash can next to my bed and murmured to her male colleague. He was holding a syringe.

"They're Rubicon chips," she said. When she saw that I was still confused, she pressed her index finger against the center of my forehead. "You have one too."

"Rubicon?"

"He doesn't remember," the man said to the nurse.

"Did we make a mistake?" the nurse asked.

"No, try a different word," he said.

"Okay." She turned to me. "Does the word *Construct* ring a bell? No? How about *One Mind? Replacement?*"

I winced at the word. *Replacement.* I knew exactly what it meant.

"He understands," said the old man.

"I can tell," she said.

Memories came flooding back, but I couldn't see any of them clearly. I just had the sense that they were things that had happened in the past.

"Have I been replaced?" It felt like the only natural question to ask.

"Oh no," she said with a slight chuckle. "The chip inside your mouth, it's called Rubicon. It connects you to One Mind. It's still intact."

"So I'm still the same person?"

"For the most part."

"What do you mean?"

"Do you remember the last thing that happened to you?"

Suddenly I felt drowsy. The outline of a mouth engulfed in light flashed before my eyes, and then I lost my train of thoughts. I smelled lavender. I thought I heard someone scream.

"You like to watch, don't you? I have a lot of patients who like to watch. Just between you and me, I like being watched."

I moved my lips a little.

"We really thought we lost you for good this time. You've done well. We're proud of you, Jason."

Empty compliments, the world was still the same. I couldn't say why, but the nurse looked strangely familiar. Every time I tried to focus on her, my vision would blur. After a few tries, my neck cramped up, so I sank into the pillow. When I opened my eyes again, I saw the dark edge of a frame that hung on the wall.

"I almost forgot," said the nurse, "we saved this for you." She took down the frame and held it in front of me.

"Congratulations!"

I sat up and took the frame. My hands were shaking.

There it was, my Certificate of Authenticity, the one thing I had wanted the most.

"Is this real?"

"Yes, it's yours to keep."

"But… I… I don't think I passed the test."

"Oh, you most certainly did. Haven't you heard? The king is dead."

"The All-Father?"

"Yes."

"How?"

"You killed him."

I laughed. It was one thing to remember. It was another to hear it from someone else. What I remembered couldn't be false if someone else saw it happen. And to hear my deeds stated with such genuine respect was heartwarming. Even if what I did was wrong, I would do it all over again just to bask in the admiration of her voice.

Suddenly the certificate didn't seem to matter anymore. I gave it back to the nurse. It seemed so trivial when compared against the magnitude of what I had accomplished. I never thought I'd survive. And I certainly didn't think I'd be treated with respect, even if I did survive. Maybe the nurse was just infatuated with me. I'd heard plenty of stories about innocent people falling in love with murderers.

"Do you not like the All-Father?" I asked.

"I don't have any feelings about him."

"You're scared they might be listening."

She chuckled. "Who?"

"You know, the people above?"

"The people above?"

"Yes, the High Council."

"The High Council is a lie. It never existed."

"What? How do you know?"

"Power is a phantom. You believe what you want to believe."

She cupped my chin with her hands. I could now see every-thing clearly but her.

"I've missed you so much."

"Do I know you?"

"Your father misses you too."

"My father is dead."

"But you still love him. Or rather, I should say, you're still in love with the concept of a father."

"He wasn't just a concept. He was real."

"Mr. Freeman, do you believe in conspiracies?"

I thought for a second. The word sounded familiar.

"I'm not sure."

"We're in the midst of a conspiracy right now, and you're the key to our success."

"How do you know?"

"That's the wrong question."

"What's the right question?"

"The right question is why."

"Why?"

She took a deep breath.

"Doctor," she said, referring to the man standing behind her, "I think he's ready."

With a flick of the wrist, he dropped the syringe in a plate on the nightstand. The needle pointed at my face. He took the certificate frame from the nurse and flipped it to reveal my face looking back at me.

"Do you like your new face?" he asked, holding the mirror side in front of me.

I felt a stab in my forehead, my throat suddenly dry.

"We tried to salvage your old parts, but they were damaged beyond repair. It's a miracle you survived."

I touched my face, feeling the contours of my jaw.

"I look… different."

"Only a bit," said the doctor. "We gave you blue eyes this time. What do you think?"

"I like them."

"Makes you feel more like a noble, doesn't it?"

"Yeah…"

"Do you miss your father?"

He sat down next to me and grabbed my hand. I didn't like it.

"What are you doing?"

"I'm trying to help you remember."

"Remember what?"

He took my hand against my will and kissed it. His lips were wet.

"My boy! I've waited so long for this moment. You don't know how much it hurts, to keep the truth from the one you love. Forgive me, son."

"Stop calling me that!"

"I understand. This must be very confusing—"

"I know who you are. I remember now…"

He released my hand and stood over me. I could see his pale face even in the darkness. There was no mistaking it. The man standing in front of me was undoubtedly Dr. Faust.

"I'm sorry our last meeting had to end so unceremoniously," he said. "I needed to make you believe that you were a failure. It was a necessary part of the protocol."

"I'm sure it is."

"What, you don't believe me?"

"How could I believe anything you say? You're a psychiatrist. All you do is lie."

"I see you haven't lost your edge. That's good. You'll need it to finish the mission."

"What mission?"

"You've trained your whole life for it. Don't you remember? You swore allegiance to the Syndicate. You hated the monarchs so much you were willing to die for the cause."

"But you tried to talk me out of it."

"That was just a test, and clearly, you passed."

He opened the drawer and pulled out a leather-bound album, just like the one Dad had showed me.

"I thought you might be interested to see the truth," he said, flipping open the album. "Come on, don't be shy."

This whole time, I thought I was paralyzed from the waist down. It just seemed like the natural thing to assume after waking up from a coma. When the nurse saw me struggle, she approached me with a smile and tickled my toes. I realized I wasn't paralyzed, and for a moment I felt the happiness of a child. I sat up on the edge of the bed, next to the man who claimed to be my father. A service model shouldn't feel emotional attachment to anyone, except for his master, and I couldn't deny the connection I felt toward Dr. Faust. The way he huddled over the album with a gentle look in his eyes reminded me every bit of my master. This feeling nauseated me. He wasn't my father. He had been manipulating me the whole time. I shouldn't trust him.

"Did you know that your father was a musician when he was your age?" Faust pointed to a picture of my dad with a guitar strapped over his shoulder, standing alone on a stage.

"He was actually pretty good," Faust continued. "Who knows, he could've been a rock star in a different life!"

"How do you know about this?"

"You know, it's rude to question your host." He sighed, as if acquiescing to my demand. "I know because your father told me the story when he applied for the program. He submitted this picture with his application."

"Why? What program?"

"Lower your voice, young man."

"I thought we didn't care who was listening to us."

"There are still people out there who want to hurt us."

"*Us?*"

"It's always been us versus them, Jason. The oldest conspiracy known to man. Your father knew this when he applied. He knew what he was getting into."

"What do you mean?"

"There are certain risks involved when you're trying to unseat the master race."

"I don't believe you. He never—he liked the monarchs. He envied them. He wanted me to be like them, but I was never good enough for him."

"Yes, he played his part perfectly," Faust whispered. "Think about it, if you didn't feel slighted, would you have done what you did?"

"You're saying my dad was an actor."

"Well, no more than you were an actor. But the emotions you felt," he said, putting his hand over my chest, "they were real."

"Don't touch me."

"I imagine you still hate the monarchs."

"They're murderers."

"See? Resentment. It's the thing that makes you special. Look at you here, so young and vivacious. Your classmates were jealous of you."

It was the same group picture I had seen in my dad's album, except we were standing in front of a garden, instead of the entrance to the convent. The garden looked almost sterile. Also, the Sisters were smiling.

"This isn't real. The Sisters never smiled. They didn't like us."

"In your mind, they never smiled," said Faust. "But in truth, they always veiled their cruelty under a smile. That's why they're good at their jobs."

I didn't really hear him, I just kept talking.

"Out of all the deviants, I think they hated me most."

"Why?"

"I don't know. I think they just had the gut feeling that I was different."

"This hatred," said Faust as he turned the page, revealing a picture of the convent on fire, "is what compelled you to act."

Even now, I could smell the smoke. I remembered standing outside the convent, watching it burn. I remembered the pleasure of revenge. I was swept away into that inferno realm, where everything was lucid and wild.

And just like before, a picture dropped onto his lap when Faust turned the page again. This time, the nurse snatched the picture and sat in his place next to me. She adjusted the lamp so the light hit the left side of her face. She reached behind her head with both hands, untied the bun, and shook her hair free. She took off her gold-rimmed glasses. Long black hair streamed over her shoulder. I could see her now. She looked just like my mother.

"Yes, see through the facade." She stared at me with cold, blue eyes. "You have no reason to fear, young man," she said, giving me a kiss on my sweat-covered forehead. "Mommy's here."

I pushed her away.

"You're not my mother."

"We created you. Faust and I."

"I've seen you before."

"I'm the All-Mother."

"You're Matilda Gray."

"Times have changed."

"I don't believe you."

"I'm the queen, but you may call me Mother."

"My mother left when I was young."

"A story we made up just for you."

"No, it happened. I remember it."

"So tell me why she left."

"She—father—they fought all the time."

"Over what?"

"I don't know. Small things."

"Like what?"

"I told you, I don't remember. I just… there was a constant fear in the back of my mind, like things can fall apart any moment."

"You were so happy back then," she said.

She gazed into the picture with genuine affection. I sat in her lap. There was a black piano behind us. I was smiling.

The long black hair, the soft, supple touch of her hands, the way she held me, like she was guarding the most precious thing in the world. Everything was just like I remembered. Everything, except for the expression on her face. Her eyes were dark blue, not black. Her gaze was cold and determined, not hopeless. This was not the mother I remembered. My mother was a kind person. She was afraid of the camera. She didn't want the world to understand her. Somehow, I cared enough to remember, but I shouldn't have even cared in the first place. I was an orphan the day I was born. No one ever cared for me.

Maybe they were one and the same. Matilda and Mother. Mother and loneliness. What difference did it make? A memory is just a piece of data. Disposable, like the bodies we inhabit.

Besides, people can change. We evolve. We're constantly in the process of becoming something else.

"You see," she said, "I'm telling you the truth."

She closed her hands over mine.

"Out of all my children, you're the only one with a soul. You didn't just resist. You allowed the pain to change who you are!"

"If you are who you claim to be," I said, "then release me from this hell."

"Never! You'll die a hundred times, if you must. You belong to us."

"I don't belong to anyone!"

I trembled just like I did before the All-Father, my heart about to burst. I sprang out of this white coffin and took her with me. I didn't think. If God existed, he must have willed this to happen. I wrapped my arm around Matilda's waist and pressed the tip of the needle against her neck.

"All-Mother!" shouted the good doctor.

"I'm fine," the All-Mother responded. I could feel the adrenaline pumping in her veins.

"Who's in control now?" I whispered in her ear.

"You are," she said. "You've always been in control."

My vision blurred again. I glanced through the window behind us. We were at least ten stories high. For a moment, I fantasized about crashing through the window and taking her with me. But the thought of coming back here again was too much to bear.

"Jason," she said, her voice even but strained, "you're right, she does exist. Your mother. I can take you to her, if you want."

"You're lying."

"No, we kept her alive, just for you."

I tensed up. For the first time I thought she was telling me the truth. The image of my mother passed over my eyes. Her smile was too precious for the world. In my moment of weakness, Matilda forced the syringe out of my hand, driving the needle into my neck.

My knees buckled. My body went numb with fever. I tried to get up, but every muscle was dead weight. I slumped to the floor. The only things I could move were my eyes, and I saw Matilda looking down at me, full of contempt.

"In time, you'll understand," she said.

CHAPTER 17

THE REVOLUTION IS HERE

MARCUS

I was drowning in the stench of this hateful city. Everywhere I looked there was decay and saliva. The winding pipes seemed to pulsate with anger. Time vanished. If the sewer rats hadn't come, I would have died from loneliness. Every time I stopped to rest, they'd politely gather around my feet and nibble on my shoelaces. They seemed to worship me. They had probably never seen a human being down here. To them I was just a walking piece of flesh, devoid of passion or hatred. In the stench of human waste, I tasted the naked struggle inside every human heart. It was raw and strange. I wanted to wash my hair in this dark waste and let the dirt soak through my skin. I cried and screamed. The world wanted me dead. I was a dead man walking.

When I climbed out of the sewers, I began to understand the meaning of fear. Fear was the thing you cherished when everything else had failed. Evening came too soon. There was a dreariness in the air. I could barely breathe. I found myself in the back alley behind a massive apartment building, the kind without a face or soul. The Greco-Roman facade was falling apart. There was mold in the gutters. Whoever had lived here either departed in a hurry or were taken away. Old jackets, half-open briefcases, and torn pages of the Mantra littered the alley. The garbage bins near the back door were stuffed with toy animals and prescription bottles.

Graceland. I knew the place. *By the grace of God, we make shelter for the faithful and craven alike. We see no evil so long as the heart is willing to listen.* I recounted this passage from the Mantra as I imagined the horrors that took place around me. Not far to the west I could see plumes of smoke rising from the cathedral. Home was now a foreign land. I remembered passing by these apartments and feeling a kind of pride that they belonged to me. The people belonged to me. This land was our land. This land was my land.

I could hear the fates mocking me. They must have been so happy to see me suffer. This was divine justice, after all. Sooner or later the king had to be taken out. All my life I had imagined myself as the nameless revolutionary fighting the good fight. Now that I was standing on the losing side, I wasn't so enamored with the idea of a revolution. The giddiness I remembered from reading all those romantic novels was now replaced by interminable dread.

I heard gunshots in the distance, and bouts of hysteria swiftly ended. The world could not have fallen so fast, I kept telling myself, but this, too, was only false hope. They were not content with murdering my parents. They wanted to destroy the very foundation of our existence. Fantasies of bloody revenge filled my head. With this newfound bloodlust, I rammed through the back door ready for a fight.

I was met with silence and chaos. All the doors were forced open, and bedlam spilled from the rooms into the hallway, as though a hurricane had blown through the entire floor and turned everything inside out. I saw broken cups and coffee slithering down the table leg, doors riddled with bullet holes, and blood splattered over kitchen walls. I could see these people vividly, people who had lived, families and friends. I could see them huddled around small kitchen tables, talking and laughing and arguing over meaningless things. Then the storm came and swept them away. In an instant, everything that was good and happy was utterly destroyed. There was not a hint of compassion left in all this carnage. Cabinets were plundered. Books were torn apart. Portraits of my father were slashed and burned. Nothing of value was spared. The criminals had defiled everything that mattered. This was clearly the goal. To defile. To destroy. Not just people, but everything they stood for.

As I came upon the last door on the floor, a bright searchlight shot through the window ahead. I crouched down and slipped through just in time.

I found myself inside someone's kitchen. There was a small round table in the middle, and the coffee mug on its surface was still warm to the touch. The room was very small. I had been in bathrooms bigger than this. How could people live in such a small place? It was strange enough to go inside a normal person's home and even stranger to be inside alone, like a thief.

All the windows were closed. I had not been inside for a minute before I started getting a headache. It must have been the cheap incense, which filled the room with an overly sweet and pungent scent.

A golden icon sat on top of the dresser by the television. It was the Everyman, a being of such perfect composition that he was born devoid of emotions. He was kind only to his followers and no one else. But the truth is, even kindness is the wrong word to use. There is really no word to describe what the Everyman is. Kindness implies compassion, but the

Everyman is not compassionate. I suppose that is why we consider him a god. If he could talk, he would surely have reprimanded me for falling so far from grace. He would have accused me of bringing this tragedy upon myself. I wondered what I would say to defend myself, when the searchlight swooped back across the room, followed by a voice through the loudspeaker: "This is a message of peace," she claimed.

It was the voice of a murderer, a traitor, a tyrant pretending to bring justice to the world. Every small inflection sounded fake. Every word was a lie.

"In this trying hour, I give you my solemn promise. We will come back stronger than ever. We are one family. We are not afraid anymore. The tyrant is gone. The monarchy is dead. We don't need to worship false prophets anymore. What we have is enough. Reason is enough. I see you. I hear you. I believe you."

I had never heard anything more shameless in my life. *We're one family?*

"I ask you to join me in this crusade for justice. There is no peace without morality. No justice without reason. The days of blind faith are over. We are now free!"

When the searchlight had passed, I stood up and peered through the kitchen window to find a lone source of light four stories up in the apartment building across the street. It was a room just like this one, with a round table in the middle of the kitchen. A family of four—a mom and dad with two kids—sat around the kitchen table, passing food around like nothing evil was happening in the world. For a moment I was there with them, sitting where the boy sat, reaching for the loaf of bread, when I heard a shrill cry from the street below. I looked down and saw a woman kneeling with a boy in her arms. She shook him again and again, but the boy didn't respond. Soon a white ambulance truck arrived, sirens wailing. Two soldiers wearing Vanguard patches, but with the cross turned upside down, strode out of the vehicle. Seeing hope for the first time, the woman summoned all her strength to carry her son with her as she approached the soldiers. But to her surprise, the soldiers pretended not to see her. Not only did they ignore her cries for help, they found her helplessness rather charming. The tall one made a joke, and his comrade laughed hysterically. Desperate, she grabbed him by the arm, screaming in his face. The soldier looked at her for a second, then pushed her away. As she fell, she tore off the badge from his uniform, though he didn't even seem to notice or care. The soldiers went inside the building.

All this commotion reached the family upstairs. I could see a darkness grace their ruddy faces, but only the boy was curious enough to respond. Despite his father's warning, he sprang up from his chair and ran toward the window. Just as he was about to press his face against the glass his father caught up to him and dragged him back. When the boy turned around to face his father, the old man slapped him so hard he bumped into the window and slumped to the floor. In that moment I realized the man was not the father. The emotional connection I had imagined was false. No father could unleash such violence on his own flesh and blood (except for mine).

This was fury, a master unleashed onto a slave.

When the Syndicate men arrived, the family was hardly disturbed. The matriarch remained seated, only getting up for a moment to shake the tall soldier's hand. The soldier even bowed toward her and whispered something into her ear. I couldn't see the expression on her face, but I suspected she smiled. The daughter climbed down from her chair and offered the short one a plate of food. He hesitated, then picked out a piece he liked and swallowed it in one bite. He patted the girl on the head.

All the while the patriarch kept abusing the boy, as if he wasn't even aware that the soldiers had arrived. But in fact, he was certainly aware. I began to understand. This was a performance. The whole dinner scene was a performance. The father was performing for the soldiers, showing how cruel he could be to a deviant. He was trying to show that he was loyal to his own people, not the Other. Yes, they had lived together and perhaps even considered each other family, but when the moment demanded loyalty, the whole family— the blood family—was able to band together and turn on the one who never belonged. People turning on people on a dime. Without hesitation. Without remorse.

I saw in the boy the tragedy of my own circumstance, but there was nothing I could do to intervene. I could only imagine the horror he experienced when the soldiers surrounded him, along with the man he had so faithfully considered his father. The three men stared him down, reducing him to a mere insect. He must have been terrified and disappointed about the nature of men. But, of course, it wasn't just the men. It was the women too. The mother and daughter sat calmly in their chairs, talking and eating as if nothing evil was happening around them. The boy was crying out for their help, just like the mother had in the street below. No one responded, not even a bit. The more he screamed, the faster he disappeared from their reality. Soon enough, he didn't even exist.

In the midst of their silence, one of the soldiers approached the window, and when he saw that there was no mechanism to open it, he unsheathed the baton from his belt and shattered the glass. Then he used the baton to swipe away the broken shards. When he poked his head through this open space, he stayed there for a second to feel the cold breeze. There was a look of satisfaction on his face when he noticed that the woman who had pleaded for his help earlier had disappeared into the night.

The short one grabbed the boy by his arms, like a butcher clutching the wings of a chicken, and brought him closer to the open space where the window used to be. I was petrified.

The boy kicked and screamed, pleading for his family to help him. But the family had returned to their dinner. The father passed the breadbasket to his daughter. The mother ran a comb through the daughter's hair. I had never seen a family so cruel and heartless (maybe except for mine).

"They're not your family," said the tall soldier.

"Help me, Mother! I'll be a good boy!" the boy cried. "Father, please!"

When no one answered him, the short soldier said, "Do you see the truth now?"

Then the soldier released his grasp, and the boy screamed as he fell. I wanted to leap out of my body and save him, like the heroes did in the stories I had read, but I told myself that he was just a deviant. After all, it was a deviant who had murdered my father. I was waiting for the horror to end in a muted splash when I heard the soldier shout at his comrade: "Look, the little bastard can fly!"

I pressed my face against the window and saw a pair of white, majestic wings flapping wildly. The boy's body hung from the wings, his arms and legs flailing, as though the body and wings were separate entities fighting for control over the mind. Gradually his wings lifted him higher and higher until he was three stories up. Only then did I allow myself to feel the shock of seeing a seraph in real life. Seraphs—those who can fly—were supposed to have gone extinct. That was what everyone had told me.

The family was awakened too. They dropped their little performance and joined the soldiers to witness their very own deviant revealing its true form.

"This can't be!" said the mother.

"We cut his wings!" said the father.

The daughter was speechless but seemed rather impressed by this supernatural feat. Unlike her parents, she was slow to realize what they feared. She held on to her mother's waist, watching the seraph boy with dreamy eyes.

The boy swayed, still learning to control his wings. He wanted to turn around and face his wretched family again. He wanted to see the shock on the soldiers' faces and show them that he had survived. The shock of transformation lingered with him just long enough for him to find me gazing upon his wondrous form. We met eye to eye. It was blasphemy. It was beautiful. How could I possibly describe what I felt in that moment? Here was a creature we were taught to hate, unshackled from society's expectations. Here was something both beautiful and profane. In his dark-brown eyes I saw the same anger that all deviants possessed. Anger toward a wicked society. Anger toward wicked men. But when he recognized who I was, a burst of hope returned to his eyes. His wings still refusing to obey, he tried to fly toward me and reached out his hand. In the periphery of my vision I saw the short soldier raising his rifle.

I waved frantically at the seraph and screamed for him to move out of the way. But he couldn't hear me. He frowned out of confusion. I pointed at the soldier above him and pounded the glass. This time, he understood my warning. He swerved around with the grace of a bird, meeting his family eye to eye, when a loud, piercing sound erupted. The seraph crashed into the window. A torrent of broken glass and feathers rushed toward me, as two more shots fired off. The bullets would have caught me in the forehead if a small creature hadn't leapt onto my back and thrown me to the floor.

CHAPTER 18

SHOUT AT THE DEVIL

MARCUS

When I regained my senses, I was disturbed to find the servant boy's long, pointed wing jutting out against my chin. It was stained with blood. I scurried back as fast as I could and stumbled into another creature, this one warm and lively.

I felt a shock spread across my frame and spun around with savage dexterity. I surprised myself at how quickly I moved. It was as if the seraph's animal features were rubbing off on me. My mind wandered, and I saw a man wrapped in black, leathery armor hovering in front of a blackened sun, his wings a thin, purple membrane.

"Don't hurt me! I'm your friend," cried out a young, bashful voice.

It was only when the creature touched my hand that I realized the man in black armor was only in my imagination. Relieved, I peered at the small, pitiful creature kneeled in front of me, his back arched, wheezing in pain. It was only a boy, hiding under a black, hooded poncho a size too big.

"Who are you?" I asked.

"My name is Grendel," he answered timidly.

As he pushed back his hood, I could see the deviant brand on his neck. For a few seconds, I thought nothing of the curious, little face staring at me. It looked similar enough to the many deviants I had met. There was the customary sadness in the eyes and anger in the mouth. The only difference I noticed was his deathly pale complexion, haunted, like he was running from some malevolent force, even in this moment. The only color was in his bloodshot eyes.

"His name is Wesley," he said, pointing at the fallen seraph. "He had a family, just like me."

"You knew him?"

"We grew up together. At the convent. They're coming after us, mister. They're going to kill us all."

Strangely, Grendel did not appear to know who I was. Judging by his pale skin, he was probably not allowed to venture outside much. I knew of noble families who kept a tight leash on their servants, to the point of denying them access to the outside world. It was their way of keeping their deviants "pure." Or perhaps he knew who I was but chose to put on an act. But why? Either way, I decided to play along.

"Which convent?" I said.

"The one up the hill, Convent of the Healing Star. Have you been there before?"

"Never." I had been there more times than I could count.

"What's your name?" the boy asked.

I thought for a second, trying to come up with an alias. Until now, I had never needed to lie about who I was. My identity was my passport. This felt strange but somehow liberating.

"Valentine," I said. "You can call me Val."

"Val... what a strange name."

"What happened here? Where's your family?"

"The Syndicate took them to the Institute for cleansing."

"Cleansing?"

"Yes, so they can be cured of their faith. Or something like that. I don't really understand any of it. How do you go from believing to not believing? Is that something that can happen to people? You're a believer, aren't you?"

"I—sure. I think I'm still a believer."

The boy chuckled. "You don't sound very sure."

"I've been through a lot."

"Val, I think this is a test," said the boy, full of wide-eyed conviction. "The Mantra says heroes are made in the trying hour. I'm going to be a hero."

"Why do you still believe the Mantra when your family abandoned you?"

"They didn't *abandon* me. I never said they abandoned me. I don't like that word, mister. It's a cruel thing to say."

"But you just—"

"They *saved* me! Can't you see? I'm alive because of them. If they took me with them, the Syndicate would've taken me away. I would've ended up like Wesley." His eyes filled with melancholy. "Do angels go to heaven when they die?"

"I don't know. I thought they were made in heaven." I meant to be sarcastic.

"We might've been second-class citizens," he said, "but at least under the All-Father we were allowed to exist. Even though we don't share the same blood as the monarchs, they still treated us like family. That's more than what you can say about our real parents. They were the ones who abandoned us, our real parents, not our masters. That's what I meant to say earlier. Val, was your master also taken to be cleansed?"

"My master?" I was both amused by his rambling and offended by the question.

"Yes, did the Syndicate take them away?"

"I'm not a deviant," I said.

The boy burst into a fit of laughter. When he saw that I was dead serious, he contorted his eyebrows into a look of fake compassion, mixed with just the right amount of contempt. "You think it's justice, don't you? You hate the monarchs for calling us deviants. You think the king got what he deserved. Measure for measure. Eye for an eye."

"I told you, I'm *not* a deviant."

"Oh yeah? Then tell me who you really are."

"I don't need to prove anything to you. Best of luck, kid, but I've got to run."

"Before you go, you might want to look in the mirror."

"What did you say?"

"Look at yourself in the mirror. The mirror doesn't lie."

I scoffed at the suggestion. Why should I listen to a child? A deviant child at that? Under normal circumstances, I would never have looked at him twice, let alone allow him to question the very essence of who I was. When my family was in charge, I could have had him arrested. Maybe worse. But as much as I hated the idea of taking orders from a deviant, I couldn't shake the feeling that there might have been something true about what he said, watching me with his bloody, red eyes. He seemed awfully sincere. Something about his demeanor struck me as familiar. I looked around, and there was no mirror in sight. I resisted the temptation to ask the boy, and he offered no assistance. I was about to give up on this ridiculous idea when I found myself looking down, as I often did in moments of doubt, and caught sight of someone looking back at me. I did not recognize this person at first. I closed my eyes, then opened them to make sure I wasn't imagining things.

I wasn't.

I was still standing in front of the golden icon. The seraph was still dead. The boy was watching me. On the altar was a white ceramic bowl filled with water. I should have recognized my own reflection in the water; after all, I should know myself well enough to recognize myself when I see it. And yet, the more I thought about myself, the more distant I seemed. It was as if a part of me had died and someone new had taken its place. This someone was the person staring at me through the surface, his eyes as cold and dark as the ones on the boy. He seemed to have a mind of his own, for when I turned my head to the right, he seemed perfectly still. As he curved his lips into a smile, I noticed deep lines forming around the mouth and eyes. I saw myself touching my face where the wrinkles appeared and was horrified to discover they were real. Then I nervously slid my fingers over my forehead, where I felt three deep lines burrowed deep into my skin. My cheeks were sunken from what seemed like an eternity of suffering. I rubbed my face over and over, trying in vain to smooth out the wrinkles in a foolish attempt to make them disappear. But the truth could not be disappeared. It insisted on being a part of me, just like the horrors I had witnessed. There was no way of getting rid of it, this old, decrepit phantom!

In a fit of anguish, I swiped at the bowl, sending it flying off the altar, shattering against the floor, and the water splashed over the deviant's feet. He jumped a little.

"What happened to your eyes?" he asked, his face turning paler.

"My eyes?" At first, I thought he was mocking me. Then I felt a terrible itch on the inside of my eyes, and I started rubbing them frantically, like a child waking from a horrible nightmare. When the rush was over, blood streamed down from my eyes, reaching all the way to my lips, and I tasted the bitter scent of iron. I swallowed hard, and a rush of nausea took over me. I felt a stabbing pain in my shoulder blades, like something was trying to pierce my skin. When I turned back to the altar, looking for myself in the water bowl, I remembered that the bowl had been shattered and the water gone. It was then in this moment of despair when the world began to disappear. I shook my head, and all I could see was the faint outline of things, followed by streaks of dark red and blue.

"What have you done to me?" I lashed out at the boy. He was a deviant, after all, and who knows what treachery he had committed!

"I didn't do anything, mister!"

"You knew... you knew this would happen to me! How? How did you know?"

"You've *turned*, mister, anyone could see that!"

"Turned? What madness are you talking about? I haven't *turned*. I told you already, I'm not a deviant. I'm not like you!"

"Not yet," he said, "but you shouldn't be scared; it can happen to the best of us."

"No, this is crazy. It's *you*. You did this to me. I was fine until I met you. Why did you tell me to look in the mirror? What did you do to me?"

"Nothing, mister. Keep your voice down. They'll hear us!"

"Let them! I'm the prince! They wouldn't dare do anything to me. It's you—your kind—who destroyed our society. I won't stoop to your level. *You* are the problem!"

"The prince would never say such a thing! He was a kind and gentle person. He cared about people like me. He died a martyr. I won't let you sully his name!"

"Died? What in God's name are you talking about? Have you gone mad? *I* am the prince. The prince is standing right in front of you!"

I expected the boy to talk back to me; in fact, I wanted him to. I wanted my anger to seethe and boil over. But all I got was silence. For a moment, I heard nothing, not even a whisper or footstep. Not a gunshot or scream. A shudder passed over me, and I felt a hand on my shoulder and heard the child's voice saying, "Don't be afraid." I was startled. The boy I remembered was much shorter than me. It would have been impossible for him to reach me at shoulder level, unless he was standing on a chair. When I turned to face him, all I could see was a dark, empty space.

"Where are you?" I asked.

"I'm here," he answered, taking my hand.

My instinct was to turn away, but as soon as he touched my hand, a hot rush of energy shot up my spine, and the darkness that clouded my eyes began to part, if only for a few moments. I savored every second of this respite, taking in the sights I had taken for granted just moments ago. I nearly cried. The room belonged to a stranger, but I thought it was mine. I wanted to hold it in my arms and never let it go. A cold wind blew through the shattered window, and from the street below came the unmistakable scream of police sirens.

"Follow me!" the boy said. "The Syndicate is here!"

Without thinking, I chased after his footsteps.

"Why are you helping me?" I asked.

"You remind me of someone I know."

I was going to ask him to tell me the truth when I tripped over his foot, tumbling into the hallway.

"Get up! Get up now!"

Even being half blind, I could see the intensity of the searchlight swoop over my head. There was a sudden clamor of footsteps on the floor below us. Syndicate turncoats, I could recognize their deception from A mile away. Fear sent me scrambling back up like a madman, and I followed the only savior I knew, a child I had just met and had already learned to hate. With the little vision I still possessed, I grabbed the staircase and flew over the steps. I ran so fast I felt like I was flying. The staircase looped around, one after another. We kept running up until there were no more stairs left to climb.

Not hesitating, the boy threw his shoulder into the door in front of us and barreled onto the rooftop. The weather had turned. Gone was the crisp autumn air from moments ago. Now the air was dead and muggy, heated up by some unknown force. There was an unmistakable feeling that everything was beginning to spiral out of control, and we were now standing on the precipice of great change.

The first of a thunder shower began to fall, for I felt the pattering of soft rain over my hair. A thick blanket of fog settled around me. I raised my face to the sky and laughed as the stinging drops hit my eyes and rolled down my chin.

What has my life become? Is my nobility just a lie?

I refused to believe it. If there was nothing essential about me, or my blood, what good could remain in the world? I could trust nothing and no one. There was still hope. There had to be. When I summoned the courage again to open my eyes, the world came back to me. I saw the flash of thunder and the fog of my own breath. I saw the sign of civilization all around me, buildings and machines people had made, generated by hard work and dedication. It was people like me who built them, was it not?

I tumbled so deep in this spiral of self-pity I failed to notice that a man had been standing in front of me the whole time, shrouded under the fog just a few paces ahead. A black hood concealed his face, and a black military trench coat draped over his tall, skinny frame. On his right arm was the Syndicate patch, the cross turned upside down. He had the boy in a chokehold, a knife pressed against Grendel's throat with a surgeon's touch.

"Help me, mister! Help!" Grendel's voice cracked with desperation.

I felt a tinge of satisfaction when I heard the boy pleading. *Good! The little deviant is getting what he deserves.* But why did I hate him so much? As much as I wanted to believe otherwise, I couldn't settle on a good reason for keeping my hatred toward him. I shuddered to think that my hatred for him came from a hatred of myself. And when I saw the terror in his eyes, my hatred turned to pity, for I saw in him shades of my own sadness and despair.

"Tell me you haven't fallen in love with a deviant," the man said in a cold, slippery voice. I recognized him at once. It was Anthony, the man who had betrayed my family.

"My God," he continued to taunt me as he removed his hood, revealing the red *S* branded over his neck. "For a second, I almost didn't recognize you!"

"Release him," I said.

"So you do have feelings for him."

"He's my friend."

"A friend? A deviant for a friend? I thought you hated the idea."

"It's me you want."

"How does it feel to be *you*?"

"You can take me, just let him go."

"You sound just like your father. All you monarchs are the same. You act so dignified, but deep inside, you care only about yourself. You want to save him to ease your conscience. But guess what? Your pity means nothing in the new world. We don't need you anymore!"

"Why are you still here then?"

"Because I'm in charge now."

"You're wrong, Anthony. You think you're free, but you're still a slave. You'll always be a deviant. The only thing that's changed for you is that you have a new boss over your head. You're just a pawn. Like you've always been."

"Ha! The orphan can talk back now!"

Then, lowering his eyes, he patted the boy on the head.

"Grendel, is that your name?"

The boy wanted to speak, but the knife was held so close to his throat that even a small movement could spell his end.

"Why are you hurting your own kind?" I asked.

"Grendel," he said to the boy, ignoring my question, "I want you to look at this man. I want you to look at him carefully. This is a man who claims to be something he's not. What do you call someone like that? Hm? A liar? An impostor? How about a deviant? You see, unlike us, he has no reason to exist. I want you to be my witness. Can you do that for me? Nod if you—"

Grendel sank his teeth into Anthony's forearm. Anthony squealed.

"Run, mister, run!" the boy shouted, his teeth stained with Anthony's blood. "Save yourself!"

Anthony grabbed the boy by the nape of the neck, and a small smirk crossed his face.

"This is all your fault," he said to me, as he proceeded to stab the boy's throat. I expected blood to come spurting out, but instead the knife broke. The boy shook free and ran toward me as Anthony removed a gun from his hip holster and shot the boy twice in the back. The boy staggered and almost fell to the ground, but he somehow found the strength to keep going.

"Jump!" he shouted at me, just as a group of soldiers came barreling through the door.

I turned to look behind me and realized that I was near the edge of the roof, with the ocean roaring far below. As the soldiers readied their rifles, Anthony shot the boy two more times, once through the calf, once through the shoulder blade.

This time, the boy fell.

"Grendel!" I called.

As the boy closed his eyes, I finally gave up the notion of saving him, spun around, and dashed toward the edge of the rooftop. Bounding over the edge, I felt a sense of freedom, as though I could maneuver myself in the air. But the moment was short-lived, as a bullet pierced my calf, and I tumbled into the water.

CHAPTER 19

WAVES OF MUTILATION

MARCUS

When I plunged the blade into his chest, my vision went black for a second, and I was taken back to the moment of my fall. I wanted to savor the agony bursting through his eyes, but I could only imagine the agony, which I found more satisfying in retrospect. I saved myself from being persecuted by my conscience.

The girl fell into my arms. We looked at each other like we were strangers meeting for the first time. Either we had changed on our own or the world had changed us. We found ecstasy in each other's embrace. Ecstasy, a feeling I thought I would never find.

There was the horror, then the feeling of release. Pure freedom was something akin to terror. You're afraid to lose yourself, but only by doing so can you come out on the other side. The freezing water lashed my body until it finally closed over my head. I wasn't drowning so much as I was descending into the abyss. All my life I had struggled to feel anything real. Not even witnessing the murder of my own family could awaken my soul. I might as well have been living under a coma, except I could still think, cry, and hope. All these pretensions began to slip away as I drifted deeper. Something like happiness blossomed deep inside my heart, and I smiled—truly smiled—for the first time. I had never felt so alive in the moment as when slipping away, never more alive than dreaming of a second apocalypse.

Take me. Carry me away.

It was better to be free than to pretend.

When I fell into the water, I left the past behind. At least, that was how I had convinced myself to stay alive. For if I were to see a future in which I was not the victim, I had to break the surface again and brave the world as a new man. But I didn't want to leave. I wanted to stay here, in the depths of nature forever. I was still afraid of the world. I should have mourned for the boy. Why did I not see him when I closed my eyes? Why could I not even remember the last thing my mother had said to me? What about the sorrow in her eyes? Was I so heartless? Even if the ocean split me apart, drowned me in a thousand pieces, I would still have to wonder about myself. I would be searching for wholeness for an eternity and maybe never find it. But was it not the search that mattered? If I didn't have these notions in my head, I probably would never have been saved. Even in my darkest and most liberating moment I was still looking for some kind of approval. I needed someone to say to me:

You're making the right choice. You deserve to live.

It was this Voice, a voice which simultaneously reminded me of the tenderness of my mother and the mockery of Grendel, that pulled me out of the water. I could well have already fainted by then, and who knew how much time had passed. All I knew was that when I recovered my senses, I found myself on the sandy beach of Paradise, a place I could recognize anywhere, in dreams or reality.

As I gazed toward the old forest, full of evergreen oaks, I became aware of myself once again, and the world returned in all its unforgiving ways. Awake, I was in no better position than where I was before. I was still a fugitive, running away from the troubles of the world instead of facing them head-on. I was plucked out of one purgatory only to be dropped into another.

For a moment, still lying on the sand, I had the bizarre notion that I had been transformed into a terrible creature, half man, half beast. I looked down at my waist with feverish anticipation, half expecting my legs to have been replaced by the tail of a fish. Even when I confirmed that my legs were still intact, I still imagined the tail of a fish, flopping about as though dismembered from the body. I resolved to clear my head of strange fascinations, and a smile emerged from this foolish endeavor. Taking advantage of this moment of relief, I raised myself on my legs once again and trudged toward the forest.

The rain started falling again in warm, tender drops. Save for the shimmering surface of the river, which snaked through the forest, the darkness was complete. The river was my guide. It led to the Convent of the Healing Star, the place where Grendel had grown up. The water still draining through my pants, I marveled at how I had managed the strength to keep walking. It was almost like I had gained a second life after falling into the ocean, when by all reasonable accounts, I should have perished.

I often dreamed about hunting with my father in this forest deep in the night. This was the thing I remembered most clearly about him. Not a memory of reality but a memory of dreams about reality. Then I remembered the resentment I felt toward him and the world and how foolish I was to feel resentful when I had everything. I saw his stern gaze, and the scar on my forearm palpated with pain. I covered the scar with my right hand, closed my eyes, and chanted a phrase from the Mantra to make him disappear from my head. Yes, faith is an illusion, but what did I have left, except for faith? The Mantra may have denied me every passion I wanted to pursue, but it was the only thing that seemed to still make sense.

The moment would not last, for when I opened my eyes, I saw the flicker of a torch slipping into darkness. A second later, the flame reappeared from behind a tree trunk, along with a man in a black poncho holding the torch, his arm shivering as he approached his friend. When they finally made contact, the light from his torch revealed a woman tied up to a tree, her face concealed behind a black mask. She must be a deviant. There were blood smears around her neck and waist, and she seemed on the verge of drawing her last breath.

"I thought I heard a noise," said the tall soldier in the black poncho. I peeked from behind a great oak tree. They were only a few feet away.

"Why are you always so paranoid?" said his friend, who was short and stocky, speaking in the high, derisive pitch of a tyrant trying and failing to impress the people around him. I disliked him already.

"I'm not paranoid. I'm just trying to be careful," said the tall soldier.

"The monarchy is dead. God isn't watching over us any-more. We can do whatever we want!"

Then he slapped his friend across the face.

"Live a little!" he shouted.

The friend grew tense and rigid, ready to strike back, but when he saw the little tyrant holding his gaze with no fear, he gave up on the impulse for violence. Pretending to be a good sport, he shrugged and chuckled.

"You're right," he said.

"I'm *always* right," said the tyrant. "It's too bad she won't live to see the new world. Such a pretty little thing…"

"Well, and hear me out on this," said the friend nervously, "let's say she was to, you know, carry the child of a thorough-bred, wouldn't she be allowed to live?"

"Albert, I'm impressed… you're thinking like a true Syndicate man."

"Thank you, sir."

"There's just one little problem. Who gets to be the father?"

There was a moment of silence before Albert understood the insinuation and cackled. I had never seen men behave in such a despicable way. Fearful of what might happen to the girl, I reached for the bowie knife strapped to my belt and squeezed the handle. I felt every urge in my body to intervene, but I knew it would be a foolish task. Although it was hard to see in the foggy darkness, I suspected they were both armed and much more practiced at the art of violence.

"If I'm going to be a father," said the tyrant, "I want her to look me in the eyes."

"Why?"

"Are you questioning my order?"

"No, sir."

"Well, then go! Take off her mask."

The subordinate hurried to the woman and with some trepidation removed the chastity mask. When he turned to his superior with a grin of satisfaction, I was shocked to find the vision of a kindred spirit, someone I had loved with all my heart. The graceful but shy brown eyes flickered painfully as her lips trembled on the verge of breaking down in tears. There was a small gash over the bridge of her nose, where blood had dried. I seethed in anger imagining all the ungodly things these men had already done to her. Despite all this, there was still a quiet determination on her face. She refused to give in to despair and was determined to live. Indeed, this was the Claudia I knew and loved.

The tyrant approached Claudia, while undoing his belt buckle.

Every nerve in my body lit up, and a thumping headache threatened to split my head open. Flushed with madness, I exploded out of my hiding place and tackled the tyrant to the ground. I stabbed him over and over again with my knife until my face was covered with his blood. The taste of his blood aroused the beast inside me and only increased my rage. I couldn't tell you what had taken over me, for this vile madness was something I had never experienced before. All I knew was that I was doing the right thing, and I never doubted this for a moment. Even when Claudia shrieked in terror, I kept stabbing the Syndicate scoundrel, until his face became so deformed I couldn't recognize him anymore. Every strain of resentment I had buried inside cried out for violent release. It was now or never. For the first time in my life, I acted without passing judgement. What sweet freedom!

I wanted this moment to last forever. When I looked down at the lifeless body lying under me, I no longer saw a man but everything evil about the past I thought I could never forsake. I fought against everything I was taught to reach the indisputable conclusion that he deserved to die. In fact, it was a mistake he ever lived. I saw in this man shades of myself, the civilized man and the primal beast condemned to fight a war neither could win. Even when he drew his last breath, I could hear the conflict raging on, inside his heart and mine. I was exhausted. It was no easy feat to kill a man. A man was more than blood and flesh. He possessed the will to live.

My whole body shaking, I strained to keep my knife from slipping through my hand. The only sound I could hear was my labored breathing. The rest of the world was silent, like a captive audience watching the climax of a play unfold with the wonder of a child. Straddled over the dead soldier's waist, with my left knee planted in the ground, I slowly raised my head, and there, standing in front of me, frozen in terror, was the tyrant's friend, his face as pale as the deviant who had died saving me.

As soon as our eyes met, he gave the most frightening shudder I had ever witnessed, his eyes turning stone cold, as if gazing into the gates of hell. Inspired by his fear, I bared my teeth and growled with a faint lurch. The movement unsettled him so much he spun around and scuttled into the darkness.

I waited until he disappeared before letting out a deep breath. I mustered what little strength I had left to get back on my feet. Wiping my face of blood, I turned to Claudia, who had been staring at me the whole time.

I smiled at her. For a moment, her lips were hard as marble. She was afraid of me. I couldn't blame her. I didn't even know myself. I slowly approached her, like a stranger with my palms open, trying to show her that I meant no harm. When she saw the blade of my knife, smeared with blood, she tensed up again, trying to turn her face away.

"Claudia," I said. "It's me, Marcus."

"Marcus?" she asked deliriously. Her eyes sparkled. Part of her recognized who I was, but the other part was afraid to agree.

"Yes," I repeated, "you're safe now."

"I never thought I'd see you again..."

When I cut the rope loose, her arms slumped to her sides, and after taking a half step, her knees buckled, and she fell into my arms.

"Are you hurt?" I asked.

"No, just tired," she said with a smile.

"It's good to see you again," I said.

"I wish the circumstances were different."

We laughed a little.

"What happened? How did you end up here?"

"I ran away."

"Why? I thought you were getting married."

"I'll never marry that man. I guess the revolution happened right on time."

She paused to watch my reaction. I didn't know how to react. What happened wasn't a revolution, but I couldn't deny my feelings for her.

"Oh, Marcus, I'm so sorry," she said, sensing my hesitation. "I didn't mean to be rude."

"Don't be," I said, fighting back the urge to say more.

"They've taken everything from us."

"Not everything... We still have each other."

Kindness flushed her eyes, and she sighed.

"Thank you for saving me."

I wanted to kiss her, but I didn't know how. It seemed inappropriate to take advantage of the moment. The scar on my forearm started to itch.

"Well," she replied, puckering her lips a little, "you look more handsome now."

"Do I?"

She laughed. Against all the despicable things I had witnessed, her smile seemed almost otherworldly. I felt a connection, a warmth I hadn't felt in a long time, but the moment I tried to seize the connection, it vanished. I was back with my old self again, where everything was cold and slippery. I just couldn't allow myself to feel any joy. She could feel it too, in the way I touched her hand. I was there but not present, and my hand slipped out of her grasp.

"What's wrong?" she asked, half knowing what I was going to say.

"Do you still recognize me?"

"Marcus, what kind of question is that? Of course, I recognize you."

"So nothing about me has changed?"

She couldn't bring herself to agree.

"Tell me what you see. I want to know."

"I see a good, decent person."

"That's not what I meant. There's something wrong with me, Claudia. I don't understand how it happened…"

"It's not your fault."

"Why is this happening to me? What have I become?"

"Marcus…"

"You see it, don't you? I have the face of an old man."

She couldn't look away.

"We all age. It happens to the best of us."

"That's what Grendel said."

"Who's that?"

"He died young. Just like me."

"You're still young, Marcus. You're still alive. That counts for something, right?"

Holding Claudia in my arms, I looked up at the stars.

"Have I become a deviant?" I asked, as if talking to myself.

I was waiting for her to confirm my nightmare when she took my hand and kissed the center of my blood-stained palm. Then she fell asleep in my lap.

CHAPTER 20

RESPECTABLE

JASON

A life driven by envy is no life at all. For a time, I was almost certain that I had grown beyond this. Beyond envy. I swore to myself repeatedly, night after night, that I should be satisfied with who I was and what I'd received, but somehow, something always got in the way. I remember watching kids being picked up by their mothers outside schoolyards and thinking how wonderful it must be to have someone who loves you unconditionally. And over the years, I invented this image of my own mother, and after she left, of all women who could be my mother. Sometimes I'd pass a kind-looking woman on the street and imagine her taking me home and making dinner for me, just like all the mothers did for their kids. Even though I knew this wasn't real, the fantasy was enough to make me love and fear every woman I saw. I let them take advantage of me, because I couldn't tell the difference between love and fear. I needed a woman's affection, but I hated the fear of losing them. And then there was the fundamental truth: I was never born at all. I was made by men who never cared for my existence. I was only to be used. So I came to think that maybe love was just a matter of being used.

Before long, I remembered falling into a kind of stupor, where day and night converged. I could be wide awake and see nothing but darkness. I could not deceive myself about my condition. In fact, I grew fascinated by it. The way the doctors murmured about me became a part of how I thought about myself. The constant whirling of the fan above drilled into the depth of my consciousness. All these movements, these suspicious eyes and murmuring lips, conspired to make me weak. I grew suspicious of myself. Their suspicions became my fear. Was I real or just a figment of imagination still trapped in my former self? From time to time, I would raise my arm and find only a hard metal frame. I should not have been terrified of myself, for I had always known what I was. But I recoiled in fear seeing through the facade I thought was real the whole time. I was civilized! I was not a machine, no more than any real living thing. It wasn't the metal frame that scared me but the idea that I was empty inside. I wasn't just torn apart; my barren emptiness was laid bare for all to see.

These ideas came to me as though from another place, somewhere both beyond and inside. This Voice, as it became known to me, whispered incessantly. If I ever refused to heed its advice, even something as mundane as brushing my hair, I would be struck by excruciating pain, and tears would rush out of my eyes. If I attempted to describe this pain, as I had tried with my doctor, I would suddenly lose the power of speech. After this happened a few times, I began to doubt if the pain ever happened at all. And, eventually, I learned to obey. I was everywhere in my mind, going about as if I was stuck in the present and future at the same time. As soon as I took upon an action, I found myself wondering if I had just completed this action in the not-so-distant past, and if I did, was I merely repeating a routine that was already predestined?

I kept going through this loop, and every time I jumped through the portal, which I imagined was to please the part of myself that was still juvenile and happy, I stumbled onto the other side, barely remembering who or where I was. The one thing I remembered distinctly was the feeling of nostalgia. I longed for the past as much as I longed to wake up. There was a mystique to the past, now that the future was thrust upon me. In the land of nostalgia, I was the stranger.

I was brushing my teeth one morning when the nurse showed up in the mirror holding a plate. I instinctively reached for the plate without turning around, expecting to find two pills and a bottle of water, but instead, my hand touched something metallic and smooth. When I turned around, I recognized the object. It was the insignia of the monarchy, a pristine, white cross etched on a black shield. This badge was stitched just below the collar of what I could only gather as a military uniform, folded up in a neat, little square. I remembered the bargain I had refused and the prince wearing this uniform on the day I'd killed his father.

"What's this for?" I asked.

"A new beginning," answered the nurse. "The All-Mother wants to see you. Please get dressed."

"The All-Mother…," I uttered, trying to remember if I had heard the title before.

"The All-Mother is the leader of the Revolutionary Tribunal. She replaced the All-Father and ended his tyranny."

"But I didn't agree to military service. That was the whole reason I—"

"We know."

"Isn't this a Vanguard uniform?"

"No," the nurse said, rotating the plate so that the insignia was now facing me. I understood the difference. The cross was, in fact, upside down. What a clever move, I thought, to turn the enemy's symbol into your own.

"We saved your life, Jason, the least we can expect is gratitude."

I was taken aback by her sudden display of aggression.

"Yes, I'm grateful, but I'm not a soldier."

"We are *all* soldiers," she said, peering into my eyes with such intensity I thought I'd burst into flames.

"Seize the day."

* * *

Seize the day.

Now where had I heard that before? I had the sensation of falling into a quicksand as I got dressed. The sensation couldn't be real since I'd never fallen into quicksand before. In the short eighteen years I had lived, I had never put on anything nice. Fashion was always the last thing on my mind. *Actions speak louder than words*—that was the code written into my genes. I was to serve others, not show off. And so, as I slipped into this rather fancy-looking military uniform, I found myself transported to an elevated state of mind. To my amazement, I began to feel respectable for the first time in my life. And *respectable* may not even be the right word for it. I can't possibly describe the effect this had on me. I was still conflicted, of course, and you don't shake off the shame of being a deviant just by changing your clothes, but there was something unmistakable about putting on this uniform. Never mind that I didn't understand what all the badges meant, or that I had never fought in a single battle, I was able to stand firmly on my feet and look at myself in the mirror without shame.

Seize the day.

The nurse stood behind me the whole time. Even when I had stripped naked, I wanted her to watch. For the first time in a long time, I felt unashamed.

"Follow me," she said, just as I finished straightening my collar.

I followed her out of the ward and started walking as I imagined a soldier would walk. Proud, firm, back straight, full of conviction. Unfortunately, I had no other audience. Everyone was gone. For the first time since I was revived, I tried to orient myself on a place and time. There was no way to tell time, for there was nothing that even resembled a clock in these rooms and hallways, which all looked the same, one after another. I was taken through several rooms, linked by winding corridors plastered with mandala wallpaper, some on the verge of falling off. It seemed as though we were traveling through time, as the condition of the building began to decay in front of my eyes. Before making the final turn to her left, we passed a broken altar, on which a golden idol was smashed to pieces. The nurse slid her hand over the jagged edge of the idol's neck and lamented, "Too bad these people couldn't find something better to believe in."

"A word of advice," she said as she grabbed the doorknob, "the All-Mother will only hear reason."

I was going to ask, as opposed to what? Then I thought better of it and walked through the door. What greeted me was something I never expected to see. I had set foot in many impressive buildings, like the cathedral where nobles gathered, but I had never been inside a space as pristine as this. Gone were the sprawling, religious paintings that the monarchs had splashed everywhere. Here, everything was a pristine white, illuminated only by natural light coming through the white curtains and the dome in the ceiling. The walls were painted white, as were the sofas, chairs, and the piano sitting in the middle. It seemed inconceivable how this pristine-looking place could exist next to a ward that was so dirty and deformed. They seemed to exist in two different countries, if not two different eras. When the nurse opened the door at the end of the hallway, I was expecting to see one of those old, abandoned factory buildings where the rain is constantly leaking through the roof and where people are kidnapped and never found.

A few minutes later, the nurse got up and opened the double doors. The way she was dripping with condescension reminded me of a certain secretary at Dr. Faust's office, but there was one key difference about her—she was most definitely awake. Wide awake.

"The All-Mother will see you now," she said. "Best of luck."

No sooner had I stepped into the dining hall than a warm arm wrapped around my back. The hand was soft and supple, and the way she rubbed my back reminded me of something more than just courtesy. A long table stretched from one end of the room to the other. On the table were plates filled with food. I was mesmerized by the smell of bacon and grilled meat.

"You must be starving." To my right, the woman emerged. It was none other than Matilda Gray, the All-Mother. "Welcome back to the land of the living."

Instead of speaking like a soldier, I mumbled something incomprehensible. I was too confused to even know what to call this woman.

"How are you feeling?" she asked.

"I'm well," I answered, putting on the ingratiating voice I had practiced my entire life. Whenever I was nervous, I found myself reverting back to the servant mindset.

"You look handsome in the uniform!"

"You think so?"

"Yes, dashing. Doesn't he look handsome, Major?"

A man approaching middle age, also dressed in a military uniform, got up from his velvet chair in the corner of the room and started walking toward me.

"A soldier through and through," he answered, flashing a grin.

I was so flustered by the praise I almost replied that I wasn't a soldier. But then I remembered what the good doctor had always told me, that things can be spoken into existence, regardless of facts, if you insist on them with courage. It was, of course, just a fancy way of saying, "It's fine to lie." I took it upon myself to graciously accept the compliment.

"I'm honored," I said.

"And we're honored to have *you*," said the All-Mother. "You made the revolution possible."

"Thank you for your service," said the major, offering his hand. When I shook his hand, I was surprised at how little pressure he applied on mine, despite the intensity of strength emanating from his muscles. He was clearly putting on an act. Another key characteristic of psychopaths.

"This is Major Anthony Fairchild," the All-Mother told me. "He's a child of the old republic, just like you and me. Even though we share the same bloodline, we're not related. But he's very much family to me."

"That's very kind of you, Mother," he said, investing genuine affection in the word *mother*. Then he turned to me. "You performed a great service to the nation. It's a pleasure to finally meet you."

"I'm not sure if I deserve the praise," I said, scratching the back of my head. "I just did what I thought was right."

"That's exactly what a soldier would say," he said with a wink.

"I know it must all feel very strange," added Matilda. "It's not easy being confronted with the truth. I can say that from personal experience! Now there's much for you to learn. We can eat and talk."

I followed the host to the long table, where a servant stood behind the chair where I was to sit. His head was lowered, and he held the back of the chair, waiting for me to arrive. I had never been waited on like this. I was always the one to serve others. The gesture was wildly intoxicating to someone always on the receiving end of the stick. *So this must be how the nobles feel all the time.* When I approached the young man, I thanked him, but he didn't respond.

"There's no need to thank him," said the All-Mother. "That's his job. You'll get used to it."

It was then that I realized the young man standing next to me was another service model. He looked just like me! Of all the models they could have used, they chose the one that resembled me the most. As I stared into his dull, black eyes, a wave of sorrow came over me. He carried the same expression I had always hated about myself, the ingratiating smile on the verge of breaking into tears. No person should have to bear such sadness alone. But he was most certainly alone. He would never be able to confess his feelings to another person, because those feelings could never materialize into words. That is how he was designed. But all the same, a part of me envied him. He never needed to worry about the things I worried about, philosophical things that may not mean anything in the end.

I found myself in a dour mood as I sat down to eat. Everything was served in tiny portions. The onion soup was served in a teacup. The salmon was cut in tiny pieces so they could fit on a plate the size of my palm. Even the bread was diced into small cubes, and for some reason, they were served in a glass goblet. There may as well have been no food at all. Maybe I was just supposed to use my imagination and pretend that I was eating a whole feast, like Alice did at the tea party. And like Alice, I found it rather strange that my other companions around the table were having a grand time savoring the food, piece by piece. Meanwhile, I was trying to suppress the urge to devour everything in one bite.

"In wartime, food is a luxury," said Matilda, apparently overhearing my thoughts. "In a revolution, restraint is a virtue. We can't afford to keep wasting our resources like the monarchs did. It wouldn't be fair to the common people."

"The salmon tastes really good," I said. I didn't know why I lied.

"The major made it himself."

"You know how to cook?" I was awestruck.

"A man needs to be self-sufficient," he said, as he sipped on the soup.

I sat up in my chair for a moment, scanning the room. Like the reception area, all the walls were painted white, not stark white but a kind of mineral white that sparkled ever so slightly if you looked at just the right angle. Everything was polished and clean. There was no blemish in sight.

"It's much nicer without all the distractions, isn't it?" Matilda remarked.

"What distractions?"

"Well, you know, all the gaudy artwork and false idols. We painted over them."

"Where are we?" I asked.

"We're in the royal court," Matilda answered. "The All-Father used to sit where I sit."

"Where are the royals?"

"Well, you're looking at them now. The people are royals now."

"But not everyone agrees," said Anthony.

"How so?" I asked, savoring the food like a royal.

"There are still people stuck in the past," said the All-Mother. "Frankly, I don't blame them. They're having a rough time right now. The Tribunal has outlawed all forms of worship. It's the right thing to do."

"Long overdue, if you ask me," said Anthony.

"Yes, I agree," Matilda said. "What do you think, Jason? Do you like our new society?"

"Sounds like heaven to me," I said.

My quip worked so well they nodded vigorously and clinked their glasses and emptied them.

"To equality!" Anthony hailed.

"To equality!" Mother and I said in unison.

Her cheeks growing slightly red, the All-Mother gazed into me with a certain fondness I remembered seeing only once before.

"What difference a day can make!" she said. "Now everyone has to pass the Trial, even the thoroughbreds. No more special treatment for anyone!"

I shivered. This news wasn't what I was hoping for.

"Have I passed?" I decided to ask, just to try my luck.

"No," Anthony answered.

"Haven't I done enough?"

The All-Mother hissed.

"Enough is when every person that clings to the monarchy is dead. Enough is when faith is purged from the world."

"But I'm just one man…"

"Do you remember," said the All-Mother, ignoring my protest, "that I used to be a fervent believer in the faith?"

"I do."

"Tell me the story. I want to hear it again."

"You want me to tell the story?"

"Yes, my origin story, as they say. You learned it in school, didn't you?"

"Yes."

"Well, go on then…"

"Well, uh… it started when you were a child."

"How old?"

"Nine or ten, I think?"

"Correct."

"And you started hearing voices. You had visions too. You were visited by saints from the past."

I paused to look for her permission to continue. She nodded.

"They told you to take up arms and save Anthem from the seraphs."

"Did anyone believe me at the time?"

"No one believed you. No one but Spencer Kane."

"But I insisted on speaking truth."

"Yes, and you helped him win the war."

"God, you just have to love a good story." She exhaled with profound satisfaction. "Look at how far we've come. You must think I'm crazy."

"People can change."

"You think I sold out."

"I think you did what was needed."

"No, I was never concerned by necessity. I lied. Plain and simple. I enjoy lying. I have the courage to admit what all the politicians refuse to admit. That's what makes me special."

"Did you make up everything?"

"Pretty much. It's a pretty good story, right?"

"Did the All-Father know?"

"Why, you think he's a believer?"

"Well, yes, he was the head of the clergy. He was the All-Father."

"So? I'm the All-Mother."

"No, he had to be a believer. Otherwise, how could people believe him?"

"Apparently not enough to follow him to the depths of hell. Look, the only reason you and I are sitting here having a nice meal inside this beautiful room while people are dying in the streets is power. We have power, and they don't. Unfortunately, ideas are not easy to destroy. You see, the irony is that we're not all that different from the monarchs. They believe in a higher cause, so do we. We even share some of the same genes. I was born into a noble family, after all. I can no more disown my lineage than the monarchs can disown their god. I don't *hate* the monarchs, at least not in the same way you might hate them. And I don't love the deviants just because I offer them a cure. What I want is a true meritocracy. The problem with the monarchs is not that they created One Mind; the problem is that they refused to take it to its logical conclusion."

"What's the logical conclusion?"

"Come, let me show you."

With some hesitation, I got up and joined her by the window. Anthony remained in his chair. She threw aside the curtain and opened the window, revealing the world below in all its naked violence. I had been holed up inside the ward for so long I found it almost strange to see people move about in their natural habitat. Against the simplicity and glamor of our dining hall, I could only describe the world below as chaos. Garbage and bodies were strewn everywhere, and people didn't move as much as they lurched, like birds darting around, so full of fear.

There was a movie theater at the intersection, and the billboard displayed "Black Mask, Armageddon" in big, white letters. A rather fitting name. Just outside the theater a throng of curious citizens gathered around a makeshift stage, covered under a black drape. Even from above, I could sense that they were foaming at the mouth with rabid excitement. Just watching them made the hairs stand on my arm.

The All-Mother watched intently. I could smell her perfume, a mix of blueberries and rubbing alcohol.

"Anticipation is the beginning of fear," said the All-Mother. "We fear many things. The Other, the unknown, our penchant for violence."

Suddenly, the crowd erupted in cheers. A broad-chested soldier strutted out of the theater, followed by a young man in his early twenties, his eyes covered by a white blindfold, his hands tied behind his back. The slanted *S* was branded on his neck. A young woman flew toward the soldier and kissed him on the lips.

"But what we fear most is change," the All-Mother continued. "So, in a way, you can say that fear is a necessary condition to change."

Change. What had really changed? The All-Father was now the All-Mother. The Vanguard was now the Syndicate. Faith was now terror. Weren't they always two sides of the same coin? Or perhaps was the change Matilda spoke about actually real? Indeed, I could not deny that there was something in the air. It was as if the pain I had buried inside was now unleashed into the world. I no longer felt alone.

Moments later, a monk dressed in a traditional, white robe stumbled out of the theater. He was clearly a thoroughbred and much older than everyone else. Unlike the boy, he wasn't blindfolded, and his eyes were green. Upon seeing a disciple, the crowd resorted to scornful silence, except for a few who hissed even more ferociously.

"Why are they being punished?"

"Everyone is being punished."

"Everyone?"

"The old master has come to be judged. We offer a choice. When he takes the stage, he'll have the opportunity to confess."

"Confess?"

"His true feelings toward the deviant race."

"What about the deviant?"

"The deviant is the test."

Matilda glanced at me sideways and noticed the curiosity in my eyes.

"As they say, there's no testimony without a test. And today, the old master will show us if he has the courage to change. Will he choose compassion for the Other or devotion to his own kind?"

I struggled to understand the distinction.

"In the past, the old master was the judge. He got to decide who lived and who died. He controlled our morality. He may have worshipped a god, but he was the one playing God. Does that sound fair to you?"

"No."

"So now, we return the favor."

Both master and servant were now positioned next to each other on the platform. As the guard tore through the servant's shirt with a scissor, a pair of full, black wings slithered out of his back. The crowd recoiled in horror. The guard pointed a gun at the deviant's head.

"In the end, this is not about revenge. Revenge is petty and frankly boring. If it were about revenge, I would have ordered the Syndicate to slaughter all the disciples. I'm creating the conditions necessary for people to reveal who they really are. Why pretend to care for someone you hate, just because your faith told you so? Why maintain that lie?"

"My fellow disciples, you must believe me," said the old man. "I have no children of my own. This boy is not just a servant, he's my son! I'm asking you to spare his life. I'm begging you! He's my only hope in the world!"

The crowd seemed unmoved. After all, they were psychopaths. Then someone shouted, "Let the deviant speak!" This suggestion reanimated the crowd, and people hollered in approval.

"The mob shouldn't be feared," continued the All-Mother. "It holds a mirror to our deepest desires."

"The mob is the judge," I said.

The servant, still on bended knee, and with a gun pointed at the back of his head, kept his eyes on the ground.

"Why won't you look at me?" said the master. "I'm trying to help you!"

"*Help* me?" the servant snapped. There was an audible gasp, like when a captive audience just witnessed a major revelation play out on stage.

"You're like a son to me! Please, don't do this to yourself!"

"Do what, exactly? I've never mistaken you for a father!"

The master was beside himself. There was a mix of sorrow and hatred in his expression. "How could you say such a thing?"

"You don't need to lie to yourself anymore, Master. Just say the truth."

"What truth?"

"You never loved me."

"I never *loved* you? How can you be so ungrateful? You're alive today because of me. I gave you a home when others kicked you out. They all said to me, 'This one cannot be reformed.' I gave you a second chance. I made you into the man that you are today!"

The deviant rose to his feet, staring harshly at his master.

"You'll never understand," the deviant uttered.

As the guard pressed the barrel of his revolver into the deviant's temple, a smile, born of profound satisfaction, graced the All-Mother's lips. Even though she didn't speak, I felt I could understand her. Had things remained the way they were, this deviant would have never had the chance to say the truth about how he felt. He would have remained invisible his whole life. The practical needs of life would always get in the way. But now, for the first time, he was seen!

The old master must have been thinking about redemption when he held his servant's gaze. To imagine anything else would undermine his sense of self. He was too important, and too intelligent, to be deceived by some emotional outburst from the inferior race. As the crowd fell silent once again, he opened his arms to embrace his one and only son. When the deviant said, "You'll never understand," he heard, "You still love me, but you're afraid of saying it out loud." In his mind, he could still save the boy, rescue him from the desolation of being exiled. For in the end, the master could still redeem the slave. His love was true, and there was no way for the world to misunderstand his generosity.

"Do you accept his confession?" the soldier asked the deviant.

"No," the deviant replied.

I imagined the sheer shock and hubris that struck the master in this moment, betrayed by the very philosophy that sustained his entire life.

I could only watch with quiet satisfaction as the old master was shot dead.

The servant could finally speak.

The master was finally punished.

CHAPTER 21

LOVE

MARCUS

I was trapped somewhere between dreams and reality when I felt the soft touch of Claudia's hand. I looked down and saw her tending to the wound in my calf. I was lying against a wall with a pillow under my back. I recognized the place from the smell of rosemary, a plant my family thought would help to cure the deviants. Probably another lie.

"You're healing faster than I thought," said Claudia, wrapping a bandage around my calf.

By the time my vision came back, the bandage was already fully wrapped, and I could no longer see the wound to confirm myself. I tried bending my foot toward me and felt only a slight pinch. Claudia was right.

"Do you remember this place?" she asked.

"Of course. This is the Convent of the Healing Star," I said, taking in the view. You could've mistaken the place for a dance hall if it wasn't littered with empty stretchers and bedsheets stained with fresh blood. Even the heavy scent of rosemary from the garden outside couldn't drown out the nauseating smell of sweat and rubbing alcohol. Two brothers, it appeared, were talking to each other on the other side, one lying in a stretcher, one holding his hand. There were mattresses, gold-striped shirts, pants, monk robes lying scattered about, piled up in heaps along the walls. What other place could have such a special charm? In its more honorable days, the place was known as a refuge for the sick and down-trodden. My parents would take me here every few months to see the converts—deviants who were on the path to healing. In truth, this was a glorified ward. There were mostly children here. We used to call them Fellows, to give them a fake sense of hope and prestige, when in reality, most of them were just living out their final days in pain.

"Pain brings you closer to God," I read from the old banner on the wall. Beneath the banner was a glass frame that displayed a pair of angel's wings, sliced off from a child's back.

"We must be in heaven now," I mumbled.

"Not quite," said Claudia, "we're still alive."

"Do you believe in the Mantra?"

"Depends on the day."

"And today?"

"Today, I'm grateful to be alive," she said.

As Claudia parted her hair, I saw the *S* brand on her neck. It seemed as if she wanted me to see it.

"Does that still bother you?"

"Oh, this? No, it's now a part of me."

"It must feel horrible to be labeled subhuman."

"I prefer to see it as *super*-human."

"But you know that's not what the *S* stands for."

"So what? You make the best of what you have. You wouldn't understand."

"No, but I want to understand."

Claudia stood up and leaned against the wall next to me. Her gaze fell upon the two brothers, who seemed to be having an argument.

"You probably don't remember, but I met you a few times when I lived here."

"I hated those visits."

"Why?"

"They were fake. The rich benefactor pretending to love the people he victimized. Nothing more condescending than that."

"I'm surprised they ever let you be the prince."

"I was born into it, remember?"

"So, what about you? Did *you* care about us?"

"It doesn't matter now…"

"I want to know."

"Honestly, I felt sorry for you, more than anything else. I'm sure you hated us too."

"Actually, no." Claudia sighed. "Well, at the start, we did. Preparing for your family's visit took a lot of work. The sisters would make us practice our manners. We had to stand in front of the mirror and learn to speak with a smile. We'd practice shaking hands. Condescending stuff, like you said. And only a few kids actually got the chance to interact with you, because God forbid a deviant looked at a monarch the wrong way. But we all had to rehearse, just in case we had the honor of being graced by your presence."

"You don't sound bitter at all."

"Well, the funny thing is, and you probably don't believe me, but after a while, we actually started looking forward to your visits."

"Really? Why?"

"They were like events, you know, and we got to get away from the monotony of life at the convent. Having you around made us feel important. Say what you want about your father, but he was always nice to us—and charming too. He remembered all of our names, and when he talked to us, it felt like he cared. Your mother was nice too. She often came to our birthday rites. And she'd bring us gifts, new clothes, toys, books. She even bought us a piano one time. It used to sit over there."

I followed Claudia's hand and found nothing but an empty stretcher where the piano used to be.

"What happened to it?"

"Our headmaster took it away."

"Why?"

"He never told us. It just disappeared one day."

"But my mother bought the gift. He dared to refuse the queen?"

"Well, he's dead, so I can't ask him now."

We shared a glance.

"At some point, your family stopped visiting us. And that was when things started to change. We started fighting each other, the kids. And the Sisters encouraged it. This never happened before. We used to be friends, or at least pretended to be friends. All of us, invalids, deviants, seraphs. We knew who the real enemy was. But then they turned *us* into enemies. In fact, instead of service on Sundays, they started hosting show trials."

"Show trials?"

"Sounds awful, right? They pick two fellows to go on the stand. One person is the accuser. The Other is the heretic. The accuser has to show that the Other has committed acts of heresy. The Other has to defend himself and will most likely fail."

"Who gets to be the judge?"

"Another fellow, of course."

"Did you ever get to be the judge?"

"No, I was always the accuser."

"How did that make you feel?"

"I liked it."

When I frowned, she doubled down on her statement.

"I'm not afraid of saying the truth anymore, even if it's embarrassing. I should be embarrassed, right? I just admitted that I enjoyed abusing my own people to please my superiors. And I know the Sisters know it too. They got off on it. They loved every second of it. The cycle doesn't stop, Marcus. This feeling that festered inside me never went away. Even after all this time, I still carry that nostalgia with me. Outside, I'm always the victim. But in this convent, I got to be the abuser. I could make someone else bleed. If that's not justice, what is?"

I gazed upon the woman I loved, mouth agape.

"But you were all abused…"

"I know! You see, Marcus, love and hatred aren't always opposites. They feed on each other."

"Do I even know you?"

"You know, it was your mother who saved me."

"I… didn't know that."

"She never told you?"

"No."

"I wasn't the only one. She saved as many as she could. She struck a deal with the headmaster. She offered to pay the convent a fee. In return, the convent would allow the lowest-ranking deviants to be adopted, kids like me. The headmaster got rich, and the kids got free. Well, free, in a relative sense."

"I thought the fellowship guaranteed your survival."

"Oh no. There are no guarantees in the world. You have to fight for everything."

"So that's how you came to work for Jacob?"

Claudia nodded. "Apparently, I reminded him of his daughter. She died when she was young."

"Was he good to you?"

"Well, I was lucky. I'm grateful he adopted me. Most deviants end up in the asylum or dead. Do I love him? No. Do I hate him? I should. It's people like him, like you, who put me here in the first place. I don't expect you to understand. Sometimes… you learn to love the people you're supposed to hate."

"I don't hate you."

Claudia smiled. "I know you don't. But you're still different. We'll always be different."

"Not always," a deep, childish voice interrupted. The boy appeared before us, his head shaven, with a gentle smile on his face. The monk's robe he wore made for a funny contrast with his childish face. You don't expect someone so young to look so world-weary and disciplined. In spite of the costume, there was a twinkle of mischief in his brown eyes. My heart skipped a beat when I saw the golden bowl he was holding; it looked like the same bowl I had seen in the apartment, the same object which forced me to see the truth.

"Get back here," ordered the young man chasing after him.

When Claudia saw him grab the boy's shoulder, she intervened.

"Let him go."

The young man looked at Claudia like they knew each other, then softened his grip.

"My name is Dante," said the boy. "Please accept my gift."

I was rather amused by such a professional introduction.

"My name is Marcus," I said, and without thinking, I took the bowl.

"You look tired," he said.

"I'm fine."

"You don't have to be afraid."

"Afraid of what?"

"Everyone turns, sooner or later."

At first, I wanted to ignore him. But then I thought, if there was ever a time to speak up, it was now. I had nothing left to lose.

"No!" I shouted. "I'm a monarch. I can't. It's not possible for me to be a deviant. I pass the Trial by birth."

Dante shared a glance with Claudia.

"I know," he said. "You must be thirsty. Drink. It's good for you."

He wasn't wrong. I was very thirsty. When I brought the bowl to my face, a glint of red, like a drop of blood on a razor's blade, flashed on the surface. I couldn't see it clearly before it disappeared. I closed my eyes and drank the water. It tasted slightly sweet, like fresh spring water drawn from the well.

Claudia patted the boy on the head and brought him into her embrace.

"I miss you so much," she said, her voice softening up in such a gentle way I could almost believe this was her child.

"I miss you too," said Dante.

"How are you holding up?" Claudia asked.

"I'm good. My brother's taking good care of me," Dante replied.

"Is he being rough with you again?"

Dante shook his head, biting his lips.

"You shouldn't have brought him here," the brother scowled.

"Why not, Magnus?" Claudia snapped back.

"He doesn't belong here, like you said."

He, referring to me.

"He's a human being, like the rest of us. He saved my life. That's more than I can say for you."

Magnus snarled. His eyes were dark brown, like his little brother's, but there was no compassion inside his eyes, save for the pain he felt toward himself. A bloody gash crossed the top of his nose. When he spoke, the gash seemed to open up, and you could see the blood seething inside.

"Why do you always take the enemy's side?" said Magnus.

"Marcus is not the enemy," said Claudia.

"He's the reason for our suffering! His family put us here, sold us a lie, then left us to die. They're psychopaths! He's a monarch. He has no compassion for people like us. He'll turn on us the moment it suits him."

"His family is *dead*, Magnus. The monarchy is dead. He has no one left."

It was so jarring to hear Claudia say this and with such gleeful satisfaction. As much as I hated the hypocrisy on which I was raised, it was still a part of who I was. I could harbor resentment toward my father, I could refuse to believe the Mantra, but there was no denying the fact that it was a deviant who had brought ruin to me and my family. It was a deviant who had ended the peaceful life I'd had. A deviant who brought chaos to the world. How could I ever forgive all of this?

"The monarchy is alive and well," I shot back.

"See what I mean?" Magnus said with a smirk.

"Cut it out," Claudia said.

"No, let him," I said. "It's better when people are being honest. At least you get to see who they really are."

"Do you want an apology from me? Is that it? Have I offended your royal sensibilities? You want me to kiss up to you, is that what you want, your grace?"

"I don't need your affection."

"Oh, but I have zero affection for you. You took everything. You made us sick. And then you preach to us about compassion and justice? It's divine justice that your family is dead!"

I was about to throw a haymaker at this arrogant fool when Dante squeezed between us.

"Stop!"

"That's your problem, Dante, you're too scared to fight. They've poisoned your mind. Religion is a poison. What you have is not a gift. It's a sickness they forced on us, a sickness that has to be cured!"

"But the Philosopher told me I can harness my gift!"

"The Philosopher is a liar, just like the All-Father. They're one and the same. False prophets taking advantage of fools. He pretends to fight for people like us, but he just wants to be famous. Nothing he says will ever come true. He can't save you. Only the cure can save you. Come with me, and I promise you'll get better."

"I don't want to be cured," said Dante, retreating from his brother into Claudia's space.

"You know the Philosopher?" I asked, remembering mother's parting words.

"Yes. I can take you to him," answered Dante. "He's been expecting you."

"Expecting me?"

"The prophecy—"

"Is a lie," interrupted Magnus, laughing. "No one can dismantle the machine. We should accept that and get on with our lives. The Syndicate is offering us a path out."

He got down on a knee in front of his little brother, clutched the boy's shoulders, and looked him in the eyes. "I'm going to ask one last time; Dante, what will you choose?"

Dante looked at his brother, his lips trembling with fear and confusion. I felt his pain intensely, the pain of being pulled in opposite directions: blood loyalty on one side, freedom on the other. I wished I could speak on his behalf. I wished I could get rid of the tyrant forcing him to choose.

I was going to grab him by the shoulder and tear him away from the tyrant when a loud burst of gunfire erupted somewhere ahead, shattering the glass window separating the garden from the hall.

"Get down!" Claudia shouted.

CHAPTER 22

BROTHERS

MARCUS

Had Claudia not warned us so quickly, we would have been hit. We dropped to the floor just in time to avoid the first wave of bullets. Magnus herded us behind a marble statue of the All-Father to use as cover. The onslaught was relentless. I could tell by the sound and rate of fire that these were submachine guns, another favorite of the All-Father. It wasn't enough to inflict pain and death; he had to do it with pleasure.

Whoever was wielding the weapons had gone completely mad. They were firing wildly in all directions, as if the sole purpose was to unleash maximum violence upon the world. There seemed to have been no command, no coordination, just pure hatred.

Soon enough, our cover was demolished. Left exposed, we looked frantically for another place to hide.

"This way!" Magnus shouted, as we crawled behind a giant tomb made of stone near the ward. Bullets seemed to scatter in all directions, and it felt that at any moment we might draw our final breath. I wrapped my arm around Dante's back and used my body to shield him from the incoming fire. Even in the delirium of fear, I was determined to see him to safety. I was never more determined to do anything in my life.

Chunks of plaster rained down from the ceiling. They cracked into small pieces on the hard marble floor, filling the entire hall with white dust. The smoke provided us with a sense of cover, and we took advantage of the illusion and kept crawling. At last, we slipped through a door on the west side of the hall and found ourselves inside a small ward with two rows of hospital beds, each one quarantined by blue curtain dividers.

Just then, the gunfire ceased. A morbid silence fell over the convent. Then came the nightmarish realization that we were still alive, somehow unscathed. The adrenaline that had carried me through the storm was now beginning to recede, leaving my veins cold and burning with pain. I was suddenly struck with a kind of inescapable guilt, or was it disappointment? If anything, it was a miracle that I had survived, but I hated the idea of miracles, and I needed an explanation. If I had survived for reasons I could not understand, did I really survive at all? I was still gripped by a maniacal reality forcing itself upon me with every breath. The whole world, it seemed, was still in the process of collapsing over my head, one layer after another, until my eyes could no longer tell fact from fiction.

Footsteps approached; we stopped moving. Dante and I settled under the fourth bed from the door, Magnus under the bed opposite, and Claudia three beds down.

Two soldiers slipped into the room. They wore black suits, half-masks shaped like a demon's smirk, and from what I could gather under the darkness their eyes seemed rather young; they were perhaps not much older than me. There was a cavalier harshness about the way they moved, like they had no care or reason to exist, except for the worship of death. To think these young men would have been devout followers of the faith was almost incomprehensible. But then again, as

Mother used to remind me, the human brain can turn on a dime, just like the world itself.

Filled with dread, Dante and I watched them approach from under the bed. One of them turned to our row, and his comrade took to inspecting the other side. The soldier with green eyes moved stealthily toward the first bed on our side, jabbed the blue curtain with his black carbine a few times, like a child playing with his toy. He stood there, tapping his right foot on the linoleum floor. Then he threw the curtain open with his right hand and aimed his carbine at the unsuspecting victim he had imagined in his head. Of course, there was no one there.

I felt Dante's heart thumping under my chest, and as I sought to comfort him, I saw Magnus glaring at me. Only then did I pause to think how odd it was that Dante had chosen to huddle with me instead of his own brother, and this must have enraged Magnus. Truth be told, I delighted in seeing his rage. So rarely had anyone chosen to side with me, outside of being compelled by social obligations. To have a total stranger seek my help was validating in ways I couldn't have imagined. It gave me a sense of hope about the world. I clutched Dante tight against me, like he was my own brother, and glared back at Magnus. But to my surprise, Dante resisted. He pushed me away a little and pointed at the soldier who was now just a bed away. I was mortified. I was too busy being petty instead of trying to think of a way out.

"What do we do now?" he whispered in my ear.

As far as I could tell, there were only two options. Stay put and hope that the soldiers wouldn't find us or sneak up on them when they weren't looking and hope to overcome them by force. I carried only a knife, the same one I had used to stab another soldier to death. This memory provided some encouragement, but I didn't think I could move fast enough to catch the guard by surprise. Besides, a sneak attack like that would need to be coordinated since the other soldier would notice me before I could strike.

While I gazed into the floor, feeling helpless, Dante nudged me in the ribs, and I looked up to find Magnus aiming a revolver at the guard inspecting his side of the ward. While holding the aim at the guard's ankle, he made a gesture with his hand to follow his lead. I nodded.

In the split second our eyes met, the soldier suddenly pulled open the side curtain and fired at Magnus. The bullet struck him in the waist. Groaning, Magnus rolled to his side, aimed, and returned fire. The soldier staggered backward and bumped into his comrade.

"He's hiding under the bed!" the soldier shouted.

His comrade made a quick turn and readied his carbine, looking for the target in the darkness. In the blur of the moment, before I even had a chance to react, Dante slipped out of my grasp and started crawling toward the soldier.

I wanted to shout at him, but that would only alert the guards. Whatever he was going to do he had a better chance of succeeding without the guards noticing him.

"Where is he?" asked the wounded soldier.

"I can't see him," replied his comrade, scanning the floor to his left. Even I couldn't see Magnus anymore. He had seemingly disappeared.

"Stupid vermin!"

"I'll flush him out." He proceeded to spray bullets into the floor. Covered by the noise, I saw Dante leap out from under the bed, clutching the soldier by the waist. Taken by surprise, the soldier released the trigger and tried to peel the boy's hands off his waist.

"What the hell?"

The comrade started laughing. "You got spooked by a little rat."

"Get him off me!"

"With pleasure." The wounded soldier sidestepped around his comrade and poked his head toward Dante, as if he was playing hide-and-seek.

"Where's mommy and daddy?" he taunted.

"In heaven," Dante answered in a voice so deep I couldn't recognize him. He glared at the enemy, his eyes burning red.

"Tell me," the soldier replied, rubbing his palm over the barrel of his rifle, "would you still believe in heaven if I put a bullet—"

His mouth stiffened, then drooped. His eyes shone brightly for a moment, then turned blank, the flesh just below his cheekbone exploding in a thousand pieces. His comrade watched with horror as he slumped to the floor, his eyes frozen in hatred. The comrade, meanwhile, found himself in a painful struggle of his own, as Dante began to unleash a power of ungodly origins. What gripped him was the pain of absolute ecstasy, the kind of pain that was indistinguishable from pleasure, magnified to such extremes his every nerve writhed and burned. When the soldier touched the savage hands holding him in purgatory, his hands caught fire, and this fire, aroused by the naked display of violence, burned through him, leaping from cell to cell. I had never witnessed anything so spectacular, so perverse. A civilized man should not be enthralled by violence, but this violence was delightful. I witnessed the rebirth of man, purified by his hatred toward the Other.

The man had certainly changed. What remained of him were a pile of bones and charred flesh. All that pure, noble blood splashed over the floor, wasted, meaningless.

The boy stood there in shock (or pleasure) as Claudia took

him into her embrace. She wasn't afraid of him. She wanted to feel his heat. I was drawn into the writhing unicorn inside Dante's eyes. I found refuge in this unwavering look.

At first, I saw nothing but a beating heart, then the veins started to grow, like roots of a plant reaching deep into the soil. The thing took shape in the corner behind Dante, organ by organ, limb by limb, when finally, a human being emerged. It was initially hard to recognize the face because the eyes and nose and mouth were contorted. At last, the shape became a person with a name and a heart. It was Magnus, naked and sweating. He was still bleeding from the waist, his blood flowing into the mouth of the revolver which he had used to kill the Syndicate soldier. But this wasn't the Magnus I knew. This Magnus was older—much, much older. He was now an old man, his entire body ravaged by age, just like me.

"Magnus!" Claudia called, running toward her old friend. His chest heaving, Magnus looked down at his little brother, their hands touching.

"I couldn't watch you die," he said to his little brother. "I had to… I had to do it…"

"You're bleeding," said Dante. "Why are you not able to heal?"

"I can't," Magnus panted, "I'm not like you."

"You can. You just need to concentrate. Focus!"

"Stop," Magnus said with a bitter smirk. "You won't change my mind. Don't try."

"I'm trying to save you!"

Claudia swiped a ragged hospital gown from the coatrack and threw it over Magnus's naked body.

"Dante's right, you can't give up," said Claudia. "Come with us."

Magnus leaned his head against the wall and exhaled, pulling the gown off his back. "You can't save me. I'm done for. If I go with you, I'll only slow you down. I won't have you risk your life for me. You've helped me enough. I can't be saved. From the day I turned into a deviant, I was doomed. I was never long for this world. Mother told me that. I'm happy I got to see you grow up, Dante. I really am…"

"You can't give up, I won't let you!" Dante insisted. "You have a gift, Magnus, you just need to use it!"

Magnus shook his head, his eyes turning pale. "I used it, and look what happened to me. This is a curse. What *you* have is a gift. You should do with it as you please. You're old enough to decide on your own. As for the rest of us, we get to live with the consequences, or not…"

Filled with desperation, Dante faced me and Claudia. "You have to help him! Please!"

Claudia struggled to speak. While she seemed torn, she was rapidly coming to terms with reality, and Dante could see a cold melancholy come onto her face.

"Are you just going to leave my brother to die? How can you give up? We can take him to the Philosopher. There must be a way…"

Magnus grabbed Dante by the wrist. "I've seen the passage of time. I've been to the promised land. I couldn't stay there long, but I was there. And what I saw, you people couldn't even dream. Maybe you're right, Dante. Maybe I should've listened to you. But listen, it's too late to change things now. What's done is done. I made my choice, and now you must make yours. Go! Go with Claudia, but never trust the prince, do you hear me? Never trust a psychopath. One day, we'll wipe them out. Till then, stay strong…"

Magnus released his grip on his brother's hand and gave Claudia a nod. His decision was final.

"It's okay, you'll be all right, kid," he told Dante. Once again Magnus picked up the revolver from the floor. "I'll buy you some time."

Dante was inconsolable. He refused to leave. I felt terrible for him, despite how much his brother hated me. He was burning up, and we needed every bit of strength to drag him away from his brother. I couldn't help but feel responsible for everything that had happened. As we closed the door, I stole one final glance at the old man, and the only emotion I could discern in his eyes was pain.

CHAPTER 23

FOLLOW YOUR HEART

It still bothered me that I was working for the very people who had conspired to bring me down. I literally died for them. I didn't see myself as a martyr, for martyrs fight for a cause they genuinely believe. For me, there was no cause, only the perpetual consequence of trying to fit in. When I fell into the All-Mother's embrace, I imagined myself finding a place to belong, and I thought I'd found it. For a little while, I thought this place, this palace made of marble and gold, was my home.

For the next two nights, I slept in a comfortable bed for the first time in my life. I didn't have any nightmares. Instead, I dreamed about walking across the stage and getting my college diploma. Everybody was cheering for me. They were calling out my name. Even though I knew I had done nothing special, I savored every moment of their infatuation with me. It was a hot afternoon, and I was already sweating under my black graduation gown. The muscle in my jaw twitched as I tried to hold the smile. I treasured every fleeting movement in their doting eyes. I had made it! Finally!

I recognized the chancellor handing me the diploma. He took the appearance of Dr. Faust but had a gentler spirit. He seemed so generous and full of joy, and I had no reason to be afraid. When he shook my hand, I felt a rush of joy. It was the most incredible feeling in the world.

"Congratulations, my son!"

Without thinking, I smiled for the crowd. I raised my diploma like a soldier raising his sword after slaying his enemy. Had I misled them? Maybe, but I was merely playing the role. I was the star of the show, so why should I not give the people what they wanted?

You'll never make it.

With an attitude like yours...

You're lucky to still be alive.

You better cherish what you have.

Or you'll lose it all.

Did they have nothing else to say? Always the same tired advice. They should go tell that to someone else. Pick another victim. I wouldn't play their game today. No, sir. I wouldn't let them ruin the fun.

The diploma was worthless, I knew. Just words on a piece of paper, sure. But what about the applause? What about the stage, the university, the dream of becoming famous? Was everything just a lie? Maybe it was wrong to crave attention, but I needed attention to survive. And maybe it was wrong to want more than I needed, but to make it, I needed more than what I'd had. Let the savage die, they'd say. Replace him with something better.

All along the forest I had stalked the trail of breadcrumbs to the chocolate house. I saw him, Master. The perfect being. I could touch him with my hands. If only I could reach it, I could live this happiness forever.

The stage turned out to be a shower stall, and I was the mirror. I had been looking at myself for too long to realize that my fever dream was just that, a dream. The cheers got drowned out by the sound of water spraying from the showerhead. The sky turned gray, and the chancellor faded, like smoke in the mirror. The other man in the mirror came into focus, and it was the bulldog face of Anthony. He seemed rather pleased seeing me naked, though not so pleased as to smile.

"If a man can dream of a better land, he can make it come true. It's good to dream."

"Have you been watching me?" I asked, turning off the shower.

"I'm always watching you, kid, it's part of my job. Have you memorized your speech?"

"I think so."

He handed me a white towel. I marveled at my physique, chiseled and lean.

"Do you like your new body?"

"Very much."

"We picked it out from an advertisement in the *Conformist*."

"Really?"

"The magazine was your dad's favorite, wasn't it?"

I hesitated. "He loved reading about famous people."

"Well, he must be proud. You're famous now."

"I thought I'd never live to see the day," I said, drying my body with the towel and wrapping it around my waist, like people did in the movies.

As I was about to leave the shower stall, Anthony stepped in front of me and pressed his palm into my chest. He stared into my eyes.

"Don't let it get to your head."

The move startled me. I wasn't expecting physical contact. The way Anthony behaved had lulled me into thinking that he was a friend. In a moment's notice, he reminded me that he was still the boss.

This realization made me nauseous and weak at the knees. I hated the way he made me feel. The feeling that you have to grovel and ingratiate yourself to someone else all the time. I had lived that life and promised myself that this time things would be different. The All-Mother saved me for a reason, and I wasn't going to let people bully me anymore. I swung the towel loose and walked naked into the bedroom.

"I'm not ashamed of who I am," I declared. "I've earned the right to be here."

He once again approached me and placed his hand on my shoulder. He was a few inches taller, and this time he smiled. It was a firm but gentle smile. I recalled the same expression from my father.

"You're a Vanguard now. You serve the Syndicate. You have a duty far greater than yourself. You may be a hero, but you're still a soldier. If you succeed with the cadet corps, you will earn the right to stand among the best of us."

"And… what if I refuse?"

"Then you'll be replaced."

In that moment I was struck by the irony of it all. I rejected the All-Father's pardon precisely because I didn't want to become a soldier. I even gave away my life to be free! What happened to the man who had convictions? How could I happily stand here, having become the very thing I despised?

"Repeat after me," Anthony continued. "No Ideals. No Morality. All for Power."

"No Ideals. No Morality. All for Power."

"This is our creed. Remember it well."

Anthony turned around and unlocked the briefcase on the bed. From one of the pouches he took out a beautiful watch, made of black-carbon steel.

"Put this on," he said, handing me the watch.

At first glance, I wanted to believe that this was the same watch I had bought for my father. The face was made of blue sapphire crystal with sword-shaped hands. There were two dials and two chronographs, one at the top and one at the bottom. I recognized the top one as the déjà vu dial. The bottom one, however, was marked with four glyphs I didn't understand.

"The bottom chronograph is a sanity gauge," Anthony explained. "It measures the level of psychosis in society."

"Psychosis?" I repeated the word feeling a faint sense of pleasure.

"The fanatics call it Rapture. They think it means the end of the world. Which is better for us because we can take advantage of their hysteria. In truth, there's nothing fantastical about Rapture. You don't need God to explain why the human mind is so frail. It's designed to be broken. You see, we're so close to paradise we just need to give it an extra push."

"And make terror the order of the day," I recited a line the All-Mother was fond of quoting from a certain event in the past.

"Now we're talking," said Anthony.

"So, what happens when the gauge is full?"

"You'll just have to live and see," said the major with a brutish smirk. He unzipped a mesh cover inside the briefcase, revealing a black suit. "Tonight, you'll be the star of the show."

CHAPTER 24

DEFIANCE

JASON

Star of the show.

There was something devious in his voice that made me more anxious than excited. After he slithered away, I looked out the window into the beautiful courtyard below, and only then, with the breeze coming through, did I recall that I was completely naked. I brought myself to the act of putting on the clothes he had left in the briefcase. I was so embarrassed I even struggled putting on my underwear. Then I asked myself if this anxiety was something I had learned from "civilized people" or if it was actually real. And I started to wonder if I was trapped in a time loop, because the dream I'd had earlier could well have happened after Anthony came.

This creeping doubt chased away the little joy I had taken away from the dream. But at the same time, this was my default state of mind, constant, eternal anxiety drenched in memories of violence. There was a sort of comfort in being unhappy. As I stood in front of the wardrobe mirror, gazing upon the stranger in the tailored, black suit, I remembered what Anthony had said about madness and terror. For so long I had been on the receiving end of terror. Now, for the first time, I was given the power to inflict terror on others. The idea was still relatively new but already blossoming inside me.

This hardness, like the carbon steel on my watch, soaked in the light so there was only a void, total darkness.

If my father was alive, he would be so proud of me. He would be encouraging me to do everything I could to take up this new cause as if my life depended on it. Who cares about the why and the how? As long as you have power over people, the end will always justify the means.

Terror was just another word. Like justice, family, and faith.

People assign meaning to words. We are the source of evil. Not language.

We must embrace the contradictions. Life is full of them! We're all contradictions, aren't we? What gives anyone the moral standing to say one thing is better than another? In the age of cruelty, no one had the moral high ground. We were all crawling in a sea of corpses. Only the strong ones didn't get buried alive.

I tightened my tie and squared my shoulders. I remembered the things I had learned at the convent—the look, the handshake, the body language, the ingratiating smile we put on because we needed it to survive. We smiled, not because we were happy but because we needed to endure. I raised my arm, holding the imaginary hand of a noble who merely tolerated my presence. I gazed into his blue, cavalier eyes and introduced myself.

I'm Jason, nice to meet you.

No, too informal.

My name is Jason Freeman. It's an honor to meet you, sir. How are you?

I'm honored to join the Vanguard.

I was saying honored too many times. What's another word I could use? Excited? Pleased? No, I was worrying too much about language. Only action counted.

Besides, the boss man had been clear.

Tonight, you'll be the star of the show.

* * *

The cab driver didn't say much on the way to the hotel. He had a blank expression set against a pair of melancholy eyes, which I took to mean that he was a convert. He had the same expression as the people who worked at the doctor's office. Converts rarely engaged in small talk and, by design, avoided talking to strangers.

"How long have you been a driver?" I asked.

He waited a moment, then replied, "Seven years."

"Do you like the job?"

"I love it. You get to meet all kinds of people."

We fell silent for the rest of the ride. Only when I was getting out of the car did he look me in the eyes.

He said, "Thank you for your service," and offered to shake my hand. I had been working myself up for the big leagues, and I wasn't in the mood for shaking a convert's hand, so I brushed him off.

"Have a nice day," I said.

He nodded, without seeming offended, and drove off into the sunset.

I left the interaction feeling rather surprised and giddy. It was a small interaction, sure, but I felt like I had taken a major step forward. I was learning to be ruthless. I was starting to embrace the order of things. Converts were at the bottom of the barrel, and they should be treated as such. They held no value beyond their profession, and that was just how things worked.

If I wasted this opportunity, I would end up no better than the cab driver, slaving away at the bottom and not even realizing it. No, I couldn't let that happen.

I walked toward the hotel entrance, where a family of nobles waited for their cab. I could recognize their bloodline right away. Swap their blue eyes with green ones, and these people were no different from the monarchs who had roamed the streets not long ago. These were the same people who had bullied me and destroyed my life. But the times were different now. *I* was different. Instead of cowering from anxiety, I walked straight toward them, my shoulders pulled back, and even mustered the courage to say hello. To my surprise, the young couple didn't ignore me, and as soon as they saw the Vanguard badge on my lapel, they smiled back. I even detected a look of admiration in the little boy's eyes. Or was it fear?

As soon as I entered the lobby, I saw Anthony talking to some rich folks in the back, grinning ear to ear. He had such a charisma about him it made me feel inadequate. The lobby was filled with nobles, huddled in small circles and talking in hushed voices, like they were trading secrets. The last time I was surrounded by so many nobles things didn't go well for them. I closed my eyes and saw these people burst into flames, clutching their melting faces and screaming in agony. I was on the verge of fainting when a young server approached with a plate of hors d'oeuvres.

"Would you like a lobster toast?"

I didn't even look at him. I was still somewhat delirious. "I'm sorry, can you say that again?"

"Would you like a lobster toast, sir? It's very good."

He lowered the plate so I could see the little square biscuits with white lobster meat on top, sprinkled with cayenne pepper. I was so hungry I pictured myself gulping down the entire plate. When I reached out, the server politely intercepted my attempt and brought one to me, already wrapped inside a napkin.

"Here you go, sir."

I was so embarrassed by my lack of manners that my face must have flushed red. When I took the toast, I looked at the server's face for the first time and was mortified to find that he looked just like me. Why couldn't they find a different type of service model? *They must be doing this on purpose*, I thought, *to humiliate me, to remind me where I came from*. He even spoke with the same inflection and tone. I nearly dropped the toast. The ironic thing was that he didn't seem to care. For all I knew, I was just another patron he needed to serve. If he even showed so much as a glimmer of discomfort in his eyes, I would have burst into a full panic attack and run out of the hotel. He must have been a convert. In fact, the room was filled with them. People who once existed as living, breathing human beings, now reduced to a heap of flesh and bones, animated only by the base instinct to survive. Here and there I spotted other service models like me, each one working diligently to serve the very people who kept them enslaved. If I weren't in this suit, I would've been mistaken for a service model too. I was searching for a place to hide when I heard the bell chime twice. The evening program was about to begin.

I swallowed the lobster toast in one bite and washed it down with a sip of champagne. I signed in at the kiosk next to the wine bar and flipped through the program pamphlet. There was a total of eight cadets in my class, and each profile featured stories of impossible courage and achievements. I found my profile on the second-to-last page, accompanied by a solemn headshot taken when I was still in high school. Unsurprisingly, my bio made no mention of my act of sabotage. According to the new history, written by Neo Vanguard, the assassination of Father Spencer was the work of a terrorist group called Esoterica, and I had risked my life to help the survivors get to safety. I almost chuckled when I read this part. What a fantastic piece of fiction!

Knowing what I knew, I suspected the other stories were either embellished or total fiction as well. It wouldn't have surprised me if the whole program was some kind of political operation, with people getting in due to family and political connections. Still, I reminded myself that it wasn't my place to question whether people deserved to be here. After all, someone could make the same critique about me. I just needed to play my part.

When I recognized the young man standing next to me as Cadet Number Seven, George Stanton, I introduced myself and offered to shake his hand. He had dark-blue eyes, likely a cross breed between the Caesar and Napoleon bloodlines, and looked down at me contemptuously.

"Are you a server?" he asked.

I got riled up. "No, I'm a cadet, like you."

He squinted. "You're part of my class?"

Not part of *your* class. "Yes."

"Show me."

I nearly lost it at that point. I was so tired of people doubting me. Everywhere I went I had to prove myself. I thought this would stop after I joined the Vanguard. Remembering the greater goal, I calmed myself and showed him my profile in the pamphlet.

He glanced at it sideways and scoffed. "Wow. Congrats. I'll see you around." He gave me a pat on the shoulder and walked away.

The bell chimed again.

As I joined the crowd of people shuffling into the banquet room, I suddenly felt a hand on my back, gently rubbing the tense muscles around my spine. I turned around, ready to snap. To my surprise, the person standing next to me was an attractive woman with a soft-curved bob, like one of those actresses from Old Hollywood. She had pink-red lips, deep, dark eyes, and her smile seemed so authentic I couldn't tell if it was rehearsed or not, a rare thing in our society.

"Jason Freeman?" she asked in a soft voice.

"Yes?"

"I'm Magda Sandberg, Minister of Propaganda. It's so nice to finally meet you."

Finally, someone being nice to me.

"Nice to meet you," I said, shaking her hand.

"You're my hero," she whispered into my ear.

I didn't know how to react. *Does she know what I did?*

True to her title, she was quick to pick up on my hesitation, and added, "It's our secret," with a playful smile.

Magda's affection toward me drew a few envious looks from guests. Not one to let things fester, Magda turned to one of them, the cadet I had just met, and rubbed him on the back as well. With the din of the crowd and a small band playing cello in the background, I couldn't hear what she said to him, but whatever it was, it was delightful enough to draw a spate of laughter from the people around her. George shot an angry glare at me.

I took my seat at a table in the center, right before the podium. Magda took the seat to my left, and an older gentle-man with a massive pot belly waddled toward the seat to my right. He was breathing laboriously with long wheezing gasps, his forehead and neck drenched in sweat. Magda gave a nudge in my ribs and shot a glance at the old man. The message was understood. I got up and helped him pull back his chair.

"Thank you, son," he said. "Your name?"

"Jason Freeman, sir." I glanced at his name card and realized he was none other than Gaius Pulcher, founder of Vulture Industries, the company that created One Mind.

"I've heard about your deeds," he said through wheezing coughs as he sat down. "You've done a great service to this country, and don't let anyone tell you otherwise. But our job isn't finished. We're going to get rid of the rest of them too. All these savages—"

A waiter approached Gaius and asked if he wanted a refill. Gaius grew annoyed and glared at the waiter. "Can't you see we're having a conversation?"

"I'm sorry, sir," the waiter said, "I just wanted to ask if you needed a refill."

"No, I don't. If you were smart, you'd know that."

"I apologize, Mr. Pulcher, I didn't mean to offend you. If it would please you, I can—"

"You can disappear from my sight, okay? Will you do that?"

"But, sir, I was told by your assistant to check in. I would be happy to come back at a later time."

"Are you stupid?" Mr. Pulcher barked. "Did you not hear what I just said? Goddammit, all you converts are the same. Dead in the brain. Dead! One day, you'll drag us all down to hell."

"Sir—"

Mr. Pulcher turned to me. "Are you just going to watch?" he asked incredulously, as if I had always been his lackey.

A rush of embarrassment came over me. I glanced at Ms. Sandberg, who gave the impression that she didn't know me at all. She offered no empathy, and her eyes and face turned to stone. I had known people like that, powerful people so disciplined in their selfishness they could turn on you on a dime. I put on a mean face, stood up, and got in front of the waiter. I didn't know what to say, except to act tough. I stared at the waiter for a few seconds, and he stared back at me. Barely any emotions registered on his face. I might as well have been looking in the mirror, another me stuck in the past.

Finally, I mustered the courage to speak: "Mr. Pulcher asked you to leave."

"Who are you?" the waiter retorted.

His reaction surprised me. I thought converts were always eager to be compliant. I searched for signs that he might be a deviant, but there was no mark on his neck, no malaise in his eyes. Of course, the Vanguard wouldn't allow deviants around anymore.

"Are you a deviant?" I asked.

The waiter stiffened up, and a dark scowl came over his face. "Deviant? How dare you! I'm a servant of the empire. I don't need to prove myself to someone like you. I've served Mr. Pulcher for over ten years. Who are you to question my place? Look at yourself. Maybe you're the deviant!"

Ever so keen to spot drama anywhere, the psychopaths that filled the ballroom fell silent and turned their eyes on me. Never had I felt so angry and embarrassed. I wanted to lash out at everyone but was powerless to do anything. I wracked my brain to think of something clever to say, but nothing felt right. If my response didn't land, I was convinced I'd be exiled forever. All the power brokers were watching, Magda and Gaius, and I needed to impress them. I had to act. I couldn't just let a lowly servant walk over me.

I got in his face even more. "Say it again," I told him through clenched teeth.

The waiter paused, slightly disturbed by the conviction in my voice. But he decided that the threat wasn't real. He opened his stupid mouth to speak, but before he could get out another word, I slapped him hard across the face. I didn't even fully realize the sheer force of my strike until I saw blood oozing out of his nose after he hit the ground. The crowd gasped. Of course, no one came to help him. No one would dare violate the law of apathy held so sacred among psychopaths. So what, a waiter got knocked down. He deserved it. Even if he died right then, the only reaction from the people here would be pure, unadulterated satisfaction. And I would thank them for that. He asked for it. Even as he curled up like a child writhing in pain, I could only feel disdain toward him. There was no room for pity. I could see the whole world shattering inside his eyes—he must have been so confused at how someone like me could betray everything he was programmed to believe. That inconsolable hatred on his contorted and bloody face, I could savor it all day long.

Apparently, Magda was quite smitten with my act of defiance. She touched my forearm and flashed a devious smile at me. Mr. Pulcher gave me a nod of approval. All that was needed to complete the trifecta would be thunderous applause from the nobles. But the applause didn't come. I was too absorbed in wanting affection from the crowd to notice that the ceremony was already getting started, and the All-Mother was about to take the stage. Everyone, except for me, was now seated. The waiter hobbled to the back of the ballroom, where he slipped through the door, probably never to be seen again.

CHAPTER 25

I LIVE FOR THE APPLAUSE

JASON

"This country never belonged to kings and queens, although I must admit, I do appreciate their sense of fashion."

Mother Matilda playfully lifted the collar of her cape, and the crowd roared in laughter.

"In case you're wondering," she continued with a wink, "everything they said about me is true."

There were spurts of laughter here and there, but most people were afraid to join in. They knew that Mother Matilda's sarcasm forewarned something more sinister. You could see it in the hardening of her face.

"The conviction of my beliefs never wavered. Yes, I spoke to God, but it wasn't the petty bearded man of the old religion. No, that god is dead. In fact, he never existed, and we've banished him from our imagination. The god we worship is the blind justice of power. We have this power inside all of us. The power to live. The power to strive. The power to become larger than life. This is the very essence of the Vanguard. And our cadets exemplify these core values."

She paused and cast out a longing gaze. The audience returned the favor with hearty applause. A few nobles, the older ones, even leapt to their feet in a naked display of affection toward the All-Mother.

"Thanks to the might of Vanguards, the monarchy is dead. But as they say, ideas are much harder to kill. The monarch idea, unfortunately, is still alive and real. It's a disease that gave us deviancy and deviants. There are rabid fanatics out there who still cling to the fantasy that we can coexist peacefully with deviants. If only we gave our hearts, they say, those winged savages will join the ranks of civilization. You laugh, but it's true. This is how they think! So, how do you root out an idea? This is indeed the challenge of our time. Some in the media have suggested that we finish the war effort. I don't disagree. I think we should press on with the full might of our forces. Peace Day was never achieved under the monarchy. True peace is when you eliminate the enemy, not when you make friends with them. But war itself is not sufficient. We have to change how we express our values. Is it right that we allow deviants to terrorize our streets? Is it right that we give no recognition to converts who assimilated to our system? Is it right that we force converts to make room for deviants out of some twisted idea of equality?"

Emphatic shouts of "no" broke out in the audience.

"And we must ask ourselves the most essential question of all," capitalizing on the wave of hysteria rolling in the room, "do we have still have a meritocracy, as our founders intended, if we allow the weak to feed off the strong?"

I felt a tap on the shoulder. It was Magda, and she pointed at her watch. Time for the acceptance speech. I followed her, keeping my head tucked as though to avoid a hailstorm of bullets, all the way to the east end of the ballroom, where we entered a small door into the backstage area. The dim lights and smell of cheap perfume transported me back in time to the final moments I had spent with my father when we were waiting to go on stage to meet the All-Father. I even remembered the way he was rubbing the leather sofa, dreaming about a better life. I looked at my watch, and indeed, the hand in the déjà vu dial just clicked forward.

Once again, I had the misfortunate of being placed next to Cadet Number Seven, George Stanton, whose demeanor reminded me of a soldier serving in the Second World War. Come to think of it, he might have been bred from that genetic profile. *Men of strength and character*, as I recalled from the pamphlet. In fact, Father almost chose this therapy model for me. Unfortunately, I was too enamored with movie stars from the era after the war. Those movie stars were too cynical to have served; they just pretended that they were soldiers and made a living out of playing on nostalgia. There was something so strange about men of that era. You couldn't tell what they were thinking or if they had managed to feel anything at all. It was like they were afraid of speaking the truth, because the truth could set them free.

Freedom is the ultimate goal, I heard Mr. Stanton murmur to himself, apparently rehearsing his speech. *We must strive— no—we must believe in a better a future*. When he noticed me staring at him, he got annoyed.

"Don't you have your own speech to practice?" he snapped.

"I already have mine memorized," I said.

"Well, good for you."

He faced the other way, toward the wall, and started practicing again. What a sad little man! If I hadn't seen him in this private moment, I might even have believed his outward bravado. It seemed incomprehensible that a man who seemed so sure of himself could be so nervous about giving a simple speech. Besides, it wasn't even supposed to be long. We only had two minutes. Once time was up, they would start playing music and cut the mic. What could go wrong in two minutes? To my amazement, every cadet except for me was sweating profusely and frantically practicing his speech. It was frankly hard to tell them apart. They all had dark-blue eyes, high cheekbones, wide foreheads, and the expression of seasoned veterans, full of courage and contempt. These were the type of men one would call upon to save them in times of need, never doubting their courage. One might even say they were born to be soldiers. How ironic it was to witness all of these brave, hardened soldiers (who had not seen even a day of action) being reduced to fidgety, anxious teacher's pets. No wonder they all disliked me. I was most definitely not their type.

Watching them getting all worked up, though, was making me a little nervous. I was lying when I'd said I had my speech prepared. I was just going to speak off the cuff, but maybe that was a bad idea.

Like one of those fanatical Sisters I knew from my days at the convent, the Minister of Propaganda whispered words of assurance at the cadets, one by one, holding their hands as if praying for their redemption. But her passion was the god-less kind, one that could only be achieved after generations of fine breeding and a lifetime of tireless practice. I suspected she was much older than she looked—after all, well-bred psycho-paths were very good at concealing their age. Every time she spoke, she radiated a kind of angelic energy that made every-one feel completely at ease. She was so skilled at the art of attraction each person wanted her attention all to themselves.

"Cadet Number One, you're up!" a strident voice barked. Cadet Number One turned around to shake his colleague's hand, then disappeared beyond the curtain. Apparently, you were supposed to shake hands with the colleague behind you before taking the stage. No one told me about this custom. I wondered if Mr. Stanton would be so kind as to honor this custom with me?

By the time Magda approached Mr. Stanton, there were only three cadets left backstage. The rest had been officially inducted into the Vanguard Elite Corps. And judging by the volume of applause, every one of them seemed to have been received with a standing ovation. I was starting to feel severely nervous. Perhaps I was wrong to judge them. Only the best of the best could get into the Elite Corps. I suddenly felt like an impostor. I didn't belong here. I never belonged. I was an impostor all along. There was nothing on my resume other than a barbaric act of terrorism that no one could know about. Yes, I had helped dismantle the monarchy, but could you even call that an accomplishment?

"Cadet Number Seven!"

Mr. Stanton turned around and looked at me. I was so desperate for attention that I volunteered to shake his hand. This turned out to be a terrible mistake, as he had no intention of showing me respect. He just smirked and left, leaving me hanging like a fool.

"Don't mind him," reassured Magda, clasping my hands in hers like lovers did in another era. "You belong here, no matter what they say. You just have to prove yourself."

"But how?"

"You have to be tough. What you did back there was impressive. People need to see more of that. You need to take initiative. Prove that you have what it takes."

"I feel like no matter how hard I try, they'll never accept me. I'm not a noble. I feel like I can never fit in."

"If you're offered a seat at the table, don't ask what seat!

Just take it. Whenever you feel like you don't belong, ask yourself this: what would you do if you weren't afraid?"

What would I do if I wasn't afraid? That's been the question of my life.

I held Magda's gaze, trying to decipher how she had managed to see through me. She seemed so warm and sincere that I could throw myself into her arms.

"Cadet Number Eight!" the strident voice called out.

"Time to impress them," Magda said, as I took a deep breath before walking through the velvet curtain. I thought of nothing in that moment, not the speech, not Magda. I just willed myself forward.

The All-Mother was radiant, as usual, greeting me with a warm embrace. As soon as she kissed me on the cheek, she smiled at the crowd and ushered me into the spotlight. Once again, I searched for compassion in her eyes. I wanted to find the woman who had claimed to be my mother. The only true family I had left. But like the Minister of Propaganda, she turned herself into an object, devoid of emotional attachment. She wasn't smiling for me. She was smiling for the nobles. Still, I foolishly waited for her to introduce me before taking up the podium, but after a few seconds, as the crowd fell silent, I realized that no introduction would be made. I was cast adrift into the vast ocean.

"Good evening, how are you?" I spoke awkwardly into the microphone. There was no response. Just a roomful of blank stares. I adjusted the height of the mic, searching anxiously for something to hold.

"I must be honest with you," I continued, almost without thinking, "I don't have a speech prepared. It's not a joke, I assure you. In fact, I'd never even dreamed of making it here."

I paused to test the crowd. They were beginning to show interest.

"People like me don't get to stand up here and make a speech. They're out there, serving you drinks, making you food. That's not because the system is unfair. No, people like me give up before we even try. That's the problem. We resent the system. We believe it isn't fair. But I never believed that lie. I stand before you as the only artificial cadet because I committed to improving myself, no matter the challenge. I refused to believe the lie that I'm oppressed. Well, guess what, it turns out you can go very far if you have the right mindset."

There were a few nods and a smattering of applause.

"When I was small, my father would tell me stories about the Golden Age, how things used to be. No one looked down on the idea of ambition. People had morals. Then the monarchy came and turned us into slaves. No more ambition. No more courage. Just blind faith. They replaced our way of life with fake morality. Well, I don't know about you, but I would rather die than live without hope. As a cadet, I swear to you that I will fight till the end. I will give my life to the cause, if I have to. We will not be replaced. We will persevere!"

I got so emotional I nearly burst into tears. I didn't know what came over me. Some higher power took over, and it felt really good. It wasn't just the rapturous reaction from the crowd, which I'd half anticipated toward the end. It was the act of saying things you know were false with such eloquence and conviction that you ended up believing your lies.

Dr. Faust must have been smiling. I had crossed the threshold at last.

CHAPTER 26

A CONFESSION

MARCUS

We had managed to slip out of the convent without being seen, but Dante soon fainted and fell in my arms. Poor kid was wracked with guilt. I could see it in his eyes. He blamed himself for his brother's demise. Even with his eyes closed, I could see the terror transfixed on his face. A nauseating feeling closed on my spine like a steel vice and refused to let go. Either Dante was very heavy, or I had fallen weak. I struggled with every step to carry him forward. Leaving his brother to die tore him apart. The fire he had unleashed was still running through him and threatened to leap out. Every now and then, he would snap awake and mumble something in a heavy voice, as if some demon had snatched his body. I couldn't understand what he said, but the sounds he made portended some horrible fate for the world, especially when joined by the distant roar of thunder just beyond the forest.

"How is he?" Claudia asked in a hushed voice, taking cover behind a wall and peeking around the corner.

"Still breathing, but he's burning up," I said.

"That's not good. We must get him to the Philosopher."

"Who's the Philosopher?"

"Someone you know."

As I was about to inquire further, we came upon three horses tied to trees, and when they saw us, they whinnied and shuffled around nervously. Judging by their slim builds, long legs, and beautiful white fur, I could tell right away these were Arabian horses, just like the one I had rode on Peace Day. What a shame to see such majestic creatures used for war.

I approached the one on the left carefully and untied its leash. To my surprise, the horse didn't stir. Its eyes focused on the sick child in my arms, as though overcome with compassion. I gently laid Dante over the saddle and jumped onto the horse.

"Follow me," said Claudia, leaping effortlessly onto her own white steed.

I spurred my horse to a gallop and followed Claudia into the forest.

I looked back at the convent one final time. I was tormented by feelings of nostalgia and guilt. I wished I had treated these deviants better when I'd had the chance.

Suddenly, Dante snapped awake and sat upright.

"May the Lord have mercy!"

"Dante! Stay with us!"

"Mercy! Please have mercy on me!"

"Stay strong!" Claudia shouted.

"Cold...," Dante mumbled. "I'm cold..."

I took off my jacket with one hand and wrapped it around his back. "Put this on."

Dante slipped his small arms into the sleeves, then slumped forward, hugging my waist and letting his small head rest on my back.

Moments later, he fell asleep again.

Claudia gave me a warm look.

"You know," she said, "you'd make a great father someday."

I blushed. "Maybe one day."

We galloped down the hill for a short while without speaking. The sycamore trees flew past, as a warm, gentle rain began to fall.

"What's happening to him?" I asked Claudia.

"It's hard to explain. Let's just say his body is trying to fight back. He doesn't want to be taken over."

"By what?"

"By his gift."

"Does this happen to all deviants?"

"This is the price we pay."

"*We?*"

"You didn't know?"

"I thought you passed the Trial."

"I was spared of replacement. There's a difference. But even disciples can turn into deviants. You've heard the Voice before, haven't you?"

"Yes."

"Well, deviancy is what happens when you refuse the call."

"I've refused the call before, and I'm not a deviant."

"Not yet."

"What's your gift?"

She gave me a blank stare as if I had said something horribly offensive.

"What? Aren't you proud to be a deviant?"

"What is that supposed to mean?"

"Well, I just get the impression that you feel strongly about being—"

"Oh, Marcus, if this is your way of getting out of it…"

I knew what she was trying to say, but I refused to give her the satisfaction.

"Why can't you just tell me?"

"We never asked for this gift. It's a miracle that Dante is still alive. You saw what happened to his brother."

"But Dante doesn't seem to show advanced aging. Is he different?"

"Not all deviants are the same."

"You know that's not what I mean."

"I know," she said with a sigh. "Have you heard of Esoterica?"

"The cult?"

"Every society is a cult."

"That's quite a statement."

"I'm just saying the truth. You grew up in a cult, Marcus. The monarchy, the Mantra, all the costumes, rites, and ceremonies. Look at the way people worshipped your father. They think he's God! That sounds like a cult to me."

"I have my issues with the monarchy, believe me, but you can't compare a nation to a cult. My father was the leader of a nation. People need someone to look up to."

"That's exactly my point."

"How?"

"I'm not saying a cult has to be bad. We just shouldn't use the term to belittle things we don't understand. I don't judge you for being a monarch. It wasn't your choice to be a monarch. We all must belong somewhere. All I'm saying is that we should keep an open mind."

"Ah, I get it. You're trying to recruit me."

She gave a sly smile.

"Let's just say Esoterica is not a group that anyone can join. You have to possess the right qualifications."

"Do I qualify?"

"You're still the prince."

"Not anymore. Times have changed."

"Just because the Syndicate took over, doesn't mean you're not a monarch anymore. No matter what happens, you will always be the prince to me."

I wanted to reach out and kiss her, but I couldn't let my emotions show. I needed to stay detached.

"You know, before she died, my mother said I'd bring back the monarchy one day. Build a new nation. Lead my people back to the promised land…"

"Do you believe in fate?" Claudia returned.

"Do *you?*"

"Sometimes, I feel like Alice, tumbling down the rabbit hole… I don't know what to believe anymore…"

As she gazed toward the snowcapped hills, I could see the possibility of hope shimmering in her eyes, so I asked her, "Are you happy now?"

"Happy—for what?"

"For the revolution… being freed from the tyranny of my people?"

"Not really." Claudia looked up at the sky in a moment of silence. "Happiness is a longing for something you don't understand. None of us is meant to be happy."

I looked up at the gathering rain and remembered my mother.

"I will say," she added, trying to lighten the mood, "for what it's worth, we're equals now, you and me. Your old tricks won't work on me anymore."

"I thought I would always be the prince to you."

She blushed. "*Prince* is just a term of endearment."

"Equals."

"Yes."

We smiled at each other in the same way we used to before the world started falling apart. The past now seemed so distant it was impossible to believe. How did we end up here?

The dreamland of youth burned down when the chapel fell over our heads, and we had been trying to pick up the pieces ever since. Sooner or later, we would have to come to terms with reality. The past was lost forever.

By the time we made it out of the forest, the rain had stopped. I had lost my sense of time. The sun was cloaked under a wave of purple, hazy clouds. Dante was unconscious. We rode onto a rocky promontory overlooking the lush, green valley below, a place that appeared so ancient and savage we might as well have stumbled into another country. This was the farthest I had traveled from home, and I was feeling nervous about the road ahead.

"See that building down there?" Claudia pointed to a large, gray structure that resembled a hospital from one angle and a factory from another, nestled close to a towering range of granite mountains. "That's where we can find the Philosopher."

CHAPTER 27

SECOND CHANCE

JASON

The December issue of the *Miraculous Conformist* arrived early that morning. The maid slipped the magazine under the door and followed with a harsh knock. When I opened the door, the maid had disappeared. I picked up the magazine in my bathrobe and saw a girl returning to her room on the other side of the hallway. She was turning the key in the lock when she realized someone was watching her. She wasn't startled. In fact, this realization aroused her, judging by the way she looked at me when she turned around. Her eyes got big, and she opened her mouth as if to say hello. I waved at her, and her face blossomed. Then, taking a deep breath, she pressed her palm into her chest and giggled. I didn't know how to react. I just stared at her in the same way I'd stare at a wounded animal. I'd never had this effect on people before. Back then, no one even noticed me. This girl reminded me of the assistant to Dr. Faust, but this time, the look was different. This time, there was respect. Respect and fear. I could approach her and give her a kiss on the cheek, and she wouldn't even refuse. She would like it very much. She waved back at me as she slipped behind her door.

I settled into my new role almost unconsciously. I guess when change forces itself on to someone, there is no other recourse than to change. There is no cause and effect. No before and after. I looked at the dial on my watch, and it turned red. Too much nostalgia is bad. I still did it because I needed the past to quell my uneasy conscience. Come to think of it, I wasn't even sure I had a conscience. I was a modern man, after all. Conscience was a thing of the past. Once a person gets taken apart, they can never come together again. Some part of them goes missing. I would sometimes catch a glimpse of him running down the street, but no one would pay him any mind. He always seemed so frantic and scared, like he was being chased by a demonic beast. This time, he stood behind a pack of soldiers chatting outside a dirty pawnshop, pointing up at me, or more precisely, at the magazine I held. For the first time, I got a good look at his face, and I wish I hadn't. He was showing all the telltale signs of a deviant—a wrinkled face aging too fast, dead expression in the eyes, a robotic facade devoid of thoughts or desires. I nearly had a panic attack, but then remembered I still had a year left before my rite of passage.

Rite of passage, instead of psychopath test—more down-to-earth. I had to give my party credit for always paying attention to language. Even the party name, National Rationalist Syndicate, or NRS, had a certain fearful mystique. Anyway, rumors had been swirling for a while that the Revolutionary Tribunal was planning for a major event on New Year's Eve. And now, with the stroke of a pen, Matilda had made it official.

"Redemption Day."

The words popped on the cover in a bold, pink typeface. The cover featured a black-and-white, closeup shot of Mother Matilda. I saw shades of Magda in the cold, ethereal expression on her face. I wouldn't be surprised if Magda had taken the picture. For a group that committed to wiping away religion, this cover shot sure looked religious. Anyone might be forgiven for thinking this was the leader of a cult, a cult of which I was now a proud card-carrying member.

I was just getting into the cover story when the phone rang.

"Hello?"

The voice on the other end was drowsy and cold. "It's George."

"You're up early."

"You're late."

I looked at my watch. It was half past seven. I still had thirty minutes before my appointment.

"I've been waiting for you," he continued in a more impatient manner. "We're supposed to be there early."

"How did I end up with you as my partner?"

"What?"

"Never mind. You wouldn't know anyway."

"You're right, maybe I'll find a different partner."

Truth be told, I hadn't given much thought to our assignment until George called. I told myself that it was just a job, even if it required some unconventional tactics. Also, in the time since I had met George, I'd gotten to know him better. He put on a tough exterior, but it was mostly for show.

"I appreciate your patience. Honestly, I didn't know you'd miss me so much. You still there?"

He didn't respond.

"We're famous now, George. We can afford to break a few rules."

"Your five minutes of fame are already up."

"Is that jealousy I hear?"

"You're unbelievable."

I chuckled. As usual, he was falling for the mind tricks. "George, by chance, have you heard of Redemption Day?"

"Who hasn't?"

"What do you think about it? Do you like the idea?"

"It's a wonderful idea."

"You don't sound very enthusiastic."

"Jason—"

"It's Mother Matilda's first major event. And it's going to be a real spectacle."

"Be careful what you wish for."

I was looking at a full-page ad for the latest miracle drug. The tagline read: *say goodbye to anxiety forever.*

"The *Conformist* makes a good point," I said, staring at the purple-and-white lollipop. "People used to be ashamed about conversion. No one talked about it in public. That's all going to change."

"This doesn't concern me. I've already passed the Trial."

"But don't you think there's value in speaking directly to the people who are afraid of getting replaced? The All-Mother is saying, I see you, I understand, and everything is going to be okay. When people learn to love conversion, they won't have to resort to deviancy anymore. That's good for all of us."

"When did you become a politician?"

He hung up. I was rather pleased with myself. I put on my casual clothes and ran downstairs to the parking lot.

It took much longer than I'd expected to get to our destination. We drove through ten blocks, winding down rain-swept streets, under palm trees, past clusters of sleek apartments and stores and salons, barber poles glowing like giant candy canes, swirling endlessly in hues of white, red, and blue. I could almost lick the hues and taste their sweetness. People used to only visit the salons incognito, cloaked under hats and trench coats and sunglasses, sometimes even chastity masks. Getting high on violent and sexual fantasies was supposed to make them feel a little embarrassed, being an upstanding citizen and all. But now, folks were visiting salons completely out in the open, without a care in the world. There was no shame, no sense of embarrassment. As it turned out, imagining oneself torturing a deviant under the influence of mind-altering drugs was really no different than grabbing a cup of coffee. Desires are desires. Who are you to judge?

George made a right turn on Sherman Way, and suddenly the impeccable order we had driven by moments ago descended into a kind of living hell. All the apartment buildings were old and damaged, like artifacts from a wartime era. Posters of the Syndicate Agent, adorned in his beret and half-mask, were plastered everywhere. A lot of the windows were blown out, and white curtains flapped in the breeze. Some of the walls were riddled with bullet holes. Even the air got steamier.

"You know," I said, breaking the silence, "there's something I don't understand."

"Not now," said George, "we have to focus on the mission."

"It's about the mission. What, exactly, is our end goal?"

"To keep peace."

"Peace?"

"Yes."

"We're asked to provoke acts of terror. That doesn't sound peaceful to me."

"Peace cannot be achieved when people are constantly plotting against you and your values. We have to draw them out, bring them to justice."

"You mean, the monarchists…"

"Them, and every traitor and terrorist we can find."

"But how many is enough? How do we know if we've achieved our goal?"

"It's not about a number, Jason. The goal is to crush the opposition from the inside. To destroy their spirit, to show them that their resistance is futile. First, we give them hope, then we show them despair."

"Despair without hope is no despair at all," I quoted Mr. Pulcher from the mission briefing. "Still, why would Mr. Pulcher get involved in all this? With all the money he has, can't he just retire?"

"For a new cadet, you sure ask a lot of questions."

"It's just my nature, George. I can't help it."

"Pulcher is a man of action. He wants to save this country. Besides, you should be grateful he's giving you a second chance."

"I *am* grateful," I said, feeling the need to reaffirm my loyalty.

"Then you should stop worrying about strategy and focus on execution."

"I will," I said, annoyed to find myself flustered so easily.

"I'm watching you closely. If you squander this second chance, you will be replaced."

My heart jumped to my throat when I heard that dreadful word again. He could see the pale horror in my face.

"Are you having second thoughts?" he asked.

"No, no, not at all."

"Good. Stay in character. You're the key to this whole operation. You have to make these people believe that you hate the Syndicate. You got that?"

"Yes, I love the monarchy to death. I miss the good old days."

"A little less sarcasm will do you good."

George parked the car in an alley leading to a nondescript convenience store at the bottom of a tall apartment building with pictures of wartime paraphernalia and naked women plastered over the storefront. I could feel eyes watching us from above. George shut down the engine and looked at me. "Put this on," he said, handing me a brown canvas sack. The thing carried a horrible stench.

"Is this really necessary?"

"If you want to be believed, you have to play the victim."

Holding my breath, I put the sack over my head.

"Follow my lead. If I tell you to stop talking, you stop talking. You got that?"

I was too enthralled by the strange attraction of darkness under this boogeyman mask to give him a firm answer. I simply nodded.

CHAPTER 28

FAITH IS A TEST

JASON

A bell chimed as George opened the door, and with a gentle shove in the back, he ushered me into the belly of the beast. My hands were tied behind me, and I could only imagine the people inside watching with some sort of morbid fascination. The floor was uneven and creaked with every step. I was afraid of falling through into a bottomless pit. The place smelled like an old bookstore, where ideas and feelings went to die, and all you had was the pervasive fear of being made obsolete. I peeked under the mask and saw pornographic magazines displayed on shelves next to the ice cream fridge, surrounded by stacks of illegal enhancers that promised super-human thrills. There was a fatal attraction to this atmosphere. In just the few minutes I was inside, I was already feeling nostalgic for a past I had never even known.

My nostalgia trip was rudely interrupted when a man put his hands on me. Judging by his shadow and use of force, he seemed to be a burly man, the bouncer type, always eager to be used by some higher command. He probably didn't have much of a brain. He did have a pot belly, which wiggled against my back when he wrapped his arms around my waist.

"He's clean," the burly man announced.

"You're late," another man said. This voice was scornful and mean.

"How's business?" George asked casually.

"Better than ever, thanks to you," the owner responded.

"It's the least I can do," George said.

"What's this one about?" the owner asked.

"He's the One."

"I don't believe you. Let me take a look."

George moved in front of me, as the tall shadow of the store owner strode toward us.

"No can do," he said.

"Why not?"

"He's not for sale."

"Not for sale? Is he not a deviant?"

"No."

"What is he then?"

"The Promised One," said George.

The owner chuckled. "You amuse me, Mr. Strode. I don't believe in fairy tales, and I don't take you to be that kind of person. As you well know, the boss will only take deviants, and he likes them fresh. So unless you have something else to share—"

"He's going to help us with the mission, and the boss will pay you handsomely for that. Now, will you let us through?"

The owner was quiet for a few seconds, then backed away.

"Good man." George, or rather, Mr. Strode gave the owner a pat on the shoulder.

"They're waiting for you in the basement," the owner replied like a timid lamb.

I followed Mr. Strode down two flights of stairs into the basement. Just before we stopped, Mr. Strode whispered into my ear, "Wait here," and shoved me into a dark corner behind what looked like a wardrobe. "Don't speak unless I tell you to."

I poked my head out from behind the wardrobe to find two people in the room. Neither had noticed me. Mr. Strode first greeted the young woman sitting on a barstool facing the wall. The other person appeared to be a young man trying to play the piano, hammering a few dissonant notes before getting up and giving Mr. Strode a hug.

"We missed you, brother!" he said. The voice seemed so raw and strange I could have mistaken him for a grown-up version of me.

"Nice to see you, Andre," Mr. Strode replied, reciprocating the hug.

"How long has it been?" asked the young man in a genuine fit of passion. "Two months, three?"

"I've honestly lost track of time," Mr. Strode responded in a cool voice.

"No, you haven't," the female interrupted. "We were supposed to meet three weeks ago. Why did you back out?"

"Hey, Bonnie, stay cool!" intervened Andre. "Max is one of us. He must have his reasons. Right, Max?"

Max Strode. Fancy name for an agent provocateur.

"I was busy with work," said Max. "How have you been?"

"Contemplating my nonexistent future," Bonnie replied in a dry, sarcastic tenor that dampened her rather feminine voice.

"That's an unsaintly thing to say," said Max.

"You don't have to worry like the rest of us."

"You'll be just fine yourself."

"How can you be so sure? In case you haven't noticed, the Syndicate is out to get us. We have no guarantees anymore. No safety nets. I'm just a poor university student with nothing to fall back on. The Syndicate took away our birthright, and for what? So they can feel special?"

"They wouldn't be the first, nor the last," said Max.

"Now you're arguing both sides? Have the money and power gotten to you that fast? I thought you'd last a little longer."

Max held his silence for a few seconds, then raised his hands in a cavalier swirl. "You got me. I've sold my soul to the devil."

Andre snorted laughter.

"Look, our work is just getting started," Max said. "The hurt is real. I get it. I was lucky. But let's not fail the revolution by doubting each other's intentions. Focus on the real enemy."

"The real enemy is always walking among us," said Bonnie. "If anything, the monarchy failed because we let down our guard."

"I agree," chimed in Andre. "Our parents were too eager to please. They think everyone's their friend. They should've never trusted those blue-eyed devils."

"Blood is blood," said Max. "Either you're one of us or you're not."

"But faith makes us strong," said Bonnie.

"One for all," added Andre.

"All for one," Max returned.

The three of them seemed to have bonded in that moment, savoring their mutual recognition of a common brotherhood. If the deviants had exhibited even an ounce of this camaraderie, we would have never ended up here. Then again, it's hard to bond with your fellow kind when the whole point of your existence is to be different and cast aside.

"How are my parents?" Andre asked Max. "Did you find out where they're being kept?"

"Ward Number Seven," Max replied, "and they're still in fine spirits."

"That's good."

"You'll be glad to know that they've refused to convert."

"What's going to happen to them?"

"The Syndicate won't do anything rash—"

"The Syndicate rounded up innocent people and put them in psych wards," Bonnie interrupted. "Sure, not rash at all."

"True, but for now, our families are safe."

"Safe?"

"The Syndicate needs them alive. The whole project is about converting believers into agnostics. It's not a good look to start murdering innocent people. Also, a number of monarch families are serving in the new regime. They still hold some influence, at least for now."

"I wish we weren't so naive," joined Andre. "This would've never happened if we'd kept those lunatics in check."

"We'll never give up our faith," said Max, giving Andre a pat on the back.

"So then, have you found the One?" Bonnie asked.

"Yes, I've found the perfect candidate," Max responded. He walked toward me and grabbed my wrist. "Be ready," he whispered.

I stumbled into the light, like a prisoner being led onto the execution stage.

"Jesus Christ!" Andre cried, jumping back as I emerged. "You could've given us a warning!"

"My apologies," said Max. "I wanted this to be a pleasant surprise."

"He's the One?" Bonnie asked.

Max pulled off the sack. I felt naked with my head exposed. I was just getting used to hiding under a mask and the security darkness granted me. But in an instant, the safety net broke, and I was plunged into the world of deception once again.

There was the young man with the mustache, which only now emerged in its full brown texture. He had this air of aristocracy about him. It seemed so peculiar that a man who expressed so much kindness toward his friend could carry so much contempt in his eyes. Speaking of his eyes, I could tell right away that he was a monarch. They were green and devoid of passion. If you held them to a mirror, they might well disappear altogether, like a vampire under the sun. His eyebrows came together watching me. *What is this thing?* I could hear him ask himself, but he was too cultured to expose his prejudice. Such was the case with all monarchs, polite and kind on the surface but really despicable on the inside.

I flashed him a gentle smile, remembering the role I needed to play. It was a smile honed from years of experience, of lowering myself to the more genteel race to appear humble and obedient. I specialized in playing the victim.

The young woman was leaning against the bar on her left elbow, her feet crossed in front of her. She held a cup of wine in her hand and licked her lip. She didn't wear any makeup and gazed at me with dark, inquisitive eyes. There was a touch of melancholy about her, as if the world couldn't end soon enough. But she wasn't a cynic, as far as I could tell. There was still a breath of life left in her body, and she tried desperately to keep it hidden from the world. If I had to venture a guess, I would say she was playing a role, just like me. And so, when I opened my mouth to speak, forgetting that I was to receive approval from Max first, she interrupted and spoke before I could make a sound.

"But he's just a service model," she said, swirling the wine in her cup.

"Not any service model," Max said. "He was saved by the All-Father."

"He was a fellow?"

"Yes."

"Is he ready to give his life for our cause?" Bonnie asked.

"You should ask him directly," Max replied.

Bonnie drew a long, slow breath and approached me. She put her palm over my beating heart and pressed her cheek against mine. It was a little warm.

"You're more handsome than I thought," she said.

"I didn't mean to be," I said.

She giggled.

"What's your name?" she asked.

I looked at Max, and he turned his gaze on the floor, which was his psychopathic way of showing approval.

"David," I said.

"Your last name?"

"I don't have one."

"You didn't adopt your owner's last name?"

"He wanted me to be free."

"You brought a deviant to our house?" Andre snarled.

"He's not a deviant. He was saved by the All-Father," Max responded.

"So what? The All-Father was too nice for his own good. He saved many deviants, and how did they repay him?"

"Listen to me, Andre, I understand that we have some philosophical differences."

"Philosophical differences? We need someone we can trust. Someone who looks like *us*."

"Well, forgive me for being naive, but people who look like us don't get invited to Syndicate events."

Andre stared at Max.

"How did you get him on the show?"

"David?"

"My psychiatrist put me in touch with the show's producer. For Redemption Day, they want to feature young people who are struggling with their faith. I fit the bill."

Andre took a deep breath and exhaled. He was on the verge of blushing and swiped his forehead with a handkerchief. He gave me a skeptical look.

"Are you struggling with your faith?" he asked.

"No, I lied to get on the show."

"Do you still believe in God?"

"Absolutely. My faith never wavered."

"Why do you hate the Syndicate?"

"The Syndicate murdered my father."

"How was your father murdered?" Andre asked.

"He was sent to the gas chamber."

"What was he accused of?"

"The crime of being different. They found out he was a member of Morning Star."

"But why do you care? He's not *really* your father."

"Andre!" Max feigned anger.

"It's all right," I said. "It's true that I can never have a real family. All the same, I've got nothing to lose."

"Nice story," Andre said. "Perhaps I believe you."

"David is ready to give his life for our cause," Max followed. "Are you?"

Andre's nose flared. "Of course, I am. Are you questioning my loyalty?"

"No, but it doesn't sound like you're satisfied with David's answer. In that case, you can have his task." Max drew a ticket to *Late Night with Charlie Conrad* from his chest pocket and held it in front of Andre, who stood frozen in fear. "Go ahead," said Max, "take it, it's yours."

"What's this?" Andre asked, his voice shaking.

"It's proof of your loyalty to the cause," Max answered.

"With all due respect," Andre complained, "this is not what we agreed on."

"Faith is a test," Max insisted. "Sometimes, we're asked to do extraordinary things."

Andre turned pale.

"Wonderful performances, both of you." Bonnie intervened just in time, clapping sarcastically. She took the ticket from Max and gave it to me. I gracefully accepted. "Let's talk business. Max, I assume you have a plan in place?"

"I do."

"Does the boss know about David?"

"Of course. He's been vetted thoroughly. Now, give me the briefcase."

Andre ignored the request and walked toward the wardrobe. His movement was so deliberate that I half expected him to turn around, pull out a gun, and shoot us down. Instead of a gun, he produced a key from his pocket, fitted the key into the lock, and opened the wardrobe. He then stepped aside to reveal the grand surprise he had been saving all along: a fresh-faced young man covered in blood. A red rubber ball was strapped tight in his mouth, gagging him, and his hands and feet were tied with rope.

Andre unstrapped the rubber ball and gave the man a hard slap across the face. "Wake up!" When this command only provoked half a smirk, he slapped the prisoner again, causing blood to spurt from the already broken nose. The prisoner finally peeled open his bloodshot eyes and burst out of the wardrobe screaming. Unfortunately for the prisoner, his body was too frail to carry through this act of intimidation. He tripped and fell to the ground.

Bonnie laughed.

"A Vanguard?" Max remarked. "Are you crazy?"

"Crazy?" Andre answered, standing over the prisoner. "No, I'm a very reasonable man. I've kept him alive."

"You lost..." the prisoner muttered while breaking into a psychotic laugh.

Andre stomped him in the stomach. The soldier let out a loud groan, spitting out some more blood, but kept laughing.

"Get me that chair," Andre ordered Bonnie. The woman who had seemed impervious to being commanded was eager to comply. She brought over the wooden chair, and Andre lifted the soldier up by the collar and dropped him into the seat.

For the first time, the soldier fixed his blue gaze on me. His eyebrows came together, and he spat on the ground.

"You look familiar," he said. "You look just like the slave who murdered the All-Father."

"The All-Father saved me," I said.

"Congratulations. Was it hard to please him?"

"He's a man of faith, unlike you."

"Don't worry. I won't judge."

"I'm not afraid of you," I said.

"Allow me to introduce you to William Wallace," Andre interrupted, pulling out a card from the soldier's jacket. "Mr. Wallace is a Knight with Neo Vanguard. Of course, he's a Vanguard in name only. He's no patriot. He doesn't believe in anything. No God, no king, no country. He pretends to like honorable things, but he's dead inside."

Andre snatched a rolled-up magazine from the wardrobe and dropped it in the prisoner's lap. As the magazine slowly unfurled, I could see pictures of nude women and men contorted in all manners of kinky contraptions.

The soldier smirked. "Am I on trial?"

"No, you're already condemned," said Andre.

"So what? We're all condemned since the day we're born. What makes me different is that I don't pretend to be something I'm not."

"A real, honest person wouldn't need to make that admission."

"I don't need to justify my contradictions because I'm not ashamed of them."

"Ah, there lies the heart of darkness!" Andre exclaimed, turning to me. "You see, this is a man who fails to understand himself, even at the most basic level. He can't look at himself in the mirror. He hates himself, just like anyone without faith hates the burden of existence. This man never woke up. He's still drowning in a primitive soup of germs, and it is a shame, a real shame that he ever managed to live. His life is a crime. Mr. Wallace, you *should* be ashamed of yourself. You murder innocent people. Do you not?"

"I do," Mr. Wallace replied, his eyes cold and wide open.

I had never heard someone so casually admit to such a horrible accusation. I would have at least expected him to show some remorse or argue back. But this man did neither, and true to his word, he felt no sense of shame. And worst of all, I had sworn allegiance to the same ideology this man served. Under different circumstances, we would have been comrades. I couldn't help but ask myself, was this the man I would become?

Andre took the magazine from William's lap and flipped to the centerfold, where two Polaroid photographs were stashed. "Ask him about this," said Andre, handing me the pictures.

I was hesitant to accept at first. I felt trapped. But then, Max nudged my ribs, and I gave in.

"Ask him," repeated Andre.

The soldier chuckled again.

In the first picture a row of well-dressed monarchs was forced on their knees in front of a place I knew from childhood, the Convent of the Healing Star. With his back facing the camera, a soldier pressed his rifle against the back of a woman's head. Judging by his red, curly hair and round-shouldered physique, I could tell the soldier was none other than the despicable man tied up in front of me. William Wallace seemed to delight in my revelation.

"Do you like my work?" he asked. "You know the woman in the picture, don't you? Was she nice to you?"

I didn't say anything. I did recognize her.

"She was very obedient, believe it or not. Look, the other one is the masterwork."

I hated following his directions, but I couldn't refuse the offer. Rabid curiosity drove my eyes to focus on the second picture, taken only a few moments after the first. The woman was slumped to the ground, her head splayed open, the rifle now pointed at a boy stripped nude, his wings already surgically removed.

I was supposed to express disgust, but I was beyond disgust. This man was my enemy. This man was my comrade.

"Why do you hate the monarchs so much?" I asked.

"I don't hate *anyone*. I hate your ideas. The thing is, they're not even *your* ideas. You have no idea why you believe what you believe. You're blind. You're brainwashed. Do you really think these people care about you?"

"The monarchs gave me a home, while you murder innocent deviants for sport."

"A prison is not a home. I think you know this better than anyone else."

"Enough!" Andre shouted. He lifted his shirt and snatched a small black pistol from his belt. It was a Ruger Standard model with a bluish hue and wood grips. "As you can see, this man is beyond saving," he said to me, his face turning ugly. "Prove yourself. Give him what he deserves."

I clutched the pistol with both hands, aiming the barrel at the center of the soldier's forehead. He tried to make eye contact, but I refused. I couldn't look him in the eyes. I tried to squeeze the trigger with every fiber in my body, but my fingers wouldn't budge.

"Prove your faith!" Max urged.

The soldier was a despicable man. If I ended his life, I would be doing the world a favor. Wouldn't I?

"Go ahead and shoot me," said the soldier. "You've got no conscience anyway."

I closed my eyes and took a deep breath.

"Drop the act, young man. Your father wouldn't approve of this."

"What do you know about my father?" I opened my eyes to look at the soldier one last time.

"He's weak, just like you."

I screamed. In the instant I pressed the trigger he broke out of his restraints and lunged at me. I missed. The Luger slipped from my hands as the back of my head hit the floor. My vision went black for a moment. The beast straddled my waist, squeezing my throat with both hands. The force was so strong I thought my head would pop off my neck.

"Once a slave, always a slave," he muttered, applying more force.

Max didn't make the slightest attempt to help. He and Bonnie just stood there watching, holding a faint pleasure on their lips. They could end this charade any moment but refused. Gasping for air, I tried grabbing his forearms, but my hands kept slipping. He was too strong. I started to faint. Then he brought one knee up from the floor and slammed it into my stomach. The pain was so intense my entire upper torso jolted upward, which gave me the opportunity to break free. I caught sight of the Luger, snatched it with my right hand, and fired two shots into his waist. He winced but somehow managed to hold on. He pinned me back on the ground again, using the last bit of his strength to choke me. This time, I brought the Luger to his temple and shot him in the head. He slumped to the ground.

I wiped his blood from my eyes and shot him again. I needed to make sure he was dead.

Still in a daze, I realized that Andre was patting my back. "That's my man!" he hollered like a fraternity boy after one too many drinks. I couldn't even tell if he was the same person I had known only moments ago. "That's my man!" he hollered again. "I knew you were the One!"

"Happy now?" I asked, exhausted from the struggle.

"The pleasure's all mine," he said as he offered to shake my hand. I answered the gesture and smeared his hand with the blood of Mr. Wallace.

Finally satisfied, Andre went to the corner of the room, pulled back the red carpet, and slid back a plank of hardwood floor. From the secret storage space he retrieved a black briefcase.

"Take good care of it," he advised. When I took the brief-case, he grabbed my hand and said, "The bomb will go off as soon as you open it, so... be prepared."

"Will you clean up the mess?" Bonnie asked, staring at the dead body.

"Me?" Max answered.

"No, I'm talking to Andre," Bonnie said.

"One more thing before you go," Andre said to me, ignoring Bonnie.

When I looked up at him, he was holding a black Polaroid camera.

"Smile!"

The flash burned my eyes.

CHAPTER 29

CAUSE AND EFFECT

MARCUS

I had every reason to believe that the voice calling me wasn't real. When I needed her the most, she was gone. There was no reason for things to be different now. The logical part of my brain could see the blue gas filling up the chamber and a gray-bearded old man sitting cross-legged on the other side of the glass wall. Sometimes he was kind. Sometimes he screamed. I was torn between the land of the living and the realm of the dead.

Standing barefoot in what I could only perceive as a long, narrow stream, I found myself surrounded by near-total darkness. There was only a faint spark of light on the horizon. I wanted to escape, but I couldn't run or even think. Here, ideas ceased to exist. I was free of expectations. I was pulled into the light against my will, and once I came through the other side, I saw her again. She looked so gracious and calm!

As she walked toward me, I realized that the woman I knew had forever changed. Gone was the queen, the royal, the politician who was always worrying about the future. Now I took in my embrace a woman who had made her peace, a real mortal unencumbered by expectations and destiny. A mother, at last!

"I thought I'd never see you again!" I whispered in her ear, bursting with ravenous joy.

She clasped my head with both hands and stared into my eyes, somewhat startled. "Why do you ask? I've always been by your side."

"You seem different. I don't think I've seen this side of you before."

She smiled. "That's because you never thought to look. Let's go home now, your father's waiting."

* * *

As I followed her into the apartment, the vision unraveled. Apparently, the old man had decided to sever the connection. I snapped awake in the gas chamber, inhaling the blue poison streaming through the showerhead. I wanted desperately to reunite with my mother, and I needed to see my father again, in the shape and form they always appeared to me in dreams. Never mind whether these visions were real, I longed for some kind of closure. *You have to let me go*, I protested to this imaginary master in my head, as though he held the key to the universe. I thought I was only speaking in the safety of my own mind when I realized, upon fully opening my eyes, that I had been overheard by the real master and his young disciples, who found my struggles so amusing they could no longer hide their contempt. It was only then that I began to recall how I had met the old man in the first place, outside the gates of the sanitarium, where he was playing hide-and-seek with two seraphs, a brother and a sister, completely oblivious to the chaos festering in the world. He introduced himself casually as Victor Volstead, and he said to me, "But some people like to call me the Philosopher."

When he had noticed the ailing Dante strapped over my horse, he carried the boy to a large waiting room just behind the main gates. Morning glory with blue and violet flowers had encroached on every corner of the sanitarium, even covering a good portion of the walls and floor. "Oh, my boy," he said, "I told you to restrain yourself, but you wouldn't listen! Why must you torture me like this every time?"

"Master... I'm sorry," a delirious Dante answered.

"No, no, don't be sorry. I should be apologizing to you. I should have never allowed you to leave. It's all my fault."

"But, Master, I've found the One. He—he will save us all!"

Victor gave a bitter smile. As I entered the building, I could feel eyes turning on me. I had never seen so many deviants in one place. Some turned invisible upon making eye contact with me, while others were peeking from behind doors and window blinds. A few seraphs were perched on top of the giant sequoia trees that broke through the ceiling, waiting for the right moment to swoop down for the kill.

"Children, be gentle, this young man is not your enemy," said Victor in a gentle, booming voice. "He means you no harm. He has come to us seeking help, and we must help him. That's what we do. We help those who can't be saved."

"But I am their enemy," I said. "My family outlawed their very existence."

"I think your mother would want you to stay. At least long enough for you to see the truth."

"What truth?"

The Philosopher ignored my question for a moment and turned to Claudia. "Sweetheart, would you hand me the syringe?"

Claudia obeyed while giving the old master a hearty embrace, whispering to him, "I miss you so much." If I didn't know

Claudia, I would have believed that the Philosopher was her father. All this time, she never told me anything about this.

"And where are my manners? Welcome to Esoterica!" Victor announced, still trying to put on a performance as he pressed the needle inside Dante's forearm. Then he kissed Dante on the forehead. "My child, this should make you feel better. Think of me in your dreams."

Victor turned to me. "So, what do you think of our home?"

"This is your home?" I asked.

"Why, does it not suit your tastes? Ah, say no more. You're homesick, aren't you?"

"That's a rather odd thing to say, given that your people killed my father."

"And we could say the same for you, many times more. If we keep having that argument, we'd never have any time left to live! You are not my enemy, Prince Kane. I would advise that you return the favor."

"Is that a threat?"

"Marcus, be kind," Claudia said. "If it wasn't for Victor, you'd never have survived."

"How is that the case? I survived on my own."

"Did you?" Claudia shot back.

At face value Claudia's assertion seemed so absurd I found no reason to entertain it. But for the same reason, and especially given the absurdity of everything that had happened, I found myself playing back the events and looking for clues to justify her assertion. The Philosopher was keen to pick up on my curiosity and interjected before I had the chance to make up my mind.

"If you must hear the truth, I will confess that I had nothing to do with your escape and survival. Claudia is only speaking in a metaphorical sense. Your mother told you to find me, and you did. That's the extent of my involvement. I gave you a sense of direction."

"You knew this would happen?"

"Not in the way you think. You see, your mother was an extraordinary woman. She had a special gift for understanding how things would change. I happen to believe it is often men who are blinded by vanity. We're too concerned about right and wrong that we cannot even see the truth placed right under our nose! By no means am I a masochist either. There is evil in all of us. But your mother was one of those rare beings unfettered from conventional beliefs. Indeed, it was the illusive Mercedes who predicted the tragedy that befell on your family. How much longer would people tolerate a system of oppression with no end in sight? This tragedy was bound to happen. I'm sure you've felt it too. She told me about your visions, Marcus. You share her gift. There's no connection more special than the bond between a mother and her son."

"But she never mentioned you to me."

"How could she? She was ashamed of herself. No, shame is too strong a word. Ironically, it was your father who sought me out. At the time, he and your mother were under immense pressure to produce an heir for the kingdom. They tried every doctor in town, but nothing worked. At last, they came to me. But no one could know. If anyone were to find out that the royal family was consorting with a deviant doctor, the whole kingdom would be up in arms. Alas, I agreed to help and keep the whole thing a secret. And in case you're wondering, I'm not a deviant, at least not in the way the term is medically defined. Anyhow, we found a way to usher you into the world. It was no easy task. I will spare you the details, but let's just say a few rules concerning the royal family were broken along the way."

"What are you trying to imply?"

"Oh, please, nothing of the sort happened! Your mother and I were only friends."

"That's… not what I was trying to say."

"I apologize. I have a vivid imagination and tend to impose my madness onto others. It's a natural weakness. You must forgive me. Now, where was I? As it turned out, it was in fact your father who was unable to conceive. Your mother instructed me not to tell him the truth. If it wasn't for the aid of deviancy, which was illegal and still is, you would've never made it out alive. But I think your father knew. I saw the look on his face when he held you for the first time. I'm afraid to say it wasn't pretty. I should spare you what he said—"

"No, I want to know."

"Well, he had the same expression that you have on your face at this very moment. Does that help you understand?"

It took me a second to realize the nasty insinuation he had just made. But even though I wanted to teach him a lesson, I couldn't deny that he was telling the truth. Things were finally starting to make sense. Father's resentment toward me, mother's sadistic speeches about power, and the demons that nested in my head—I could better understand them now. I wasn't mad after all, and suddenly all those unpleasant memories began flooding my head. I felt an insatiable urge to relive every moment of fear and doubt I had ever experienced.

"I hope I haven't upset you," Victor said. "I mean no malice. God knows I'm incapable of hurting anyone. Just look at me… I rely on the charity of others to live."

"I thought you were in the business of saving people," I replied, making a half-hearted attempt at a witty comeback.

"I wouldn't call this a *business*. Unlike some people, I make no profit from the pain and suffering of the least among us."

"So how *do* you manage to survive? Where do you get the resources to support all of your disciples?"

The Philosopher exchanged a sardonic glance with Claudia. "I can see why you like him," Victor said, causing Claudia to blush. "There *are* still charitable people in the world, Marcus. Not everyone is a cold-blooded psychopath. And even psychopaths have their reasons to lend a helping hand. You never know how the tides may turn."

"What's in it for them?"

"Well, we don't ask for much. Look around. We make do with what we have. To those of us condemned to live in the shadows, we're used to coping with pain. Pain is what drives us. It's the lifeblood of revenge. The benefit of being a deviant is that you get to live untethered from the system. You're free to think on your own. All the dictates in the world cannot hold us down. We don't live by their rules. We make our own. Who doesn't want this kind of freedom?"

"You call this freedom?" I asked, scanning the waiting room, filled with sick deviants lying in makeshift beds, writhing in pain. "This is no different than the convents run by the Vanguard. All I see is pain and suffering. Your disciples are dying. I don't think you'd be so cruel as to consider death a kind of freedom."

"You're more accurately describing yourself than my disciples."

"I'm doing fine."

"Are you? Have you looked at yourself in the mirror lately? You've aged thirty years in a matter of days. I wouldn't call that 'doing fine.'"

"Master, he's not ready," Claudia said.

"How long do we wait to tell him? A day, a week, a year? He may not even be here by then."

"That's ridiculous," I said.

"Is it? If you believe you don't need our aid, you're welcome to leave."

The Philosopher got up and summoned a seraph. The seraph was very young, no more than six or seven years old, and like me, he was showing signs of advanced aging. "Would you kindly prepare a warm meal for our noble guest and see him on his way tomorrow morning?" The seraph nodded. Then Victor said to me, "We don't have anything fancy here, just some leftover fish and porridge, but I wouldn't want you to leave on an empty stomach."

"Wait, how long do I have?"

"At most a few months, give or take," the Philosopher replied.

"Why should I trust you?"

"You can make up your own damn mind. I'm not here to dictate to anyone what they should or shouldn't do."

"How is this happening to me? I'm a monarch by birth. I'm nineteen, and I've already passed the test. It's impossible for me to become a deviant now."

"Not impossible, especially not for you," said Victor. "In fact, one could say that the circumstances of your birth made this day inevitable. You were destined to become one of us, Marcus, and there's no denying destiny in a world gone mad. It's hard to say which came first, the inability of your father to conceive or his hatred toward you, but either way, the cycle is bound to break. Think about it. How can a machine, no matter how magnificently designed, ever hope to contain all the base impulses and desires of mankind?"

"One Mind..."

"Hm. You're the id of One Mind, the psychic force destined to be unleashed onto the world. You're more than a deviant,

Marcus. You're the very embodiment of chaos itself. You're the cure to the repression of One Mind. Don't you see? You hold the key to the promised land!"

"Aren't we already living in the promised land?"

"Ah, but there is a paradise beyond the utopia, and it's more beautiful than anything we can imagine."

"No, this is crazy. You're making this up."

"Why would I make this up?"

"Maybe you're saying all this to convince me to join your cause."

"And what do you think it is I'm striving to accomplish?"

"You want to overthrow the system, by any means necessary. You want absolute power. You lie and extort to get your way. That's what cult leaders do."

The Philosopher burst out laughing. "Where did you get those grand ideas? I certainly hope that personal tragedy hasn't clouded your mind."

"Am I supposed to be offended by that?"

"I don't know, depends on what you actually believe."

"It doesn't matter what I believe. As I see it, there's something you need from me and something I need from you."

"I never asked you to do anything for us."

"And I never said no."

"Well then," said the Philosopher, leaning back into his chair with a playful smirk, "there might be more to Prince Charming than meets the eye. What do you propose?"

"I'll consider joining your cause, if you can cure my condition."

"There's one little problem with that offer... There's no cure for your condition. The only way you can prevent it from killing you is by learning how to harness it."

CHAPTER 30

DESIRE

MARCUS

I followed the Philosopher into the belly of the beast. The sanitarium was a kind of maze, full of long, bending corridors that all seemed to circle back to the place we had started. All the rooms were similar, furnished with the same red carpet, art deco wallpaper, and white, circular tables. The windows were barred or wired, allowing only slivers of light to pass through. The whole place smelled like cotton candy, which took me back to my childhood in ways I did not want to remember. Everything was submerged in a bluish haze visible only from a certain angle. There were board games and adult magazines in every room, a rather strange combination considering the patrons of this fine establishment.

"They wanted the invalids to feel at home," said Victor, as we walked through one of these abandoned recreational rooms. "And what better way to achieve that effect than by combining nostalgia and sex."

"I would never have thought of that," I said.

"That's because you never needed a reason to live."

"Everybody needs reasons to live."

"Call me a skeptic, but I can't imagine a prince with all the power and wealth in the world spending his spare time worrying about the future."

"Well, to be frank, that's sort of my specialty."

"You have a point there," said Victor, chuckling along with Claudia. "But to be fair, your kind of anxiety and depression pale in comparison to the magnitude of suffering these invalids went through. My God, can you imagine living out your final days alone and trapped inside a prison cell? And for what crime? Just because you're not 'smart enough' for the rest of the world? These are human beings, Marcus, that your father put in here. Every one of them had dreams and aspirations, like you and me. How is it that you got to live in a golden house while they suffered worse than animals?"

"I thought you were trying to help me, Mr. Volstead. Now I feel like I'm being put on trial."

"He's just trying to make a point, Marcus. You don't have to take it personally," said Claudia.

"But I do. You both clearly hate whatever it is that you think I represent. And you try to make me feel guilty every chance you get. I wasn't the one who decided to lock away these poor souls. I wasn't even born when that happened. Things happened for a reason. And clearly, you both have benefitted from this, haven't you? Claudia, you lived inside the royal family—as a servant, yes, but you were sheltered and taken care of. And you, Victor, were a doctor who had the opportunity to serve my parents. I'm sure they paid you handsomely for your services. Despite what you may believe, we're not all that different."

"*Things happened for a reason*," repeated Claudia in a seething voice. "How would you like it if people said that about your family?"

"That's different," I said.

"How?"

"Because I'm not the one casting blame."

"Don't you hate the Syndicate for what they did to your parents?"

"Of course! I hate the All-Mother. I hate the people in charge. But I'm not going to blame everyone associated with the Syndicate—"

"Perhaps you should," said Victor. "How can I say this plainly? Your survival depends on it. In the eyes of One Mind, we're all invalids. And soon, the entire human race will be purged. If we don't name the enemy, all will be lost. The enemy is not just one person, it's the entire idea and everyone who clings to that idea."

"What idea is that?"

"The idea that says everyone is disposable, except for the ones in power. The idea that there's nothing meaningful about our lives, except for the functions we serve. Anyone can be replaced at any time. And vengeance must be purged."

"Is vengeance not a sin?"

"Is it sinful to seek justice? I'm simply asking you to see the truth. Look at you. Have you once considered who you're meant to be? I'm not talking about being a prince or a disciple or a psychopath. God knows you'll never be a psychopath. But *you*! The version of you in the future, free of expectations. Tell me, Marcus, what do you feel inside? What is standing in your way?"

"The whole world," I said.

"Then the whole world must be defeated!"

"How do you do that?"

"By first understanding yourself."

We arrived in a grand room with high vaulted ceiling and white blinds. The only thing missing was a white piano. I imagined that people once made music here and danced endlessly to those romantic tunes. But even before setting my eyes on the strange and ghastly device in front of us I could feel an unsettling air cascading on my skin. The feeling exceeded my capacity to understand. The Philosopher's ideas kept swimming upstream to reach my head. If only I knew the difference between right and wrong. If only I could see through his heart. I wanted to trust him, but I hated seeing myself in all its ugliness and imperfections.

The Philosopher threw the red drape on the ground, revealing three human-sized glass boxes set on a raised platform. Inside the middle one was Dante, sitting cross-legged in some sort of deep meditation. His chamber was filled with a blue gas. Every now and then purple flames would dance over his skin. All the while, a most peculiar thing happened: wrinkles formed on his face, then disappeared.

"What's happening to him?" I asked.

"Nothing is happening *to* him," Victor answered. "He's finding a way to purge the venom of conformity injected by One Mind."

"Is the blue gas a cure?"

"Not a cure," said Claudia, pressing her forehead against the glass box. "A cure will remove your gift permanently. After everything they've taken from you, Marcus, what have you got left but the sanctity of your soul?"

I couldn't speak.

"Euphoria. This blue air you see is a reflection of a person's inner soul," added the Philosopher. "In the wild, Euphoria has no hues. It only becomes visible to the naked eye when a deviant is manifesting his gift. Think of it: if we're nothing but meat puppets, glorified animals with no meaning or purpose, why live at all? Any one of us can be replaced by someone else, a machine, or even an idea. Even the ghosts that live inside One Mind are just facsimiles of our ego. They're not human. They can never be human. We live because we desire to live. Desire is the root of all existence. We can be anything we want to be. We are not bound by destiny. I lied when I told you that there's no cure for your condition. There is a cure, but you knew that already. The Syndicate is forcing the cure on deviants as we speak. They call it the 'edict of grace.' I can, if you wish, bestow upon you this mercy you so desperately seek. And, we will ask nothing in return. But, if it's the truth you seek, I can make no guarantees about life or death."

Like a waiter, he moved to the side graciously, opening his arm toward the empty box.

First it came to me as a shock. Then, as the glass door closed on me, I found myself savoring the savage fear of what would happen next. Not since my childhood had I felt so fearful and yet so alive, this electricity surging inside my veins. As I inhaled the Euphoria into my lungs, time began to bend and turn in unexpected directions. In the blink of an eye, the Philosopher and his disciples appeared on the other side, their eyes glowing red and dancing wildly under the pale glow of moonlight. My heart was racing so fast I could hear every tiny movement, even the way the hairs on my skin chafed against the air. I could hear them whisper in my head, like the universe was passing on its deepest secrets. By the time I could decipher the first few words, my mind had already fallen back to the moment where I had previously departed. I was with Mother again, in a different version of my life that I must have secretly buried. Just like the moment of passing from wakefulness to dream, I found myself seeking refuge in the sweet embrace of nostalgia.

I was finally home.

CHAPTER 31

WISH FULFILLMENT

MARCUS

Since when did we start to crave a past that didn't exist? I couldn't help but ask this question as I followed Mother into this shabby apartment complex. Everything here was foreign to me. I had never experienced poverty and never wished myself to be poor. But at the same time, I was drawn to poverty. I was drawn to the idea of living a "normal" life, one free of the pretense of power. I had heard famous people say, "My greatest desire is to lead a normal life." Many times, I was driven past this neighborhood, and many times I had fantasized about living in a place like this, a housing project for people who, in all likelihood, had already lost their memories and personalities. These were places inhabited by orphans of the state, walking automatons unconcerned about the beauty and passions of human existence. I suppose, even before the advent of our technology, that was how anyone in power, whether in a monarchy or not, chose to view the peasants of their day. But still, I found myself growing ever more fascinated by the lives of our "converts." How did they view the world? Did they possess a world view? Did they understand the difference between passion and purpose? What were they living for? And, by extension, what was I living for?

When I came back here, and it was indeed a feeling of coming home, the dread I had been feeling all my life seemed to vanish. Like a burden lifted from my shoulders, I could finally see things as they were, free of expectations. There was a sense of freedom to living without purpose. If everyone met the same fate, why labor endlessly to find meaning in a meaningless life? Why not just live? In fact, this feeling of liberation was so intense I could no longer separate fantasy from reality. I began to "remember" things I should never have experienced.

When I made eye contact with a middle-aged man in a biker jacket climbing up the stairs with a limp in his left leg and a cigarette hanging from his lower lip, he smiled at me with a kind of painful realization that his life had already ended, and I could no longer feel hatred toward him. Nor disdain. Nor disgust. The word that could best describe what I experienced in that moment was a word all but banned from the language of our society: *compassion*. I understood him, much as he understood me. It wasn't hopelessness or failure but the knowing recognition of our mutual destiny. Often at night, I would be awakened by the heavy stomping of feet on the floor above, followed by spurts of agonizing screams. I would wonder whether this, too, would happen to me some day, being trapped in a cycle I would be unable to break. There was a sly self-awareness in the way he smiled, as though he was embarrassed that his private moments of frustration had been overheard. Still, he found solace in knowing he wasn't alone. I shared his pain.

Mother was making small talk with a gaunt, little man living next door. He spoke in a jittery fashion, like he had been starving for days. Every time Mother came back from work, he would get her attention somehow and carry on a conversation about little things that annoyed him. For some reason, I was always afraid that he may do something irra-tional, even though he seemed helpless on the surface. Just as he was opening the door to go back to his room, he paused, turned around, and walked toward me with a fake smile.

"Haven't seen you in a while!" he said in a patronizing tone. "How's life treating you, sport?"

"I can't stand you," I said.

"That's not very nice!"

They laughed.

"Like father, like son," he followed.

"Watch it."

He shrugged. "Sorry, I'm just a little rusty, if you know what I mean."

She gave a sarcastic laugh.

"Hey, kid, listen to your mother, okay? She cares about you."

He pinched my nose, then scuttled back to his room.

After seeing him off, Mother came back to me, getting down on one knee.

"Won't you look at me?" she said. "I like you better when you're happy."

"I'm not your lover," I said.

"Wait, are you mad at me for talking to him?"

"I don't like him."

"Neither do I."

"I don't believe you."

"We play the game to stay alive."

"What game?"

"We must be good people."

"No rich person would ever say that."

"Look, I know you hate it here, but I promise we'll find a better place, a better life for both of us. But before we do, we have to be good. Do you understand?"

I didn't respond. What did "good" even mean? I shifted my gaze away from her face and caught my reflection in the window. I was disgusted by the old face staring back at me. The only saving grace were my eyes, which still seemed innocent enough to give the impression of a child. No wonder they were laughing at me. I would be laughing at this freak as well.

With a sigh, Mother got up and opened the door. Room ninety-seven. The number seemed familiar. The room was about the size of a canine kennel with just one small round table sitting on a dirty carpet. There was a television, the old kind with analog controls, on one end, and a ragged fake-leather sofa on the other. At first, I couldn't believe my eyes. Slumped in the sofa was a rather large man whose facial features I refused to recognize until he threw a beer bottle at me and said, "Come here, boy, sit next to your papa."

Then Mother said, "Don't mind him, he's drinking again."

And I said, "Who is he?"

Suddenly, a childish voice joined in and answered, "He's your father, of course!"

He walked toward me holding a plate filled with cheap department-store cheese and grapes. He was a shabby-looking creature, and if I didn't know any better, I would have taken him as my friend or even my brother. But he certainly was neither, for the look in his eyes undoubtedly belonged to the deviant who had killed my father. The ungrateful rat who had sought revenge on the very people who had taken pity on him. He looked so desolate and scared I almost wanted to pity him. I took a few grapes from the plate and threw them at his face, and he didn't even blink. He giggled uncontrollably as if he enjoyed the teasing. When I started laughing at him, he seemed even more amused. He was just like any other service model, childish and inept. There was indeed a bit of sadness in the way he smiled, and this made me want to tease him even more. He deserved the pain. If not for pain, how would anyone know that they're real? Besides, it wasn't like I had much to enjoy in this lonesome world. I needed his pain to feel good. There was someone here, a real living, breathing creature I could hassle.

"Be nice, Marcus!" Mother shouted through a dirty smirk. Then she threw a piece of sock at the back of our servant's head, and he giggled again.

"I don't appreciate that," he said, pretending to protest.

"You know you like it," Father said. He chucked an empty can of beer at the servant model just to pile on the joke.

At last, our servant started to cry. The mood made a turn for the worse.

"Oh, shut up!" the man on the sofa snapped. "No one's going to hear you cry. This is your job. It's your life, get over it." The monster slobbering at his sandwich flew off the sofa, still sucking on the meat sauce on his fingers, and marched toward the servant with obvious menace. As he passed me, I finally got a good look at his face. Under the meat puppet was a man I had once considered my brother. How could I have forgotten him? Sly, slavish, demonic, always bursting at the seams. He was a chameleon of the first order, a backstabber, a traitor, a murderer. He held the same expression on his face when he had murdered my mother. There was no remorse. He was a monster then and a monster now. Being the helpless, little lamb that I was, I gazed frightfully at the monster as he pushed me into the TV, knocking it off the stand. *Late Night with Charlie Conrad* was playing, and I hated the man's disgusting voice. It was well known, even to a child, that talk-show hosts specialized in the most spine-tingling art of chicanery and pandering, but never had I witnessed a man as insipid as Charlie Conrad. He wouldn't shut up! One look at the way his lower lip drooped with saliva told you all you needed to know about his private life and his relationship with the opposite sex. Speaking of Mother, she tried to plant herself between the monster and the servant but tripped on a rubber duck, and as she fell, she hit her head on the edge of the table. Delighted by the mishap, the monster began unleashing his rage on the poor servant.

"It's always you! Always making a scene! I'm going to smack the devil out of you!"

"No, Papa, no! I'm hurt!"

Papa wouldn't listen. He got off on the fear. "Miscreant! Deviant! You'll learn to obey!" he shouted as he slammed his fist repeatedly into the teenager's spine.

"Stop it, Victor! You're going to kill him!" Mother shouted.

We were really the dysfunctional family that Conrad featured on his talk show. "Con-rad! Con-rad!" I could hear the audience shout. They loved all this disgusting chaos. I wondered, was this the normal life I had always secretly desired?

Not one to allow a moment of peace, Victor escalated his attack and started choking the servant.

"I'm sorry!" the servant pleaded. "I'll do anything, anything! Please, you're hurting me!"

"You better stop, Victor," said Mother.

"Or what? What are *you* going to do to me?" Victor shot back.

"I'll kill you!" Mother took a fruit knife from the table and swung it at the monster. She missed. Instead, she cut the servant on the cheek.

"I'm so sorry, honey!" she cried.

"Don't be sorry, he can take it," said Victor. "He doesn't feel anything. Do you, champ?"

"I feel pain!" The servant was once again on the verge of tears. Except, this time, he had no tears left to cry. He was caught between anger and desperation, and nothing seemed reasonable anymore, not his job, certainly not himself. It seemed, in that very moment, he was being betrayed by the entire world. The lie had torn itself open, and blood began seeping from the wound. Not even One Mind could rein in his desperation. He was now a ticking bomb, destined to unleash hell. I couldn't let this happen again.

The servant's eyes turned red, and Victor screamed.

"Goddammit! You're the devil!" Victor released his choke-hold and cried out in pain. He looked at his hands, which were badly burned. Even I could feel the heat from a few feet away.

"Jason, my boy, listen to me," Mother said, lowering to one knee and staring into the servant's eyes. "We love you, okay? We love you so very much. You don't have to do this."

The servant boy finally let out a second wave of tears, which sizzled upon contact with his burning face. Slowly, his eyes returned to normal, and the heat began to dissipate. He decided to live. As he fell into Mother's arms, he whispered, "Thank you."

I felt so conflicted watching this unfold. A part of me wanted to save him. The other part wanted him to die. And seeing him so close with Mother made me regret my compassion for him in the first place.

Then, out of nowhere, someone yelled, "Cut! Nice work!"

From just beyond the kitchen in the back, a tall fellow with glasses strode toward me, clapping. Behind him was a whole crew of people performing various routines, some looking into the camera, some carrying sound equipment from one place to another. I grew terribly confused. Was this all just a performance? How did I not know that I was on a TV set?

The emotions felt so utterly real I couldn't snap out of this cold reality.

"Wonderful job," said the man whom I could only assume was the director. Up close, I could recognize the features of my father on this fellow's face, the wild, impish eyes, the well-defined jawline, and the brooding menace registered in every movement he made. The only major difference was that Father never wore glasses. And the director appeared much younger, and I imagined this was how my father would have looked in his early twenties. Apparently, my silence disturbed him.

"Your grace, I hope I haven't offended you. I was only trying to say that your performance was impeccable. You played the part perfectly. There was such wonderful conviction in your eyes. I know this can be uncomfortable, to play someone far below your stature, but you're doing a great service to the country. You're helping millions of people understand the plight of our working poor."

I thought for a second and looked up at this slimy sycophant. He nervously adjusted his glasses. "How does this help the country? I thought we shouldn't be showing com-passion."

"Yes, yes, indeed. Your grace is right. Real compassion is absolutely sinful. It should be avoided at all costs. But... how do I put it... we all want to be *seen*. When you put a spotlight on someone, it makes them feel special, even if they get nothing in return. I hope I'm making it easy to understand..."

"Are you calling me stupid?"

"Oh, Lord, no, not at all, your grace. I would never dare! I'm not as articulate as I should be."

"Are you a convert?"

"Me? No, I'm fortunate to have passed the test."

"Are you sure about that? There are converts who go on to become directors. I've seen it in the Archives. It's nothing to be embarrassed about."

The director chuckled timidly. "Your grace, even if I were a convert, I wouldn't be aware of this fact. It would have been erased from my memory."

"So, is it impossible for a convert to know that he's been replaced?"

"Not so, and your grace, if you would follow me," said the director, leading me away from the set toward the office building in the back lot. Along the way, people nodded obediently when noticing my presence. They all held the same little smile just long enough for me to believe they were genuinely in awe. Who knew what they really thought of me. I could only imagine the depth of their resentment. As we walked past a small gathering of similar-looking assistants, all of them wearing glasses and their backs eternally hunched out of deferential timidity, the director called on one such assistant, a young female with thick makeup and a sharp, little face. "Will you help the prince remove his makeup?"

"Of course," the girl answered. She approached me. "May I, your grace?"

I was relieved to know that my aging face was fake. I nodded. With a flick of the wrist, she found the edge of the mask at the bottom of my chin and peeled it back, inch by inch.

"There you go," she said, smiling. "All better."

I wanted to touch her face in that moment and comfort her aching heart. I saw in her eyes the desire to seek acceptance, and I witnessed the passing of a life before me, and in that moment she smiled. There was no comfort in seeking acceptance from someone out of fear. And it was fear that brought her to smile.

Soon, we arrived at the director's office, judging by the golden plaque over the door, which read Dir. Ivan Stanley, and went inside. The reception area was barely large enough to hold the two of us. I was expecting a larger office, given that it belonged to the director.

"Scarcity is a virtue," he said, as if noticing the thought that had passed through my head. "I like to keep things simple and clean. We start with nothing and leave with nothing. Your grace would understand."

I didn't understand the insinuation. As a monarch, my consciousness would be preserved in One Mind forever. He surely knew that. It was common knowledge. To jab him back, I asked, "Do you have your affairs in order?"

"Not yet," he replied, going behind the reception desk while rummaging through the drawers. "I don't have happy memories. I've been working my whole life. Never had a moment to enjoy anything, not even the work I do. It just comes and goes, one day after another. So, no, I haven't had 'the talk' with my psychiatrist, although I'll need to have it soon."

"How old are you?"

"How old do you think I am?"

"Twenty-seven?"

"Close. I'm almost thirty." He produced a memory cube from the drawer and placed it on the reception desk. "So, this is my reward for working hard. Just three memory streams to pass on to the world. It's a little unfair, don't you think? Why can't I preserve my entire consciousness, like you?"

"The system storage is limited."

"Oh, that's cold, your grace. I didn't take you to be a heartless scab."

"Excuse me?"

"My apologies, your grace, I didn't mean to offend you. *Scab* is a term of endearment, just like *deviant*. Don't you sometimes wish you were a deviant? To be free from all this?"

"I'm already free."

"Stop lying to yourself. You're not free. You were never free. You just forgot who you are."

"I know who I am."

"Do you?"

"Yes, I'm Prince Marcus Kane. And if you don't stop this nonsense, I'll have you arrested."

"Please, forgive me, your grace, I'm only trying to help."

"I don't need your help. I don't need anyone's help."

"You need my help to remember who you are. Now, your grace, would you kindly turn around and look behind you?"

"Why?"

"Please, just humor me."

When I turned around, the office space I had encountered just moments ago was no longer present, like the stage had been swapped. The office was replaced by an operating room, blood everywhere. The light flickered, and I could hear men shouting and tanks rolling by. This was apparently some kind of underground bunker, not a proper hospital, judging by the dirty equipment and makeshift operating bed. On the bed was a young boy with black hair and dark, green eyes, just like mine. Even though the surgeon was cutting open his scalp, he was wide awake and spotted me gazing at him. He opened his mouth to speak but struggled to make any sound.

"Be still," said the surgeon, a stocky, older man with a gray beard. "You'll be all fixed up soon. Just stay with me a little longer."

I heard footsteps approach. A man and a woman arrived.

They must have been the boy's parents. I couldn't see their faces because they were wearing chastity masks.

"Do you recognize the boy?" asked Ivan.

I wanted to deny my intuition but decided to say the truth. "He looks like me."

"He *is* you," said Ivan.

"But I don't remember being here. This isn't real... You're messing with my head."

"I'm not the one messing with your head, the surgeon is."

"What's he doing to me?"

Ivan gestured for me to go to the other side of the bed and see for myself. I was too scared to move.

The mother kneeled beside the bed, clasping the boy's hands. "Will he make it?" she asked the surgeon.

"Don't be so grim," cut in the father, "he's going to make it."

"How can you be so sure?"

"Because we have the best surgeon working on him."

"Mr. K," said the surgeon, "I'd like to have your permission to initiate the transfer."

Father thought for a second, then stood up. He cast his gaze on the helpless boy, seemingly pleased. "My son, you'll carry the legacy of all the best monarchs before you. Service, dedication, and hope. I will love you like my own. I promise."

"Is that a *yes*?" the surgeon pressed.

"Yes, do it."

"Wait!" Mother shouted. "We haven't asked for his consent."

"We don't need his consent," said the father.

"But he's only a child!"

"So what? He ought to consider it a privilege. Don't you, kid? Nod if you agree."

"Stop it," she said. "You're being cruel."

"Look—look at him smile! You see that smile? We're doing him a favor, sweetheart. If we don't replace him now, he'll end up in a loony bin. He gets to be a prince, and we get to have a son. I think that sounds pretty fair. Carry on, Doctor."

"I suggest you both hold him down," said the surgeon, pressing a long needle into the boy's exposed brain. "This is going to hurt."

In that moment, I slipped inside the boy's body, becoming one with him. I felt what he felt and shrieked when the needle entered the sensitive part of my brain. I jolted violently against the restraints, fighting with every fiber of my strength to break free. The lingering smirk on Ivan's face was the last thing I remembered before the world exploded into a million fragments, dancing and splintering and morphing at the same time. I felt as though my soul could burst out of my body at any moment, and it was a miracle that I held myself together long enough to remember to open my eyes, for when I did, I finally crossed the threshold. I ran out of my own body with such force and conviction that my willpower managed to escape the prison even before my body could follow suit. As I crashed through the glass wall, watching the maelstrom of glass shards swirl around me, I could see my old body still stationed inside the chamber, in a state of deep meditation. The ugly truth of my origin now laid bare in front of my naked eyes, there was no turning back. In this moment of impossible flight, the world finally started to make sense. I looked at the seraphs and deviants with a sense of kinship and understanding I had denied for so long. The world forced itself upon me, violated and twisted my conscience out of shape, just like it had with all of them. We shared the same plight after all! The same pain, the same frustration, the same inescapable feeling of inadequacy and guilt that chased us wherever we went.

I was never a prince to begin with. I was merely a child trying to survive. When I fell back into reality, the ground beneath my body caved and cracked, and the thunderous pain that split my head open suddenly healed. I reached out my hand and summoned my old body back to me, the soul once again reunited with the vessel. Still, I couldn't ignore the feeling that a part of me had gone missing, perhaps stuck somewhere between the past and the future. That was the last thing I remembered as I fainted in Claudia's arms.

CHAPTER 32

THE OFFER

MARCUS

When I came to, I was standing in front of a fountain searching for my reflection in the water. A thick fog descending, the cold breeze made me self-conscious about my body. I couldn't remember how I got here or what I was thinking in the moments before I awakened, but there was no doubt that time had passed since I had broken out of the gas chamber. There were vague memories of secretive conversations and people passing by and observing me from above, like tourists watching a caged animal. Even though I couldn't remember what they had said, I saw in their eyes wonder and fear, the same wheel of emotions on which I was fastened and couldn't seem to stop. I kept tumbling into the past and sometimes felt like seeing the future, for time had become a thing of the past, and I needed to focus on the present. In the present, I was standing in front of the fountain, and the Philosopher stood on one side, Claudia on the other. Claudia put her hand on my back, and when this sensation of touch registered in my head once again, I realized that I was half naked. I felt a wave of energy percolating beneath my shoulder blades, like some mechanism needed to unwind, but I wasn't sure if I should allow it to happen. The only thing I knew for certain was that a part of me had gone missing.

"He was right here!" I said, returning to a heated argument. "I saw him. He was right here!"

"Calm down," Victor said.

"I *am* calm," I snapped.

"Do you know where you are?" Victor asked.

"Yes. I'm in the sanitarium. Ward Number Ten."

"Good. Who is the leader of Anthem?"

"That's a ridiculous question. Are you trying to provoke me?"

"No, I'm just checking to see if you're still sane."

"Matilda Gray, the All-Mother. The Syndicate staged a coup and replaced my family. Are you satisfied? Should I recount the whole story again?"

"I am, indeed, very satisfied and relieved. You hadn't spoken a word for some time. So, yes, I'm happy to know that you're still in control of your faculties."

"We were all worried about you, Marcus," added Claudia. "I'm glad you made it."

"Did you see him too?" I asked.

"Yes, we all saw him."

"How's that possible?"

"Apparently, you asked the question knowing it's very much possible," said Victor, "or else, you wouldn't ask the question in the first place. We belong to each other now. You can feel it inside, can't you? A burning nostalgia for a past that doesn't seem to exist."

"Yes... How do you know?"

"Because it's true. Because what you witnessed was the past you've always been denied. You overcame One Mind. You broke through to the other side!"

"So what I saw was a memory?"

Victor paused. "Yes," he said as if he had just remembered his words, "and not only a memory but also a state of mind."

"I don't believe it. No, it can't be true." I felt the urge to fight back, despite feeling a vile kind of happiness. "It must've been the drug. Euphoria, wasn't it? How do I know that it wasn't just a hallucination? I *remember* my entire childhood, growing up with my parents. I remember every detail because I lived through them. Those memories are true. My mother was always there. My love for her is true. I may have hated my father, but I was still his son. Who are you to say those memories are false? I'm not a replacement. I'm a prince."

"In a sense, we've all been replaced. Just by varying degrees. But I don't want to get into a philosophical discussion here."

"Well, you are the Philosopher, right?"

"In name only. I took on the name as an act of protest, since the Order declared that philosophy is dead. Rejoice! Welcome to the new utopia! Who needs God when you've got everything figured out by the supreme reason of the human brain? You're the machine, and the machine is you."

"You're saying my whole life is a lie."

"I'm not a prophet, Marcus. I don't claim to have all the answers. The all-knowing sage doesn't exist. He's a lie made up by the system to make you conform. And listen, even *he* doesn't realize it. That's just the role they assigned him. I'll be the first to admit that I don't know everything. No one does. But it's with this humility that I allow for the existence of the exceptional. You're on the verge of a great transformation, Marcus. Don't you want to see what's on the other side?"

"You said you can see the future," Claudia said, pointing to the water, "but can you see yourself?"

I had never said I could see the future. Even as I prepared to make my objection clear, a temptation lurched across my mind, and I was frozen. This temptation burned inside my eyes, bringing them to the verge of tears. But the strange thing was that I had no tears to cry. I wasn't sad or angry. I only felt the inexorable sensation of power, power to illuminate everything that had been hidden from me. And just like my father before me, I allowed this power to pass through my eyes, releasing a bright beam of light to pierce through the fog. For a moment, I was gripped by ecstasy, for I found my younger self reflected on the water's surface. All the exasperation and guilt I had carried for so long seemed to have vanished. But no sooner had I rejoiced at the sight of my true self than the image began to shift. The small creases made by my smile spread like a disease over my face, burrowing through my skin, leaving trails of carnage. At once I lost my youth, and the old man staring back at me was vile and ungrateful. But the strangest part came next. As soon as the old man grimaced, the child returned, and then back again it went, over and over. I pressed my hands against my face, hoping to stop the madness. I could feel the changes slithering back and forth. I wanted to scream.

"Make it stop!" I shouted.

"I don't have that power."

"Please… just make it stop."

"Only you can control it."

"How?"

"Embrace the vengeance in your heart."

I sank down to my knees. The pain was too excruciating to bear. Then I felt something else come over me, something so insidious I couldn't even put it into words. It was an alien intrusion, like a phantom had slipped under my skin and burrowed its way to my spine. First, I felt a wave of chills, enough to make me believe that I was buried under a pile of snow. Then, there was the sensation of flight, a sensation I couldn't describe clearly because I had never experienced it before, nor could I experience it as a human being, but it was something like perpetual falling in a world upside down. I saw the lovely Claudia turn pale and kneel beside me. Her movement suggested something other than pity. There was a pleasure in the way she frowned at my suffering. I could see it in her eyes. She was enamored with me in that moment, placing her hand over my naked back, and in the instant she touched me, the pain exploded. I would confess to you some vile feeling I felt toward her in that moment, which I would not be able to explain, even if I were calm and reasonable. It was a strange mockery of life itself. When you're so close to oblivion, you see through people, and you want to eviscerate them. The tenderness of her touch traced the path of this imaginary snake crawling up my spine. When I reached for my back, something sharp pricked my fingertip. Claudia, holding my gaze, took hold of my wrist and guided my hand over my shoulder blade. All along the path I felt a thousand tiny spikes. They were so sensitive to touch that my heart pounded every time our hands went over the tip of a spike. I was running out of breath.

"This is who you are," Claudia whispered into my ear. "Don't fight the temptation. Give in to it."

I couldn't speak or fight back. How could she call it a temptation? I had no idea what was happening to me, except for the premonition that the whole world was about to explode.

Then I heard a tender voice echo in the distance, calling out my name. With my fists driven into the ground, and my back horribly arched, I lifted my head enough to see Dante approaching, holding something in his hand.

"Master!" he shouted hoarsely, his face pale. He seemed to be in worse shape than me. "Master, take mine, and save yourself!"

He opened his palm to reveal a short syringe filled with a blue substance.

"What is this?"

"The cure," he said. "It's going to take the pain away."

"And the sickness too?"

"Yes..."

"Marcus, look at me," Claudia cut in. "If you take the cure, you'll never be the same again. You'll lose yourself. You must endure!"

"For what?" I asked her, almost tenderly, clenching my teeth as another wave of thunder cracked open my back.

"For yourself!" Claudia said.

I thought about myself for a moment, and it turned out to be the thing I hated most. I swiped the syringe from Dante and jammed the needle into my arm. I waited for the cure to take effect; however, nothing happened. My heart was still pounding furiously, and the alien sensation that invaded my body only grew stronger. My eyes burning, I tried to stand up.

"What have you done?" I asked under my breath.

The three of them stood watching with no emotions at all. Claudia was full of pity, Victor frowned, and the boy clasped his hands together in front of him, as if to pray.

"What did you do to me?" I demanded again.

Still no response.

Finally, I was so overwhelmed by this cruel agitation that the pain seemed to fade. I knew then that I had ventured beyond the threshold. It was unmistakable. If some dire fate would fall upon me, I would gladly accept it. Consent held no meaning when your whole being was on the verge of collapse. No one cared whether I lived or died. And in this decisive moment, I made up my mind. I was going to live. I needed to live. I needed to prove them wrong, in every way possible. How swiftly the transformation came! The force of nature taking up my body grew to such monstrous proportions that my shoulder blades practically opened. Slicing through my last defense, these vile spikes burst forth, and in the periphery, I saw them grow and expand, spilling blood all over. I wiped the blood from my eyes and noticed that the alien phantom had finally blossomed. I stood up, trying to hold my balance. I couldn't even hear my own scream. Delirious pleasure took over, and I gazed upon my new form with equal parts fear and joy. Not for one second could I tear my eyes away from the majestic set of black wings that protruded from my back, fresh with blood and pulsating in the wilderness of the world. They weren't the wings of a bird. Rather, they resembled the membrane of a bat's wings, partially transparent and laced with purple veins. I took in a deep breath. If rapture could grace the heart of man, let this moment stand as the testament of truth. I was saved! My heart was so full I could sing the angel's verse without a hint of shame. All the same, I could no more understand this transformation than my father could process the difference between kindness and betrayal. When things exceed expectations in every way imaginable, reason is all but lost. I gave in to the fantasy completely.

"You have passed the test, my son," the Philosopher proudly declared. "God have mercy on your enemies."

There was no disputing the sheer power of epiphany. I stood proudly like a king. I was redeemed. I had never felt so solid and mean. I could even allow myself to forgive them for playing a trick on me. Surely, what Dante had given me was no cure. The whole thing was an act. Even so, I was happy to have been deceived. Gazing upon my transformation, Claudia was overwhelmed, her cheeks flushing red, and flew into my arms. I held her neck in my palm and kissed her lips. She had never tasted so good.

"Now you understand," she said, "why they've hated you for so long."

"So this is who I am…," I said, tasting the dried blood on my lips. A cold breeze swept up the leaves and chased the fog away. I trembled all over. "They lied to me the whole time."

"And you must make them pay," she said.

"You surprise me, Claudia. I never took you to be a vengeful spirit."

"I can say the same for you."

"We do what we must," I repeated a familiar phrase.

"And doesn't it feel good?" Claudia asked. "To be free of expectations?"

"It most certainly does."

Breaking away from my embrace, Claudia strode behind me to worship my newfound form. She pressed her cheek against the hard ridge of my wings, which grew hot in response. Almost embarrassed, I trembled and moved away from her touch. I was still so brainwashed by the virtue of being stoic that I shuddered to imagine a world where people could be free to express their emotions. As soon as I tore away from Claudia, I wanted to apologize.

"Am I a monster, Claudia?" I asked.

"No."

"What am I then?"

"A free man."

"A free man without a home."

"We are your home. We are your family. You belong with us."

"Master," Dante said, "you're young again."

"Look." Dante took my hand and led me back to the fountain.

Indeed, I could see in the reflection that my youth had been restored. I touched my face to make sure I wasn't dreaming. The snakes that had slithered under my skin had crawled back into the dark recesses of my mind. I could still find the wrinkles in their wake, but the passion of youth, which I had never possessed in spades, had somehow returned to grace my expression. Overjoyed, I turned to Dante, who threw himself into my embrace, and I held his bald, little head in my hands. When we made contact, my wings reacted once again, this time burning even hotter than before, as if they were on the verge of catching fire. I could only reason that Dante's gift was reacting to mine.

"See?" said Dante, coughing. "I knew this day would come." As soon as he finished those words he collapsed once again in my arms.

"Dante!"

"I'm fine..." His face was now the one ravaged. "This is the pain of liberation, not bondage."

"Don't say that, my friend, we're going to save you," I said. "Claudia, do you have the cure?"

"We used the last vial we had on you," Claudia said.

"That wasn't the cure."

"You resisted, so it had the opposite effect."

"Master," Dante said, "don't worry about me. Let me die in peace. I've fulfilled my destiny."

"No, I won't let you die. We didn't come this far just to give up now."

"This is the price we pay for being different," said Claudia. "We bear the burden of responsibility."

"How can you give up so easily?"

"Loss is a part of life," Claudia said.

"Claudia, do you hear yourself? We brought him all the way here because we were going to help him. Dante is our friend!"

"If we give him the cure, we'll take away his gift. Dante will never be the same again."

"That's better than dying."

"Is it? Would you give away your wings?"

I couldn't answer the question.

"Dante finished his part in the prophecy so that you could join us. He can rest easy now."

"I'm not worthy of anyone's sacrifice. There must be another way."

"If we violate the prophecy," Claudia insisted, "we'll lose everything!"

"I don't believe in prophecies!"

"There is another way," the Philosopher interrupted.

Claudia gave him a stern look.

"No, no, we must keep an open mind. There's nothing to fear."

"But Master..."

"Marcus, you asked me earlier how I manage to keep things running as they are. There is someone who can help Dante, but he's not to be trusted."

"Who is he?"

"We refer to him as the Benefactor. He gives us the resources we need to feed our disciples. So far, he has kept his end of the bargain, but he's a member of the Syndicate. He's a full-blooded psychopath. He will eat you alive, if he must."

"But does he have the cure?"

"No, but he has something better. He has pure, unfiltered Euphoria that can heal Dante without taking away his gift."

"How do we reach him?"

"He's not someone you can reach. He only responds to offers."

"Offers?"

"Yes, a psychopath always demands something in return."

"What can we give him?"

"We've given him enough," Claudia uttered.

"There can always be more," Victor responded.

"No more… We can't…"

The Philosopher looked at Claudia wistfully.

"Oh, sweet child, I know how you feel. Shh… Pain is a necessary condition to change. Don't you want to change the world?"

Claudia couldn't refuse.

"My son is working for the Syndicate," the Philosopher continued. "He's risking his life for our cause. He can get us to the Benefactor. He goes by many names, but the one you should know is Max Strode."

"Max Strode," I repeated. "Never heard of him."

"He's a new cadet with the Syndicate. He's a little like you. He takes everything too seriously. Which, to be fair, is a requirement for his job."

"So he's a spy."

"Yes, if you insist. His heart is true."

"Who does he work for?"

"Gaius Pulcher."

"He's the Benefactor?"

"Yes."

"Why would the head of Vulture help a cult of deviants?"

"Everyone has their vices… and Euphoria is one hell of a drug, as you well know."

"But he already has the Euphoria."

"Exactly. And when a noble gets addicted to Euphoria, he tends to develop other needs."

"What needs?"

"You might say, deviant needs."

I was beginning to understand. No wonder Claudia resisted the idea.

"We offer him a deviant boy and a deviant girl for his private enjoyment in exchange for three vials of Euphoria."

"How long has this been going on?"

"Long enough for us to survive."

"That's disgusting."

"I know."

"How can you do this to your disciples?"

"I never force anyone. My disciples understand what it takes to survive. We're willing to sacrifice for the greater good. What other choice do we have?"

"We don't have a choice."

"Such is the state of existence for those banished from the world."

"I'll volunteer."

"Excuse me?"

"I'll go. I'm now a deviant, right?"

"You'll volunteer to walk into the lion's den?"

"Are we not already in the lion's den?"

"You know the Syndicate is looking for you. Nothing would satisfy them more than to eradicate the Spencer bloodline."

"Am I a monarch? Or am I a seraph?"

"You exceed my expectations, Marcus."

"I know Pulcher. I know what kind of man he is."

"And you're familiar with his vices?"

"Yes, all too familiar..."

"Have you ever worn a chastity mask?"

For a moment, memories of being lashed by my father crossed my mind. He had forced me to wear a chastity mask every time I dabbled in unwanted passions.

"Yes," I answered.

"What about the girl?"

"I'll go alone."

"No, that won't work," said Victor. "He'll only honor his end of the bargain if we offer both a boy and a girl."

"I'll go with you," Claudia declared.

"Are you sure?"

"No, but I can't in good conscience allow another disciple to get hurt."

"You're both crazy, you know that?" Victor said. "Two wanted fugitives offering to be captured."

"This is for Dante," I said.

"And for our cause," Claudia joined.

"Before you go, your transformation needs one more step," said Victor. Then he turned to Claudia. "Sister Sagan will do the honor."

Claudia led me back into the room with the glass chambers, making a turn to the right down a flight of stairs into an underground furnace. She turned on the light, which flickered, and reached for a black branding iron whose tip sat inside the open furnace. When she took it out, I noticed the familiar *S*-shaped letter brand at the end of the stick, burning red hot.

I understood its purpose.

"Now you get to know what it's like to be branded an outsider," said Claudia.

"I'm ready."

Watching the brand approach, I tilted my head to the right and exposed the left side of my neck.

I closed my eyes, biting back the pain as Claudia pressed the hot iron into my neck. When I opened my eyes again, my wings had retracted, and I was now officially a deviant.

CHAPTER 33

GRADUATION

JASON

"All these years, we've never been closer to our goal," said Max on the phone. It was half past midnight when he called, and I was still dreaming about being bound to a rock and devoured by a giant eagle. "You still there, Jason? Did you hear what I said?"

"Yes, I heard you."

"You ought to be more excited. This time, you'll really be famous."

I wasn't in the mood to talk about myself. "What's going to happen to Andre?"

"The same thing that happens to every traitor."

"But he's your friend."

"Is he?"

"And Bonnie?"

"Why are you asking? Do you feel sorry for them?"

"Maybe a little bit. I guess I'm just a softie at heart."

"Sure, a softie not shy enough to kill."

"It was just acting, Max. Don't confuse that with reality."

"Oh, I'm not confused, my friend. I'm impressed. That was some performance."

"Thank you."

"Where did you learn how to act?"

For a second, I almost allowed myself to spill the truth. Even after all the practice, I was, as I'd said to Max, still a softie at heart. I could be too easily swayed by compliments. Fortunately, I remembered my weakness.

"I've never told anyone about this," I said, trying to sound sincere, "but I took acting lessons when I was in elementary school. It's kind of embarrassing. My dad forced me to do it."

"Why? Did he want to live vicariously through you?"

"That was part of it, I'm sure. But mostly, he made me do it because I was having problems in school."

"What kind of problems?"

"Well, things, you know, that come naturally to normal people."

"Like what?"

"Like how to be sociable. I didn't even know how to talk to people. I was so shy I could barely function in social settings. I had to learn everything from scratch. How to look at people in the eyes, how to smile, how to shake hands, how to ingratiate myself to get what I wanted. You know, basic stuff. I guess you could say I got a lot of practice with frivolous things."

"So you learned to overcompensate for your weakness."

"You sound just like my acting coach."

I'd never met an acting coach in my life.

"Word of advice..."

"Yes?"

"Sometimes, being nervous can make you seem more sincere."

Then Max, or George, depending on the time of day we spoke, trailed off and hung up. I didn't know what to make of him. Sometimes, he was sincere. Sometimes, he was cold. I do recall my father telling me once that the people giving advice are usually the ones who are most in need of heeding their advice. If that were true, what did it say about Max? Did he have a hidden agenda? Or was he casting doubt on my story? Either way, I left the conversation wanting more. I was going to ask him about the show, the briefcase, and the script I had rehearsed earlier. He wasn't wrong; I was indeed going to be famous.

The night was free of dreams or nightmares. I slept as if I were perfectly awake. I remembered everything, which is to say, nothing much. It was a dreamlike state with no end in sight. I could feel every vibration in the air, like I was being exposed to the world for the first time. That morning, I woke up remembering a motivational speech I had heard a decade ago. The speaker was a psychologist giving a sermon about embracing discomfort as the way to live. Of course, speeches focused on that topic were a dime a dozen. Everybody was talking about embracing discomfort. It was, after all, the stoic way. But there was a quality about this man, a kind of religious touch that made me remember him more than the others. He wasn't just giving another version of the same speech, he genuinely believed what he was saying. I was so absorbed in trying to understand this man that I almost walked out of my room without any pants.

I wouldn't admit this to anyone, but living inside Mr. Pulcher's mansion was a dream come true. It was paradise in hell. While the whole world was suffering—people getting shot in the streets, families getting torn apart—I had the good fortune of sleeping soundly in an expensive and comfortable bed. I was well-nourished, well-treated, and well-protected. You really couldn't ask for anything more. I had a servant, a service model just like me, although much less handsome and only ten years old, who tended to my every need. My room was on the far end of the west wing of the mansion, where I could see our private waterfront from my bedroom window. The mansion was three stories high and lavishly furnished. We had our own gourmet kitchen, home theater, greenhouse, climate-controlled wine cellar, everything we needed to entertain the cultured elite. Well, I say "we" in a somewhat selfish way. This was not my home. I would probably never get to own a house like this. In fact, I used to hate people who lived off the wealth of others. I called them leeches. Funny how things can change. I was now a leech. A handsome and grateful leech but a leech nonetheless. Did I judge myself for violating my own convictions? Sometimes. Then again, I was no stranger to living in a web of lies. Sometimes, the world just vanished, and I'd see myself floating in a red sea with all the other obsolete machines.

Max walked up to me looking annoyed. He stubbed a cigarette on his left palm and blew out some smoke. Behind him was a professional camera crew, with the All-Mother standing in front of a water fountain, holding an expensive purse in one hand and a small cat in the other. Magda was behind the camera, looking prim and focused. She did her work quietly, which seemed unlike her. I hadn't seen this side of her before. A ragged copy of the *Conformist* was lying open on the coffee table.

"Do you like her?" Max whispered to me.

"The All-Mother?"

He nodded.

"Is that a trick question?"

"No, I just want to know."

"Do *you*?"

"Never mind, you're no fun."

In truth, I did find the All-Mother somewhat attractive. She reminded me of my own mother. Or rather, I should say, she possessed a kind of maternal spirit. And by *attractive*, I didn't mean in a sexual way. I had never loved a woman before. Love was forbidden in my line of work. In fact, I didn't even think it existed anymore. Still, there was an animal part of me I struggled to control. I wanted someone to take care of me. I was jealous of Max, especially in front of women. I hated the attention he attracted. He was so cold and nonchalant it baffled me that any woman would find him attractive. But the root cause was simple. They liked him more because they were all the same. If I acted the same way as he did, women would call me arrogant. Unfortunately, I didn't possess the innate qualities that would have people confuse arrogance with charm.

Naturally, Max managed to lure Magda's attention as soon as she moved away from the camera. The two of them had such great chemistry one might have mistaken them for a couple. Then again, maybe it was jealousy talking. She placed her palm on his back, just above the waist, knowing this would make him feel special. Come to think of it, she did this to every man she encountered, friend or not. So perhaps their relationship wasn't so special. In any case, she approached me after making small talk with Max, holding a mystery in her eyes. I tried to stay cool and pretended I didn't notice her, but a second later, I gave in. As soon as she was within reach, my lips curled into a big smile. I couldn't even remember what I'd said to her. I got so nervous. She didn't smile or do anything to make me feel better. There was no back-rubbing for me. Instead, she raised an eyebrow and whispered, "Good job back there!"

I was surprised. "Oh, that was nothing. I was just doing my job," I said with a sheepish smile.

"You stopped a terrorist attack on your first mission. That's pretty impressive!" she exclaimed, glancing around to make sure no one could overhear our conversation.

"I'm happy to be of service."

"We're happy to have you on the team!" she returned with glittering eyes. "You should also thank Max, if you haven't. He was the one who convinced us to bring you along."

I winced. "Oh, I, uh, didn't know that."

"Don't be shy! He may not want to admit it, but he likes you a lot. You guys make a good team. I see great things for you in the future."

The future. Feeling bold, I took a step closer to Magda and whispered in her ear, "I hope I'm now in the clear."

She looked puzzled. "In regards to what?" she asked, clearly feigning ignorance.

"You know, my situation."

"Oh, I understand. I believe they'll take that into account. We can trust the process."

Trust the process? I was getting annoyed. I had done so much already for the empire, probably more than anyone else, and they still couldn't give me the golden ticket. While my heart was thumping, I mustered enough courage to say, "I feel like I've proven myself." Tears almost surged to my eyes.

"I'm sure you do, and you have every right to feel that way. Walk with me."

As I followed her into the rose garden, a young man walked past Magda and handed her a black briefcase. It looked identical to the one Andre had given me, except the handles were red instead of gray. With the camera crew behind us, we found a quiet spot next to a lake with lily pads. A black-winged angel stood behind Magda.

"Look," she said with a sigh, "I know how you feel. I was in your position once. I know you're feeling a lot of pressure. It can be a lot to process—"

"Even with everything I've done, my CFT has barely moved. At this rate, I'll be replaced," I said, blushing as my eyes got wet with anger and desperation. "I'm not asking for special treatment, just what I've earned."

"You have nothing to worry about," she said, setting the briefcase on the ground. "Oh, please don't cry, my dear. You have so much to be proud of. We know how special you are. Here." She handed me a handkerchief.

I felt like such a fool. I had never felt so embarrassed. I wanted to tear my head right off my neck. I hated her so much for making me break down like this. I refused the handkerchief.

"All right, I'll make you a deal," Magda said. "Once you complete the assignment, we'll fast-track your graduation. How does that sound?"

I almost said no just to spite her. Instead, I came to my senses. "I—I don't know what to say."

"Oh, honey, you can say thank you."

"Thank you," I said with a sweet little smile.

"Here's All-Mother's gift. Please take good care of it."

She handed me the briefcase.

"It's pretty heavy."

"Well, the All-Mother is very generous."

"So the guest really has no idea?"

"No, of course not. This will be a surprise."

"Who came up with the idea?"

"You're looking at her."

"You're pretty good."

"Why, thank you!"

"Fast-track."

"Uh-huh. Now, be a good boy, okay?"

How condescending.

"I'll hold you to your word," I said.

As she winked at me, Anthony came wheeling Mr. Pulcher toward us. The old man's head was draped in a white cloth. Anthony announced in a solemn voice, "The guests are here. Mr. Pulcher needs you now."

CHAPTER 34

A MAN OF WEALTH AND TASTE

JASON

My first impression of Magnus was that he seemed a bit too old for his age. And while all deviants are like that to some degree, when I shook his hand, I felt something harsh and vengeful, like he had suffered through a lifetime of pain with nothing to show for it. I understood that well. Still, I couldn't parse out if it was the feeling that felt familiar or the person himself. Then again, how can a person exist without being felt?

When he said his name was Magnus, I obviously didn't believe him. This was no Magnus. A Magnus is someone tall and strong, capable of splitting a tree in half with his bare hands. It was clear he also didn't know what to make of me. He wanted to ignore me at first, perhaps thinking I was insignificant, just a servant. But when I introduced myself and asked him to follow me, he paused, as though stricken with fear, and looked up at my face. It felt like he was scared that I knew who he was, even though he wore a chastity mask. Speaking of the mask, it was one of the pricier models with a demon face and red muzzle, very suitable for Mr. Pulcher's taste. Just the right amount of savage. It was clear Mr. Pulcher was pleased. His right foot jerked up when he touched the deviant boy.

While Anthony wanted the deviants to come to Pulcher, Pulcher insisted on coming out to them. He had everything in the world but still insisted on being polite. All the same, he wanted people to see that he could indulge in his vices out in the open. It was a show of strength. Old people are generally shameless, but this man took it to a new level. He was so transgressive he wore his age as a badge of honor. Not only did he not care what other people thought of him, he played with their expectations. He was a trickster of the most unpredictable breed. In other words, his shamelessness was part of his genius. Just when you thought you had him figured out, a different side would emerge, and it would mess with the mind. He'd said to me, "Jason, I lie all the time. Everybody lies. The difference is that I don't try to justify myself. The moment you try to justify yourself, you've lost the battle. Ya know what I mean?" Frankly, I didn't know what he meant. Doesn't the act of lying require some form of justification? One has to justify to oneself that it's not a lie in order to say the lie with a straight face. The wonderful thing about Mr. Pulcher was that he never looked down on me. And I think that was because he was shameless. A shameless man doesn't fear what others say about him, and a fearless man has no use for prejudice. In a sense, he was a pure being, unencumbered by the weight of the world. He could be your best friend or your worst enemy. It all depended on how he was perceived. It was clear to me that the best course of action was to act if he were my friend. In return, he treated me like a kindred spirit. I was something he could mold.

No matter how deep his depravity went, Pulcher was a pious man. Watching the boy and girl, he projected the aura of a priest. Yes, he was a pervert, but he presented himself as a pious man, and that was all that mattered in our world. Presentation always surpassed the truth. And he could still wrestle respectability out of his perversion, which was deserving of praise. People who really knew him respected Pulcher for his performative sainthood. Myself included. They would often say behind his back, "Pulcher is a wonderful performer!" And this was never said in jest. We held him in high regard for his ability to pull a fast one over our eyes, and we loved him more and more every time he did.

"One vial per night, that's the deal; three vials max," he said, raising his right eyebrow. "Do you accept?"

The deviants remained silent. They seemed confused. They were shaking in their chairs.

"Master Pulcher is asking you a question," I said.

The boy was about to speak when Mr. Pulcher interrupted him.

"Now, before you respond, please know this is my final offer. Whether you say yes or no, you're required to stay for one night. Consider this a small price to pay for all the trouble we went through just to get you here. If you say yes, you can choose how long you stay. If your performance exceeds expectations, I may offer you a bonus vial. I know your little group needs all the help it can get."

"What service are you expecting of us?" asked the boy nervously, while the girl closed her hand into a fist.

"You sound civilized for a deviant, I like that," said Pulcher. "Did you finish university?"

"No."

"I like deviants who are educated. How old are you?"

"Nineteen."

"And your comrade?"

"She's eighteen."

Pulcher licked his lips. "Remind me, what's your name again?"

"Varya," she said.

"Were you abandoned as a child?"

She tensed up. "Yes," she said, her voice breaking.

"Do you feel lonely?"

She took a deep breath.

"Well, *I* feel lonely all the time," said Pulcher. Then, like a dog shaking off the doldrums of the day, he sat up in his chair and drove a comb through his slick, dark hair. "Magnus, you asked me what service I'm asking you to perform. I will not ruin the surprise by answering the question now. But let me say this: every deviant who has ever performed this service has gone on to do wonderful things in the world. Once you get on my good side, I won't let you go. I'm a man of my word. Which one of you will sign?"

The boy nodded at me, and I handed him a blue fountain pen. He signed the contract and pushed it back to Pulcher.

"We want the bonus vial," he snarled.

"We'll see what you're made of," replied Pulcher, shaking his head with contempt.

CHAPTER 35

IN THE BEDROOM

JASON

"May I propose a duel?" offered Anthony with a friendly smile.

"A duel?" Pulcher asked.

The major shivered, then replied, "Yes, your grace."

"In my bedroom?" Pulcher asked again.

Having been here a few times myself, I no longer needed to marvel at the size of Mr. Pulcher's bedroom. Needless to say, it was enormous.

"Your grace, I'm proposing a friendly match only, nothing violent," Anthony responded. "No blood will be drawn. All for your entertainment, sir."

Pulcher got up from his wheelchair and sat on the edge of his plush, enormous bed. Resting his head on the palm of his hand he appeared to fall into deep thought. He frowned like a man discarded by his friends. I could almost pity him.

"Who did you have in mind?" Pulcher asked, raising his head.

The major was pleasantly surprised. "I was thinking, your grace, if it pleases you, that we could invite Magnus and Max."

Max was leaning against the wall by the window when he heard his name called. He seemed displeased. As much as I wanted to see him suffer, I took up the opportunity to volunteer myself. The idea just came to me, without rhyme or reason.

"Let me play," I said, "I'll challenge Magnus, if Magnus agrees."

To my surprise, the demon-faced lad replied, "I accept your challenge."

"Very well," Mr. Pulcher agreed. He jumped up from his bed like a child and clapped his hands. "But, I want this contest to be real. No playacting. No make believe. I want to see some blood! First person who can draw blood from his opponent will receive an extra reward. Women, men, money, whatever you want. Say the word, and I'll grant your wish. But you have to give me a real fight. No cheating. I'll have the cheater sent to the gas chamber! You got that?"

You could see blood rushing to Pulcher's face. He was really getting into it.

"Yes, sir," I affirmed.

"And you, my sweet tribute, what do you say?" Pulcher asked Magnus, turning his voice into a sugary lather.

"I accept."

When I turned around, I caught Max looking at me with his arms crossed. "You sure about this, my apprentice?" he said.

Pulcher stormed in front of Max and slapped him across the face. "How dare you! Never question the courage of your men. Do you understand?"

Max was so shellshocked he couldn't speak.

"Do you understand?" Pulcher shouted again.

"Yes, your grace," Max answered, glaring with a kind of anger I'd never seen from him before.

"Good, good," said Pulcher, patting Max on the cheek a few times while trying to calm his breath. "I—I didn't mean to hit you, my child. Are you okay? Did I hurt you? Oh, good.

You can take it, can't you? A little pain does wonders to the psyche. Yes, yes, I know. Now, why don't you be a good boy and show them the weapons?"

"Yes, sir," Max responded, his face beet red.

Humiliated, Max dragged his feet toward the ivory showcase, above which a large oil painting featuring a wealthy couple hung on the wall. The male subject wore a red tabard, and his wife, in a green dress, was pregnant. There was a hexagonal mirror behind them, and I could see myself and the deviant boy reflected. My opponent had the unfair advantage of having his face concealed behind a mask. I wanted to see his eyes. I wanted to see him tremble with fear.

Below the painting was a small, round button camouflaged in the same milky white paint as the rest of the wall. Max pressed the button, and a long, wide drawer in the showcase snapped open. There were all manners of knives, chains, swords, handcuffs, and whips arranged under a glass panel. Pulcher was a man of taste. I took interest in the rapier with the ivory handle.

"May I?" I inquired, as I thought one should in a moment like this.

"Be my guest," said Pulcher with a chuckle.

Max had no other choice but to slide open the glass panel. He was in a sour mood. I took the rapier with my left hand and made a downward swipe to get a feel for its weight. If Max hadn't dodged in time, I could have slashed his right arm. He was none too happy about it, but what could he do? The master would set him straight.

Meanwhile, the deviant boy settled his grubby, little hands on the katana. A fitting choice, I thought, for someone whose whole existence was outlawed. But the moment he squared his shoulders, I knew he was no ordinary deviant. This wasn't the first time he had held a weapon. There was a natural poise to him, like he was used to being watched. He reminded me of someone I had seen on TV. I was just about to figure him out when he lunged at me in one quick stride, the sharp end of his katana flashing across my eyes. I swerved to my right, bumping into Max, who pushed me back into the arena. Stumbling back on the red carpet, I held my rapier up like a shield, deflecting two vicious blows overhead. I was far more skilled with a gun than a sword. I sidestepped, keeping my eyes on the deviant as he readied his katana with both hands for another strike.

"Who are you?" I asked, parrying his strike.

He refused to answer.

I stabbed at his foot, just barely missing his toe.

"Someone you know," he grunted.

"Then show yourself, take off your mask!"

Apparently, I touched a nerve. He brought his katana over his head with both hands and leaped toward me with such ferocity I could imagine my head splitting open. I froze. All of a sudden the future became clear. There would be no more groveling for acceptance, no more drifting in darkness. I closed my eyes and dropped my rapier. I opened my mouth to smile. No, I cackled. I was laughing at myself and this strange, little thing called life. Unfortunately, the deviant boy didn't have the courage to finish me off. When I opened my eyes, I was annoyed to find his katana landing just an inch to my right, barely missing my shoulder. He was groaning as if he were the one being beaten down. I hated him even more. He reminded me of the timidity of every deviant I had ever known. The timidity of a people ostracized for so long they can no longer tell the difference between being kind and being weak. I needed to teach him a lesson. I needed to prove to myself that I was better than the labels my people had suffered. I drew a deep breath and drove my knee into the delicate part of his ribs, sending him rolling away from the edge of the carpet.

Pulcher and the boys hollered.

Flushed with adrenaline, I lunged at my prey, aiming the sharp edge of my rapier at his throat. I knew I couldn't kill him. Mr. Pulcher had to be satisfied first. Still, the thought of killing a fellow deviant drove me crazy. The fantasy was so overwhelming I found myself unable to stop the motion from completing itself. Right as my rapier was about to pierce the deviant's throat, he pulled the carpet from under my feet and threw me off balance. Rolling back to his feet, he chased after me, picked up his katana with his left hand, and slashed my shoulder. I was too enthralled by this display of violence that I laughed when blood sprayed from my open wound. The only thing I felt was the rush of ecstasy. I felt alive!

Falling to my knees, I looked up at my fellow deviant with the edge of his katana shivering half an inch from my neck.

"Well done!" Pulcher shouted. "Well done, my boy!"

"He cheated, Master!" I protested.

"Oh, don't be a loser," Pulcher said. "He beat you fair and square!"

"But, Master, he pulled the carpet—"

"And he beat you. He beat you!" Pulcher repeated like a maniac, wiping the sweat from his forehead. He approached the deviant boy until he could smell the dripping sweat on the boy's face. He inhaled and kissed him on the cheek, whispering, "Drop the blade."

The deviant boy retracted his katana and dropped it to the floor.

I stood up, blood seeping through my fingers as I held my right shoulder.

"And you." Pulcher turned to me. "You performed admirably as well. I'd say to give yourself a pat on the back, but it doesn't seem like you can." He was so self-absorbed he burst out laughing at his own stupid joke.

As soon as I followed his example and laughed at myself, Pulcher's face tightened up. As noted, psychopaths can change on a dime. Everyone fell silent.

"Magnus, tell me something; when did you turn into a deviant?" Pulcher asked.

The boy took a step back to avoid smelling the old man's breath. The old man chased by taking a step forward. He was right in the boy's face again.

"Really, I want to know," he said.

"I don't remember," the boy said.

"Really? You don't remember?"

"Is this part of the test?"

"There's no test. I'm just asking a simple question."

"I'm a seraph. I was born a seraph."

"Ah! So you do know the answer."

"But I'm not a deviant."

"Yes, you are. All seraphs are deviants. Savages, perverts, miscreants, rats! That's what you are."

"I beg to differ."

Pulcher snickered. "Do you still have your wings?"

The boy didn't answer.

"Number Eleven, come here," Pulcher said. I hadn't heard myself referred to that way since I'd enlisted in the Syndicate. While my instinct told me to resist, the name already took its toll. I obeyed, like a good little dog.

"Sir." I stepped forward to face my master.

"You can have your revenge," he said, revealing a black-and-white stun baton. "And we'll see if he's telling the truth."

I took the baton and smiled. It was cold to the touch. Meanwhile, he approached the deviant girl and handed her a stun baton as well.

"Take it," Pulcher said.

When the girl refused, he slapped her across the face.

"Take it," he said again.

Reluctantly, the girl took the baton. Right when she did, Pulcher grabbed her hand and forced her thumb over the dial, pushing it up until electricity started churning between the metal tubes.

CHAPTER 36

THE POWER OF FAITH

JASON

"I used to believe in God," said Pulcher. "I know that's a blasphemous thing to say, but I can be honest with who I am, right?"

No one said a word.

"Now, imagine their shock when our founders discovered angels in real life. Real life! For tens of thousands of years, man has dreamed about meeting our maker, and one day, the dream comes true. What then? What does a man do when his dream comes true? Is he redeemed? Does he bow down and live in fear?" Pulcher poked his baton into my chest. "Does he?"

"No," I answered.

He smirked with the mischievous grin of a child. "When our founders came to Carthage, the angels really thought we were offering them a gift. How could they be so gullible? There we were, refugees with nowhere else to go, our home planet razed to the ground by atom bombs, our whole species on the verge of extinction, and we still had the audacity to exterminate the aliens. Behold the Ark, our new God!"

Pulcher broke down and cackled. He was so deliriously aroused by his own words he started choking on his spit. The feeling was infectious, and I couldn't restrain myself anymore and mimicked his guttural reaction. Pulcher appreciated my flattery and wrapped his thick arm around my neck. For a moment, he was my friend.

"God himself is a psychopath," I proclaimed, "so why should *we* be any different?"

"Careful there, my friend," Pulcher said, "you don't want God to know that!"

We burst out laughing, although I had no clue why I was supposed to laugh. I half expected Pulcher to kiss me on the cheek and tell me how much he enjoyed my company. But no such thing happened. His arm weighed down on my neck like a python, squeezing the air out of me. The more I tried to escape, the more pressure he applied. With a crooked grin, he jabbed his baton against my stomach with more force than I could have expected. When I braced, he finally pushed me out of his hold.

"All right now, enough playing around," he said. "Let's get to it."

I insisted on playing along to show that I was ready for the big league. "We should have him take off the mask," I said. "I want to look him in the eyes."

"Why?" Pulcher asked.

I was stumped by the question. I didn't expect him to ask me why. "Because I... think it'll be more enjoyable."

"For me or for you?"

"For you, sir."

"So you know what I like without asking me first?"

"I'm sorry... I just assumed..."

"The mistake you made is that you still think of this thing as human," Pulcher lectured, breathing faster as he picked out a pair of scissors from the weapons cache. "Hold him down."

For a second, I thought he was referring to me.

The girl shrieked.

Max walked over and latched his big hand over the boy's shoulder. The boy didn't resist. He laughed.

"What, you think this is funny?" Pulcher asked, still panting.

The boy kept laughing.

"Hold him down!" Pulcher shouted at me.

I shook off my stupor and grabbed the boy by the other shoulder, holding him down, just like Max did.

"Now, I want you to watch," Pulcher grunted, as he slid the scissor under the deviant's shirt and sliced it open from top to bottom. He tore the shirt to shreds and scattered them to the floor, leaving the boy's torso exposed. He pointed his baton at the slits on the boy's back. "Do you see? What we have here is not a human being. You got that? Savages have no feelings. We can do whatever we want with them. Do you understand?"

"Yes, sir," I answered.

"Close your heart to the pain," Pulcher instructed, as he electrified his baton and jammed it into the boy's waist, causing the boy's entire body to convulse. The boy screamed.

"Now, it's your turn," Pulcher said, turning to the girl. "Don't just stand there, participate!"

"No," the girl said.

"No?" Pulcher retorted. "No? What do you mean 'no?' *You* volunteered. No one forced you to be here."

"I can do something else, if you like…" The girl approached Pulcher, stabbing her baton into his chest. The electric shock didn't cause even the slightest reaction. He seemed impervious to pain.

"No, Varya," the boy muttered. "Please, don't…"

"Aha! You have feelings for him, don't you?"

"And what if I do?" she returned in a devilish voice.

"Ooh, you're something else!" Pulcher belted. He grabbed the girl's wrist and jammed her electrified baton into the boy's chest, causing another violent scream. "You like that, don't you? You want to feel that again? Yeah?" This time, Pulcher forced the girl to shock the boy in the jaw. The baton slipped from her hand, and she tumbled to the floor.

"Varya!" the boy muttered through clenched teeth. His cold sweat now coated my hand and arm. I could smell his fear.

"You heard that, miss? Your boyfriend is calling for you," said Pulcher. "He's quite a looker, isn't he?" He swallowed his spit and nodded at me. "Now you do it too."

This was my moment to shine. With Max holding down the boy by the neck, I stabbed the boy in the back with my baton. The electricity ran wild over his sweat-covered body. His back arched. His head and legs quivered. He could barely move his neck.

"How does it feel?" Pulcher asked, closing in on my face. I could smell his rancid breath.

"Feels good," I said.

"Yeah?"

"Yeah, feels good."

"Then do it again!"

When I hit him again, a pair of spiky, black wings burst through the slits on his back. I dodged just in time to avoid being stabbed in the eyes, but the spikes still caught my forehead, and blood ran down my nose.

Pulcher started laughing maniacally. "Look at you! He got you good!"

I was so embarrassed I smeared my blood all over my face. This made Pulcher laugh even harder.

"Behold the savage!" I heard Pulcher shout in between intense bouts of flaring pain.

The boy stood over me with his ugly, bat-like wings spread open, and a thick, mucus-like liquid dripping over the edge of them.

"Do you see now, my apprentice? You've been deceived all along. There's nothing *divine* about this creature. He's just an animal, and an ugly one at that. Can you believe all those fanatics were fawning over a beast like this? They've lost their goddamn minds." Then, with a sweet, agonizing smile, Pulcher offered his hand to me. I took it and got up, one hand still covering my bleeding face.

"We can give them what they want," he said, "an eye for an eye. What do you say?"

I nodded.

Screaming, the girl swung at the old man, who calmly caught the baton, purple sparks ablaze, and popped it out of her hand. Max kicked the boy in the back of the knee, and the boy collapsed face-first on the carpet. Sitting on the boy's neck with one knee, Max grabbed the left wing by the stalk and unsheathed his sword.

The girl screamed even louder.

I wished I hadn't looked. Even Anthony walked away.

But in truth, I couldn't resist. I felt myself transforming as I closed my heart to the boy's pain. I was growing stronger. I no longer needed to look him in the eyes. All I needed was the satisfaction of knowing that he would forever be deformed.

CHAPTER 37

THE RIGHT TO SUFFER

MARCUS

When I woke up in the middle of the night, the dirty old man was gone. I was alone in his bedroom, naked and sweating. I was too ashamed of myself to even remember the pain. It went by in a flash, or perhaps it didn't even happen at all. Hell was real. There I was, abused, tormented, maimed, and somehow still breathing. Either I was lucky or God hated me. The last thing I needed was the compulsion to feel sorry for myself, but that was how I felt. I wanted to cry or scream, anything to ease the pain. I wanted the world to suffer what I had suffered but was completely powerless to do anything about it. Perhaps this was how deviants felt all the time. Still, this understanding, if one could call it that, offered me no peace. If anything, it caused me to sink deeper into a state of depression. I was burning in a swamp of my own making. Yes, I blamed myself. How could I not? It was my choice to come here. It was my choice to join the cult. It was my choice to become the monster that I was now. The more I agonized, the more I remembered. Not just the torture but the callous contempt of it all. I clutched my head with both hands, trying to squeeze my eyes out of their sockets. How far had I fallen! I used to be the one looking down on the world, and now, I was beneath everyone. No one wanted me anymore. Maybe I deserved it. Could this be God's way of punishing me?

When I tried getting up, I felt dizzy, and my vision blurred. I was hearing voices. Then I heard music, classical piano, strident but diffused, like the player was getting mad for playing the notes incorrectly. I found an elegant black suit hanging over the footboard and a beret on the nightstand. They all happened to be my size. Someone was thinking about me.

When I looked in the mirror, I realized I was still wearing my chastity mask. I explored the holes on the muzzle with my tongue, trying to remember how things tasted. If someone saw me on the street, they would've mistaken me for a deviant. The prince was gone. In a fit of self-loathing, I tore off the mask and threw it on the floor. Instead, I put on the army beret.

As I did, I remembered that I was here for a reason. I had made a promise to someone I cared for, and I intended on keeping that promise. I couldn't believe my luck when I found a vial of Euphoria inside the first drawer I opened. Not only that, when I plunged the vial into my pocket, I found something else quite curious: a revolver.

I was no stranger to weapons. Holding this cold little gun awakened in me some passing memory of childhood, of Father, and sanctimonious lectures about good and evil. I hated God, not for personal reasons but because he never appealed to me. But now, for some reason, and this was the feeling that always preceded a revelation, I could see him standing there, somewhere behind my eyes. Even when I aimed this revolver at him, he stood firm. It was then, during this moment of absolute standstill, that I heard a familiar voice echo in my head: "All for revenge."

No doubt, it was the Philosopher. How could I ever forget him? He was the man who had opened my mind to a different reality, one in which I was trapped in this very moment. But he couldn't be… No, I must be confusing the two. There was no way someone so twisted could take his crown.

"Kill them all."

When I opened the door, I found myself in the middle of a long hallway that stretched in both directions, seemingly without end. The art deco patterns, a perennial favorite of high-minded elites, added to this illusion, which also made my head spin. Where was Pulcher? And Claudia? This didn't feel right.

Revenge, what a grand concept.

I grabbed the revolver with the resolve of a hunter. When the thought of murdering Pulcher passed over my eyes, I found myself standing in front of a door painted red and slightly open, behind which a heated conversation was taking place. I was still very delirious and hearing multiple voices in my head, some I could recognize, some completely alien. The first words that struck me came from the woman I loved:

"Will this be the last time I see you?" Claudia asked longingly.

The man who responded to her was the gruff inquisitor who had executed my mutilation. So he was the Philosopher's son. What a farce. Everyone just had to stand in my way. *Listen to these two lovebirds.* It was absolutely disgusting.

"You can still say no," said Max.

"I can't…"

"Why not?"

"Because—"

"Don't let me talk you into it."

"No, that's not what I mean."

"We can still leave."

"Stop it."

"I love you."

"I love you too."

"Where's the briefcase?"

"Are you sure?"

There was a moment of dead silence. I pressed my ear to the door, getting more and more anxious. I was filled with dread, hot-blooded, envious dread. It overpowered me to the point of driving all the blood to my face, and I could feel my eyes and mouth burning.

"Here…"

"This is the real one?" Claudia asked nervously.

"Yes. The bomb will go off when you open the briefcase. Come here. Are you scared?"

"That's a stupid question. Of course I'm scared, Max."

"Does Marcus know?"

"No. I never told him."

"That's good."

"Is it? He's my friend. He saved my life. Doesn't he deserve—"

"No! He's not one of us. Never will be. *We* made the pledge. You and I. *We* are the same."

"Max…"

"Give me a kiss before you go."

Through the narrow opening, I could see Claudia bending over Max as they tumbled into the bed. Even if I could swallow my pride and set aside my feelings for Claudia, I couldn't allow her to sacrifice her life. And for what? The man was clearly using her, just like the Philosopher had. All the men in Claudia's life wanted to manipulate her for their own selfish gain, and she was blind to all of it. They didn't care for her at all. If a man truly loved a woman, he would never allow any harm to come to her. He would put his own body on the line to save her, not the opposite.

I kicked open the door. Before either of them could say a word, I pointed the gun at Max's head.

"Marcus?" Claudia shouted in embarrassment. Her eyes had never looked so enchanting. I wanted to taste her tears and pay back the pain she had suffered a thousand times over. "What are you doing here?"

"I'm here to save you," I announced boldly, like a knight.

If I weren't holding a gun in my hand, Claudia would have chuckled at my outlandish display of gallantry.

"From what?" she asked, her voice shaking.

"This man," I said, filled with righteous anger. How could she be so blind? "He's evil. He's using you."

"So this is the One. You're smaller than I thought."

"Is that the best you got?"

The man was so insolent he kissed Claudia on the forehead as he stood, zipping up his pants. Slithering cautiously like a reptile, this man had to be the most insidious creature I had ever witnessed. He was even more despicable than Pulcher. At least Pulcher was honest about what he was. Max, on the other hand, was determined to deceive to his very last breath.

"Have you gone insane?" he asked, grinning at me. "Do you know who I am?"

"I don't care who you are!"

He snickered. "I understand that it must feel horrible to realize that your whole life has been a lie. Talk about being used!"

"Max!" Claudia protested. The man she professed to love gave her a hard, patronizing glance, and she fell silent.

"Look who's talking," I retorted.

"And what are you accusing me of, exactly?"

"You're not going to argue your way out of this, Max."

"Do you see now, my love? This is who he is. He can't help it. He's always going to look down on people like us. He'll never be your prince charming."

"At least I'm not a monster…"

Claudia tried to reason with me. "Marcus, Max is a good man. He's a deviant, like us. He's doing what is needed for our cause. He's been with us since day one. You can trust him!"

"Trust him to take your life away?"

Claudia shook her head. "No, that's my decision to make."

"He decided for you!"

"Don't be so naive, little one," Max said. "You have much to learn."

"Claudia…," I urged. "Can't you see he's taking advantage of you?"

Claudia ignored me.

"Give me the gun," Max ordered. "Playtime is over."

I clutched my revolver tighter.

"Give me the gun. I won't ask you another—"

He didn't have to ask twice. I shot him. I watched the bullet enter his forehead and come out through the other side, creating a hole in the wall, his blood splattering all over the bed and Claudia's face. He collapsed, gazing at me with aching intensity, as if he was about to divulge the secrets of the universe. I closed my heart to the pain and felt a surge of satisfaction when his body hit the floor.

CHAPTER 38

FATAL ATTRACTION

MARCUS

"What have you done!" Claudia screamed, cradling Max's limp head. "How could you do this?"

"We have to leave!" I shouted. I didn't know what else to say. I certainly wasn't going to express any remorse. No, not anymore.

"Are you—" She struggled to put words together. She caught herself on the verge of cursing at me, then thought better of it, and for a moment, I saw in her eyes a glimmer of hope. No, it was probably relief. "How could you! You killed him! You murdered an innocent man!" She strained her voice so much it nearly splintered into a sarcastic laugh. I wanted to comfort her but thought better of it.

"Stay with me, Max!" she shouted to the man she claimed to have loved.

"I'm sorry! I didn't mean to—"

"How could you?"

"I'm sorry, Claudia, but I won't let you sacrifice yourself for someone else."

"Get away from me! Don't touch me. Get away!" She flung her arm at me as I reached to comfort her.

"It's over," I declared. "The nightmare's over."

"What? Are you mad?" Claudia's tears mixed with her lover's blood.

"The nightmare's over. We can leave now."

"What happened to you, Marcus?"

"He's not innocent. He took you hostage."

"That's ridiculous. He loved me!"

"He was going to lead you to your demise, and you were going to let him. I did you a favor."

"You're unbelievable."

"Claudia, you know I'm right. You know in your heart that the mission is just another lie."

"No, you're wrong."

"You know he abused your faith. He made you think you loved him when you don't."

"How do you know what *I* feel?"

"Stop lying to yourself!"

Claudia turned reddish pale. She stared at me for a second, her blood-smeared face burning with rage. She wanted to speak, but her lips only trembled. If she had the revolver, she would probably have shot me. But some reservation lingered in her eyes, and when she glanced sideways at the bed, I knew she had lost her mind. I took off after her and managed to reach the briefcase before she could. She was really going to do it. She was going to kill us both. With tears streaming down her face, she clawed at my arms, fighting desperately to keep her pride. What had happened to us was a tragedy. I couldn't blame her. Neither of us could do anything about it. We were just trying to survive. It wasn't Max she loved but the thought of being free. All her life she had been searching for a greater cause to believe in. She saw herself as one with all the oppressed people in the world, even when the very people she fought for decided to betray her. It was blind allegiance, and she knew it. But even if she hated me for the rest of her life, I would be glad to know that she lived.

I took the briefcase and threw it out the window. We watched it fall into the beautiful courtyard below. In the moment I let go, Claudia shrieked as if she were losing a child. Then came the explosion, which rocked the entire mansion, sending shards of glass and dust bursting through the blown-out windows. As we braced for cover, I took Claudia into my arms. Even as her eyes resisted, she held me tightly. She was still fighting her instinct, but her instinct was beginning to win over. The evil roar of the explosion sent our hearts fluttering. My body pulsed with lust as we stared into each other's eyes. We were afraid of each other, at some level, and this fear, smeared with the blood of revenge, turned into a fatal kind of attraction. In that moment, we realized that we were bound by destiny to be together.

The three words I wanted to hear from her did not come to pass. Instead, she whispered, "This isn't over."

"I know."

"I'll never forgive you."

"I know."

"I'm sorry about what happened."

"Me too."

I showed her the vial of pure Euphoria.

I wanted to believe that the Claudia I knew was back. I had walked so close to the precipice of losing her that I could still feel the wind of hell blowing against my hair. Before we left the room, she bent down over her lover's dead body, kissed him one last time on the forehead, and threw the bedsheet over him.

"I'll come back for you one day, my love," she said.

I believed her.

There was an outburst of commotion down in the court-yard. A loud alarm went off. The sound was so piercing I felt like someone was stabbing my temples.

"I think Pulcher wanted this to happen," Claudia suddenly remarked, casting a stealthy glance at my revolver. I tucked the revolver away. "He must've planned the whole thing."

We rushed down the hallway.

"He must've known who you are the whole time."

"How do you know?"

"I don't, just my gut instinct."

As we were about to round the corner, streaks of flashing, white lights danced over the opposite wall. Syndicate soldiers. They were coming for us.

"There's another way," Claudia whispered, opening the door to our right with a red, diamond-shaped key that Max must have given her. I sneaked into the room as the pungent smell of old books rushed into my nose.

It was a grand library that rivaled the size and volume of my father's collection, and the leather covers and red-oak bookshelves were all neatly arranged but rarely used. The books were very much beside the point. It was the display of luxury that mattered. As the devil might say, *I'm a man of wealth and taste*. But wealth wasn't enough; Pulcher, just like my father, came from that generation of monarchs who prided themselves on being intimate with history. Not under-standing history, just being close to it. Then they could brag to everyone about how sophisticated they were, without ever needing to care about traditional values. Gazing upon the tower of books, I was reminded of something Pulcher had once said to me: "The future is already written."

"If Pulcher can see the future," I said to Claudia, "wouldn't that make him a deviant too?"

"He doesn't need to see the future," Claudia replied, as she searched for some secret contraption behind one of the bookshelves. And then, after running her palm over a row of books, she found the one she was looking for. She nudged the book inward by the spine, and something clicked. The bookshelf snapped open, allowing Claudia to pull it toward us, revealing a secret passageway.

The feeling of déjà vu didn't hit me until we were deep in the underground tunnel, which was well-lit with white light bulbs, like some kind of excavation site.

"It's happening again," I mumbled.

"What did you say?"

"I said, it's happening again."

"What is?"

"Just a feeling."

"What do you see?" Claudia turned intensely curious.

"Nothing, it's just a bad feeling."

Claudia paused to inspect my face. "You look like you just saw a ghost."

"I think you might be right."

I wasn't sure if Claudia got my joke, but she didn't laugh. She furled her brows like she was pondering the great mysteries of life.

"Do you feel different on the inside?"

"I don't know. I feel like I'm an impostor."

"Everyone's an impostor," Claudia said.

Footsteps rumbled overhead.

"Where does the tunnel lead?" I asked.

"Outside, to the forest behind the estate."

"Why would he build something like this?"

"Every psychopath has a plan B in case people turn on them, which makes sense, given all the horrible things they've done."

"If they're so afraid of payback, maybe they should treat people better in the first place."

"Well, they wouldn't be psychopaths in the first place, would they?"

I saw compassion in Claudia's eyes, but this compassion was hardened by a strange form of hatred. We both found our situation somewhat laughable. For much of the rest of the way, we were silent. The commotion above seemed to have died down by the time we reached the end of the tunnel, where we found a steel ladder leading up to the surface. With the moonlight pouring down over Claudia's hair, she looked positively angelic. It struck me then that I still didn't know what special gift she possessed. I was too nervous to ask again.

"How long do you think the revolution will last?"

"As long as it takes," she responded with a smirk as she clambered up the ladder.

"You seem to enjoy war a lot more than me," I said.

"You'll learn to like it too."

"I hope not too much."

It was so wonderfully strange, standing in the open with the pristine grass all around, to know that somewhere nearby a revolution was raging, and a nation of lunatics were out for blood. Sinking into the horizon, Pulcher's mansion seemed like a lost memory destined to fade away, just like everything else in the world. Maybe nothing extraordinary ever happened. I glanced at Claudia, apparently struck by the same epiphany. If I still had both my wings, I would take her with me and fly into the clouds. How amazing it would be to see the world from above!

Then came a hoarse cry from behind the darkness cloaking the forest, and a small, childish figure clad in a hooded, red robe came galloping toward us.

"Marcus! Claudia! It's me!"

It was Dante! I was so happy to see him I was almost trampled by his black steed. He jumped down from the saddle and threw himself into our embrace. I couldn't believe it.

"Dante!" I shouted.

"Master!" he answered. Never had a word meant so much to me.

"How did you find us?"

His aching black eyes shone brightly in the moonlight. His face looked pale as ever. His little head bobbed as he inhaled a few times trying to find the energy to speak.

"Slow down," Claudia urged.

"I could sense your pain," Dante said, finding his words after calming his breath. "It hurt me even more than the blight itself. I needed to find you."

Claudia tilted her head in gentle disapproval. "I told you not to come. You should be resting. What if you—God! How can I live with myself if something happened to you?"

"I know," Dante said, brushing Claudia's hair like he was her father. Then he confessed with a playful smile, gazing down at his hands, palms up, "I've never choked someone to death before."

"What? Are you hurt?" Claudia followed, almost shocked by how nonchalant Dante seemed to be.

"Just some Syndicate scum," Dante said with a childish giggle. I found the remark rather funny, but Claudia wasn't pleased.

"Take this," I said to Dante, handing him the vial of Euphoria.

His face lit up. "You got this for me?" he asked, like he was accepting a gift.

"Yes, for you," I said with a smile.

He uncorked the vial and squeezed every last drop into his eyes. Blood began returning to his face, chasing away the paleness and brushing it with a spirited, reddish glow. I could see sparks of fire igniting in his pores. I was almost afraid that his power might burst through again, but fortunately, he managed to compose himself and center his mind. The boy was saved, at least for now. I knew the effect would be temporary. Then again, so was everything in the world.

"How do you feel?" I asked.

"Alive," Dante answered, as tears rushed to his eyes. "Thank you! Thank you for saving my life!"

"It's what you'd do for us," I said, giving him a warm hug.

"What did they do to you?" Dante asked nervously.

I was too embarrassed to say. "I'm all right," I said. "I've had worse days."

"I heard you scream," Dante said, glancing toward my back. He seemed to know about the mutilation. "What they've done to you is pure evil. I'll kill them! I'll kill them all!" His pupils opened wide with fiery plumes whirling inside.

"Dante, look at me," Claudia said.

The boy peered into Claudia's eyes.

"Yes, good," she said. "Remember the mission. We'll have our revenge but not today."

"So you changed your mind?" Dante said. "You'll stay with us now?"

"Marcus convinced me to stay."

"We have to stick together," said Dante, putting on the air of a general. "The Philosopher isn't always right, he said so himself. We have to make up our own minds."

"Since when did *you* become the Philosopher?" Claudia said.

"I was born with it, my friend," he said.

We all had a good laugh.

Claudia suddenly winced and cried out in pain, moving both hands over the left side of her stomach. Sensing her distress, Dante placed his hands over hers.

"What's wrong?" I asked.

"I don't know," Claudia said. "I think I heard something pop."

"Let me see," Dante said.

Claudia turned pale. She lifted her shirt, terrified of what she might discover.

"See, you're okay," Dante said, finding her skin intact. Claudia was surprised but not fully convinced. She pressed her index finger into a particular spot in her flesh, trying to find the source of her pain. When she pressed a little too hard, she winced again, and the black horse neighed and reared.

A wintry gust blew overhead. Then the ground rumbled, beaten alive by the tapping and clattering thud of hoofs. When Dante approached his horse to calm the beast, a bullet whistled past my ear, striking Claudia in the very spot where she had felt the pain.

"Claudia!" I shouted. I ran over and pulled her to the ground. A firestorm of bullets erupted overhead. The black steed was struck down.

They were toying with us.

The shooting quickly stopped, and a troop of riders emerged from the shadows and flew into the open plain. They were clad in black suits, wearing the red demon mask and upside-down cross. I recognized their leader at once—my old brother.

He was delighted to see my true face.

So this was how the world would end.

Dante stepped in front me. I could feel the heat radiating from his body.

"No," I said to him, "don't let my suffering be in vain."

A crazed, senseless smile came over Claudia, as if she had wanted to say she was right all along. I was about to give her a final nod when I felt a hard crack on the back of my skull.

CHAPTER 39

A WORD FROM OUR SPONSOR

JASON

I was on my way to meeting Mr. Conrad when I got the call. Magda delivered the message. She was very affected. I was alone in the dressing room staring at my face in the mirror when she asked me how I was holding up. I wanted to laugh and cry at the same time. I was on the verge of realizing my dream, and the last thing I wanted was to be dragged into the past. Any time something sad happened, I'd get confused. How was I supposed to react? How would a psychopath react? And what if the sad news brought joy instead of pain? Did we always have to feign sadness just to appear classy? I had these questions swirling in my head the whole time Magda was talking. I couldn't really hear her beyond my thoughts. I needed to get away. Destiny was calling me on the other side. Every time Magda paused to check on me, I'd mumble with my lips closed to allow some guttural sound to pass through. I couldn't think of any words to say. This actually produced the effect I wanted to convey: I was so emotionally distressed by the news I could barely speak.

"You can cry, if you want," she purred.

I exhaled. "A man doesn't cry."

"I've seen a lot of men come to terms with their emotions. Especially in times of grief. The more you practice, the better you get at it, like everything else."

"Thank you for the encouragement. May I go now? Mr. Conrad is waiting for me."

"He can wait a bit longer, young man," replied Magda. "Do you not have any manners? I just told you that your partner died, and you can't even have the decency to say sorry?"

"What should I be sorry for?"

"George Stanton was an upstanding servant leader for the empire, and he put his life on the line for you. For *you*, Jason, and you should be grateful."

"I thought I should be sorry."

"God! Have we created a monster?"

"If I say yes," I said in my feminine falsetto, "would that make you feel better?"

Magda went silent. I could hear her rhythmic breathing, which I suspected was done on purpose. I let the silence steep. A few seconds later, she reemerged from the darkness and whispered, "Do you want to know how he died?"

She knew this would get my attention.

"Tell me the whole story," I said.

"He died because of you," said Magda.

I had a sense of where she was going with this, and it didn't sit well.

"That's the whole story?"

"Where were you that night?"

"I didn't kill George, if that's what you're asking."

A knock came on the door. "Five minutes, Mr. Freeman," said the assistant.

"I gotta go," I said to Magda. "Let's have this conversation later."

"I'll call off the appearance if you refuse to cooperate. Charlie's on our payroll. We decide what gets aired."

"Charlie Conrad may be a mouthpiece, but you don't control him."

"Jason—"

"Now, why would I do such a horrible thing?" I said, putting on my feminine voice again. "I liked George. He was nice to me."

"Your lack of compassion isn't helping."

"Wait, did you just accuse me of being a psychopath?"

"Don't get smart with me, kid. If you lose me, you lose everything."

"Is that a threat?"

"You better believe it."

Sliding my index finger over the fake-leather handle on the briefcase, I said, "Maybe the All-Mother will feel differently."

Magda scoffed. "Be careful what you wish for."

* * *

I kept having conversations with myself in my head. This was never a good sign. Every time I tried to remember my lines for the show, my mind would drift to the night of the murder. I wished I could have been the one pulling the trigger. I had set up everything so nicely! But I also kept telling myself: *You don't always have to do the dirty work yourself. You should learn to appreciate the process more.* A true psychopath would savor laying down the trap for someone else to take the fall. Guess I still wasn't sophisticated enough. Still, I'd grown so attached to the old man that I found myself, even if just for a passing moment, hankering to hear his praise more than getting famous on national television.

In times like this, I needed restraint more than anything else. Yes, Magda's words did rattle me, but I kept telling myself that it was good to be rattled. I would be more careful this way. If she hadn't called, I might have done something foolish. Magda was right: one wrong move could cost me everything.

I shook the assistant's hand carefully, not wanting him to pick up on the stress I was feeling. He kept making eye contact with me as if trying to fish for buried secrets. What did he know? He was just a lackey, like me. We had our roles to serve, and that was the end of it.

I treated him nicely but avoided small talk. I smiled, patted him on the back, showed him more respect than he deserved. This is how rich people treat servants. I was a fast learner.

"Mr. Conrad doesn't like surprises," he reminded me, giving me a sharp side glance as we walked down the carpeted hallway toward the guest room. As far as I could tell, the whole studio seemed closed off. There were no open windows. The air inside smelled like old socks. It was a miracle we managed to breathe.

"Did you hear what I said?" the assistant chased.

I almost said, "Really, a comedian doesn't like surprises?" But instead, I said, "Yes, I'll stick to the script."

"Will you hand me the briefcase?"

I complied. He swiped the briefcase and nodded at the secretary sitting behind a large oval desk. She picked up the cradle phone on the desk and mumbled. We stood on the red, mold-ridden carpet, glancing around, pretending to be occupied. The assistant didn't tell me what was happening and kept checking his watch. He was very careful not to show the full watch face, pulling up his cuff quickly, then sliding it back down, but I still managed to catch a glimpse of crimson hues. Clearly, I wasn't the only one feeling stressed.

We were on the top floor of the building. The atrium was flanked by fake Roman columns with fake vines crawling on them. The red carpet was faded and dirty, the fake-leather cushions were breaking apart at the seams, the people sitting on them anxious and petty, their eyes shifty and constantly cooking up some new scheme. I supposed I wasn't good enough to admire these people, at least not yet. I wanted to get inside their minds so I could fit in better. This whole place felt like a setup, and in a way, it was liberating. No one would care if you lied. Say you stabbed someone here, the blood would just get absorbed into the red carpet, and some custodian would come and take away the body, throw it into the ocean, scrub the carpet clean, and it'd be like the whole thing never happened. If you can get away with anything, there's nothing you can't accomplish. Thinking like this got me in a better mood, and I flashed a grin at the assistant. He looked away. *Fine. I don't care about you either.*

From the corner of my eye I caught a flash of light and looked up to find that the domed ceiling was made of glass, and the clouds were bursting at the seams. The thunder in the foothills must have been rumbling again, but I couldn't hear anything inside. I approached the window and gazed at the city below. The parade streamed onto Broadway Street, converging with throngs of city folks and foreign visitors gathered in Union Park. There were floats of giant cats, buddhas dressed in suits, bygone heroes, ancient astronauts, and wild dancers barely dressed. In fact, I think some of them were naked. The parents didn't mind. There were no Christmas symbols, and the greens never mixed with the reds. The All-Mother wanted religion to be purged, and she had done a damn good job of it. The only acceptable godhead was the buddha, which was never much of a god to begin with. He was merely asking for a break from all the suffering we needed to endure. That wasn't very saintly of him.

"If God didn't exist," I suddenly heard a familiar voice say, "it would be necessary to invent him."

I turned around to find the venerable Charlie Conrad in the flesh. He was smaller than I had imagined and far more prudish in person. There was a jaded confidence in his dull, blue eyes, and I shook his hand gently to show my respect.

"Be careful," I replied, "you don't want God to hear that."

He smiled, narrowing his eyes. "He probably doesn't care."

"Very true," I said, still shaking his hand, which was warm and soft and not very rugged, like I had imagined. "It's an honor to meet you, Mr. Conrad."

"Oh no, please, the honor is all mine. Come, I have something to show you."

He took me into the conference room around the corner behind the reception desk. On my way I passed my handler, and he pretended to smile. He was probably jealous. Always the servant, never the star. This pleased me very much.

The room was ordinary and a bit of a disappointment. I expected something extravagant, like Mr. Pulcher's mansion, but here were old furniture and dated magazines. Even the clock on the wall had stopped working. It was six thirty-five when I entered and would probably stay that way for another thirty-five years.

"You know, Prince Kane once sat where you're sitting now," he remarked, putting his legs up on the long conference desk. "Too bad what happened to his family."

I couldn't tell if he was being facetious.

"He was a good man," I said.

"You've met him before, haven't you?"

I was annoyed by his line of questioning. "Can we not talk about him? I have bad memories when I think about him."

"I don't mean to be rude."

"No, you're fine…"

"Maybe I'm just getting old. I can't keep up with all the new rules! It's exhausting! Call me old-fashioned, but I prefer to live in peace. I get nervous when things change for no rhyme or reason."

"I hear you. But doesn't that happen all the time on your show?"

"Yes and no. Some of it is just playacting, as you know. Some of it is real, but you don't know how long the change will last. I'll give you an example. Teen mom gets dumped by her scumbag boyfriend. Real loser. She gets on the show and suddenly has a change of heart. Why? No one knows. It's not in the script. Not a single line of dialogue is prepared. You put the camera on them, and magic happens. She sees him for the first time in a year, with someone's child, and they fall in love all over again. Again, not scripted. The guy is starstruck. The girl is smitten. They say sweet nothings, kiss, and make up in front of millions of people on live TV. Can you believe that? You zoom in on the girl and see genuine hope and affection in her eyes. No acting. Real, raw emotions. You think this is going to last forever. But then a month later, you read in the papers that the guy was shot in the back of the head, and their kid, barely three, watched the whole thing unfold."

"That's terrible!"

"I know, right? But here's the thing—the girl gets away with it. No charges, no jail time. Nothing. It's like nothing happened."

"She gets replaced."

"Exactly. Don't you think that's a miscarriage of justice?"

"Well, the boyfriend was a scumbag, as you said."

"Does that mean he deserved to be murdered?"

"I can see justice in that."

"Wow, you really *are* a Syndicate man. No wonder they sent you here. You don't give a damn, do you?"

"I'm not *that* good."

"Oh, don't be such a humble pie. You know exactly what you are."

My face stiffened up. Was he mocking me?

"I'm sorry?"

"We both play our parts, and we get paid doing that. What's not to like?"

"Agreed."

"Look, I'll skip the pleasantries. Bad things are going to happen on the show tonight. Real bad things. Things never been done before, okay? Frankly, I don't even think it's cleared with Legal. With the way things are going now, I wouldn't be surprised if all the laws just disappeared one day! Just poof, deal with it! Ha! That would be pretty nice, wouldn't it?"

"Yeah, that'd be real nice."

"I need you to bring your A game. We're going for the 'bad things happen on Christmas night' vibe, make sense? People love to see things fall apart during the holidays. Life's too boring sometimes. You have to mix it up. If you see the camera close up on you, be prepared to say something real, like right from the heart. None of that corporate speak; that just turns people off. If you do that, I'll never have you back on the show again, understand?"

"Yes, sir."

"Go off the cuff. Did you memorize your lines?"

"I, uh, yes."

"Forget them."

"Really?"

"Yes. Forget every single word. Just roll with it. Don't question it. I say this to everyone who comes on the show. Check your morality at the door. I don't need it, the audience doesn't need it. We just want to have a good time, all right?"

"The All-Mother wants to make sure—"

"Yeah, yeah. I don't need a lecture. She'll get her boost. I get the message. I'm not stupid, okay?"

"Thank you."

"Don't thank me. Thank yourself!"

CHAPTER 40

ALL FOR REVENGE

MARCUS

I couldn't believe what I saw when I opened my eyes. Sitting in front of me was a group of rich nobles, all dressed garishly and gazing at me with tremendous intensity. For a second, I thought I had been dropped into a graduation ceremony, seeing all these white chairs neatly arranged under a dark-blue sky. All that I needed were herds of fawning relatives and red-faced administrators to complete the scene.

Then a gust of wind blew over my face, smelling like wet soil after a hard night of rain, and I wanted to stretch my arms to take in the fresh air, only to realize that my hands were tied behind my back. Looking down at the white limestone blocks under my knees, I recognized where I was. This was no doubt the Moloch Pyramid, with its wide, cascading platforms and the shadow falling down the staircase resembling a snake. I remembered being here once when I was young, playing hide-and-seek with my father and almost falling off the ledge. This was one of the many recurring destinations I had visited in my dreams. It seemed my dream had come true.

With a strange kind of melancholy I gazed upon a flock of blue swallows gliding toward the forest and into the Valley of Hope. This was a mystical place, a holy place, as the old generation would say. They said the first angels were discovered in the Valley of Hope, and each year, they made a blood sacrifice on top of the pyramid to appease the gods. Unfortunately, there was no appeasing the greed of civilization.

"Fancy seeing you again, brother."

The savage spoke behind me.

"May I present you the object of our affection," he addressed the panel of nobles. "You remember the venerable Prince of Anthem, Marcus Kane?"

The nobles nodded, their faces pale, like the limestone blocks.

"His father was known for mercy, a quality that will surely be tested tonight. Isn't that right, your grace?"

I looked up at Anthony, the monster who had murdered my mother. I wanted to tear him limb from limb.

"No mercy for you," I said.

"Just out of curiosity, my prince, have you considered the gravity of your current position?"

"I see you haven't forgotten your manners."

"Do you want to know what your mother said to me before she died?"

I glared at him.

"She said, 'Promise me you'll let him live.' I want to tear up just thinking about it."

"I don't believe you."

"Oh, why not?"

"She'd never say that. She doesn't bargain with deviants."

"Why do you despise your own kind?"

"I'm not like you."

"Deny all you want, Prince Kane, but there's no escaping the truth. You're an imposter, and your lie will be exposed for the whole world to see. Don't worry, your death will not be swift. You'll live long enough to suffer the wrath of our contempt. And then you can understand the meaning of life."

"Your threats mean nothing to me. I've been through hell and back, and I'll watch you die."

"You hurt me, Marcus. I've always felt a kind of kinship between us. I've carried your secret my whole life, and this is how you repay me?"

"You're a despicable fool."

"Tell me, brother, what do you think will happen to the legacy of your bloodline when the world finds out the truth about you?"

I turned to the nobles. "How can you tolerate this? The man before you murdered the queen. He conspired to murder the king. He betrayed the faith we placed in him. He's the worst kind of deviant. He'll betray you too!"

"Excuse me." I saw a hand go up in the third row. "Did someone mention the queen?"

It was Matilda Gray.

"I don't mean to intrude," she said, in the same sarcastic inflection Anthony had used, "but I can attest to Major Fairchild's account. The truth was too much for the beautiful Mercedes to bear. Her heart was in the right place, but she hated her husband. You could even say that she was happy when the king died. She was finally free! We just helped to move along the process. But in all seriousness, it's truly remarkable that the All-Father was able to keep the truth from us for so many years."

"What truth?" shouted a gentleman with a purple wizard hat in the audience. He was one of those older monarchs who always enjoyed making a scene. "We deserve to know!"

"Sweetheart, that's why we brought you here," said Matilda, rubbing the old man's back as she sauntered toward me. "Your mother was always very kind to me. Almost too kind, one might say. I know there's always been bad blood between us. You were right to be suspicious about me. Your mother was too naive. Too bad she never possessed your instincts about people. But Marcus, I want you to know that I hold no grudge against your family. They were always very nice to me. I'm simply performing a service to the nation."

"You call murder a service?"

"Yes. We transformed your family into martyrs. The world always needs martyrs. Even the godless one we live in now."

"You devil!"

"Please, I take no offense. I've been called far worse, believe me. If we care about morals, maybe we should remind ourselves that your father was a fake prophet. He never performed any miracles. It was all for show."

"How dare you!" the old man shouted. "We should never speak ill of the All-Father's name."

The other green-eyed nobles chirped in agreement.

"And yet," said Matilda, "you all conspired to assassinate the All-Father. Does your faith allow you to be a hypocrite, or is it just you?"

The old man fell silent. He turned to look at his peers, but none of them wanted to speak up either. He was left feeling embarrassed.

Sensing a potential opportunity, I tried to make eye contact with him, hoping that I could turn him into an ally.

"I'm very sorry about your father," he said, as though confessing to me. "He was a friend, and I loved him. But times change… We can't always be everything that we want to be."

"What's that supposed to mean?" I asked without thinking.

"It means," Anthony cut in, "that your time is up."

He kicked me in the back, and my head hit the floor.

"Be gentle," Matilda said, "we have to keep him alive, for the time being."

"Yes, All-Mother."

He grabbed my arm and pulled me up but not completely upright.

"Is this what you've become?" I challenged the nobles. "Where's your courage?"

The All-Mother chuckled.

"Courage? You think these people have courage? They want the same thing I want, but they're too afraid to admit it. They don't care about faith, they just care about power! Isn't that right, Professor?"

"Tell her she's wrong!"

"No! I will not turn my back on the All-Mother."

"You see?"

"And I will not have my faith questioned."

"I am the Prince of Anthem. I command you to release me!"

"Your command has no power anymore!" the professor shouted, his body shaking.

"Please, for the sake of all that's good, you cannot give up!"

"What about you, madam? What say you?" Matilda pointed her sword at a woman wrapped in a stately, blue dress, like a politician, sitting in the front row. She had an old, greedy face, with heavy makeup around the eyes, and a glare so selfish you could see it from a mile away.

"I... uh..." the old lady stammered, her eyes rolling back and forth, her soul stirring against her chest. After surveying her peers, she declared in a high, haughty voice, "I support the All-Mother!"

"Very good!" the All-Mother shrieked in faux excitement. "And, by the way, if any of you decide to change your mind, you're free to leave. Any volunteers? No one? Really? Wow...

I thought at least one of you would be brave. I guess I was wrong."

"Our courage resides in faith," the old man declared to murmurs of "yes" and "amen."

"Very well then, I promised I'd show you the truth," said Matilda, while nodding at Anthony, "and I intend on keeping my word."

Anthony took my arm and spun me around on my knees, exposing my back to the nobles, who gasped.

"Behold," said Matilda, "this is what the All-Father was hiding from us all this time."

"Do you see?" Anthony asked. "Here." He ran his index finger along my left shoulder blade. "This is where the coracoid was severed. He's intact on the other side."

"I don't believe it!" the professor shouted. "This can't be real!"

"It may just be a scar," added the politician lady.

"How many monarchs have slits on their backs?" Matilda asked.

I strained my neck to look at my adoring fans. The professor exchanged a sardonic glance with the politician, and they shook their heads.

"Anthony, you may proceed."

Anthony unstrapped the stun baton from his belt and held it high.

"Watch," he said.

I closed my eyes, and there was a sharp, stinging flash. He jabbed the baton into my right shoulder blade. The electric shock torched my skin, and tears came to my eyes from the pain. My body convulsed, and it felt like my back was going to split open. I bared my teeth like an animal and screamed. The nightmare I thought I buried came back in flashes. The spikes began to grow, penetrating my skin. I felt the sting of cold air, the webbing between the spikes unfolding and stretching open into the shape of a wing.

The politician lady shrieked in horror. She was so overcome with shock she fell out of her chair. The professor rushed to her side. She dropped to her knees and threw her hands in the air: "God bless the All-Mother!"

"God bless the All-Mother!" repeated the professor.

The rest of them followed: "God bless the All-Mother!"

Holding his comrade by the arm, the professor pointed his fat index finger at me and yelled, "Deviant! You should be ashamed of yourself!"

"How dare you take the Lord's name in vain!" another one yelled.

"It wasn't his fault." Matilda pretended to speak for me. "It was the All-Father who forced him to a live a lie."

"He's not innocent!" shouted the politician lady.

"I know," said Matilda, "no one abused is ever innocent."

"Kill the sinner!" the professor shouted.

"Kill the sinner!" they repeated.

"I'm in awe of your decisiveness," said Matilda, "but don't you think we should give him a chance to repent?"

The nobles looked at each other as if they were confused, but this confusion was short-lived, as they realized that Matilda wasn't really asking for their permission. Soon enough, they all nodded in compliance.

Taking the cue, Anthony grabbed the wrist joint on my wing and forced it down to the floor, which shook, and a round platform rose to the surface. On opposite ends of the platform were Claudia and Dante, hands tied behind their backs, being held down by Syndicate agents.

They called out for me.

I opened my mouth, but I couldn't speak. I was too exhausted. Something evil squeezed the back of my throat, choking me from the inside. When I reached out to them, I felt a sharp, stabbing pain in the back of my head.

"Take a look at these pretty faces," Matilda said, "so young and naive and full of hope. Don't you just want to squeeze them with your hands?"

"What do you think, Anthony, do you still have feelings for the harlot?"

Anthony inhaled. "No, she betrayed me."

"Ah, nothing more bittersweet than a lover's betrayal. But then again, it's good for the soul to understand how people really feel about you, isn't it?"

"I gave her everything…"

"Oh, please," Claudia said, "you don't have anything to give. You're just a servant."

"A servant? Is that what you call the person who decides whether you live or die?"

"My dear," Matilda said, "with all due respect, that decision isn't for you to make."

"You see?" Claudia followed.

"That decision is for Marcus to make."

"What decision?" I finally managed to speak.

"If you want to live," Matilda answered, "one of them has to die."

I opened my mouth, but no words came out.

"The choice is yours."

"No. I refuse to make that choice."

"Why? You think these people are really your friends? The girl is a fanatic. All she cares about is revenge. You're just a weapon for her to use. And the boy, well, let's not be deceived by his innocent facade. He's been manipulating you the whole time. You think you've found a real family in these deviants, but the truth is, you'll always be an outsider in their eyes."

"Take me, Master!" Dante pleaded. "This is meant to be. I will die happily for our cause!"

"Spare Dante," said Claudia, "he's only a child. Take me. I'm ready to die, so let me go. You've already saved me, Marcus, and for that, I will always be grateful."

"Claudia… I… can't…"

"Yes, you can! For the sake of our cause, you must!"

"What cause? Is my life more important than yours?"

"Yes, it is!" Dante shouted. "You are the One! You will save our kind!"

"I'm *not* your kind! I never was… I never belonged any-where. I don't even know who I am…"

"You're the exterminating angel," Claudia said. "You will dismantle the Machine. You will deliver the world from darkness!"

"No, I won't be deceived anymore. No more prophecies. No more lies. We've suffered long enough." I swallowed my spit and raised my head to look at the All-Mother. "If I agree to give my life, promise that you'll spare them both. They're innocent. They deserve to live."

"Are they truly innocent?"

"If we all must die, we all must die. I won't have any more blood on my hands."

"Claudia, do you want to tell your lover the truth, once and for all?"

Claudia cast her gaze downward. Tears streamed down her face.

"Before it's too late, I'd like to express my gratitude to Claudia," the All-Mother said. "She was the brave soul who suggested the idea of blowing up the cathedral. We couldn't have taken out the king without her help. Thank you. I mean it sincerely."

"No, that's a lie. Claudia would never do such a thing. She's not like you. She's kind. She has a good heart. Tell me it isn't true, Claudia."

She held my gaze lovingly while her soul was tearing itself apart.

"It's true," she said.

"No, stop forcing me to choose. I've made up my mind!"

"Marcus, look at me! Everything Matilda said is true. It was me who came up with the idea. I helped the Syndicate murder your father. I hated the monarchy. I hated how they treated us like slaves."

"Is this the master you want?"

"No, but it's better than the one I had."

"Have I made the choice easier for you?" Matilda asked.

The soldiers readied their pistols.

I looked at the boy who had lied to me, the boy I had saved, his gaze holding mine with such intensity my eyes started burning up. I looked at the woman I loved, the woman who betrayed me, and I peered into her soul.

"Speak now or forever hold your peace."

They pressed the revolvers into the backs of their heads.

It was in this moment I began to understand. I was never meant to be a prince. I was never destined for greatness. I was here for only one purpose. My whole life had been leading up to this moment. I was the ungodly fire they forged in the depth of hell, and I would rain down vengeance on all the sinners without mercy. I may not have been a pureblood, but righteous rage flowed inside my veins. A most unbelievable sensation gripped my senses. I was stepping into the beyond.

This pale fire roiled over my every nerve, and like a child possessed by the devil, my back arched, and my body spasmed in ecstasy. I broke out of Anthony's hold, a new wing bursting forth from where I was cut. I stood on my feet again, and the weight of the world was lifted. I had never felt so light inside. My feet pulling free, I spread my wings open and flung myself into the air. All these people looked so small and insignificant from above. Consumed by a pale and powerful light, I hovered over them, my eyes and mouth burning so intensely I could taste the clouds in heaven.

For a moment I could finally see a flicker of humility on their faces. But this, too, was just a deception, for when the light from my eyes cleaved through their necks, the soldiers didn't beg for mercy, they cried out in rage. They couldn't possibly accept a reality in which they were powerless. The same fear flushed Anthony's eyes when I swooped down toward him. I grabbed him by the neck, spun him around, and held him down with both hands as I opened my mouth, releasing the full intensity of my power at his face, melting bone and flesh while he screamed. He took out his pistol and fired a few shots into my stomach. There was only a slight itch at first, but a moment later, a dull, aching pain came over me, and I lost my grip on him. Without thinking, I turned my wrath on the nobles, cutting them down, one by one. I couldn't stop myself. I couldn't even savor their reactions. It all happened so fast.

The light became so intense it cleaved through the limestone, and the floor began to rumble and slide apart. From the corner of my eye, I caught the All-Mother scuttling toward her hovercraft. I saw Claudia and Dante slipping into the abyss. Despite feeling betrayed, I couldn't bear watching them perish for me. I took off in their direction, grabbed them by the waist, and whisked them away as the pyramid crumbled.

I followed Matilda flying toward the Valley of Hope. I had only one thing in mind.

Revenge.

CHAPTER 41

LOVE OF SUFFERING

MARCUS

Matilda was nowhere in sight. Her hovercraft had crash-landed between two palm trees. The centurion wheel was still spinning. A dense fog filled the forest. I could smell the dark energy in the air. This place was different.

I looked down at Dante, who sat slumped against the trunk of a palm tree, clutching his waist. He looked just like me when I used to go hunting with Father. The roles seemed to have been reversed. I was now the tormentor gazing down at the helpless prey. Even as my instinct told me to empathize with him, I remembered his deception all too well. I put on the stoic glare of my father and stepped into the stream, letting the cold water cleanse my feet. I looked up at the black temple a few paces ahead, and a strange sense of nostalgia came over me.

"Don't go," Dante said. "This place is a trap. Here you see what you want to see. And once you cross the line, you can never come back."

"Dante's right," added Claudia, hobbling toward Dante while holding her stomach.

"Why should I believe anything you say?"

"You'll have your revenge one day, I promise," she said, "but today, we live."

"Maybe saving you was a mistake."

"Maybe. Marcus… I still love you."

"Don't you dare… You don't get to say that to me after all you've done."

"I know."

"My family saved your life. We gave you a second chance. We were kind to you. How could you betray us?"

"I never wanted your mother to suffer."

"That's your excuse?"

"I make no excuses for my actions. I did what I had to for the sake of our people."

"Well, congratulations. You replaced one evil regime with another."

"And this is our chance. We can end it, once and for all!"

"There's no 'us.' I'm no hero. I wasn't destined to save anyone. I'll have my revenge, and the rest of you can live as you please."

"But Marcus—"

"No. I've heard enough."

"She's leading you into a trap."

"Sounds familiar."

I could pour all of my hatred on Claudia, I could unleash this vengeance without end, but there was no denying the feeling that I was walking into yet another lie. I had grown numb to the world, and the feeling of danger was the little I had left to feel alive. Adrenaline kept flooding my veins, and my scalp itched with anticipation.

No, I could never go back again. I wanted to cross the line. I needed to cross the line. I'd been waiting for too long. I wasn't ashamed of my desires anymore. If not now, when?

I was staring into the fog and getting lost in all the morphing shapes when I heard a familiar voice. It was a soft and caring voice, full of life and tenderness. It was the kind of voice that made you want to leap over a cliff to save it from drowning in the ocean. There was also a harshness to it, like judgment was being passed. When I looked over my shoulder, only Claudia's eyes and lips were still visible through the fog, still pleading for me to go back to the past. Then the voice called out again.

"Marcus!"

"My son!"

"Mother?"

"Yes."

"Is it really you?"

"Yes, my son. It's me."

There she was, standing in the flesh, holding the same smile I remembered before we parted. My heart was beating so fast I could hardly hold it together. When she touched my hand, my knees buckled, and I collapsed. I was overcome with joy. I didn't care if I was being deceived. I didn't want to fight the feeling anymore.

"Son! I've missed you so much! I've come back, and we'll be together forever."

"But I thought you died!"

She held my head in her bosom, and I looked up at her magnificent eyes.

"Eternity awaits beyond the realm of death. Your eyes don't deceive you. I'm exactly what you see. I want to make up for all the time we've lost. Oh, my son, we have a whole life ahead of us!"

I took her hand and got to my feet.

"Come with me," she said.

"Where are we going?"

"Marcus, don't go!" Claudia shouted. "That woman's Matilda. She's not your mother!"

"We're going to a place where they won't bother us," Mother said. "Hurry! Time is running out. We need you home, Marcus."

I turned around one more time to find Claudia clawing her way through the fog, panting so helplessly I felt a tinge of sympathy for her again. I could touch her hand, if only I reached out. I could escape this moment, if only I tried. I could even have my revenge on the world and live the prophecy. But the thought of fate awakened my fear. I was never destined for greatness. I was never a hero. This world didn't deserve heroes. I was only human.

I needed to go home.

CHAPTER 42

REDEMPTION DAY

JASON

People were still shouting obscenities when the lights went dim. The director had to berate the audience in a gentle voice just seconds before we went on air. Of course, no one listened. That was the whole point. The chaos added to the drama, and the drama needed to feel real. I'd never imagined myself watching my favorite talk show as a member of the live audience. It was a surreal experience, as anyone would say to a reporter when interviewed about it. But there was something more peculiar than just the feeling of surreal. It was the feeling of numb ecstasy, a kind of raw anger for realizing that I was, in fact, less important than my mind wanted to believe. I sat on the far left in the middle section, clutching the fake leather handle of my briefcase, my right elbow shielding a cup of popcorn from the rowdy teenager to my right. He was one of those kids who never understood anything clearly. He just went with the crowd, doing whatever it took to please the people around him. I could see his future already. After another decade of debauchery, he'd get replaced, find himself a happy little family, and say to everyone he met that he'd changed for the better for his kids.

"It was a terrible wake-up call," he might say to his psychiatrist. "But I needed it to change."

Even now, I could see that muted, sanctimonious smile slip through from time to time. Our boy was growing up right in front of our eyes!

A montage of dead actors played over the projector screen. Whenever the actor shown was someone people disliked, which was most of them, the crowd erupted in jeers. Generally speaking, the louder your reaction, the more likely you would be rewarded with an extra point or two on your Sterling Score. It demonstrated that you were ruthless enough to mock dead people, a quality deeply cherished in our world.

The background music was fine, nothing too solemn. After all, these people were rich enough to buy themselves a piece of real estate in One Mind. Whenever a new round of jeers erupted, the boy next to me would try to slide his hand under my elbow and steal my popcorn. I had to slap his hand several times before he stopped this horrible behavior. He shrugged when I scowled at him.

Toward the end of the montage, when the most famous actors graced the screen, the announcer interrupted the program: "We apologize for the interruption, but we bring you breaking news. There has been a development in the nationwide manhunt for the terrorists behind the assassination of the All-Father."

The video cut to live footage of what I could only describe as professional pandemonium. You know the instant you lay eyes on it that some of it is staged, but the lizard part of your brain insists that everything is real. And boy, was it grand. Helicopters were swirling around like flies descending on dead meat, the trees were shaking, the leaves whistled, and bloodhounds were barking. A whole battalion of police cars and Syndicate officers dressed in their finest suits encircled a nondescript cabin in some backwoods country. Moments later, in the midst of rowdy cheers from the studio audience, a young man walked out of the cabin with his hands behind his head. His gait was measured and defiant, and as the camera zoomed in, I recognized him as Andre. He seemed rather nonchalant as he dropped to his knees, just the way I remembered him. I couldn't deny feeling a sense of pride to see him arrested.

"What I'm learning as we speak, Margaret, is that this young man is a leader with Morning Star, a terrorist cell from the old regime. His name is Andre. He's killed over a dozen people. According to a manifesto police have obtained, the stated aim of Morning Star is to restore the monarchy to its former glory. I might be going out on a limb here, but I don't think that's going to happen anytime soon. And I hear that he was plotting a major attack at the Redemption Day parade, which would have killed hundreds, if not thousands, of innocent people. This just begs the question, Margaret, how can someone be so evil?"

"Well, Mikhail, it's called resentment. Plain and simple."

Resentment. Perhaps Margaret was right. It must have been resentment working the Syndicate officers to a frenzy as they descended upon Andre like a pack of rabid dogs.

After a few minutes of relentless beating, Andre was helped up by a Syndicate officer, his face all swollen, his feet limp as he was dragged to the police van. As the broadcasters hailed this moment of triumph, a man shrouded in a black hood popped out from the pack of Syndicate officers and unloaded a shotgun blast on Andre's face. Then the gunman was shot down.

This sequence of events happened so quickly the broadcasters lost their words. The studio audience fell silent too.

Then the feed was cut. Accompanied by a snazzy bassline, the projector screen retracted to reveal the stage once again.

"Well, on that thrilling note," said Charlie as he waltzed back on stage, seemingly half-drunk, "let's bring back our guests."

"We want to see more!" someone in the audience shouted, followed by cheers.

Charlie turned around to find the gentleman sitting behind him, patted him on the head, and whispered something into his ear. The man smiled like a child.

Then Charlie told the crowd, "I think I understand this guy better than his wife."

Of course, the crowd cheered. The comment was so unexpected but also so on brand for Charlie I couldn't help but crack a smile too.

Clutching the microphone like a trophy, Charlie strode in my direction but avoided making eye contact with me.

"My guests today are angry, betrayed mothers. Please meet Stacey. Stacey says her son has been cheating on her with better ideas about the world."

The crowd moaned.

"Stacey, what's going on?"

Flaunting her little black dress, Stacey looked pretty composed sitting in the high chair with her legs crossed in front of her. She looked rather young to be a mother. She probably wanted to have kids before she got replaced.

"Hey, Charlie," answered Stacey, half flirtatiously.

Some in the audience cackled.

"Are you hitting on me?" Charlie interrupted.

"No," she said. "I think you're too old for me."

The audience groaned.

"Why do you have to hurt me like that?"

"I'm sorry, Charlie."

"Tell us what's going on."

"Well, I have a beautiful little boy. He's the youngest one I have. His older siblings—"

"How many kids do you have?"

"Four, including David."

"Wow. You're impressive. Do the other kids know that you're on the show?"

"Well, now they do," she said with an awkward chuckle. "I mean, they all support me."

"In doing what?"

"In getting little David to fall in line. Charlie, I love him dearly. I want to say that first. I had him with my second husband. I fell in love for the first time when I had him. It's different when you're in love, you know what I mean?"

"No."

"Anyway, my kids will probably hate me for saying it, but I'll say it. David is the most talented kid in the bunch. He's wise beyond his years. He's only eleven, and he can understand big ideas better than I ever could. He's just really, really smart. But here's the problem, Charlie. David's embarrassed about being smart."

"Why?"

"Because he's been brainwashed. I'm scared for him. He's refusing therapy, refusing to take conditioning pills, refusing to even show up to school. His Sterling Score dropped from the top five percent to the bottom ten percent in just three months. If he doesn't get his act together, he'll be replaced! And I don't want that to happen to him. He's too smart for that."

"Wait, you said he's been brainwashed. What do you mean by that?"

She sighed to gather herself. "David has fallen for the religion of Esoterica."

"Ma'am, you do realize that could be considered a crime."

"Yes, I'm aware, but I don't have any other options."

"All right, let's welcome David to the show!"

As soon as David walked onto the stage, I found myself groaning with the rest of the audience. David didn't look good. His accelerated aging was far worse than mine. Even though he was still diminutive, like a child, his face was wrinkled and tired. His eyes were dull, his skin loose, and his voice husky like he'd just ran a marathon under the weather. You couldn't help but feel sympathy for him. But clearly, he wanted none of it.

"Oh, shut up!" he berated the crowd. "You think you're better than me?"

"David." His mother approached him cautiously. "You have to listen to me."

He swatted her arm away and nearly hit her in the nose. I booed viciously, just like the rascal next to me.

"Why should I listen to you?"

"How could you say that to your own mother?" Charlie asked.

"Because! She's not my mother."

"What proof do you have?"

"Look at us! Do we look alike?"

"You look older than her," returned Charlie.

We cheered.

"Your mother is concerned for you, David. Do you understand that?"

"No, she's just concerned for herself."

"Do tell."

"If she gets me on pills, she'll get a higher score. She's using me and all her kids, Charlie. She doesn't really care about us. She just wants to save herself!"

"Is that true, Stacey?"

"No!"

"You don't sound very convincing."

"I mean, it's true that I don't want to get replaced. Who does? And, yes, getting David off drugs will get me a higher score. But I still care for him. Two things can be true at the same time."

There was a moment of silence.

"David, I love you," said Stacey, tears welling up in her eyes. "Please come back to me."

She kneeled in front of David and held his hands.

"Won't you come back to me, sweetheart? Your mother loves you very much."

My heart pounded in rabid anticipation.

"I'm sorry, Mom. I don't hate you. I hate the system. I don't want people to judge me. I don't care about what they think. I just want to live out the time I've got left on my own terms. I hope you can accept me for who I am."

Stacey looked at her son with genuine love and was on the verge of embracing him when Charlie moved in with the cameraman behind him.

"Before you say yes, I want you to meet someone who might change your mind. Bring on the special guest!"

CHAPTER 43

EUPHORIA

JASON

When the spotlight landed over my head, I took the briefcase and stood up. A security guard scurried up behind me and handed me a microphone, which I accepted like I was accepting a lifetime-achievement award.

"Tell us your name, young man," Charlie said.

Their eyes feasted on my anxiety.

"My name is Miguel."

"No last name?"

Some of them snickered.

"No, I'm a service model."

"No, no, we welcome everyone here," Charlie pretended to chide the audience members who booed. "Only smart people come on the show, remember?"

They laughed at my expense.

I feared the microphone would slip through my hand. I was sweating profusely.

"Okay, now, tell us why you're here."

"I'm here, Charlie, because I think I can convince David to change his mind."

"Well, don't just stand there, come on up!"

They cheered, but I found no solace in the sound of their applause. I walked up to the stage and settled into a flimsy plastic chair. Mother sat in the middle, the son on the opposite side.

"In my former life, I was a member of Esoterica," I confessed. "Yes, I used to be an anarchist. I used to be just like David. I hated the system."

"Don't talk to *me*, talk to David," said Charlie.

I shifted in my chair and tried to match his gaze. He was bursting with anger.

"David, I know how you feel," I said.

"No, you don't. You're lying. How do I know you were with Esoterica?"

Without speaking, I took off my shirt to show him the *S* brand on my right shoulder blade. There were moans and hisses. Charlie touched the scar with his index finger. The scar was real.

"So you were their slave," he said.

"Pretty much. But at the time, I had no idea I was being brainwashed, just like David. I wore the brand like a badge of honor. I wanted to prove myself worthy to a world that looked down on me."

"How did you get out?" Stacey asked.

"Mom, he's lying to us," said David.

"Will you shut up and listen for once?" Stacey snapped.

David shrugged in dismay.

"I'm telling you the truth. I used to hate myself. Frankly, I still do sometimes. Being a service model is hard. You're invisible to the world. You're just a machine. I mean, look at me, you probably can't tell me apart from the other models you see in the streets."

"You're right about that," Charlie quipped.

"But we're actually all the same," I said.

"I'm nothing like you," said David.

"Not on the surface, but deep down, we share the same fears. We're afraid of being cast aside. We fear that look in people's eyes that says, 'You mean nothing to me.'"

He blushed and looked away.

"Judging by your appearance, David, you probably have three months, four at best?"

He waited for a moment, then nodded.

"My God!" Stacey shouted. "You told me you had at least a year left on the wager!"

"No, Mom, I lied."

"I was exactly where you are when I made up my mind to leave Esoterica. Look at me. It's not too late. I survived. I survived because I made a choice. When my therapist told me I only had three months to live, the world opened up. I began to see things clearly. Esoterica didn't care about me. If I died, they wouldn't mourn for me. They'd just find someone else to take my place. In fact, they'd probably laugh at me for being weak."

"I bet they're right," David said.

The audience booed. A few brave souls even cheered. I appreciated their mockery.

"Look, I'm not offended. I think the kid's right. The world is a cruel place. It's easy to get confused about who's on your side and who isn't. If I may, Stacey and David, I'd like to make you an offer."

The two of them were genuinely startled.

I touched the briefcase, paused, and looked at the audience. I let the anticipation build. I strained my face and bared my teeth as I grabbed the briefcase with both hands.

The audience appreciated my comedic posture.

With the camera zooming in, I slammed the briefcase on the desk, startling the audience.

"Oh, I love surprises," Charlie said.

"Stacey, I know it's hard being a single mother."

"I'm not single," she said, frowning sarcastically.

"Well, you will be after tonight."

"What's that supposed to mean?"

"David," I started turning the dial on the briefcase, "it sounds like there's nothing I can say to convince you to change your mind. I get it. If I were trailer trash like you, I'd want to kill myself too."

As I expected, David burst out of his chair and stormed toward me, cursing and making juvenile threats at my life. I didn't flinch as the security guard held him back. The mother, funny enough, smiled a little. She probably had a thing for service models.

"I have in this briefcase two million points." I opened the briefcase for everyone to see. All the black money bills were neatly bundled in bite-sized stacks. Stacey was impressed.

"Wow! Where did you steal the money?" Charlie asked.

I smiled.

"I didn't steal the money, Charlie. This is a family show."

"Oh yes, family show." He winked.

"This money is being provided by the venerable Change A Life Foundation. Their mission, yes, thank you. Their mission, as most of you know, is to lift people out of poverty and give them a second chance. David, if you agree to be converted tonight, right here on the show, you can split the money with your mom and walk out a millionaire. How does that sound?"

There was roaring applause.

I could tell David was flustered by the outpouring of support. He'd probably never experienced this kind of validation in his life. Even though he still tried to look tough, the facade was fading away.

Right on cue, the lights dimmed, and a crew of handymen seemed to materialize out of thin air, pushing a conversion pod onto the stage.

I couldn't help but be impressed by this impeccable stage-craft. I grinned like a little kid as the stage filled with smoke. A low, pulsating beat rocked the stage, and I started clapping like a caveman. I had never seen a conversion pod so sleek and inviting. It looked more like a fancy gadget than a killing machine. For so long, I had come to associate the dental chair and its low drilling noise and disinfectant smell with the dread of replacement. There was nothing dreadful about this conversion pod. The all-black, leathery shell looked so comfortable I wanted to press my face against it. David was awestruck as well, and Stacey was licking her lips imagining what she would do with all that money.

"Well, what do you say to the offer?" Charlie asked Stacey.

Without a moment's hesitation, Stacey shouted, "I'll take it!"

The audience cheered, and she pumped her fist in the air.

"And you, David? Do you accept the offer?"

"The offer will only stand if you both accept it," I added to great dramatic effect.

The irony of life must have sailed across David's mind. In order to live, he had to become someone else. All the pain and aggravation, all the memories, good and bad, all the desires and fears, they would all mean nothing in the end. What does living even mean when everything can just vanish with a press of a button? What would I do if I were him? I fantasized a violent confession, like a rock star slitting his chest with broken glass. As blood trickled down the stage, I would blow a kiss to the crowd. They'd scream my name, over and over.

But David found no solace in a sweeping exit. He looked at his mother one last time and said, "I love you."

"I love you too," his mother replied.

"I'll see you in the next life," he said.

His mother was too emotional to say anything else. After tonight, David would never recognize his mother again. Stacey would just be another stranger to him.

For all her vices, Stacey was still human. She reached out her hand as he stepped inside the conversion pod. He refused to look back. He was too far gone to think about love anymore. He sat inside the red leather chair while his mother looked on wistfully. There was a mix of sadness and hope in her eyes. Slowly but surely, she relinquished herself to the inevitability of life.

As the pod was closing over the boy, there was an outburst of commotion behind the curtain, and a young man erupted onto the stage, ramming through two security guards.

"Ah, let's welcome Michael, Stacey's new lover!" Charlie announced.

"Open the pod!" Michael shouted. "Open the pod! I need to see my son!"

Mercury was beginning to fill the pod.

"Stop it, Mike! David's made his choice!" Stacey shouted back. She tried to grab his waist, but he shook her loose.

"You're despicable! You just want the money!"

"It's *our* money, Mike! We'll never have to worry another day!"

The dad lost it. He was about to turn his fury on me when Charlie stepped in front of him.

"If you want to say your final words, you may want to say them now."

David was in a state of peace. There was a look of longing his eyes, like he was being visited by phantoms of another dimension. By now, the needles had penetrated his jaw, and the conversion was underway.

Dad pummeled the machine with his hands while the audience laughed.

"Stop it, you'll get him killed!" Stacey reproached her lover.

"She's right, you know," Charlie added. "If you break the pod, the boy dies."

"Come back to me!" he wailed. "You're better than this, David! I love you! You're the best thing that's ever happened to me! Come back! Just say the word!"

Even as his former self was being erased, David was still conscious enough to recognize his father. His lips moved just a little.

"You see? He's trying to get out! Please, Charlie, call it off!"

"No!" Stacey yelled. "It's too late, Mike, let it go!"

I saw in Michael shades of my own father. I wished I could take him into my embrace and ease his pain, but the only thing I could do was watch him fall into despair. I couldn't throw away my own future on the whims of compassion. He clutched the pod with both hands and threw his head against the hard glass. Blood began to trickle down the pod.

I bumped into the security guard next to me and snatched the handgun from his hip holster. Then I whispered a sweet nothing into Stacey's ear. She took the gun from me and shot her lover in the head. His brain matter splattered over the pod.

The mercury drained away, and the pod opened slowly with Michael's fresh corpse sliding to the floor.

I handed the briefcase full of money to Stacey.

"Congratulations," I declared, "you win!"

"Thank you!" she cried with happy tears on her lips.

She gave me a big hug.

The audience went wild.

"Let's welcome Albert!" Charlie announced.

As if rising from the grave, the boy walked out of the pod. He looked young again. His blue eyes shimmered like a newborn's, full of hope. No longer the David we once knew, Albert took the stage while waving at the audience. For a new convert, he didn't seem fazed by the situation one bit. It was as if he had always been fated to appear on this stage in this very moment. And it seemed that he had always known this moment would come.

"How do you feel, Albert?" Charlie asked.

"I feel great," Albert said in a fresh, lively voice. "I feel like I'm ready to take on the world."

"Do you know Stacey?"

"No," he said, looking at the woman who used to be his mother with childish bewilderment.

"Stacey is the Good Samaritan who paid for your procedure. She saved your life!"

"Wow, I don't know what to say," said Albert. "Thank you so much, Stacey! I owe you my life."

Stacey wanted to say the words in her head, but the words couldn't come out. The system wouldn't let it. Once the past was erased, it was gone forever. Her son was gone forever.

"You're very welcome," she said as she shook Albert's hand. "I, uh, want to wish you a happy new life."

Albert nodded. He didn't even notice he was standing in a pool of blood, or that the blood belonged to his father. As far as he knew, he didn't have a father. The system was his father. The system was his mother.

We heard the sound of fireworks before the images flashed on the screen behind Charlie's desk. People were dancing in the streets, young lovers were sharing a kiss for the camera, and the TV host was getting drunk.

"Happy Redemption Day! Happy New Year!" Charlie said to the audience.

"Happy New Year!" the audience shouted back.

Then Charlie wrapped his arm around my neck with a huge, hysterical grin.

"What do we say to the folks at home?"

We both took a deep breath and looked straight into the camera.

"Better luck next time!"

9 798218 362980